Praise for
FIRST TO FIGHT

"CAUTION! Any book written by Dan Cragg and David Sherman is bound to be addictive, and this is the first in what promises to be a great adventure series. *First to Fight* is rousing, rugged, and just plain fun. The authors have a deep firsthand knowledge of warfare, an enthralling vision of the future, and the skill of veteran writers. Fans of military fiction, science fiction, and suspense will all get their money's worth, and the novel is so well done it will appeal to general readers as well. It's fast, realistic, moral, and a general hoot. *First to Fight* is also vivid, convincing—and hard to put down. Sherman and Cragg are a great team! I can't wait for the next one!"

—RALPH PETERS
New York Times bestselling
author of *Red Army*

FIRST TO FIGHT

Starfist
Book One

David Sherman
and
Dan Cragg

A Del Rey® Book

BALLANTINE BOOKS • NEW YORK

A Del Rey® Book
Published by The Random House Publishing Group
Copyright © 1997 by David Sherman and Dan Cragg

Published in the United States by Del Rey Books, an imprint of The Random House Publishing Group, a division of Random House, Inc., New York, and simultaneously in Canada by Random House of Canada Limited, Toronto.

Del Rey is a registered trademark and the Del Rey colophon is a trademark of Random House, Inc.

www.delreybooks.com

Library of Congress Catalog Card Number: 97-91713

ISBN 0-345-40622-2

Manufactured in the United States of America

First Edition: October 1997

19   18   17   16   15

PROLOGUE

"Mark One?" Gunnery Sergeant Charlie Bass asked. He gave the Terminal Dynamics techrep a hard look. "Are you sure we can catch the bandits we're hunting with a Mark One?" He gestured toward the small black box on the table.

"The Mark One, as you call it, Sergeant, is the Universal Positionator Up-Downlink, Mark One," Daryl George answered. He wore an expression of superiority. It was clear to Bass that the techrep was explaining his toy to the NCOs gathered around the table only because he thought the men were too dumb to understand without his explanation.

"Where was it field-tested?" Gunny Bass asked. Sergeant Major Tanglefoot gave him a dangerous look.

"I'm glad you asked that," George said to the assembled first sergeants and company gunnery sergeants of 31st FIST. He smoothed his pencil-line mustache with a chubby forefinger before proceeding. "You have the right to know everything necessary about the testing of the equipment that your lives and the lives of your men might depend on. The final field-testing of the UPUD"—he pronounced it "you-pud"—"was at Aberdeen. It passed every phase with flying colors." George smiled broadly, as if announcing they'd just won the lottery.

"Aberdeen—a testing range. What you're telling us is

1

that this Mark One hasn't seen action yet." Bass carefully avoided looking at the sergeant major.

"As I *said*, Sergeant," George drew himself up to his full, soft, six feet of height and thrust his jaw aggressively toward his interrogator, "it passed every phase of its testing with flying colors."

Bass's jaw locked at constantly being called "Sergeant," as if he were some damn army noncom. He wasn't in the army, he was a gunnery sergeant in the Confederation Marine Corps.

"Are there any *other* questions?" Sergeant Major Tanglefoot broke in.

Bass spoke up again. "Sergeant Major, you know, I know, and so does every other NCO in this room, that there's a world of difference between controlled tests and tests under fire. We're on a combat operation here. This is no place to be testing unproven equipment."

"Everything in the Corps' inventory had a first time under fire," Sergeant Major Tanglefoot replied. His voice said his patience was running out. "This is the first time for the UPUD."

Bass winced. "Right, Sergeant Major." He swallowed, knowing he was on thin ice arguing with Tanglefoot. "It's just I think we shouldn't use the Mark One without taking along the radios and locators that we know work. Just in case this thing doesn't."

In a voice that brooked no further discussion, the sergeant major said, "Headquarters has directed we turn in all platoon and company radios, geo position locators, and vector computers. Each company and platoon will be issued a UPUD to replace them. That's *one* piece of equipment to take the place of *three*. Company gunnery sergeants, you will turn in the old and be issued the new, personally. First sergeants, you will see to it that they do. That is all. Do it."

The twenty senior noncommissioned officers of the 31st Fleet Initial Strike Team's operational units rose and started filing out of the room.

Charlie Bass knew when to shut up. This was one of those times. But Daryl George didn't know when to stop. He said to Bass, "Sarge, don't worry. I personally guarantee you the you-pud, Mark One, will perform as advertised."

Bass turned back and glared at George. "And *I* personally guarantee *you*, if we lose one man because this thing doesn't work as advertised, *you,* personally, will pay for it."

"As you were, Bass!" Sergeant Major Tanglefoot snapped. "You *will* knock off this nonsense, Gunnery Sergeant."

"Aye aye, Sergeant Major. Sorry, sir." He gave George a look that said he was anything but sorry. Then he followed his company first sergeant out of the room.

"Careful, Bass," his first sergeant whispered.

The "bandits" the Marines were chasing on Fiesta de Santiago seemed to melt into the mountains even more easily than they had into the population in the lowland cities. By mid-afternoon of the third day, after the Marines dismounted from their Dragons to start negotiating terrain too rugged for the air-cushioned assault vehicles, they still hadn't seen anything more of their quarry than an occasional footprint.

"Where's that Mark One say we are?" Bass asked PFC LeFarge, the communications man, when the Bravo unit stopped to plan its next step.

LeFarge said, "Position mine," to the black box he carried. The UPUD was twelve inches high, eight wide, and two deep. One face lifted to expose a viewscreen. The screen flickered at LeFarge's voice, then showed a string of coordinates and a schematic map with their position marked on it.

"Any word from the Skipper?" Bass asked as he plotted the UPUD's coordinates on his paper map.

In the middle of the second day on foot, the company commander had divided his unit into two elements. He and the first sergeant took two platoons and half the assault platoon along one trail, while his executive officer and Bass followed a second trail with the remaining platoon and the other half of the assault platoon. Now communications were lost.

"Not since 0830 hours," LeFarge responded. He looked up at the boulder-strewn, wooded slopes surrounding them and casually brushed a rivulet of perspiration away from his eyes. It was over a hundred degrees in the shade. "Must be the mountains are blocking the transmissions."

Bass shook his head. This is a bad place, he thought. Real good place for an ambush. "It's supposed to be string-of-pearls communications, not line-of-sight. There's always a satellite up." He used a compass to shoot azimuths from three landmarks around the narrow, steep-sided gorge they were in, then marked the position he calculated on the overlay and wrote down the coordinates. In a pinch, old-style compass-and-map, land-navigation technics still worked.

"Check with third platoon's comm man, see if he's getting the same readings you are."

LeFarge started murmuring into his helmet mike, to the comm man with the third platoon command element a hundred meters to the rear.

Bass got to his feet to show the Bravo commander his map overlay. The positions and sets of coordinates given by both the UPUD and his compass were marked on it. According to the UPUD reading, they were in the next valley over from the position Bass had worked out.

"How sure are you?" Lieutenant Procescu asked.

Bass pointed out the landmarks he'd used to plot their positions. The valley the UPUD said they were in didn't have similar features.

"Gunny," LeFarge said, "third platoon gets almost exactly the same location I do."

"Can we find our way home?" Procescu asked.

Bass nodded. "By using compass and map, if that's all we've got that works."

"Where are we supposed to be?"

Bass shrugged. "Chasing Pancho." Maybe one of the bandits the Marines were following was named Pancho, and maybe not. It didn't matter. Anytime the Marines went up against guerrillas who were called bandits, they labeled them all "Pancho."

"Then if we've got no problem with finding our way home," Procescu said, "let's chase Pancho." To LeFarge he added, "Keep trying to raise the Skipper."

"If we need air support and the squadron tries to vector in on us using the Mark One, we may as well not even ask," Bass said to Procescu as he shouldered his pack and checked his hand weapon. "Saddle up!" he called to the squad ahead of the Bravo command element. He held up his right arm, let his chameleon sleeve slide down so his arm would be visible, then gave the hand signal that meant "Get up and move out." The resting, nearly invisible Marines of the lead squad briefly flickered into visibility as their chameleons adjusted to changing surroundings. They rose to their feet and resumed moving up the narrow gorge bottom. The men on the valley floor were easy enough to spot by anyone who knew what he was looking at—their chameleons never quite matched their surroundings; instead, they flickered through the color scale as they changed color to match the stones and earth they were closest to. The flankers in the shadows up on the slopes were impossible to see unless an observer happened to spot their faces, hands, or the uncovered V's of their upper chests.

"We're only chasing about twenty Panchos," Procescu said to Bass, "and there's forty-six of us. We won't need air support when we catch them."

A quarter hour after Bass made his location check, the reinforced platoon that was the Bravo unit reached an area where a recent temblor had tumbled many large boulders to the valley floor and uprooted most of the trees on the steep slopes. Birds from Earth and native fliers twittered and sang as they fed on the buzzers that hummed and flitted through the torpid air of the valley bottom. The barren slopes appeared empty, and it looked as if bad footing was the only problem the Marines would have until they reached the next wooded area, somewhere past the next bend more than half a klick ahead.

The lead squad and one gun team were flickering through the open and the Bravo command group was at the edge of the denuded area when a flanker on the left slope shouted "Pancho!" His shout was almost drowned out by the ozone-crack of his weapon as it vaporized the partly exposed boot of a bandit. Instantly, the other two Marines on the left slope opened fire; the cracks of their weapons, the even louder cracks of the rocks that split when the bolts hit them, and the sizzle of vaporizing flesh, nearly masked the screams of wounded bandits or those burned by flying globules of molten rock.

"Take cover!" Bass bellowed as he dove behind a nearby boulder. All across the valleyside came a scattering of cracks as the bandits began to return fire. On the valley floor, the Marines tried to return fire from cover while the gun team set up, but the shields that protected them from the bandits' energy weapons did nothing to protect them from the molten rock thrown when incoming fire melted stone. The Marines caught in the killing zone could only huddle behind the boulders, out of the way of the sizzling bolts and flying magma.

Procescu assayed the situation quickly and calmly gave orders into his communicator. "Three Actual, get the rest of second squad and the other gun on that slope to help your flankers. Send your platoon sergeant with two assault teams to the flankers on the opposite slope to lay down some suppressing fire. Remaining assault team and assault squad leader, to me."

Bass opened the switch that allowed him to listen in on all of the communicator talk in the unit down to fire team leader. He heard the third platoon commander give his orders, the platoon sergeant pull together the rest of the assault squad, the squad leader, assault squad leader, and the fire, gun, and assault team leaders urging their men into motion. The fire and gun team leaders pinned down in the open reported that they had no casualties.

Bass flicked down his infra goggles to scan the slope where the fire was coming from. He picked up only a couple of dozen man-size heat signatures. What's going on here? he asked himself. There's got to be more bandits than that. They wouldn't set up an ambush unless they knew they had us outnumbered.

Abruptly, heavier fire broke out on the left slope as Lieutenant Kruzhilov and his reinforcements reached the flank and added their power to that of the three Marines shooting at the bandits there. Over the command net Bass heard the platoon commander coolly issue orders to coordinate the fire of his ten Marines. In seconds, instead of firing at random targets, they were hosing out plasma bolts in line, slagging a broad swath of slope beginning twenty meters to their front.

The third assault team reached Procescu, and the Bravo commander added its fire to the advancing maelstrom.

Forty meters in front of the Marines on the flank, a screaming bandit leaped to his feet. One of his arms was missing, a cauterized hole was burned through his thigh, and a ball of half-melted rock had set his uniform ablaze. A Marine in the open rose up from cover and took him out with a clean head shot. The remaining bandits broke and ran.

At least they don't have shields, Bass thought.

"Cease fire, cease fire!" Procescu ordered. "Three Actual, maneuver to check that slope, make sure it's cleared. Check the bodies, see if there's any we can keep alive to question."

Bass frowned. He couldn't believe such a small force would set an ambush for a reinforced Marine platoon. He twisted around to scan the opposite slope. He saw, through his goggles, that its entire length was blotched with red—that's where the main effort of the ambush was! The bandits hadn't known the Marines had flankers on the slopes, so the flankers were able to trip the ambush early. The bandits on the left must have been a blocking force that was supposed to stop the Marines from withdrawing after they were caught in the open by the larger force on the right flank.

To Bass's right, through the trees, a line of red spots was approaching the bandit-held slope—the platoon sergeant with the other two assault teams. On the valley floor the Marines who had been pinned down were rising to their feet.

"Everybody down!" he shouted into the all-hands circuit. "They're on the right slope. Three Bravo, stop in place. Use your goggles." Bass's pulse was racing wildly. A second later he heard Platoon Sergeant Chway murmur,

"Jesus Muhammad," then issue the commands to set up the assault guns to rake the right slope.

Several of the Marines in the open jumped up and zigzagged for the cover of the trees where the command unit was. The bandits' main effort opened fire and plasma bolts engulfed two of the runners. When his shield was overwhelmed, one man simply vanished with a flash, then the other dropped, a charred husk. The rest of the Marines were forced to drop behind cover before reaching the tree line. The stench of seared flesh wafted up to where Bass lay.

Chway ordered the two assault teams into action. In seconds their oversized weapons were throwing out bolts that could melt a meter of ferrocrete. The three flankers added lighter, disciplined fire.

Procescu ordered the assault team with him to blast the far end of the slope. He ordered Kruzhilov to add his gun's fire to that of the assaultmen. The gun on the left slope began spewing out bolts so close to each other they seemed almost a steady stream. Its aiming focus twisted side to side on the slope as it burned through the far end of the ambush.

The bandits weren't sitting passively while the Marines poured fire into the two ends of their ambush. A hundred of them concentrated their fire on Chway, his assault guns, and the three flankers with them, and two platoons returned fire at Kruzhilov's gun and fighters on the left flank. The rest of the bandits kept the Marines in the open pinned down and out of the fight. Only the command group was, for the moment, unscathed. The bandits couldn't see those Marines because of their chameleons, and they didn't have infra goggles to spot their heat signatures. But they could see the glowing muzzles of the overheated weapons and began to concentrate their fire on them. A scream on the right flank was cut short when several weapons converged on one Marine. Another didn't have time to scream before seven weapons overwhelmed his shield and turned him into carbon vapor.

Through Bass's goggles, the first fifty meters or more of the right slope was a solid sheet of red from the fire Chway's Marines had put onto it before moving onward. Nobody could be alive in that area. But bandits were strung out over another three hundred meters before the slag that was being created at the far end of the ambush by the fire from the Marines' left flank. From the slackened fire to the left, Bass could tell that Kruzhilov's section had also taken casualties.

"Bass, to me!" Procescu's voice said in his helmet. Bass scuttled to the Bravo commander. "There's too damn many of them," the lieutenant said when Bass reached him. "We need help, and we need it now. Take LeFarge back and find a high place you can climb to. See if you can raise anybody." He looked into the intended kill zone of the ambush. "If I can get those men under cover back here, that'll help."

"Good idea," Bass responded. "Try to move them one at a time." He turned to LeFarge. "Let's go."

The volume of outgoing fire from the Marines' right flank slackened abruptly as one of the assault gunners was crisped and his weapon stopped firing.

Bass remembered a place 150 meters back down the gorge where a rock wall had left a slope of scree less steep than the gorge sides. If it wasn't too loose, he and LeFarge might be able to climb high enough to contact the rest of the company via line-of-sight transmission.

The rock wasn't too loose to climb, but it stopped at a cliff face they couldn't scale. Fifty meters to their left, however, the cliff ended in a cut or a gentler slope—Bass couldn't tell from where they were. "Think you can make it across there?"

"No problem, Gunny." LeFarge put his words into action and led the way across the steep slope.

The shallow roots of the bushes were spread wide enough to hold the weight of the two men as they stepped on their stems and grabbed hold of the branches. It took only a few minutes for them to negotiate the slope. They found a gentle rise to a notch in the ridge side another hundred meters up and clambered into it, breathing heavily from the exertion.

"See if you can raise anybody," Bass said. When he left the platoon, he had turned off the all-hands channel so he could concentrate on finding a way up the ridge. Now he flipped it back on while LeFarge set up the UPUD and started talking into it. But the steep-sided valley wound from side to side, and they had taken a couple of turns following it—there was too much rock between him and the platoon for clear communications. Bass heard enough to know that two or three more Marines were down and that only a few of the men in the open had managed to get back and join the fight. Most of the others, including the gun team, were still pinned in the open, unable to engage the bandits. He cursed silently as he fought his rising anger and frustration.

"I've got Battalion!" LeFarge exclaimed.

Bass shook his head. Battalion headquarters was more than a hundred kilometers away. How could they raise them but not get the company command unit, which was just a ridge or two away? "Let me talk to them."

LeFarge said something into the UPUD and handed it to him.

"Red Roof, this is Purple Rover Bravo Five," Bass said into the UPUD, giving the battalion call sign and identifying himself as the senior enlisted man of a group split off from Company I. "We are at," he rattled off their map coordinates, "in contact with more than two-zero-zero bandits.

Bandits are wearing chameleons and have blasters. We are taking heavy casualties. We need air support. Over."

"Purple Rover Bravo Five, that is not where your UPUD says you are."

"Red Roof, UPUD malfunctioning. Visual confirms our location. Over."

"Ay, Pancho, you think you're smart, don't you?" the battalion communications man said, and laughed. "You're not going to lure us into a trap that easily."

Bass's jaws clenched. The battalion comm man thought he was a bandit who'd managed to break into the net and was trying to get a mission launched to lead some of the FIST's aircraft into an antiaircraft missile ambush. "Negative on that shit, Red Roof!" Bass shouted.

There was a slight pause and the battalion communications man said, "Hey, Pancho, use proper radio procedure."

Bass drew in his breath sharply and cut off a withering response. "Red Roof, this is Purple Rover Bravo Five. I say again, this is Purple Rover Bravo Five. Purple Rover Bravo is at coordinates given and needs help now. Please provide. Over."

"I'll pass it up, Pancho. Red Roof out."

"Use the voice identifier, Red Roof. That'll confirm my ID," Bass said, but there was no response. The battalion comm man wasn't listening anymore.

LeFarge swallowed. If they didn't get help soon, the Bravo unit could be wiped out. "It's routine to use the voice-recognition identifier on all suspect calls," Bass said in a reassuring voice. "Let's go back and hold on until the air gets here." But he didn't feel as confident as he sounded.

"We'll hold out, that's all," Procescu said when Bass reported his contact with battalion. "We're hitting them harder than they're hitting us. Pancho'll probably cut and run before air can get here anyway."

Bass flipped down his goggles and scanned the slope. Working from the ends toward the middle, the Marines had slagged nearly half of it. But bandits in the unslagged rock had re-formed onto a line facing the Marines, and the line's lower end was on the bottom of the gorge, not higher on the slope where the Marines were concentrating their fire. He also saw that the far end of the ambush hadn't been thoroughly slagged; many targets were still fighting back. He wasn't as sure as Procescu that the bandits would run. There were probably more than 150 of them still in the fight, maybe closer to two hundred.

Bass raised his goggles to study the terrain and the eerie modern infantry battle with his naked eyes. Around him, effectively invisible men howled insults and tiny bits of star-stuff at each other, and he heard the snap of superconducting capacitors discharging, the louder cracks of ancient rock being split at sun-heat, the hiss of solid stone turning briefly liquid from the plasma bolts. But most of his mind was occupied with the tactical aspects of what he was looking at.

If the bandits extended their line across the gorge, they would be in position to assault the Marines; the Marines would have too many individual targets and they could be overwhelmed by sheer numbers. While Bass examined the ground the bandits would have to cross if they did assault, he saw gray flicker against the darker rock in the distance, moving to the left—the bandits *were* getting on line for an assault! He scuttled over to Procescu.

"Do you see what they're doing?"

The lieutenant nodded. "They're brave men, if they're going to stand up and charge," he said. "Or maybe they don't realize we can see them," Procescu added.

The bandits' fire changed its focus suddenly. Instead of shooting into the trees, or keeping the Marines still in the open pinned down, they started firing randomly at the rocks between themselves and the Marines. "They know." Bass swore. "They're sparking so many heat signatures that even with our goggles we won't be able to tell what's hot rock and what's them." Not only did these guys know what they were up against, Bass thought, they must have a pretty good communications net of their own, to coordinate their fire and maneuver so quickly.

"An assault force usually has to outnumber the defenders by three to one to succeed," Bass said. "They've got us outnumbered five or six to one."

"We've got assaulters and machine guns. They don't." Procescu's voice was neither as steady nor as confident as he wanted it to be.

"Fix bayonets, Lieutenant?" Bass gave the officer a skull-like grin. Procescu stared at the company gunny. "Numbers can count for a lot," Bass added.

"We're Marines. That counts for a lot too."

Bass grunted. On the side of his right thigh, he patted the pocket where he kept a four-hundred-year-old Marine K-Bar as a talisman. The ancient knife couldn't help now, but it somehow reassured him.

Six of the Marines in the open had made it back into the trees by the time Bass and LeFarge rejoined the unit. Two more had died trying. One of the six brought the gun with him and added its fire to that being put out by the others. But the Marines' fire was no heavier than it had been—five of the Marines in the trees were down, and one of the assault weapons was being fired by someone who wasn't very familiar with it. The last three crawled back into the trees while Bass and Procescu discussed the bandits' next move. Procescu sent one of them to each flanking position and kept the third in the middle.

Procescu looked at his handgun, shrugged. "I think we should all have blasters," he murmured.

Bass looked around. Up on the left flank three Marines had been killed. Their weapons looked usable. "Be right back," he said, and scrambled away. He was back in a moment and handed weapons to Procescu and LeFarge. Quickly, he checked his own. Out in the open he saw a swath of flesh color over a barely seen flicker and aimed at a spot just below it. He squeezed the trigger. The swath of flesh dropped out of sight. One less bandit to worry about.

Whistles shrilled suddenly through the cacophony of battle. A barely visible ripple of movement crept across the gorge. The assault began. In the middle and on the left flank the bandits had closed to little more than fifty meters before rising up to run at the trees. On the right flank the continued slagging of the rock face kept the bandits over a hundred meters away. However far they had to go, they screamed and fired as they charged.

Along their pitifully thin line, Marine officers and NCOs calmly ordered their men to pick their targets carefully, look for flesh and weapons, make every shot count, to kill, and kill, and kill before the bandits could reach them. But there were too many targets, and the Marines couldn't see all of them.

"Lieutenant! I've got Air," LeFarge shouted as he put down his weapon and spoke into the UPUD. "Call sign Flamer." He handed the unit to Procescu.

"Flamer, this is Purple Rover Bravo Actual," Procescu said into the UPUD. "What kept you?"

"Wrong address, Purple Rover," said the pilot of the lead A5G Raptor circling high above. "Looks like there's a lot of you down there. Who am I supposed to incinerate?"

"Do you see the open area, Flamer?"

"Affirmative."

"That's where Pancho is. Do him before he mingles with my positions in the trees."

"Too late for that, Purple Rover. Either you've got him so badly outnumbered you don't need us, or he's already in your position."

The bandits were indeed among them. The thud of a running foot hit the ground near where Bass lay. He looked up into a wild-eyed face above an out-of-focus area of green and brown. A blaster in the unclear area was pointing at him. He rolled toward the bandit as the heat of a plasma bolt passed over him. He rolled into the bandit's legs, knocking him over, then groped with one hand for the enemy soldier while his other reached for his combat knife. The two struggled briefly—the bandit tried to bring his weapon to bear, but Bass's knife proved to be better for infighting, and red spread freely over the bandit's chameleons. Bass rolled away to retrieve his blaster as the dead man's entire uniform turned red, as it mimicked the color of his blood.

"How close to the trees can you flame without scorching us?" Procescu said into the UPUD. Bass realized the lieutenant hadn't been aware of the hand-to-hand fight he'd just concluded only a few meters away. "That's too far away to do any good," Procescu said after a pause. "Bring it in closer." He listened, then said, "The only people standing are Panchos. With any luck the heat'll pass over us and hit them. Do it now."

A squad of bandits was directly in front of them. Bass gritted his teeth as he fired at the enemy.

"Bring it in closer!" Procescu shouted into the UPUD. Bass knew what that meant—they were going to be crisped by their own fire. Either way, from bandit fire or from their own Raptors, they were dead. At least it'd be fast, and they'd take most of the bandits with them.

Suddenly the screams of diving turbojets smothered all

other sounds and briefly stunned the combatants. Bass flicked on the all-hands channel. "Everybody *down, now!*" he ordered.

"Get as flat as you can," Procescu added, "get behind a ridge or a rock. This is going to be close."

The double-mach-plus Marine Raptors screamed almost straight down from the heavens. When the lead aircraft was still little more than a rapidly growing, shiny speck in the sky, it was stitching a line of plasma bolts from the bottom of the gorge to halfway up the left slope, barely fifty meters from the trees. Just when it looked as if it was going to follow its bolts into the holocaust in the gorge, its forward vernier jets flamed, bouncing it back skyward. Before the lead aircraft finished its maneuver, its wingman twisted to stitch bolts up the right side of the gorge.

The bolts from the Raptors' cannons were to the bolts of the assaulters what the assaulters were to hand-blasters. Each bolt vaporized whatever it struck, leaving a steaming hole nearly five meters in diameter. Molten rock pooled at the bottom of each crater. Gouts of lava flew everywhere; some landed harmlessly on rock and quickly solidified, some charred trees or set them ablaze, some killed men.

The wave of heat expelled by the explosions washed across the open and incinerated anyone in its path. The foliage on the nearer trees flashed vapor and the outermost line of trees burst into flame. For twenty-five meters into the trees, anyone standing was hit by a wall of super-heated air that seared lungs and peeled off skin. Most of the bandits were in the open or standing in the first twenty-five meters of the tree line. Not all of the Marines were behind something that could deflect the heat wave.

The stunned survivors picked themselves up and took stock. The few bandits who survived were in full flight. But Procescu was dead, as were Lieutenant Kruzhilov and

Staff Sergeant Chway and everybody who had been on the right flank with the platoon sergeant and the assaulters. LeFarge was gone—instantly vaporized—and the UPUD lay on the ground, now a thoroughly useless, half-melted chunk of slag. Half the Marines who began the day with the Bravo unit were dead. A quick survey told Bass ten times as many bandits had died in the fight.

"That's too damn many good Marines died today," Bass said to himself.

Third platoon's comm man had hidden behind a good-size boulder during the air attack, so both he and his UPUD survived. Bass used it to report the results of their fire mission to Flamer and to request pickup. While awaiting it, he looked at the black box with disgust. If the damn thing had worked right, they would have had air support before the bandits made their assault, and not so many Marines would have died.

Half an hour later the survivors of Purple Rover Bravo and the corpses of their dead—as much as could be found of them—were aboard hoppers, flying back to Battalion.

"You *what*?" Daryl George exclaimed in amazement. "No, no, no-no-no, you can't blame me for your incompetence! No wonder the you-pud didn't operate the way you expected it to. You aren't supposed to separate the satellite units from the company you-pud."

"Say again?" Bass demanded. His fists clenched and he took a step toward the manufacturer's rep.

George spoke quickly. "Only the company command unit Universal Positionator Up-Downlink uplinks to the string-of-pearls. The others communicate through it. Once you got a ridgeline between the company headquarters and your Bravo unit, you lost satcomm. It became just a line-of-sight radio. It's in the manual, right there for anyone to see: Appendix F, Annex Four, Section Q, Sub-note Seventeen. All there. It's all right there," he shrilled. "What's wrong with you people? Didn't you read the manual? You would have known that was going to happen when you split groups if you'd read the manual." George emphasized each word, pumping his fist up and down in time to the words. His normally sallow complexion reddened.

Sergeant Major Tanglefoot saw red but still put out a hand to restrain Bass. There was something more he wanted to know. "How did it give coordinates if it was 'just' a radio?"

"Through its inertial tracking system," George answered quickly. "I don't understand why it gave the reading it did—it's a very reliable inertial system. Maybe your comm man wasn't maintaining a regular pace. Maybe—"

Daryl George barely got out his second "Maybe." Bass knew every man in his platoon by name, knew their personal histories. They were more than just faces to him, they were his men. Bass remembered the ashy deposit on the ground that had been LeFarge, who had wanted only one thing out of life: a commission in the Marines. And Bass knew he would have made a good officer. And Lieutenant Procescu. Bass had known him for fourteen years, since the young Procescu had first joined Bass's squad as a PFC. The lieutenant hadn't gotten his head down quickly enough and his brain had been cooked instantly, the skull cracked open like an overboiled egg, brain matter swollen several times its normal size protruding obscenely through cracks in the glaring skull.

"I told you you'd personally pay if one man was lost because this Mark One didn't work as advertised," Bass cut in, his voice like a blaster bolt. "It didn't work and we lost a good many more than one man because of it."

It took Sergeant Major Tanglefoot, three first sergeants,

and two gunnery sergeants to pull Bass off George. But they'd given him a few seconds to work off his steam on the manufacturer's rep before they'd intervened.

It ultimately took three operations to fully restore vision in George's left eye, but the doctors declared him fit to be released from the hospital after only a week. Almost a year of intense physical therapy passed before he regained a reasonable degree of use of his right arm, though. His limp didn't last quite that long. And nobody ever notices his oral prosthesis. When the Marine Judge Advocate explained the civil charges that could be brought against him for failing to ensure that the Marines were properly informed of the deficiency inherent in the UPUD Mark I, George decided to drop criminal charges against Bass.

So Gunnery Sergeant Charlie Bass wasn't charged with attempted murder, which was precisely what he'd attempted; he was court-martialed for something many in the Confederation Marine Corps considered a much more serious offense: Article 32A(1) (b) of the Confederation Armed Forces Uniform Code of Military Justice, Conduct Unbecoming a Noncommissioned Officer. The court took extenuating circumstances into consideration before delivering its verdict. Gunnery Sergeant Charlie Bass was reduced one grade in rank. Staff Sergeant Charlie Bass was then assigned to duty with the 34th FIST on Thorsfinni's World, a hardship post somewhere out in the nether reaches of Human Space.

CHAPTER
ONE

"What does your middle initial stand for?" the recruiting sergeant asked. "I've got to have your full name."

From the age of eight, Joseph F. Dean despised the middle name his parents had saddled him with—Finucane, after his maternal grandfather. It was in that ill-starred eighth year of his life, on the first day of his enrollment at the New Rochester School for Gifted Children, that a ten-year-old upperclassman took to chasing him during recesses and after school, boxing his ears and kicking his rump, singing, "Fin-u-can, Fin-u-can, I can kick your new can!" Dean endured the torment as long as he could, and then one day he laid the bully's head open with a field-expedient cosh made from a sock and a piece of concrete he'd found in the street. The next day he was expelled from the prestigious school. Joseph Finucane Dean was not only an intellectually gifted child, but in the art of attack and defense, a precocious one.

"During your initial interview, Mr. Dean, you did not give your full name," the recruiting sergeant explained.

"Uh, Finucane, sir."

"Is that with an E?"

"Yessir," Dean answered, "terminal E," he emphasized, and then felt embarrassed at maybe sounding too pedantic.

Joe Dean was sitting in the Confederation Marine Corps

recruiting office as the result of a spontaneous decision on his part—especially since he'd always dreamed of joining the army, in the footsteps of his late father, who had been a highly decorated veteran of the First Silvasian War. He had lived and breathed army and could hardly wait until he finished college to enlist.

On a cold and blustery day, a too-familiar kind of day in the bleak and inhospitable city called New Rochester by its wearily cynical inhabitants, Joe Dean had felt good for a change. He walked lightly through the portals of the Federal Building and slipped into one of the interview booths reserved for the army recruiting office. Immediately, a computerized display activated and he found himself staring into the face of a young woman dressed in a pale green army uniform. She was very pretty, and he wondered idly if it was the image of the recruiter herself or one generated in cyberspace.

"My name is Sergeant Sewah Fernandez-Dukes of the Confederation Army Force," the image on the screen announced. "May I have your full name?" Dean felt a twinge of doubt, almost dismay. Somehow, the beautiful woman with the alluring voice just didn't fit his idea of what it was he wanted to be if he donned a uniform.

"Uh, yes, ma'am: Joseph F—"

"Gawdamn, Bulldog, I was so hungry I could've eaten the north end of a southbound *kwangduk*!" a powerful voice announced from the corridor at just that moment. Joe Dean stuck his head out of the booth and instantly the image of Sergeant Fernandez-Dukes disappeared from the screen. Two men, one short and squat and the other, the one who had just spoken, big—Dean estimated his height at about six-four and guessed he must weigh fully 250 pounds—were passing by. Both were dressed in impeccably tailored uniforms, bloodred tunic with a stock collar over navy-blue trousers. The bigger man's sleeves were adorned by huge gold chevrons worn points up with rockers underneath, so many Dean couldn't remember moments later how many there were. Other stripes marched up from the cuff in diagonal slashes to meet the lowermost rocker of the man's rank chevron. A bloodred stripe slashed down the outside seam of the big man's trouser leg, and a bronze collar device—an eagle rampant on a globe floating on a river of stars, a ribbon scroll in its beak—glinted powerfully in the light. Tucked under the big man's right arm, the one closer to Dean, was a plain ten-inch stick of black ebony capped by the same eagle device. He carried the stick wedged tightly in his armpit, his right hand grasping the stick just below the eagle's head.

The other man was short and squat with broad shoulders and thick arms on a short torso mounted on short, bow legs. He walked bent forward aggressively, his head thrust out while his arms pumped energetically back and forth, his hands balled into huge fists. Dean could see he talked out of one side of his mouth, and when he laughed, it sounded like a dog's *rark! rark! rark!*

The two men passed on down the corridor, talking and laughing loudly, their footfalls echoing sharply on the marble floor. They disappeared through a door marked MARINES.

Slowly, Joe Dean got up and followed them. Later, when he thought about that moment, it seemed as if scales had fallen from his eyes and everything he'd ever learned about the army, and all his dreams of joining it, just floated right out of his head. A man mesmerized, he drifted down the hallway past a long row of booths. Some were filled with young men and women earnestly talking to the computerized recruiters. He didn't bother to look to see which services they were talking to. The three booths at the end marked MARINES were empty. Joseph Finucane Dean slipped quietly into the first one.

"Gotta get all these details straight," Master Sergeant Riley-Kwami said, leaning back in his chair. He was the bigger of the two men Dean had seen in the hallway. From his neck hung a gold pendant on a midnight-blue ribbon speckled with silver diamonds, just like the one Dean's father had won—except the Marine's pendant bore the face of what looked like a Norse god instead of the Greek goddess on his father's. He could not help staring at the decoration. The recruiter was being patient with Dean because the scores on Dean's intelligence tests were among the highest he had seen since going on recruiting duty two years earlier.

The initial recruiting interview was completely automated. The interview booths worked up a complete physical profile on the prospective recruit while also checking, through other computer databases, every facet of the individual's life. Even before Dean stepped out of the booth, the Marine Corps knew he'd been kicked out of school at age eight and why, as well as the state of enzyme function in his stomach. Within five minutes, as he calmly answered innocuous personal questions, he had been found fully qualified and a highly desirable prospect for enlistment. Also, the first entries in his service record had been completed.

"Elly, terminate," Riley-Kwami said. "Elly's our pet name for the recruiting program," he explained. "I wanna shut her down for a few seconds so we can talk off the record. I'll turn her back on when we get back to the official stuff. She might know how to spell your name, Mr. Dean, but you gotta speak up to make sure. Funniest things happen to you when you rely too much on all this razzle-dazzle technology. Goddamn thing should've caught that during the interview and asked you to spell out your middle name." The big master sergeant shook his head. "Gotta get a tech man down here to fix that. Gawdamn army and navy's got the money to run all this crap, but what we got is real crap. Was it mine or the Bulldog's image on the computer screen in the interview booth?" he asked suddenly.

"Not you, sir. A heavyset man with two stripes over a gold star."

"Corporal Bildong, known affectionately throughout the Corps as 'Bulldog,' for obvious reasons." The recruiter nodded. "And Mr. Dean, don't call me 'sir,' for two reasons: first, I'm not an officer—I work for a living. Sorry," he added quickly as a look of bewilderment passed over Dean's face. "Old service joke, Joseph. You'll catch on. And second, because I'm a master sergeant and that's how I like to be addressed—as Master Sergeant."

Joe Dean smiled broadly, feeling comfortable and natural in Riley-Kwami's presence. He wanted to be like him.

"Finucane?" Riley-Kwami mused. There was something about this Joseph Dean that made the older man want to sit back and relax, tell a few war stories. He sensed they would not be wasted on this prospect. "A Gaelic name, isn't it," he said, a statement, not a question. "Ethnology is sort of a hobby of mine. You can get curious about that sort of thing in the Corps, because we get to so many places downstream where you gotta know such stuff. I mean *way* downstream, places the army never gets to unless there's a serious war on. So I always wonder where people come from. Languages you get to know too. You should hear me cuss in Sino-Hindi. I picked that up on Carheart's, when we were training the constabulary there, oh, twenty years ago now. Bulldog

was my fire team leader then and he's still a two-striper."
Riley-Kwami laughed shortly. "But a damn fine Marine,
Bulldog. Carheart's," he sighed, an indication that there
was more to duty there than training the constabulary.
"Hell of a tour, Carheart's. The *kwangduks* come up and
shit right in your mess kit, you don't watch real careful.
But the girls . . ." He let his voice trail off. " 'Finucane,'
huh? A beautiful sound that name has to it, Mr. Joseph
Dean."

"My mother's maiden name, si—uh . . . Master
Sergeant."

"You're learning, kid, you're learning," Riley-Kwami
said, shaking his forefinger at Dean. He looked at the
young man's red hair and freckles and decided he was
probably Irish through and through. "We don't see too
many pure Anglo-Irish anymore. We don't see many
pure anybodies anymore. Look at me: Most of my ancestors came from West Africa back before the Second
American Civil War. But some on my father's side came
from the Auld Sod during the Potato Famine. So my
family name's Riley-Kwami. You gawdamn Irish jumped
all kinds of fences these past five hundred years!" Master
Sergeant Riley-Kwami slapped his palm on his desk and
roared with laughter. "Okay, Elly," he said to the computer, "we're on again." Then to Dean, all business now,
"Mr. Joseph Finucane Dean, do you hereby honestly and
freely express the intention to enlist into the Confederation Marine Corps for a period of not less than eight
years? And do you also acknowledge that if you are
enlisted into this Corps, you receive no guarantees of
training, schooling, or assignment beyond those stipu-
lated by the Corps as in the best interests of the Corps?"

"Yes, I do."

"Then, Mr. Dean, be here tomorrow morning at eight

hours for your formal enlistment and swearing in. When you come down here tomorrow, bring only the items of personal hygiene you can carry in a small bag. Dress casually for the weather, but wear only those clothes you do not want to keep. Do not even bring money, is that clear? You will sign some papers and then be formally sworn into the Corps by the Skipper. You will then be transported directly from here to a port of embarkation to be determined in the morning. Your next stop after that will be Boot Camp. Is all this clear to you, Mr. Dean? You will be given a full briefing before you depart tomorrow. Tell your family that by midday we will contact them with information on how they can get in touch with you. Mr. Dean, you will be leaving this world for a very long time. Your training will be very hard and very long and you will most likely be assigned to duty in some of the most disagreeable places in space. You may very well die there. Do you still intend to be here tomorrow at the appointed time?"

"Yes, Master Sergeant."

"Elly, take a break." Master Sergeant Riley-Kwami reached his big paw out to Dean. Joe Dean stood and shook it firmly. "You have made the right decision, Mr. Dean." Riley-Kwami smiled. "It's a hell of a tough life, but you'll love it, Mr. Dean, you'll love it!" He grinned fiercely. Behind Master Sergeant Riley-Kwami's glittering eyes Dean thought he saw something, a wild spirit called up from the souls of long-dead tribal warriors or Gaelic clansmen that thrilled and frightened him at the same time. And then he knew: it was the thing that won you the midnight-blue ribbon with the silver diamonds.

Back at work, Joe Dean announced to his shift leader, Mr. Buczkowski, that he was quitting. "Butch" Buczkowski was a powerful man, physically hardened after nearly seventy years working out-of-doors on the lake. At eighty-two he was still a decade away from the mandatory retirement age. He shifted the cigar stub from one side of his mouth to the other before he spoke. "What the devil are you telling me, Joe?" Buczkowski squinted hard at the young man. His cigar shifted one more time.

"I went down to the government building and enlisted in the Marines, Butch."

Butch took the cigar stub out of his mouth and spat leaf fragments onto the ground before he stuck it back in. "Joe," he said patiently, "do you have any idea what the devil you're getting yourself into?"

"I have some idea," Dean answered almost defiantly.

"The devil you do!" Butch exploded. "Joe, you ever been on an interstellar ship, 'specially a goddamned troopship? You'll be cooped up in there thirty days before you get to that training world, whatever they're calling it these days—it was known as Arsenault in my time, after the guy who first settled it—but we recruits called it Asshole, because that's what the Confederation turned it into when they bought it from Arsenault's descendants a hundred years ago and made a planetary training center outta it. Yeah. Those Arsenaults were some smart people, unloading all that worthless real estate on the Confederation. Yeah. I was there during the First Silvasian War, the one where your daddy got his medal."

Butch was silent for a moment, regarding Dean. "When ya leaving?"

"Tomorrow morning."

"Jesus." Butch sighed. "I'd give you some money, kid, but you know, there won't be anywhere to spend it until you get your first liberty, and that probably won't be for another year. Hell, they might not even give you any pay until you're through with your basic training."

Butch took the cigar from his mouth and removed more masticated leaf with a stubby index finger, which he wiped on his coveralls. "I was in the army, Joe, and our depot was in the temperate region of the planet. The Marines' depot was in the tropics. We trained there for two months, and Joe, I was never so glad to see snow again! The dumb-ass Marines took most of their training in the tropical zone, except for the mandatory month on one of Asshole's airless moons—we called it the Turd—where we learned to live in near zero gravity and all that shit." Butch stuck the cigar back into the corner of his mouth.

"Hey!" Butch exclaimed suddenly. "Why the Marines? I thought you were settled on the army?"

Dean shrugged and his face reddened. "I don't know, Butch, I just changed my mind." He didn't want to explain what had happened—he didn't know if he could explain it.

Butch reflected for a moment. Dean had been working for him for five years, all through college. The young man would have quit to join the army much earlier, but when he'd finished high school, his mother wouldn't sign the papers to waive college. "Ah, well, Joe, you'll make a good Marine!" Butch stuck his hand out. He remembered the time a drunken deckhand on a Canadian hydrofoil had threatened to throw some passengers overboard. When he began roughing one of them up, Dean, only sixteen at the time, had stepped up and knocked the man unconscious with one blow. "Ah, shit, kid, I'll miss you! You'll make a damn fine Marine. Good luck to you!" They shook hands.

For the first time since he'd decided to enlist, Joe Dean felt a twinge of sadness. He never thought he'd regret leaving New Rochester, a dreary place on the shores of Lake Ontario, about twenty miles west of the site that had been Rochester, in the state of New York, before the Second American Civil War. The old city had been completely destroyed in the war and then rebuilt farther west about eighty years afterward. But he'd liked Butch Buczkowski, a rough and profane but honest and fair man.

Saying good-bye to his mother was much harder. But she had known this was coming for years and had prepared herself for it. He had not been prepared, though, and the next morning as he trudged away from the dingy complex where they lived, his throat was so constricted he could hardly breathe. His mother had refused to go with him because she knew he'd need the long walk to recover from their parting. She hugged him long and hard and silently right at the last. He had almost made it to the government building in the downtown section before the tears in his eyes had dried enough so he could see clearly.

CHAPTER
TWO

"Recruits!" Corporal Bulldog Bildong barked. "Stand at—ease!"

The slim officer who had just administered the Oath of Enlistment to the fifty-five men standing before him looked them over before saying anything further. The officer, a captain, Dean thought, looked to be about thirty-five years old. He was wearing a bloodred tunic with an epaulette on each shoulder and a high stock collar bearing the rampant-eagle device; his trousers were a bright gold. On each shoulder board was his insignia of rank, one gold orb. The captain had told them his name was Samson Malimaliumu. He began speaking in a clipped, rapid-fire voice:

"At ten hours you will depart here for the New Rochester spaceport, where you will board a shuttle bound for the starship CNSS *Private Thomas Purdom*, which is in docking orbit three hundred kilometers above Earth, for transit to the training world Arsenault. Arsenault is nearly two hundred light-years from Earth. The trip, mostly in hyperspace, will take approximately thirty Earth days. The *Purdom* has a complement of one thousand naval personnel. You will be traveling with approximately three thousand other recruits, most of them army and navy enlistees, all of them from Earth. The other recruits will be rendezvousing at the depot from other ports

31

around the globe. Once all the other Marine recruits are aboard, you'll be formed into your training company en route to Arsenault. You'll train in that company until you graduate—if you live that long. Arsenault is a very tough world and the drill instructors are even tougher. Upon graduation from Boot Camp, you will be assigned to the Fleet. Other training companies are being formed on the other worlds where we recruit and they will arrive at Arsenault at different times during your training cycle, but you won't have much contact with them, or with any Marines other than your drill instructors, until completion of your recruit training. In peacetime, Earth ships out recruits every six months. Your training will commence the moment you board the *Purdom*. You will be issued all necessary items of clothing and equipment while aboard her. By the time you reach our training base on Arsenault you will be familiar with the organization, history, and traditions of the Marine Corps; the rank structure of the Corps; the Confederation's system of military justice; the basic school of the Marine, including military courtesy, the manual of arms, close-order drill, how to wear the uniform, basic squad formations and the duties of the combat infantryman; you will learn basic weapons assembly and disassembly.

"Any questions? No? Corporal!"

Corporal Bildong came to attention facing the captain. "Sir!" he barked.

"You have command, Corporal."

"Aye aye, sir." He turned back to the recruits. "Detachment, atten-HUT!" Behind him Captain Malimaliumu marched out of the room.

At Bildong's command, the recruits tried with considerable lack of success, and many imaginative variations, to assume the military position of attention.

The corporal rolled his eyes and snorted. "Well, my

little dukbirds, at least you got a job for the next eight years!" A few of the recruits laughed at the remark and Bildong silenced them with a ferocious frown. "Okay, stand at ease," he commanded resignedly. "You'll learn all the military stuff when you get aboard the *Purdom*. Right now, here are meal chits for all of you. There's a cafeteria in the basement of this building. Go on down there, eat breakfast, and wait there for further instructions—that means don't leave the cafeteria, not for any reason. That gives you an hour to eat and get acquainted. Take your personal stuff with you."

"How soon do we get our guns and go and fight?" someone asked abruptly.

Bildong quickly fixed him with a steely look. "You want to fight?" he snarled, then continued in a calm but firm voice, "Don't worry, you'll get your chance. You'll get more chances to fight than anybody could want." He walked over to the recruit, a short, skinny, uncommonly black man. "And I guarantee you," he continued, staring into his eyes from inches away, "the first time you get into a fight, you'll wish to whatever god you pray to that you'd never heard of the Confederation Marine Corps. When Marines fight, people die. And some of those people are Marines. Maybe you. If you go into combat with the attitude you seem to have right now, you'll probably die in your first firefight." He stepped back and swiveled his head to look at everyone. "Any of you think you're tough guys? You think you know how to fight? Well, what you know is fun and games. This is no game, people. This is about life and death. A lot of death."

A long silence descended upon the recruits, fifty-five pairs of young eyes glued to the figure of the corporal. A chill had run through the room. These young people had enlisted in the Corps for the usual reasons people had been joining the military since at least the time of the

Romans: to test themselves, to get away from home, to travel, to have fun in foreign parts—both geographical and anatomical. Now, dimly, they were beginning to realize that the Confederation Corps of Marines might have its own serious plans for them that had nothing to do with travel and fun, especially not fun.

"Anybody else have a dumb question?" Bildong asked when the silence had stretched long enough to be uncomfortable.

"Uh, Corporal, when will we get the full briefing Sergeant Riley-Kwami mentioned yesterday?" Joe Dean asked innocently.

"*Sergeant* Riley-Kwami?" Bildong asked. "I don't know any *Sergeant* Riley-Kwami." Then an expression of surprised realization slowly came over his face. "Or do you mean," he began slowly, "*Master* Sergeant Riley-Kwami?"

"Uh, yes, uh, aye aye," Dean stammered, uncertain what he'd done wrong.

Bildong shuddered, then looked away and waved a hand at him. "Never mind with the 'aye aye,' you'll learn how to use the word properly later on." He looked back at Dean. "You did mean Master Sergeant Riley-Kwami?"

Not trusting his voice, Dean nodded.

"A sergeant has one more stripe than I do," Bildong explained with exaggerated patience. "A *master* sergeant has a good many more than that. We're not the army— we make the distinction." He paused to see if his point had gotten across, then continued, "Now, I believe you asked a dumb question?" He waited, and when Dean didn't answer, said, "Repeat your question."

"Uh, what about the full briefing Ma-master Sergeant Riley-Kwami said we were going to get before boarding ship?"

Bildong regarded him with wide-eyed amazement for a moment. "Sweet Jesus Muhammad, you a comedian or sumptin'?" Then he shook his head. "Recruit, you just got all the 'briefing' you're gonna get until you step aboard the troopship. Then they'll 'brief' you until it oozes outta your ears. Now go on down and get some slop. Might as well start getting used to Marine Corps food. Take the first ladder—that's what you probably call a stairway—on the left after you exit this room. When you're done, stay in the cafeteria. An NCO will join you there later to escort you to the port."

The cafeteria indeed served something that resembled "slop," and within seconds, with the fifty-five recruits crowding in, it was overfull and noisy. Fortunately, Dean was one of the first recruits in line, so he was able to find an empty table in a corner where he set his loaded tray. He took a taste of the glutinous material dished up as hot cereal and marveled at what they'd managed to do with plastic these days.

"Sit with you?" someone said. It was the skinny black kid who'd asked when would they get to fight. "My name's Frederick Douglass McNeal. But everybody calls me Fred."

"Joe Dean," he replied, and shook McNeal's outstretched hand. He was struck by McNeal's dark complexion. It seemed as out of place in this room full of shades of brown as did his own fair face. He remembered his recruiter saying, "We don't see many pure anybodies anymore." In a way, his almost-pure Irish ancestry and McNeal's evident almost-pure African gave them something in common.

"Guess we're both on Corporal Bildong's shortlist with our dumb questions, huh?" McNeal asked. Before Dean could respond, he said, "Look over there!" Dean glanced in the direction McNeal nodded and saw nothing but other recruits. "Look, look." McNeal pointed with his fork. "That girl." He indicated one of the cafeteria's counterwomen. Dean hadn't taken much notice of the cafeteria workers. This one looked pretty plain to him.

"What about her?"

McNeal leaned his head closer and whispered, "Does she shuck?"

"Huh? What?"

"You know." McNeal arched his shoulders and made an open gesture with his hands. Seeing Dean still didn't catch his meaning, he pounded one fist gently into a palm.

"Oh," Dean said. Redness instantly crept up to his hairline from under his collar. The survivor's benefit from his father's pension wasn't very much and he'd had to work most of the way through high school and college to supplement it, and didn't have much time or energy left over for an active social life. So he was particularly inexperienced with women, and in fact had never done anything more daring with a girl than hold her hand. The only woman with any meaning in his life up to then had been his mother, whom he loved, and he saw all other women in the same light.

Seeing Dean's embarrassment, McNeal apologized quickly. "I've got a big mouth."

"That's okay," Dean said. He was relieved that McNeal wasn't going to rib him about his inexperience. "Where you from, Fred?" he asked, changing the subject.

"Churchville," Fred answered quickly, then launched into his favorite topic: "They named me after a saint," he began, and enthusiastically told Dean all about himself. Dean reciprocated. By the time they were finished with what they could eat of their breakfast, the two had become friends. They were an incongruous pair, Fred McNeal, short and wiry and very black, and Joe Dean, tall and fair with reddish-brown hair and a face full of freckles.

After a while Dean leaned over and asked McNeal,

"Say, have you ever, you know, did it, uh, with a girl, Fred?"

"Hell no." McNeal laughed, covering his own embarrassment at the directness of the question. "Who needs a woman when you got these," and he held up the fingers of his right hand.

Breakfast over—the recruits were still too raw to think of the meal as "morning chow"—they cleared their trays and sat at their tables, waiting for the escort NCO to show up. And wait they did, sitting and standing around the way enlisted men of all armies at all times in all places have always waited.

"Why'd they make us come in at eight?" McNeal asked after more than an hour of sitting at the cleared breakfast table.

Dean shook his head. "I don't know. My dad was in the army, and he always complained about 'Hurry up and wait.' I guess this is what he was talking about."

"Didn't that officer say we were going to the ship at ten?" another recruit, who overheard him, asked.

"I think so."

"So it's half past now."

Dean shrugged. His father had been a career army man, and he didn't really know any more about the Marines than his companions, probably less since he'd made the decision to join the Marines only the day before.

Clearly annoyed that the recruits were lingering so long after breakfast, but unable to do anything about it, the civilian cafeteria workers tried as best they could to prepare for the noon meal.

At 10:45 a voice cracked over the hubbub. "Attention on deck!" About half of the new recruits continued their conversations.

The man who had called for attention was a sharp-looking corporal who'd entered the cafeteria quietly and unnoticed. When he saw he didn't have the room's full attention, he sighed and jumped onto a chair and from there onto an empty tabletop. "SILENCE!" he bellowed in a voice that carried more than two hundred years of parade-ground authority. Startled, the recruits turned their attention to him. The civilian workers had all heard this routine before and, since it wasn't directed at them, ignored it.

"That's better," the corporal said in a voice still powerful and penetrating but several decibels lower. He was of average height and build, with a dark complexion. His main distinguishing feature was a fierce, sweeping, black mustache. But with all eyes in the room fastened upon him, he seemed somehow larger than his actual physical size. Dean recognized the voice he'd used. His father had often projected his own that way and he called it his "command voice." He also realized that this corporal was a man used to commanding and being obeyed.

"I am Corporal Singh, and you are in my charge. From this moment until you finish your training on Arsenault—those of you who survive it—I will be with you, day and night."

"Oooh, one powerful, take-charge bozek, that corporal!" McNeal whispered into Dean's ear.

Somehow Singh heard. "Who said that?" he shouted. Again the recruits jumped at the sound of the corporal's parade-ground voice. The cafeteria workers continued about their business. "Now you people listen up," Singh shouted. "Two things I do not want to hear from any of you while I'm talking: your chow hole and your ass-hole!" The "hole" of "asshole" echoed in the corners of the room and out in the hallway, and people passing along the corridor on the floor above wondered idly who was doing all the shouting about holes. The silence that now descended upon the recruits was profound.

"Now listen up! You people may think you're about to embark on some kind of camping trip or big adventure. Well, I'm here to set you straight. My Marine Corps has been around for 225 years and we proudly trace our lineage all the way back to the United States Marine Corps, and through them to the Royal Marines of the United Kingdom—two of the fiercest bands of warriors ever to grace humanity. My job is to see that none of you screws up my Corps, and by all the prophets, I will see to it! We are warriors! That's our sole reason for existence. We fight and we kill. Believe me, that is no kind of camping trip or big adventure. For more than two centuries we have fought in campaigns and wars everywhere there has been fighting." As he spoke he paced back and forth on the tabletop. The recruits slowly edged closer to each other for protection from this suddenly very fearsome man. "Not once in our history have we been bested on the battlefield. Some of the fiercest fighters in Human Space have surrendered by the thousands without a shot being fired rather than risk being defeated by an eleven-man squad of Confederation Marines.

"People, you are about to be tested," Singh continued. "Shake all the civilian dust from your shoes. We are a proud force. We can go anywhere in Human Space and do more with less than anyone else. We go to places no one else has ever been. Beginning right now, we are going to find out which of you are good enough to qualify for membership in my Marine Corps."

All eyes were intently trained on Singh. Dean stood aghast with his mouth hanging open. For the first time he thought that maybe he should have stayed with the army's female recruiter instead of following Riley-Kwami and Bildong down the corridor.

Carefully, very carefully, McNeal nudged his new friend and, braving the wrath of Corporal Singh, whispered ever so quietly into his ear, "You trying to catch flies, your mouth open like that?" Dean's face turned beet-red for the second time that morning.

"You!" Singh shouted, and pointed his finger directly at McNeal.

McNeal's eyes widened, and he looked around. "Me?" he asked.

"Yes, you, recruit! Get over here! Now!"

McNeal stood at attention before the table.

"What is your problem, recruit?"

"I have a big mouth, Corporal!" McNeal answered immediately.

"Yes, you do, young man," Singh replied in a fatherly tone of voice. "Now assume the position!" he shouted, pointing at the floor. McNeal just stood there, uncomprehending. "Get down on the floor, on your belly, hands flat on the floor under your shoulders," Singh said in a patient, schoolmasterly tone of voice, "and do push-ups. Count each one off as you do it. Now begin. That's right, that's right. Good."

To the sound of McNeal's steady "One, two, three, four," Singh addressed the remaining recruits. "You will form up in ranks there." He pointed to the side of the large room, where there was a bare space, bereft of tables and chairs. "From here I will march you to the bus that will take you to the shuttle that will lift us to the CNSS *Private Thomas Purdom* in docking orbit. Do you understand?"

A few voices said, "Yes, Corporal." A few more voices quickly chimed in. Singh looked at the group expectantly. Someone got the hint and shouted, "Yes, Corporal." This time more than half of the assembled recruits echoed the reply.

"Let's try it again. Do you understand?"

This time nearly all of them yelled out, "Yes, Corporal."

"The *Purdom* is in a stable orbit. It can wait up there for a long time if it has to. Now let me hear it. Do you understand?"

Everybody shouted back, "Yes, Corporal."

"All right, then, do it. Over there, four ranks. Tallest to my left, shortest to my right."

The cafeteria erupted into a chaos of movement as all fifty-five recruits scrambled to get to the open space Singh ordered them to.

"Not you," Singh snapped to McNeal, who had joined the scramble. "You're doing push-ups." McNeal groaned and rubbed his already aching arms before dropping back into position.

Many of them knew how to line up in ranks, but the concept of lining up by height wasn't familiar to all of them, and that caused confusion in getting lined up. More important, though, nobody wanted to be in the front row, where they'd be close to the corporal with the fearsome voice. Instead of getting into something resembling a military formation, they wound up huddled in a mass against the wall.

Singh looked at them with an expression of amazed pain and lightly dropped off the table. He stalked toward them with slow, deliberate paces, stopped a few feet in front of the middle of the mass and drew himself up erect, facing them. "What are you trying to do to my Marine Corps?" he began softly. "Are you all political appointees? Is that it?" He began moving with brisk steps and sharp movements, bent forward at the hips, head jutted forward, sticking his face into the faces of the unfortunates in the front of the mass of recruits. His voice rose in volume as he paced and spoke. "Are your daddies and mommies influential? Influential enough to get around the law and have you enlisted into my Marine

Corps even though you aren't qualified? Did they even manage to get some politician to promise that you'd get commissions, even though the law requires that no one be commissioned an officer of Marines until and unless he's proved himself as an enlisted Marine? Well?" He stopped in front of one edgy recruit and almost shouted that last word directly into his face.

The recruit looked nervously side to side, tried to press himself farther back into the bodies to his rear, but they were too tightly packed for him to squeeze through.

"N-n-no, Corporal," he finally stuttered. "My parents didn't do that. They don't have any political friends."

Singh pulled back from him, looked disdainfully at the others. "Any of you? I want to know who the political appointees are so you can be washed out of my Marine Corps now, before you have a chance to become a blight that will rot this Corps at its core!"

Nobody spoke up.

"You're sure," Corporal Singh said. "None of you are political appointees. We'll see. I guarantee you, anyone in this room who isn't fit to be a Marine won't last out the training on Arsenault. Now, form up on me. Four ranks. By height. Move!"

The recruits milled and shuffled about, but came no closer to getting into formation—nobody wanted to be in that front rank.

"*Aargh!*" Singh finally cried out. "You, you, you, and you." He pointed to the four tallest. "Over here."

The four reluctantly went to where he pointed and clustered against the wall.

"You." Singh pointed to one of the four. "Stay where you are. You," he pointed to a second, "stand three feet in front of him. You," he pointed at the third, "three feet in front of him. You," the last, pale recruit, "three feet in front of him. Now," he said when the four were lined up as he directed, "that didn't hurt, did it?"

Singh returned his attention to the others. "You, you, you, and you." He pointed to the next tallest. "Line up next to them, an arm's length away."

One of the four sprinted to stand next to the one against the wall. The others saw him and ran as well. The slowest looked aghast as he realized he was going to be in the front row.

Singh turned back to the remaining recruits. "See, it's easy. Now, look around you, see who you're taller than, who you're shorter than, and line up accordingly. If you don't see anyone shorter than you, get to the end of the line." He moved back several paces to give them as much room as they needed and stood easy with his arms folded over his chest. It took longer than it might have, but less than it could have, before they were standing in formation. It was a sloppy formation. Hardly anybody was directly behind anybody else, and their left-to-right dress was as crooked as a broken-backed snake. But it was a formation.

"I'm not going to give you proper marching orders," Singh said when the recruits stopped milling about and were all standing still, facing him. "You wouldn't understand them and I'd only have to repeat myself." He still used his parade-ground voice, but it held no trace of anger or frustration. "You will do what I say, when I say, and how I say, and we will all be on the bus in a few minutes and on our way to the shuttle port. Once we are aboard the *Purdom*, the next stop will be Confederation Marine Recruit Depot, Arsenault. Welcome aboard, people. Start walking through the door. You too, bigmouth." McNeal scrambled to his feet and joined the rear of the formation.

On the way out of the cafeteria, Dean realized that Corporal Singh had walked into a room full of noisy, energetic young men—none of whom knew him, and most of whom were bigger than he was—and gotten them all to be quiet, listen to him, and do what he said. Singh had not hit anyone nor threatened violence—he had done it all strictly with the force of his voice. Suddenly, he knew this was something he wanted to be able to do himself, he wanted that parade-ground voice—and everything that went with it.

CHAPTER
THREE

When the fifty-five recruits finally boarded the shuttle and the flight attendants checked that the restrainers holding them into the acceleration seats were fully deployed, the recruits' anxiety about Corporal Singh changed to excited anticipation. Many of them had been off Earth before, visiting one of the orbiting recreation parks. Some had been to the moon. A few had toured Marshome on the fourth planet, or Amoropolis, on Venus. One claimed he'd been to Ceres Station in the asteroid belt, but not everybody believed him.

Joe Dean had never been higher above the surface of the Earth than a short-hop in an atmospheric flier on a class trip that took him from the shores of Lake Ontario to New Columbia District. McNeal claimed never to have flown in anything, but that was harder to believe than the kid who claimed to have been to Ceres Station. Just one day earlier, when he'd decided to sign up, Dean had taken the biggest step of his life; then he'd taken another when he swore his oath of enlistment; now he was aboard a nearspace shuttle to take the longest trip he'd ever been on, three hundred kilometers straight up and halfway around the world to a waiting starship.

A starship that would take him on a journey so far that, even though the trip would last only a month, the light he saw from the star at his destination wouldn't be seen on

Earth for nearly two centuries. Later, as a Marine, he expected to journey even farther, probably to stars so distant his great-grandchildren might not live long enough to see the light that would shine on him. The thought made him feel cosmically insignificant.

Joe Dean desperately needed to believe that at least one of the recruits he was embarking on this journey with had been at least as far as Ceres Station, even if none of them had ever been on a starship. None of the recruits had even visited a real starship before, and soon they would be boarding one.

Without warning, the shuttle began to shake as its jets whirred up. Dean looked out the nearest porthole. The air was shimmering around one of the atmosphere-jets that would lift the shuttle to the top of the stratosphere, where its ram jet would take over to lift it the rest of the way to docking orbit.

The public address system clicked, and the recruits stopped to listen—no matter what any of them claimed about familiarity with space flight, none of them had been lifted into orbit enough times to have become jaded about it.

"Good evening, ladies and gentlemen—" The P.A. voice laughed, then said, "Well, I guess it's just gentlemen on this flight. This is Captain Wu Chalmers. It's my pleasure to welcome you aboard United Atmosphere's orbital shuttle, Flight 402. We'll be lifting off in a few moments." His well-modulated voice exuded confidence and calm. "Our flight plan today calls for us to take off on a southeasterly heading and climb to Launch Point, which at this hour is a few hundred kilometers east of Bermuda. Don't bother looking out the portholes to see that island paradise, because we'll be close to fifty kilometers up and it'll just be a speck in the ocean. At Launch Point you'll experience a moment of weightlessness, but don't let that disturb you. It's normal to go into momentary free fall when the shuttle switches over from atmosphere-jet to ram. When we reach orbital altitude, which is way up there in the thermosphere, and the engine cuts off, we'll be in null-g for the rest of the trip. Along the way we'll pass within visual range of the interplanetary shipping docks. I'll let you know when we do so you can take a look. One third farther around the Earth we'll reach the interstellar docks. Flight time from takeoff to docking should be approximately seventy-five minutes.

"Take a nap, read, whatever. Just, please, remember, the Confederation Aviation and Orbital Administration rules require that you remain in your seats for the duration of the flight. If you must relieve yourself during this time, draw the privacy curtain around your seat and use the convenience console in the seat. Your flight attendants will demonstrate how to use them when they show you the emergency procedures. Thank you for flying United."

There was another click and the senior flight attendant came on to give the emergency instructions, which were almost the same as those on an atmosphere liner; hardly anybody paid any attention.

"There it is!" someone gasped.

"Where?" another recruit asked, excited.

"There," McNeal said, awed.

As the pilot maneuvered the shuttle craft, the passengers got an excellent view of the starship where it hung silhouetted above the terminator.

"My God," someone whispered.

"Is it the *Purdom*?" another asked.

"Yeah, I can see the name," his companion responded.

"How can you see the name?"

They'd all seen images of starships: trids, holos, even two-D's. But mere images couldn't do justice to what was floating before them. The ship was vaster and far more ugly than they'd imagined. The CNSS *Private Thomas Purdom* was an enormous ebony conglomeration of metal nearly two kilometers along its main axis and several hundred meters at its greatest girth. Dozens of tenders and service shuttles swarmed busily about her sides, doing maintenance or delivering passengers and supplies. On the shadow side, work parties encased in protective suits scuttled over her hull, laboring under lights as brilliant as tiny suns.

As the *Purdom* loomed larger and larger through the ports, the recruits' exuberance turned gradually into awed silence. They were overwhelmed by the sense they were in the presence of a leviathan that could live only in deep space where it had been born, never to make planetfall. When the ship became outmoded or was damaged beyond repair in the unimaginable ferocity of battles fought in the farthest reaches of Human Space, she would be returned to an orbital port like this for salvage and her reusable components incorporated into another vessel.

Gradually, as the shuttle entered the enormous shadow cast by the starship, it was engulfed in darkness. Closer up, the activity about the *Purdom* seemed to be even more frenetic. They passed by tenders shuttling back and forth, and Dean flinched at their passage, afraid they might crash into one of these other craft that so ponderously maneuvered about their mysterious business around the starship's hull. An enormous square of light loomed larger and larger in the hull as the shuttle neared, and almost before its passengers realized, they were inside an enormous berthing compartment.

Guided by two silver-suited sailors, an accordion tube snaked out of a bulkhead forward of the shuttle's wing. A loud bang reverberated through the shuttle's hull as the tube made contact with the hatch's locking ring. Thunks and pings penetrated the hull as the tube was locked into place. A flight attendant undogged the hatch and a sailor inside the tube opened it from the outside.

"Listen up, people," Corporal Singh called for their attention. "Stay in your places until someone comes to move you. I don't care how many times you've been to a disney, this is a navy ship. It's different. Very different. Stay where you are until I tell you to move."

"I'll take over now, Marine," a khaki-clad navy chief petty officer said as he swam aboard during Singh's little speech. He gave a slight push against the hatch frame and drifted out of the way of two sailors who swam through behind him. Each pushed a large, spoollike object ahead of him. "Hook 'em up," the chief ordered.

"Aye aye," replied one sailor. He hooked his spool to a stanchion and led the other sailor, who kept his spool, to the rear of the shuttle. Using well-practiced movements, the sailor with free hands pulled out the end of the thin cable wound around the spool. He attached a clip on the end of the cable to the man in the outermost portside seat. The sailor pulled out more cable. Two meters along was another clip, which he attached to the second man, and so on. The cable was studded with clips at two-meter intervals. In moments every recruit on the port side of the aisle was attached. Back in front, the sailors retrieved the other spool, took it to the rear of the cabin, and repeated the hooking process on the starboard side.

"We're going to disembark in an orderly manner," the chief announced when the sailors had completed hooking up the recruits. "As you might have noticed when the shuttle was in final approach, this ship is big. It's easy to get lost if you don't know your way around—and you aren't going to be aboard long enough to learn. That's why the tether, so nobody gets separated on the way to the troop area. Now, when I give the word, you," he pointed to the recruit in the port-side aisle seat, "will go with this sailor," he indicated one of the two ratings who'd hooked the recruits together. "When the last man on the port side reaches me, you will all stop so the first man on the starboard side can be hooked to him." He looked at the chief flight attendant for the first time since boarding the shuttle. "They're ready to be unlocked, ma'am."

The chief flight attendant did something outside the sight of anyone in the shuttle's seats and all the safety restraints unbuckled and retracted.

"All right, you, move," the chief ordered the recruit in the first seat. The recruit gripped the arms of his acceleration seat to keep from drifting away. The chief gave him a hard look. "I said 'move.' That means now. Go." The recruit looked back over his shoulder at Corporal Singh.

"Time to move out, people," Singh said. "Do it like the chief says." He grinned at the chief petty officer as the recruits started stringing out, floating not quite under control behind the sailor leading them.

The chief glowered at Singh, then returned his grin. "Maybe you got yourself a good bunch here."

Beyond the tube that connected the shuttle to the interior of the ship, they were immersed in the sounds and smells of a starship preparing for flight. The continuous stream of shuttles arriving and departing sent clanks echoing through the interior of the ship. Incoming cargo being shifted about in the airless loading bays clanged harshly through the metal bulkheads. The crews working on the ship's outer hull made a steady rain of pings. This exterior cacophony overlay the constant thrumming and thudding of machinery deep within the ship's bowels. Dollies, hoists, and monorails whined and screamed and whirred as they moved cargo and people about. Men at work shouted and chief petty officers barked a constant string of orders. The odor of fresh lubricants taxed the ship's air scrubbers. The body smells of sweaty deckhands wafted over the recruits as they rushed by them in their work.

One of the sailors grabbed a downward-passing elevator cable and hauled the first recruit in line with him. The cable only went "down" in the sense that it ran perpendicular to the deck they were on, and as far as anyone could be sure, it went "down" according to how the shuttle was oriented in the docking deck. Singh helped the chief and his other sailor link the rest of the recruits onto the cable until the chief signaled him to grab hold and go.

It seemed like a long time before the sailor in the lead stepped off the cable and started unlinking the following recruits and pulling them into a passageway that was empty of anything but them and a monorail car. Most of the noises that had assailed them on the loading deck were muted down here.

Wasting no time, the chief and his men crowded the recruits into the waiting car. As soon as everyone was aboard, he pulled himself into the front of the car, grabbed a handhold, and picked up a microphone. The handhold wasn't for decoration—the car lurched forward immediately and the chief would have sailed down the car's length if he hadn't had a grip on it.

"Listen up," he said into the mike. "This ship has twenty-five decks—that's 'levels' to you landlubbers. You're on Deck Twenty-three. You will not leave Deck Twenty-three for the duration. Remember that! Your training area for this flight is half a kilometer sternward, in Area Whiskey. Remember that! You will be confined to that area for the entire voyage. Don't worry, it'll be big enough for all of you. When we arrive there, I'll hand you back to your corporal and won't have to worry about you until it's time to jettison you on Asshole."

The monorail disgorged the fifty-five recruits into a

huge, well-lighted bay. To their surprise, at least 150 other recruits were already there, gripping handholds sticking out from what Dean thought of as the ceiling. They faced a raised dais behind which a group of Marines managed to hover without seeming to hold on to anything. They were dressed in green jackets and trousers with khaki-colored shirts. Each wore a brown-leather "Sam Browne" belt over the green jacket—the Class A uniform, as the recruits were soon to learn. That was the only uniform they were to see, except for garrison utilities, until after they graduated from Boot Camp and were assigned to the Fleet. Each of the Marines on the dais wore a kaleidoscope of ribbons fastened above his left jacket pocket.

Corporal Singh nudged and pushed his group into the rear rank of the bobbing recruits already holding on there and made sure each grabbed a handhold. He nodded toward an officer on the dais, a captain, judging by the gold orb that graced each shoulder strap on his jacket.

"At ease!" the captain shouted. "That means, shut up and listen up, in civilian," he added. He spoke with a distinct but unfamiliar accent. Silence, punctuated only by the humming of the air ducts, the creak of expanding and contracting metal, and vast booming noises far within the hull—sounds that would accompany them all the way to Arsenault and soon go unnoticed—was immediate.

The captain smiled and nodded approvingly. "You're learning. My name is Captain Tomasio and I am your company commander. Welcome to Company A, First Battalion, Fleet Training Regiment. These Marines up here with me are the company executive officer, the company first sergeant, and your drill instructors. Your squad leaders and fire team leaders—you'll learn what all those are very soon—will be selected from among you, once we get organized and get a few things straightened out. We are all going to get to know each other very well over the next six months. Now, painted on the deck in front of each bulkhead—that's 'wall' in civilian—you will see large yellow squares numbered one to four. When your name is called, you will move smartly, and I emphasize smartly," a ghost of a smile flickered across his lips, "to your designated number. That will be your platoon assignment. Later, you will be organized into squads and fire teams by your drill instructors." Captain Tomasio turned to one of the other Marines. "First Sergeant."

The company first sergeant didn't appear to make any movements to direct himself, but still drifted sharply to the front of the platform. "When I give your name and platoon assignment, move sharply." He barely glanced at the clipboard in his hands when he began calling the names off: "Abercrombie, one . . ."

The Marines had an ancient expression they used to describe what happened when the first sergeant started giving platoon assignments to the recruits: Chinese fire drill. None of the recruits had much experience with movement in null-g, and most had none at all. There was chaos in the compartment for several moments until, at a soft command from Captain Tomasio, the drill instructors took over and started physically moving the recruits from their handholds to their designated platoon areas.

Dean found himself assigned to the second platoon. Fred McNeal joined him there and the two shook hands happily.

The following hours passed in a whirlwind of hurry-up-and-wait, punctuated by moments of frenzied activity and confusion. Before they were through, all the recruits streamed perspiration from every pore. First, all personal possessions, clothing, watches, rings, even toothpaste, were confiscated and locked away, to be returned when the recruits joined the Fleet; everything they would need over the next six months would be issued to them.

CHAPTER FOUR

Second platoon's chief drill instructor was a barrel-chested staff sergeant of about forty named Neeley. The first assistant D.I. was an older man, very slim and immaculate in his Class A uniform, named Staff Sergeant Pretty. No one dared laugh when he said his name, though. His embroidered red chevrons consisted of three bars with points up and a rocker underneath with a flaming-sun device in the center. These chevrons were much smaller and utilitarian than those worn on the dress uniform Dean had seen on Riley-Kwami at the recruiting office. Corporal Singh was the junior drill instructor. The three instructors quickly put them through their paces. At the double—which was quite a trick in null-g.

"Line 'em up, line 'em up, line 'em up," Staff Sergeant Neeley cried out for what felt like the five hundredth time since Captain Tomasio turned the recruits over to the D.I.'s. "In alpha order." This time—in reality the sixth—it took only a fraction of the time it had the first; by now they knew whose names came before and after theirs.

"Name," demanded the lance corporal seated at yet another battleship-gray desk.

"Anderhalt, Shaqlim X," said the first recruit in line.

The lance corporal typed the name into his computer, then glanced over the personnel display that popped up on his screen. "Date of birth?"

"April eighth, 2427."

The date of birth matched. "Mother's birth name."

"Lahani Schwartz."

That also matched. One last check for verification—or maybe it was just for the annoyance factor. "Blood type."

"AB negative, N, Duffy," also matched.

"Put your left wrist in there." The lance corporal pointed at a buff-colored ring on top of a box on the corner of his desk nearest where his subject gripped a handhold.

Anderhalt put his wrist in the ring. The lance corporal pressed a large red button on the side of his keyboard. The ring contracted until it was in full contact with his skin. There was a muted click, then the ring expanded back to its original size.

"Next."

Anderhalt, not having been told to move, stayed where he was. The lance corporal looked at him for the first time. "You can go now. And take your wrist with you, I don't want it."

Anderhalt flushed and hastily did what he was told.

"Name," the lance corporal said to the next recruit in line.

Everyone strained to see what the shrinking ring had done to Anderhalt, but Pretty and Singh were hustling him down the passageway, and they each had to wait their turn to find out what was happening.

After his turn, Dean was still examining the featureless bracelet the ring had clamped onto his wrist when the chief D.I. called the platoon to attention.

"You have just been issued your personnel record," Neeley said when all of his recruits were looking at him. "Right now it's just about blank, because you're blank. All it contains is your personal data, your medical history, and the results of the tests you took when you enlisted. Every company office and every personnel department from battalion or squadron on up in the Marine Corps has a reader for it. Every company, battery, and squadron first sergeant in the Corps controls a writer that will update your record as things happen that need to go into your record. Every time your company updates your record, the update will also relay to the next-higher command, which will relay it to the next-higher command, and so forth, until your record is completely updated in Central Data in Saint Louie.

"You can't muck about with it. There is no way you can read the data it contains, and no way you can alter it. There are only two ways that bracelet will ever come off you. One is if you are released from active duty at the end of an enlistment, through retirement, or as the result of a court-martial that kicks your worthless hindquarters out of this man's Marine Corps. The other is if some felonious aggressor out there on some godforsaken planet you'd never set foot on if Mother Corps didn't say you had to blows your hand off.

"If anyone tries to muck about with the data in that bracelet, the bracelet will erase. If you are the one who did it, stand by for a court-martial. More likely, though, anyone mucking about with it will be a scum-sucking aggressor who had the rare good luck to take you prisoner, something that doesn't happen very often, let me tell you. If that's the case, well now, that's why the data is programmed to erase in case of unauthorized entry. We don't want any rat-snorfing aggressors getting their sklit-licking fingers on that data.

"By the way, if you should ever be taken POW, stand by for rescue. In the entire two and a quarter centuries of the Confederation Marine Corps, only one Marine has remained a live POW for more than ninety-six hours standard. In that instance, the Marine in question was on leave and it was seventy-three standard hours before anyone knew he'd been taken. A rescue mission was planned, mounted, and executed in under twenty-four hours. The only thing that went wrong with the mission was the Marine being rescued was in aggressor hands for nearly ninety-seven hours.

"Enough grab-assing for now. You've got more processing-in to undergo. Corporal Singh, move them to the next station."

McNeal wondered if he was the only one who thought it was ominous that Staff Sergeant Neeley had said only one Marine had ever remained a *live* POW for more than ninety-six hours.

"Let's sidestep briskly through that line, people," Staff Sergeant Pretty said to the line of recruits clad only in whatever underwear they'd worn when they left home that morning. "The sooner you get through, the sooner you get to stop for chow. The longer you take to do everything, the longer it will be before you get to stop to sleep. I don't need much sleep, so it doesn't matter to me if you don't get any. And I don't have anywhere to go for the next month, so it doesn't matter to me if you want to spend all that time milling around when you could be moving briskly and getting your processing-in done with."

That looks too much like a coffin, Dean thought as he approached the first position on the line. They didn't really sidestep; they pulled themselves along a chain of handholds standing out from the bulkhead. The contraption at the first position resembled a coffin only in general dimensions: a box seven feet by two feet by three feet. But it wasn't laid out flat, it stood up.

"Remember to keep your eyes closed when you're inside," Corporal Singh said to each man as he moved into the box.

Dean moved up to the box, glided into it, and flinched as the door closed behind him. He closed his eyes as instructed and didn't see the sensors as they measured him. Ground to crown. Toe to heel to ankle, height of arch and instep. Ground to crotch, ground to waist. Hip to armpit to shoulder. Neck. Shoulders, delt to delt. Chest width and depth. Waist width and depth. Hips width and depth. Chin to crown to nape. Temple to temple. Occipital bulge. Height and width of brow. Spacing of eyes. Length of nose, breadth of nostrils. Width of mouth. And more.

It was over in less than a second.

The door popped open. Dean pushed himself out of the box, handholded himself to the next station, held out his basket, and accepted the two pair of brilliant red sweatpants that were dropped onto it by the robot server. Handhold again and be issued two equally bright sweatshirts. Another handhold and receive three sets of underwear. Again, and get four pair of socks. Once more for cloth shoes, two pair. At the last position, robot hands fitted a Marine chameleon utility hat onto his head.

Back in line with the others who'd received their clothing issue, waiting for the rest of the platoon to go through the line, Dean examined his cache. The sweatshirts bore a large gold emblem on their fronts: an eagle rampant on a river of stars, the emblem of the Confederation Marine Corps—the same insignia worn on the collars of the dress uniform. The word MARINES ran down the outside of each sleeve. A gold stripe ran down the outside of each pant leg, with the word MARINES in red running its length. The underwear was utilitarian, the socks were thick, with cushioned soles. The white shoes were soft and flexible, and had rubber soles. Only the hat was different.

It was drab, almost colorless. Dean snaked an arm

through the basket's handle and used that hand to grip the handhold. With his free hand he took the hat off his head and examined it. It seemed to be sort of green, sort of gray, sort of—Dean blinked, sort of red. He moved his hand and held the hat against the side of his basket. It turned almost the same tan as the basket.

"Hey, look at this," Anderhalt exclaimed.

Dean looked at the other recruit, who held his hat against the bulkhead. The hat was distinctly gray. Anderhalt started looking around for a different color to hold his hat against.

"Belay that, people!" Neeley roared. The drill instructor was suddenly in front of Anderhalt, glowering at him, then glared down the row of recruits who had already received their clothing issues. "Just hang where you are and wait. When everyone has their issue, I'll explain everything you've been issued—including the chameleon effect." He started to return to the line of recruits who hadn't yet received their clothing, then briefly turned back. "Don't just stand there in your skivvies, get dressed."

Soon enough they all had their clothing issue and were standing in formation, each recruit a brilliant splash of red against the battleship gray of the compartment's bulkhead. Staff Sergeant Neeley stood front and center to address them.

"You will not be issued proper uniforms until we reach Arsenault," he told them. "There are two reasons for that. The first is you will undergo a strenuous physical fitness program aboard this ship, and you will be eating a diet carefully calculated to help bring you to peak physical condition. That means you will change shape—for most of you, that means lose fat and replace it with muscle. Some of you will gain weight. Either way, the clothes that fit you today won't fit a month from now. Before you disembark this ship, you will step into the coffin again to be remeasured. These two measurements, today's and on your last day, will be one gauge of how your fitness has progressed.

"The second reason is a very practical one. Shortly after you came aboard the *Purdom*, you were told that you would be restricted to this deck for the duration of the voyage." He paused to sweep his gaze across the faces of everyone in the platoon. "Let me assure you, no one else on board this ship is wearing scarlet sweat suits. Should you attempt to go to any other part of the ship, you will be seen and reported. Let's not find out what will happen to anyone who leaves Deck Twenty-three." He paused to consider for a moment, then continued.

"A number of you have examined your headgear and wondered why they don't seem to have any particular color—or that they don't seem to stick to one color. Maybe you've heard of Marine chameleons. That's what we call our field uniform, chameleons. Chameleons are only worn on combat operations, except that the head-gear is worn with the standard green garrison utility uni-form. Within limits, chameleons pick up the color pattern of whatever they are closest to. That makes a fighting Marine very hard for an enemy to see. You may well wonder why you have chameleon headgear now. Again, there are two reasons. The first is so you will get used to the idea. The second is so you will look as empty-headed as you are at this time."

Neeley looked at Singh. "Move them on to the next station."

The recruits knew their day was nearing its end when they discovered they could hardly drag themselves any farther through the maze of corridors and compartments that constituted Area Whiskey. At last Staff Sergeant Pretty led them into a large compartment equipped with bunks and personal gear lockers.

The bunks—called "racks," to the great mystification of the recruits—were fastened to the bulkheads or to vertical pipes running from overhead to deck, three high. There were just enough for the men of second platoon. Their spacing looked odd—there seemed to be exactly as much space below the bottom rack as there was above the top one.

The recruits of second platoon were told for the time being just to stow their gear in the lockers as best they could and secure the lockers with the padlocks that were part of their issue. In the morning, Pretty promised, he would come around with Corporal Singh and show them how to do it properly, to be ready for the continuous round of inspections that would soon form a major part of the routine of their life aboard the starship. "If any of you must jerk off in the night, kindly see none of it gets on the guy on the bottom," Pretty announced just before he led them to the galley for their first starship meal.

Sometime during all this rushing around, getting issued clothing, personal and hygienic supplies, personnel-record bracelets, and everything else they'd need during the one-month voyage, the starship pulled out of Earth orbit and headed for its first jump point. For this first phase of its movement, the *Purdom* rotated around its long axis. The rotation created centripetal force, which gradually restored an ersatz gravity. The transition was so gradual that the recruits were in the galley, eating solid food off plastic trays, before they realized they weren't floating anymore.

The galley was enormous, more than big enough to hold the recruits of Company A. The food was plentiful and delicious and the recruits ate ravenously. Even

McNeal was so hungry he finished his meal with hardly a word between mouthfuls.

Back in the platoon bay, Pretty announced that the time was 22 hours. "Your day while on board this ship commences at zero six hours and lasts until twenty-two hours. On Arsenault you'll be lucky when your days don't last twenty-four hours. The training schedule for this voyage allows for half a day of free time once a week. That isn't for four more days. Hop into your racks, people, the lights will be doused in exactly five minutes!" And they were.

The young men of second platoon strapped themselves into their racks. The ship's centripetal gravity kept them secure in their racks, and the straps were provided in case an inflight emergency caused the ship to cease its rotation. During the sleep period, the only light in the compartment came from small emergency lamps near the deck and the overhead to guide men in case of an emergency. Too tired even to talk with McNeal in the next bunk below his, Dean lay and listened to the ship as it groaned and cracked and hummed all about him in the darkness. From far, far away came the dim but incessant boom of the *Purdom*'s many motors, engines, and machinery.

Dean thought for the first time that day of his mother and wondered what she was doing. He thought about what he'd learned that day. The last thing he thought that first night was that he was just too excited to sleep.

The *Purdom* reached jump point in the middle of the next afternoon, and the D.I.'s herded their charges back into their compartments.

"Everybody, in your racks. Right now, right now. No dilly-dallying here. Believe me, you don't want to be standing when we make the jump. Move it now."

Pretty and Singh swam through the compartment, hustling the recruits with staccato commands of "Move, move, move," and using their hands to rush them into the racks.

"Everybody, lie supine." Singh saw someone on his stomach and shouted, "I said supine, dummy, not prone. Prone is a position for shooting and fucking. You aren't doing either right now. On your back. Everybody, on your backs and strap in."

The three drill instructors made another pass through the compartment, making sure each man was properly strapped in.

Once everyone was secured in his rack, the three D.I.'s went to the compartment hatch. "Stay where you are, as you are," Neeley said, "until we come back to let you out." He opened a small panel next to the hatch and pulled a lever concealed behind it, then hit the light control as he followed the other two D.I.'s out of the compartment, plunging the compartment into darkness broken only by the emergency lights.

"Hey, what's this?" Dean shouted as a webbing suddenly dropped from the bottom of the rack above him and secured itself to the frame of his own rack.

He wasn't the only one asking that question, but nobody could answer it. They found out a moment later when the artificial gravity shut off and the ship jumped into hyperspace.

With an abruptness so complete it seemed that it had always been this way, the universe went gray. Or was it black? Weight vanished; it wasn't a floating sensation like null-g had been, but a total absence of weight, as though mass had disappeared altogether. All the weight that ever was, was now, and ever would be, settled onto him. There was no sound. There was such a volume of sound, he thought the universe must be ending in the collapse of everything into a primordial speck that instantly exploded in the big bang.

It ended as abruptly as it began, so suddenly that it was a few stunned seconds before anybody screamed. And only a few more seconds before everybody was yelling and struggling against the restraints that held them in their racks.

The pandemonium lasted only until the three drill instructors entered the compartment and reactivated the lights. The three Marines went through the bay just as they had moments earlier, this time calming everyone down. They weren't totally successful; some of the recruits were upset by the unexpected experience, and would remain so for some time to come. When relative calm was restored, Neeley stood by the compartment hatch and spoke to the platoon.

"I know that some of you think it was unfair of us to let you experience a jump into hyperspace without warning of what was about to happen. But this is an important lesson for you to learn. Marines are warriors. We fight battles. Sometimes we know a fight is coming; we set the time, the place, and the circumstances for it and are fully prepared. But sometimes we have only a few moments of warning—or no warning whatsoever. There's a big universe out there, with a lot of surprises. Most of those surprises are nasty, and can kill you if you aren't prepared to act immediately and decisively when they happen. What you just experienced was an unpleasant surprise, but nobody got hurt." He looked at them with mild disgust. "And every one of you panicked. Try to do better next time. The next time you get surprised, your lives may well depend on your reaction. The next surprise that jumps out at you just might kill you."

Finished with his speech, Neeley turned and left the compartment.

Pretty snorted and followed the senior D.I.

Singh shook his head. He said one word, softly, but loud enough for all to hear: "Boots!" He pushed the lever that released the restraining webbing before he left, and dogged the hatch behind him, so the men of second platoon were left on their own to ponder what Neeley had said about surprises.

Only then did they notice that gravity had returned. It took several more minutes for anyone to notice that what had been the compartment's overhead was now its deck. "Down" was now toward, rather than away from, the ship's core. The racks had rotated during the jump. Now they understood why there was as much space below the bottom rack as there was above the top one.

CHAPTER
FIVE

Each day started with the shrill blare of a bugle over the public address system and the drill instructors' banging their batons against the bulkheads shouting an ancient chant: "Reveille! Reveille! Drop your cocks and grab your socks! Reveille!" Then, even before most of the recruits were fully awake, an hour of calisthenics, followed by showers, morning chow, and finally a thorough cleaning of the living compartments. After that, one hour of close-order drill.

"Close-order drill hasn't changed much since the time of the Romans," Staff Sergeant Neeley announced, "and it hasn't gotten to be any more fun since then either, but we require all Marines to be able to march in matchless formations. After we land at Arsenault, you'll probably never use this skill, and it is a skill. So why do we teach it? This, recruits, is your introduction to following orders and working as a group, so pay attention! And don't ever anticipate a command!"

Punishment for minor infractions of the rules on board the *Purdom* was to practice close-order drill between 22 and 06 hours and on the free half days. For those really recalcitrant offenders, kitchen duty—known for some unfathomable reason as kitchen police—was available.

* * *

On the second day, Dean had a medical exam by a real doctor, the one he'd been promised back at the recruiting station. He sat in the womblike chair of the examination table in sick bay, fully clothed, waiting for the physician's instructions.

The doctor sat at a desk, reading Dean's medical history, compiled back at New Rochester, on the monitor of his computer. After a moment he nodded and said, "You've been a pretty healthy lad." Dean didn't know if he was supposed to say something, so he didn't say anything. The doctor made some keystrokes and examined the screen again. Evidently satisfied with what he saw, he cleared the screen, then said, "Private Dean, did you know you have an ingrown toenail in your left big toe?"

"No, sir."

The doctor nodded and added a few keystrokes to his computer file. "Okay, Private, keep your eye on it. If it gets worse, report to sick bay and a corpsman will cut it out for you. Dismissed."

Dean just sat there, unbelieving. He hadn't been examined yet. The doctor hadn't even looked at him other than a quick glance when he told him where to sit.

"Did you hear me, Dean?"

"Yes, sir. But aren't you going to examine me?"

The doctor looked him in the eye. "What do you think I was doing with you in the examination table? You're in perfect health, anybody can see that. Report back to your platoon."

As the days flowed into weeks, the recruits became used to the routine and to the minutiae of military training. They were issued weapons with which to practice the manual of arms, and which they were expected to field-strip and clean. And clean them they did—endlessly.

"Always handle every weapon as if it were a loaded weapon, even when you personally know it's not," Corporal Singh told them the day they were issued the weapons. "This will be drilled into you once you're on the ranges and patrolling on Arsenault. Weapon safety will become second nature to you. 'Unloaded' weapons have killed more people than I care to think about. We really want to avoid having them kill Marines. Start learning that now."

They learned both the fire capability and nomenclature of their weapons. The basic infantry weapon in the Confederation Marine Corps, they were told, was a miniaturized oxy-hydrogen plasma shooter, commonly called a "blaster," but in the manuals a "weapon."

"These weapons are semiautomatic," Corporal Singh told them, "that is, they fire one bolt each time the trigger mechanism is activated. The 'basic load' for a Marine rifleman in combat," he went on, "is four hundred 'rounds,' or four power packs or 'magazines' capable of shooting up to a hundred bolts each.

"There are also handheld versions of these weapons which are carried by officers, NCOs above squad leader, and the gunners on crew-served weapons," Singh continued. "An automatic weapon is also authorized for each assault team. This is what's called a 'crew-served' weapon, because it requires three men to operate it. It can fire up to a hundred bolts per trigger pull. The crew carries a bipod, a tripod, two extra barrels, and each man carries two extra power packs that contain six hundred bolts each. You gotta change the barrel on one of those babies every six hundred bolts or it'll crystallize on you." Corporal Singh always became very animated when he talked about weapons, moving his hands as if firing at an unseen enemy.

* * *

During a break, several recruits pretended to shoot one another with the unloaded weapons. Singh was upon them instantly. The men had never seen him so angry.

"You fools!" he shouted. "These weapons are not toys! They are the most deadly killing machines known to mankind!" The veins on Singh's neck stood out clearly as he shouted at the hapless recruits. Staff Sergeant Pretty came over, took Corporal Singh aside, and they talked quietly for a few moments. When Singh came back he was calmer, but very firm, and there was no more horsing around with weapons.

After the third day they carried their weapons everywhere, and at night they fixed them into slots beside their racks. "You'll get plenty of practice firing real ammunition when you get to Arsenault," Pretty announced, "and for the rest of the time you're in this Corps, your issue weapon will stay with you always, except when you go on liberty or if you wind up in the brig. I mean your weapon will *always* be with you, when you eat, when you sleep, when you shit, and if you're lucky enough to draw duty on an inhabited world where the people don't stink worse than *kwangduks* and the women aren't uglier, you'll keep your weapon handy when you fuck!"

"Once, I pulled a month's duty on a place called Euskadi," Corporal Singh offered, apropos of the universal monosyllable just uttered by the normally straitlaced Staff Sergeant Pretty, "and all I had between me and the ground at night was one of their thin native girls." The men of second platoon had come to like Corporal Singh. He proved to be a very professional Marine, but easygoing in his manner and with a lively sense of humor that tended toward the bizarre and earthy.

"Yes," Pretty replied, "and your weapon." And that

was the only joke Pretty attempted to make during all the months he was second platoon's drill instructor.

"All right, recruits," Neeley announced one day during a classroom training session, "I'm gonna give you Neeley's Thirteen Rules for Staying Alive in Combat. You listening?

"One: Incoming fire always has the right-of-way.

"Two: Keep it simple, stupid.

"Three: Keeping it simple is the hardest thing in the world.

"Four: Never stand next to anyone braver than you are.

"Five: If things are going too well, it's an ambush.

"Six: The easiest way is mined.

"Seven: The one thing you never run out of is the enemy.

"Eight: Infrared works both ways.

"Nine: Professionals are always predictable.

"Ten: We always wind up fighting amateurs.

"Eleven: When the enemy's in range, so are you.

"Twelve: When in doubt, shoot until your magazine is empty."

Neeley placed his hands on his hips and smiled fiercely. "You remember those rules and you'll be okay."

"Staff Sergeant, you said there were thirteen of your rules," McNeal reminded him.

"McNeal! You again! Recruit, you got a big mouth! Down, down, down!" Immediately McNeal assumed the push-up position. "Give me fifty.

"Dean! I saw you standing next to this bigmouth troublemaker. Get up here and get down. Give me seventy-five! I just made up a new rule: Never stand next to anyone dumber than you!"

To the accompaniment of the pair's steady counting, Neeley, still smiling fiercely, turned back to the recruits.

"Thirteen: Remember the other twelve."

* * *

As the days passed, the relationship between the recruits and their D.I.'s began to solidify. Their company commander and first sergeant were everywhere, observing them in classrooms and in the exercise areas, making on-the-spot corrections, conferring with the drill instructors. Their own drill instructors stuck to them like leeches during every waking hour. It seemed either Neeley or Pretty or Singh would be there whenever someone made a mistake or needed a question answered. At first the recruits were apprehensive under all the scrutiny, but gradually they came to understand that the D.I.'s were there to teach and instruct, not criticize and belittle. Singh in particular used some of the most foul language any of them had ever heard, but he never used it to demean a recruit, it was just his nature to talk that way. When a recruit did something right, which began to happen more often as the days passed, one of the D.I.'s would be quick with a pat on the shoulder or word of praise. For many of the men it was the first time in their lives anybody had ever complimented them on doing something right.

Even close-order drill became fun for the men of the second platoon. Once they got the basic facing movements down pat, Corporal Singh taught them cadence counting and the ancient ditties that went along with it.

One they particularly liked went:

> I don't know, but I've been told,
> Euskadi pussy mighty cold.

When the entire company was in the parade bay practicing at the same time, the platoon commanders had their men count cadence at the top of their lungs—"One, two, three, four!"—to try to outshout the other platoons maneuvering there. Dean and his mates took to the competition with abandon, shouting until they were red in the face and the veins in their necks stood out. They made the bulkheads ring and finished their drilling flush with the belief that they had won the decibel contest. Best of all was the sense of pride in accomplishment the men derived from marching well together, instantly responding as a group to Singh's shouted commands, maneuvering as if all of them were one. Each recruit was given the chance to drill the others under the watchful eyes of the D.I.'s.

Occasionally, members of the ship's crew on work parties in Area Whiskey would come by and watch the Marines drill, and then the two groups exchanged the time-honored insults that pass between Marines and sailors. But generally the crew was not much in evidence, although navy officers would sometimes confer with the Skipper. Once, the colonel commanding the training regiment came to talk to the recruits for a few minutes. He was in his early seventies, and told them that more than fifty years before he had stood right where they were now. He emphasized that regardless of rank, every Marine had started his career doing exactly what they were doing—every Marine, from the most recent graduate from Boot Camp on Arsenault all the way to the commandant himself.

Dean was the first in his platoon to be selected as an acting squad leader. All the recruits were given a chance to practice leadership skills, as fire team leaders for a day or two or drilling the platoon for a session in the parade bay, which was called the "grinder." The most outstanding were selected to be squad leaders for one week. Dean, with his quick intelligence, even temper, and natural ability to work well with others, would have stood out even without the test scores in his record. At the end of the voyage, Captain Tomasio, in conference with his respective platoon commanders and platoon sergeants, would pick the best of the men to be acting squad leaders during the time they would be training on Arsenault. By the end of the third week they had unanimously selected Dean as one of the recruits upon whom they would confer that honor.

The personal relationships between the recruits began to take shape also. Of course, Dean and McNeal were inseparable buddies after the first day, but platoon and squad friendships soon developed. All the men were from Earth, so they had geography in common, and since English had been the official language of the entire Confederation for more than 250 years, they were able to communicate. But they also had a common culture that stretched far back into Terran history. This was due in part at least to the Borden Act of 2010, introduced by a U.S. Senator, G. F. Borden of Virginia, which provided the legislation and funding for the Library of Congress to digitize all its holdings. Not only did that make all the books in the library's collections available electronically to future generations, it preserved all the motion pictures ever produced by Hollywood. Joe Dean's favorites were those starring John Wayne, especially *The Sands of Iwo Jima.*

CHAPTER
SIX

A persistent thrumming filled the humid air about the platoon as it sat in classroom formation in a jungle clearing. They had been on Arsenault a month by then. Every day it had rained, sometimes all day, sometimes day after day. Just then there was a temporary break in the monsoon and Arsenault's sun poked through the clouds, driving up the humidity and heat in equally stifling proportions.

As the noise became louder and more insistent, the ground beneath the recruits began to tremble. The men could clearly hear small trees and bushes snapping and cracking as a large man-made object pushed its way inexorably toward them. Suddenly, a behemoth burst through a fringe of bushes and came rumbling to a stop about ten meters from the platoon.

"People, meet the vehicle the box kickers in procurement called the AASALCAC," Neeley shouted over the thrumming, which gradually ceased as the driver powered down the engine on his armored vehicle. "AASALCAC stands for Armored All-Surface Assault Landing Craft, Air-Cushioned, which is far too much of a mouthful for you to try to memorize right now. Anyway, we aren't box kickers, we're warriors. We call our equipment by warlike names, not namby-pamby ones. We call this beast the Dragon."

As the Dragon's propulsion system cut off and the heavy machine dropped suddenly several inches to the ground, the NCOs briskly but unobtrusively walked to the rear of the platoon formation, where they were shielded from the wave of muddy water that gouted up from underneath the Dragon, drenching the unsuspecting recruits, drowning out their shocked screams and curses.

"You may remember that somewhere along the line I told you something about 'unpleasant surprises,' " Neeley said calmly as he returned to the front of the formation. He blandly watched the recruits in their attempts to wipe the runny mud off their faces. "This is another lesson for you. Never assume that anything you've never seen before is benign. Especially not something big and mean-looking. Most particularly not something that says 'Marines' on it."

The normally staid and straitlaced Pretty even cracked a tiny smile as the recruits grumbled and muttered among themselves.

Three more of the vehicles roared into the clearing to join the first one. This time the recruits followed the example of their NCOs in getting behind something and avoided most of the mud bath. The machines measured eight feet high by twenty long and twelve wide. The paint on their armored sides possessed the same "chameleon" capability as the Marine field utilities, and the recruits watched, fascinated, while the vehicles quickly changed color to blend into the surrounding foliage before their eyes.

"These are the combat workhorses of the Corps," Neeley announced. "Every FIST transportation company has twenty-four Dragons. Each Dragon can transport twenty fully-equipped and -armed Marines, or fifteen with crew-served weapons. They depend on their low profile and high maneuverability to avoid enemy fire, but each has an integral plasma shield and light armor to protect it against most infantry plasma weapons. A Dragon can do 175 kph on the open road, a hundred over broken ground, and seventy-five knots or more on the water. Each weighs thirty tons. A Dragon has a crew of two: a driver and a gunner/navigator. One out of six in the FIST combat configuration carries a heavy gun.

"Dragons are climate-controlled." Neeley grinned and wiped away the perspiration dripping down the side of his face. "Now to go for a ride. Staff Sergeant Pretty?"

"Listen up now," Pretty shouted. "You will mount through the rear ramp." There was a whirring noise, and heavy armored doors lowered to form ramps. "One squad per vehicle. Once inside, fasten in. Squad leaders, pay close attention because after this morning you will be responsible for making sure your men and equipment are secure whenever you ride these things. No dukshit, people; if you are not properly secured when you hit rough terrain, you can be seriously injured, even killed. Yeah, they're 'air-cushioned,' but watch out when you don't got the air or the cushion. Now, mount up by squads as I call you out, left to right. Keep your communicators open to the platoon net. Fill up front to rear as you climb aboard."

Ten high-backed jump seats lined each flank of the Dragons inside. Each man secured himself into his seat with two heavy shoulder belts secured by a fast-release device centered in the middle of his chest. The seats were called "mummy boxes" because once inside, the rider looked like a mummy in its sarcophagus, except that the seats provided extra protection against a crash or a hit by a heavy weapon or a mine. Weapons and other items of equipment locked securely into forms molded into the seats. Mass confusion reigned as the inexperienced squad leaders tried to sort out the unfamiliar conditions.

The NCOs watched their men in silent amusement for a while. "At ease!" Corporal Singh announced at last. He stepped into the interior of the Dragon that held Dean's squad. "Now watch. I'm going to show you how all this stuff works."

It was well after dark when the platoon was delivered back to the base camp. Dean limped down the ramp, kicking caked mud off his boots. A pain shot up into his right buttock. Now he knew what Pretty had meant about not having the air or the cushion. The platoon fell into formation beside the Dragon.

"All right," Staff Sergeant Pretty shouted. "Now somebody tell me what he sees there." He pointed vaguely toward the hulking Dragon. The men stared intensely but could see only the dim interior lights inside the vehicles. "Look!" Pretty shouted. "Mud!" he screamed. "Somebody's gotta clean up those vehicles!"

McNeal groaned.

"McNeal! Front and center!"

On the shooting range, they saw their first dead man. A recruit in another platoon discharged his blaster into his own jaw. The bolt sizzled up through the man's brain and burst out the top of his head, vaporizing his face. He died instantly. His trachea lay completely exposed to the goggle-eyed recruits who swarmed around his still-smoking corpse. Little bloody bubbles, the remnants of what was being expelled from the air left in his lungs when he died, mixed with the gooey gray matter of his brain and shredded skull fragments. Some of the men gagged, and all of them held hands to their noses because the man's bowels had let loose. None had ever smelled anything so foul before.

"Whew! Closed-coffin ceremony for that boy," McNeal muttered.

Corporal Singh wheeled about and glared at McNeal, as if he was going to launch into him, but he said nothing and after a moment turned back to the dead man. Singh knew his men were learning a hard but valuable lesson. When you live and breathe death and violence, you have to deal with it somehow. Denying death by making light of it is a safety valve by which those who must face it deal with the stress.

They marched all morning through the sopping jungles, alternately drenched by heavy downpours and then steamed like crabs when the sun came out and turned everything into a sauna. Thirty minutes before they saw the stream, they could hear it. Few of the recruits could identify the sound, a dull roar punctuated by heavy thumps, the sound of boulders and uprooted trees bouncing down the stream, which was in flood, as were all the streams and rivers in that part of Arsenault during the monsoon season.

Staff Sergeant Neeley halted the platoon on the lip of a steep gorge. Ten meters below the precipice the stream roared and surged, the water beaten into a froth of white foam by the force of the current. A heavy mist hung above the banks as far as they could see up- and down-stream. The air about them was redolent with the clean, bracing aroma of wet foliage and water spray. Combined with the roar of the flood below, the atmosphere was charged with the danger and excitement of nature unleashed. Most of the recruits were from the cities of Earth and had never seen such a display. All of them were awed by it.

Suddenly, the sun burst forth from behind the overcast for a few moments and a brilliant rainbow glowed and shimmered over the gorge. Several men gasped involuntarily at the sight. Few of them had ever seen a real rainbow before—the polluted air of Earth's cities hid them from most people. In seconds the clouds rolled back over the face of the sun and the platoon was shrouded again in gray wetness, but the men remained dazzled by the display for several moments after it disappeared.

"People, this is one of the most dangerous operations you'll perform while in training here," Staff Sergeant Neeley said, shouting over the roar of the torrent. His words were punctuated by a heavy "bump-bump-bump" as a boulder bigger than a Dragon rolled by on the bottom of the streambed. Neeley nodded. "Yep, the force of that water is so strong it can roll an object weighing hundreds of kilos along like a child's rubber ball."

"You fall in there," Staff Sergeant Pretty added, gesturing over the lip of the gorge, "and we'll never find you again. Don't get too close to the edge," he warned.

"We have to get a man on the other side of that gorge," Staff Sergeant Neeley shouted, pointing to the jungle forty meters on the other side of the raging stream. "Any volunteers?" He grinned.

Corporal Singh began to unpack the platoon's single puddle jumper. Powered by energy cells and maneuvered by a system of tiny but powerful jets, it could lift a man a thousand meters straight up. The device permitted trained couriers and scouts to negotiate miles of rough terrain completely free from the restraints of gravity. Recruit training companies were never permitted more than one puddle jumper, and nobody except a man trained in its operation was ever permitted to strap it on. The recruits breathed a silent and collective sigh of relief as Corporal Singh began to climb into the harness.

"The object here," Neeley was saying as Corporal Singh fastened the jumper harness, "is to get a line across the gorge. Then each man will cross— Get away from there!" Neeley started toward three recruits standing on the lip of the gorge who'd been staring down at the rushing water. He was too late. The ground upon which the men had been standing crumbled suddenly and sent them plummeting down into the foam. They dropped so quickly none even had a chance to let out a scream.

"Goddamnit, get the fuck back from there!" Neeley shouted at the other recruits as they instinctively surged in a group toward the bank to help their comrades. Staff Sergeant Pretty immediately began speaking into his headset while Staff Sergeant Neeley and Corporal Singh herded the platoon away from the stream and had the men sit among the trees. The three NCOs conferred hastily. "We stay here until help comes," Staff Sergeant Neeley told them. Nobody suggested trying to rescue the three men; they hadn't a chance in that torrent. Within minutes, it seemed, Captain Tomasio was alighting from a command-and-control hopper followed by several staff officers. Seconds later, personnel from the battalion medical staff arrived on another hopper, followed immediately by two more that carried other platoons from the company.

"We're going to form search parties," Staff Sergeant Neeley announced. "This stream empties into a larger one about sixteen kilometers downstream. The fourth platoon will be airlifted down there to form a cordon across the water, try to catch our people if their bodies make it that far down. We'll take this side of the stream and first platoon the other and start looking right now."

The search stopped after dark and resumed at first light the following morning. The first victim, a pimply lad from Philadelphia named Schwartzer, was found about mid-morning. His mangled remains were pulled from among the branches of a large tree bobbing in an eddy.

The men gasped as his corpse was laid out on the bank. He was covered with huge gashes and abrasions, through which stuck the white ends of jagged bones.

Dean found the second man three days later. He was closest to the bank when the body suddenly rolled over in the middle of a raft of driftwood and the corpse's booted foot stuck up above the water. The body was swollen to twice its natural size, and aquatic animals had been at it for some time before it surfaced. At first Dean hesitated to touch the thing rocking obscenely in among the flotsam. He knew the three men who had fallen in, but could not recognize which of the remaining two this one was. Dean stepped cautiously into the shallow water, hesitant to touch the swollen, discolored skin surface, looking for something to grab on to that wasn't rotten flesh. Evidently all the man's clothes had been ripped off by the force of the water, leaving only the boot on his left foot. He tried to drag the body closer to shore using a stick he'd picked up out of the water.

"Goddamnit, Dean, get in there and pull him out!" Corporal Singh snarled. Everyone was on edge by then, even the D.I.'s. Dean grabbed the booted foot and dragged at the body. Under Singh's prodding, several other men jumped into the water and helped haul the body to shore. Once the corpse was fully exposed on the land, the stench of rotting waterlogged flesh was terrible. Worse, as it lay on its back, everyone could clearly see the damage done to the body by the animals. The man's face had been destroyed and his genitals had been completely eaten away. The recruits stumbled into the nearby bushes and vomited. Dean heaved until there was nothing left in his stomach. Even Fred McNeal, the acknowledged joker and wise guy in the platoon, remained stoically silent and avoided looking at what had once been a friend.

Two days later the search was given up and training resumed. The third man was never found.

The weeks of training in the temperate zones and mountains came as a blessed relief from the tropics and the zero-gravity training on the larger of Arsenault's two moons—the "Turd," to the generations of soldiers and Marines who'd been there—and was an exciting challenge, all the more so because it marked the unofficial end of Boot Camp.

Graduation Day was hot and clear. The sunlight beat down steadily on the men in their ranks; the rainy season was over. The men of A Company stood rigidly at attention in their new scarlet and blue dress uniforms. Not a man in the company had ever felt prouder of himself than he did that morning, Dean more than most, because the single golden chevron of a PFC was emblazoned on his sleeves. He was one of five men in the platoon to win meritorious promotion for conduct and achievement during the training cycle.

Presentation of the marksmanship badges was another high point in Joseph Dean's military life. He'd qualified as one of the best shots in the company, scoring High Expert. "Not one recruit in fifty has shot as high a score as you since I've been in command here," the Brigadier said as he pinned the golden cross onto Dean's blouse. "Congratulations, Marine." Dean's chest almost burst right through his tunic. He wished his parents could see him. After the Brigadier passed down the rank, Dean permitted himself a huge grin. Captain Tomasio, glancing back from where he stood next to the Brigadier, scowled ominously and then winked. With great difficulty, PFC Dean wiped the smile off his face.

* * *

"Here you go, Marines," Staff Sergeant Neeley announced, but then had to pause while the new Marines of second platoon cheered—it was the first time one of their drill instructors had called them Marines, a title they'd just spent six months striving to earn.

"Okay, okay," he continued when the shouting had died down. "Here are your assignments for specialty training: oh-one, infantry, the king of battle; oh-two, artillery, can't fight a war without 'em; oh-three, air assault, you ground fighters'll love them the first time they show up when you need air support; oh-four, combat engineer, we rely on the navy and army for noncombat-condition engineering; oh-five, armor and combat transport, you remember the Dragons; oh-six, armorer, you break your weapon, they fix it; oh-seven, aircraft mainte-nance, the flyboys can't without maintenance; oh-eight, logistics, that's rations and power packs; oh-nine, admin-istration, it's a dirty, unappreciated job, but somebody's got to do it. There are others, but don't worry about them now, because nobody gets 'em right out of Boot Camp.

"Infantry, you'll leave for the Fleet tomorrow morning. The rest of you will go to your specialty schools—right here on Arsenault." This was met by a chorus of outraged screams. "At ease, at ease," Neeley calmed them down. "Actually, outside Boot Camp, duty on Arsenault is pretty good." Several men loudly expressed disbelief. "Pretty good," Neeley continued. "You can even have cold beer in the evenings."

"Aaaah!" McNeal yelled. "I'd reenlist for a cold beer!"

"As you were," Neeley said shortly. "Here are your assignments: Anderhalt, Shaqlim X, oh-two, artillery; Clancy, Mordecai, oh-one, you leave tomorrow . . ." and on through the alphabet. Dean did not hear his name called. "McNeal, Frederick D, oh-one," Neeley announced. Neeley droned on, and each successive announcement was greeted by shouts of joy or groans of despair as the newly minted Marines contemplated their fates for the next seven and a half years. Those going to the same schools broke up into little groups and began speculating loudly about what to expect. At last Neeley was finished.

"Miss anyone?" he asked. Dean raised his hand, bewildered. "Dean, huh? I called your name, Dean, were you asleep or something? Oh-one. PFC, you leave for the Fleet in the morning."

CHAPTER
SEVEN

Everybody has traditions—planetary, national, city, family, individual, group—in all times, in all places. Traditions are important, always have been, always will be—even when they don't make sense to outsiders. They help people build and maintain a sense of identity and continuity.

On Saint Brendan's, where they don't have snakes and never did, they drink green beer every March 17. The Saint Brendan's calendar doesn't have a March 17, either—with an orbital period of 379 days, they can't use the same calendar as their cousins on Old Earth. But the original colonists were from Ireland and insisted on continuing to celebrate the patron saint of their Earthly nativity. So they arbitrarily designated every 365th day as March 17, or Saint Patrick's Day. Complete with quadrennial allowance for leap year. The second wave of immigration to Saint Brendan's consisted of Americans of Irish ancestry. They were the ones who brought in the green beer. The green beer caught on, so once every 365 days everyone on Saint Brendan's guzzles down a pint or two of green beer—it's traditional.

Saint Brendan's has been on the metric system from the beginning. Green beer on Saint Patrick's Day is the only time they use the archaic measure of the pint. That's a tradition too.

Everybody faces east to kneel and pray on Alhambra. Alhambra was originally settled by Moslems from North Africa. Like all good Muslims on Old Earth, they face Mecca when they kneel five times a day to pray. In North Africa, Mecca is to the east, so Alhambrans face east to pray. If they really wanted to face Mecca, though, they'd face in a more-or-less northerly direction, because that's where old Earth is relative to Alhambra. But it's traditional to face east, so five times a day all Alhambrans face the direction of the planetary rotation to kneel and pray.

On the dozens of worlds where their brotherhood spread, Masons still say arcane things to each other about squares, levels, and planes. It doesn't matter that few of them have ever seen any of those ancient tools, or that fewer of them are stoneworkers or carpenters. It's traditional that Masons speak in arcane terms about objects they're unfamiliar with. Don't mock them for their obscure, often unintelligible vocabulary, though. No Mason who can so identify himself is ever lost and alone on a world where he can find a brother Mason. That's another of their traditions.

Le Loi's victory over the Chinese in Old Earth year 1427 is annually celebrated on Chochet Viet, which was first colonized by a Vietnam-based mining consortium. None of the succeeding waves of immigrants were Vietnamese, and, due to intermarriage, none of the population today is of pure Vietnamese stock. Not only is there relatively little Vietnamese in their blood, the largest portion of later immigrants was Chinese, and the planetary language is mainly a derivative of Cantonese. Still, Chochet Viet maintains the tradition of celebrating Le Loi's victory over the Chinese.

Of all the worlds and all the organizations of Human Space, none are more tradition-bound than the Confederation Marine Corps.

One of their traditions has to do with making planet-fall. It doesn't matter why they're making planetfall: an assault against a hostile defense to kick open a door for the regular army to invade through; making a liberty port of call; a ceremonial landing in escort of a new ambassador; or for any other reason. Marines always make planetfall the traditional way—over the beach.

Klaxons rang and blared throughout the Confederation Navy SAT—Starship Assault Troop—*Lance Corporal Keith Lopez*. A voice intoned over the ship's speakers, "Commander, Landing Force, prepare the landing force for landing."

The navy has its traditions too. Klaxons are one of them.

On the ship's bridge the captain and the dozen officers and men of the bridge watch went through the ages-old routine of preparing to disembark the landing force.

Another navy tradition is the layout of a ship's bridge. The bridge on the *Lopez* would have looked familiar to Chester Nimitz. At first glance, that is.

"Is the string-of-pearls deployed?" Captain Bhofi asked, not that the ship was going to deploy the geosynchronous satellites around a Confederation member planet that already wore its necklace. He sat in a high chair bolted to the deck in the middle of the five-by-eight-meter room. He faced a wall of what looked like a row of one-by-two-meter windows that lined what was otherwise a featureless, battleship-gray wall. The windows gave the impression that the bridge was located above the top surface of the spaceship. It wasn't, though. Close examination of the windows would reveal that they were actually viewscreens—at the moment, the viewscreens showed exactly what was in front of the ship, but they could show whatever was in range of the ship's sensors, regardless of direction. A corner of Thorsfinni's World hung bloated in the lower quadrant of the rightmost screen. A maneuverable orbit-to-planetside shuttle was in the second-to-the-right screen and growing as it approached.

"Is the string-of-pearls deployed?" the deck officer asked, repeating the question. He stood at a deck-mounted console a few feet from the captain's chair.

That was another navy tradition: the repeating of orders.

The bridge communications petty officer pressed a button on his console and said loud and clear, "Is the string-of-pearls deployed?" into his voicelink with the communications shack. He sat at a cramped desk behind the deck officer.

"The string-of-pearls is deployed, aye, and communications established," answered the petty officer second class in the comm shack who was responsible for the commlink with the belt of geosynchronous satellites already in orbit around the globe below the *Lopez*. It wasn't necessary for it to be there, but the comm shack was located in a position remote from the bridge.

"The string-of-pearls is deployed, aye, and communications established." The reply was repeated until the captain acknowledged it.

"Establish communications with the harbormaster," Captain Bhofi ordered.

Yet another tradition, calling the spaceport boss a "harbormaster."

"Establish communications with the harbormaster," the deck officer repeated.

The communications petty officer repeated the command into his voicelink.

"Communications with the harbormaster established, aye," said the petty officer second class in the comm shack.

The answer came back and Captain Bhofi ordered, "Patch the harbormaster through."

"Patch the harbormaster through," the deck officer repeated.

The bridge communications petty officer tapped a short series of buttons on his console, echoed the command into his voicelink, listened to his headphone, then said, "Harbormaster patched through, aye."

Captain Bhofi picked up his voicelink and said into it, "Confederation Navy SAT *Lance Corporal Keith Lopez* requests permission for orbital docking."

"Permission granted, esteemed visitor Confederation Navy SAT *Lance Corporal Keith Lopez*," the harbormaster replied. "Stand by to receive pilot."

The communications petty officer punched a different button on his console and said the same thing into his voicelink. Then, softly, he added, "Let's let the local mugwug come aboard and act more important than he is."

"Helm, one point to port," the captain said. One more tradition; a compass "point" is far too crude a measure to maneuver for orbital docking.

"One point to port, aye," said the helmsman, and turned the ship's wheel to the left. A steering wheel in a starship? Maybe the navy's even more tradition-bound than the Marines.

Preparations to receive the pilot and to commence docking complete, Captain Bhofi turned his attention to the one man on the bridge who wasn't one of his officers or men, the only Marine officer aboard. "Commander, Landing Force, is the landing force prepared to land?" he asked in the voice that had caused several navy officers over the years to request a transfer from his command, and driven many a chief petty officer into early retirement.

Confederation Marine Major Longaway stood calmly

with his back to the bulkhead, near the port-side hatch of
the bridge, out of everybody's way. When the captain
spoke, he slid easily to attention and said quite calmly,
"Yessir, the landing force is prepared to land."

Captain Bhofi's glare asked how Major Longaway
could know his Marines were ready to land when he
hadn't left the bridge since the command to ready the
landing force was given.

"Corporal Doyle saw to it, sir."

"Corporal Doyle," Captain Bhofi repeated, as though
continuing to pass orders and responses. Stone-faced, he
turned his attention back to his bridge duties.

The ship's first officer looked at Longaway and wondered how he could have replied so calmly.

Longaway winked at the first officer, then calmly
turned and left the bridge.

The voice that followed the klaxons was a carefully
modulated female voice, but the effect it had in the ship's
only occupied troop hold was the same as that of a
grizzled old chief bos'n snarling out orders.

Twenty-odd Marines, the only occupants of a troop
hold designed to house the 113 junior NCOs and enlisted
men of an infantry company, stopped doing whatever
they had been doing and checked their gear, made sure
their lockers were empty, the deck around their racks was
clear, and their weapons, packs, and seabags ready to be
picked up and carried to the landing craft waiting in the
well deck.

The troop hold was right out of navy tradition. Cots
were stacked four high, with two feet of head space
between the top of one mattress and the springs of the
next one up. A stack of battleship-gray lockers separated
the head of one stack of racks from the foot of the next.
The rows of rack-and-locker stacks were separated by

meter-and-a-half-wide aisles. Even though space wasn't as scarce in built-in-orbit starships as it had been in seagoing ships, the third-to-last thing any sailor on an assault troopship wanted to do was make the Marines it was transporting too comfortable. If they were too comfortable, the Marines might want to stay aboard instead of making their assigned planetfall. If they stayed aboard, they'd probably want to take over, and the second-to-last thing any self-respecting sailor wanted was to have Marines in charge.

The last thing any sailor on an assault troop transport wanted to do was make planetfall with the Marines—if the Marines are going in, planetside is probably too dangerous.

None of the Marines galvanized into action by the voice ordering them to prepare for landing were more animated than a stocky, diminutive corporal who bounded from his rack in the NCO corner of the troop hold and barked out:

"You heard the word, people! Make sure your gear is stowed and your seabags secured." He marched through the nearly empty hold, doing his best to give everything a gimlet-eyed once-over.

"We're about to hit the beach. Anything you don't have with you when we go over the side, you'll never see again. Look sharp now."

"Who died and left him God?" someone stage-whispered.

"I heard that, Chan," Corporal Doyle snapped. In three strides he stood nose-to-chest with a PFC who was as much bigger than any of the other Marines in the hold as Doyle was smaller. "Nobody had to die to make me God. I've got more of these than anybody else here does." He tapped a thumb against the two bronze chevrons and nova device pinned to his utility shirt collar. "That makes me God. Step aside for inspection."

Chan almost managed to suppress a sigh as he took a step to the side and pivoted to face parallel to his rack. He casually came to attention.

Using a series of quick, sharp movements, Doyle made sure Chan's pack and seabag were securely closed. He opened the small locker at the rack's head to satisfy himself it was empty, then flipped the rack's thin mattress to check for anything stowed under it. Disgruntled that Chan's gear was impeccably packed and ready for disembarkment, Doyle snatched Chan's blaster from its belay at the head of his rack. Using parade-ground motions, he inspected the weapon. The battery wasn't in it—it was unloaded and clear. His close scrutiny found no corrosion, dust, or oil buildup. Disappointed at not finding anything wrong with the weapon, he thrust it at Chan so fast the big man almost didn't get his hands up in time to stop the blaster from slamming into his body.

"Square away that mattress, Chan," Doyle snarled. "I don't want any sailor-boys complaining we didn't leave this hold shipshape."

"Aye aye, Corporal," Chan said in a long-suffering voice. He was glad the trip was over and he might never again see the runt who had ridden him for the whole voyage.

"Everybody, open your lockers and stand your mattresses up," Doyle ordered. "Gear and weapons inspection." He briskly went through the small portion of the troop hold occupied by the few Marines being transferred to 34th FIST on Thorsfinni's World. Everyone was fully packed, not a strap was out of place, every weapon was immaculate.

"All right, people," Doyle said after looking them over one last time, "stand by for further orders." He spun and returned to the NCO corner, of which he was the sole occupant.

"Are all corporals in the fleet as full of crap as that?" PFC Joe Dean asked Chan, who stood next to him.

Chan shook his head. "Negative on that. Doyle's a pogue and wants everyone to think he's as tough as a real Marine."

"Pogue." That's another Confederation Marine tradition. They preserve ancient language. "Pogue" was the word twentieth-century U.S. Marines used to describe noncombat Marines—clerks and cooks and bakers and other nonfighters. A "real Marine" was in the fighting arms; an infantryman, artilleryman, tanker, recon, air crew—anyone who pulled a trigger, cocked a cannon, snooped and pooped, or dropped bombs.

"We're grunts, he's a pogue. With any luck, we'll never see him again." Chan paused in thought for a moment, then added, "I don't know how he got his second stripe. The man is in serious need of an attitude adjustment."

"Attention on deck," someone shouted moments later.

"As you were," Major Longaway said before the Marines in the troop hold could scramble to their feet.

"How's it going, PFC Chan, you ready to land?"

"You know it, sir."

Longaway stifled a smile.

"How about you, PFC Dean, ready for your first duty station?"

"Gonna get me some, sir."

"Sir!" Corporal Doyle scrambled out of the NCO corner and snapped to attention in front of Longaway. "The landing force is ready to land. I inspected the men myself."

"I knew you would, Doyle."

Doyle frowned when his rank was omitted. Some of the other Marines exchanged quick glances. Someone let out a quickly cut-off guffaw.

"We'll be heading for the well deck any minute now. Get everything ready and stand by for further orders." Longaway started to turn to leave the troop hold, then turned back. "For those of you who haven't done this before except in Boot Camp, get ready for the ride of a lifetime. It's a little more exciting the way we do it here."

As soon as the officer was gone, Doyle spun and stared each man in the eye, looking for any sign that would tell him who had laughed. They all looked innocent. He started to turn back to the NCO corner when the klaxons again rang and blared throughout the ship, followed by the melodious voice saying, "Landing Force, prepare to land."

"Fall in, people!" Corporal Doyle shouted. "Line 'em up, line 'em up, line 'em up!" He scurried along the line of Marines who scrambled to shrug into their packs, shoulder their seabags, and hoist their blasters. He snorted angrily when he couldn't find anyone who didn't have everything ready to move out. Then he took his place facing the middle of the line.

"Platoon, a-ten-hut!" he shouted.

The Marines shuffled their feet, but nobody made a serious attempt to come to attention; they couldn't in that narrow space with the loads they were carrying.

"Right HACE! Fo-art, HARCH!" Doyle had to duck back as a shouldered seabag nearly hit him in the head. He stutter-stepped in place for a moment, then realized there wasn't enough space in the narrow aisle for him to squeeze along the line of moving Marines to take his place near the head of the column.

"You forgot something," someone said softly as he

walked past. Doyle couldn't see who it was because the man's seabag blocked his view of his face.

Doyle started to snap out when he realized what it was he had forgotten. Red-faced, he scrambled back to the NCO corner to get his own pack, seabag, and weapon.

The "well deck" was at the bottom of a ladder at the opposite end of the short passageway outside the troop hold. Like its namesake in seagoing amphibious landing ships of ancient Earth-bound navies, the well deck was located in the lower, forward part of the ship's hull— though the designations "lower" and "forward" were arbitrary in starships. Unlike its predecessors, the well deck didn't open to the seas to let water in so amphibious landing craft could float out. Confederation Navy starships never settled in water seas—not on purpose anyway. Neither did the well deck contain numerous landing craft. Six "Essays," "Entry Shuttles, Atmospheric," were suspended from the well deck's overhead. Each shuttle could deliver three Marine Dragons to a planetary surface. In one drop, most of a FIST's infantry battalion could be delivered to the surface to make an amphibious assault. After off-loading their Dragons, the shuttles returned to orbit to pick up the next wave in the FIST's remaining Dragons and the ship's own landing craft, which weren't as heavily armed or armored as the Dragons, but were faster on the water. If necessary, the three Dragons in the ship's own complement would join in a landing. A single SAT could deliver an entire FIST to the surface in two waves.

Nobody waited for orders when they reached the well deck, and nobody listened to the orders Corporal Doyle shouted; they all headed directly to the one shuttle that would land them on Thorsfinni's World. Preparing to land was something the Marines had drilled on many times; everyone knew exactly where to go and what to do when he got there. Major Longaway led one contingent onto one Dragon, and Corporal Doyle shepherded the other onto the second. The other five shuttles in the well deck were loaded with supplies and equipment destined for the Confederation's military forces planetside and would follow the Marines' shuttle.

Dean grimaced at the thought of being on the Dragon with Doyle.

There were only two Dragons on the shuttle; there weren't enough men making the landing to need three— and hardly enough to justify using two. The Marines went directly to their assigned stations on the Dragons and stowed their packs and seabags in the locker spaces below the vehicle's seats. Then they made sure the seats that normally faced the center line of the vehicle were secure in the acceleration webbing that hung from the overhead and held them in a front-facing position. Other straps anchored the webbing to the deck. Satisfied, they climbed into the seats and buckled themselves in. As each man secured himself in his webbing he shouted out that his position was ready, and punched a button in the webbing to tell the computer he was ready to drop. When the buttons on all deployed webbings were punched and its own sensors in the buckles verified the messages, the computer's voice intoned to the coxswain—a navy petty officer, because these Dragons belonged to the navy and not the Marines—"All personnel secured. Vehicle ready for drop."

"Shuttle One ready to drop," the shuttle's coxswain reported to the ship, and his computer verified the message.

"Well deck, stand by for zero atmosphere," the computer voice said. Even through the walls of the Dragon and the shuttle outside it, the Marines could hear the whisper of the well deck's air being sucked out.

"Open drop hatch," the voice said.

Inside the Dragon the opening of the bay hatches beneath the shuttle was felt rather than heard by the Marines.

"Stand by for null-g," the ship's voice intoned.

The Marines tensed themselves for a sudden loss of weight.

"Null-g," intoned the ship's voice. "Three, two, one, mark."

The ship's gravity generators shut off. Everywhere in the ship and on its surface, people and objects slowly drifted upward from whatever direction had been "down" for them—anyone or anything that wasn't secured to a surface would drift away. In the Dragons there was a slight shifting of webbing as weight went away from the overhead support straps and newly floating mass was pulled into equilibrium by the deck straps. Dust particles that had been held to the ship's hull by gravitation drifted away.

"Whooh!" Clearly one of the Marines hadn't done this often enough to become accustomed to free fall.

"Belay that," snapped Corporal Doyle. He was secretly glad he hadn't been the one to make the noise—in eight years, it was only his third time in null-g.

The klaxons rang and blared throughout the ship and through the speakers on the Dragons. The computer-generated female voice said, "Land the landing force."

Waiting in nervous anticipation of his first real orbital drop, Dean told himself it was only his imagination that lent a note of sarcastic humor to the voice. But he didn't have time to dwell on the thought.

The shuttle was attached to a launch-plunger in the overhead of the well deck. On the command to land the landing force, a 100-psi blast of air ejected the shuttle away from the ship.

Dean knew he was supposed to yell when the acceleration cut in, but the sudden four-g force that slammed him toward the overhead turned his planned yell into a scream of near terror. Somehow, this didn't seem quite the way he remembered it from the practice landing they'd made from the Turd. The deck straps on the webbing straightened and went taut with the sudden movement, and made the fine adjustments needed to stop the webbing from slamming its human cargo into the overhead.

One second and three hundred meters from the closing bay doors, the shuttle's engines fired up and added three g's of forward momentum to the four vertical. The roar of the shuttle's engines, soundless in the space outside it, was loud enough inside to drown out the yells and screams of the men in the Dragons. Small rockets on the bottom of the shuttle ignited to cancel the downward motion of the entry vehicle, the aft retros firing more strongly than the forward ones to aid the main rockets in giving it a slight downward thrust. Less than ten seconds after launch, the shuttle was already past the one-and-a-half-kilometer-long SAT. Only the downward thrust from its main engines kept it from being flung into a higher orbit.

"The shuttle is clear of the ship," the shuttle's coxswain reported. "Request permission to commence atmospheric entry."

"Permission granted" was the reply. "On my mark, commence atmospheric entry. Four, three, two, one, mark."

The coxswain punched the button that controlled the topside attitude rockets. The shuttle's computer got confirmation from the ship's launch control computer and executed the command. Small vernier rockets above the shuttle's nose fired briefly to angle the shuttle downward sharply and convert its orbital velocity of more than

32,000 kilometers per hour into downward speed. Five seconds later the main engines shut off and the shuttle went into an unpowered plunge. If its path had been straight down, it would have catastrophically impacted the planetary surface in under two minutes, but its glide angle was calculated to take five minutes to reach 50,000 meters above the surface, where the wings would deploy and forward thrusters would fire to drop the shuttle's speed to something that could be controlled by powered flight.

Dean's digestive system reacted violently to the sudden drop from multi-g thrust to weightlessness. His intestines abruptly bloated, his stomach twisted and churned, his body tried to gag; he fought to keep from vomiting. He forced himself to swallow and twisted from side to side. Then he remembered to relax, concentrated on relaxing. First his legs, then his lower abdomen, his upper; next his chest, his arms, his throat; finally his head. The bloating in his intestines decreased, the twisting and churning of his stomach eased. He felt no more need to gag. He sighed. Then somebody else lost it a few feet away and Dean had to fight his digestion again.

"Clean that up yourself, Marine," the coxswain bellowed. "I'm not here to nursemaid puking buzzards."

"What the fuck's a 'buzzard'?" the man asked as he wiped vomitus from his chin.

The Marines cursed at the coxswain, but no one moved to get out of his webbing and teach the sailor his place. The man closest to the Marine who had lost it grabbed the nearest suction tube from the overhead and started cleaning up before the vomitus could settle on anything.

"Sound off," Corporal Doyle croaked from his webbing as soon as he had control of his voice.

"Aabenheld."

"Chan."

"Dean."

"Fitzhugh . . ." and so forth through the alphabet, just like Boot Camp, until each of the thirteen Marines aboard was accounted for as present and conscious.

"High speed on a bad road" was how Marines described the fall from the top of the atmosphere to the beginning of powered flight fifty kilometers above the surface. It was an apt description. By the time the braking rockets fired and the wings began to deploy, the shaking and rattling were so hard the Dragon felt as if it was coming apart, and someone screamed in fear.

Someone called out something about "cherries," and another Marine laughed.

The braking rockets and deploying wings quickly cut the angle of the shuttle's dive, cutting its speed in half by the time it reached the top of the troposphere. When the wings were fully extended, huge flaps extended from them to further brake the Essay's speed. When the wings finally bit into air hard enough for controlled flight, the coxswain turned off the braking rockets, fired up the jets, and maneuvered the craft into a velocity-eating spiral that slowed their descent as well as the shuttle's forward speed. At a thousand meters altitude, the coxswain pulled out of the spiral and popped the drogue chute. At two hundred, he angled the jets' vernier nozzles downward. Seconds later the shuttle rested on the surface of the Western Ocean, a hundred kilometers offshore from Thorsfinni's World's largest inhabited landmass.

"Ready landing craft to hit the beach," the coxswain ordered.

"Landing Craft One, ready to hit the beach," said the first Dragon's coxswain.

"Landing Craft Two, ready to hit the beach," said the second Dragon's coxswain.

They revved up their engines. The curtains fluttered, then rose stiffly around the air cushion that lifted the Dragons off the deck. The shuttle's coxswain opened the aft hatches and lowered the ramp, and the two Dragons drove out to splash onto the surface. In seconds they were zipping at top speed, across the wave tops toward the distant shore.

Aboard the *Lopez*, as soon as the shuttle was forcibly ejected from the well deck, the ship began the routine to launch the supply shuttles. Gentle puffs of air eased the shuttles out of the well deck. Gentle blasts of the shuttles' rockets pushed them into glide paths that would bring them to the planet's surface in three revolutions around it. There was no great rush. No enemy was attacking the ship, no foe threatened to shoot down the shuttles as they made planetfall. There was no need for the shuttles or their cargo to suffer the strains of an assault landing.

The Marines reporting to the FIST on Thorsfinni's World could have landed in the same sedate manner as the supplies and the later shore-liberty runs that ferried the ship's sailors planetside. But the Marines have an image to maintain, a reputation to uphold. They make planetfall the traditional way.

CHAPTER
EIGHT

The Dragons didn't stop on the beach, or even just beyond it. They continued inland off-road at an acute angle to the shoreline, the coxswains gunning them as fast as they dared over the moderately rough terrain. The sailors were determined to demonstrate they were just as tough as the Marines. It was a ride of the kind all the Marines had experienced at least once before: no air and no cushion.

At a flip of a lever on the coxwain's console, the seats swiveled down and around into their ground mode, vertical, facing the center line of the vehicle. The webbing that held the Marines into their acceleration seats withdrew.

Dean groaned with the change in attitude. The upright seats seemed to magnify every bounce and shudder of the vehicle.

"Hang on back there," the coxswain yelled to his jouncing passengers. "The ride's going to be *rough* from here on."

"Rough?" PFC Chan yelled back. "On a highway like this?" He laughed.

The coxswain grinned through gritted teeth, floored the acceleration lever and held his thumb pressed against the overdrive button. A red light began flashing on the console. The coxswain ignored it and kept his thumb mashed against the overdrive button. Since it was an assault vehicle, the Dragon didn't have an automatic override that would kick in when the driver exceeded safe speed for the terrain. The bounces became higher and the jounces harder. The Dragon screamed, then shuddered violently when an undercarriage air nozzle slammed onto a rock. The Dragon veered wildly, and the coxswain had to release the overdrive button to fight it back onto a straight path. Sweating and hoping there was no damage, he kept his thumb away from the overdrive after that. He couldn't afford to get in trouble with the chief.

They reached Camp Major Pete Ellis without further incident or damage to the Dragon. At the main gate they were met by two military police vehicles that led them to their destinations. One Dragon went directly to FIST headquarters, as its passengers were all being assigned to the squadron, artillery battery, or transport company, or to the headquarters of the FIST itself. The other headed straight to the infantry battalion's headquarters.

Chan complimented the coxswain on the smoothness of his driving as he dismounted from the vehicle. Then the thirteen Marines joining the 34th FIST's infantry battalion got into formation on the windswept parade ground in front of the headquarters building. The wind smelled of fish.

Gunnery Sergeant Mason, the battalion's assistant S-1—personnel chief—had too much liberty the night before and didn't feel quite up to matching replacements' skills and experience with the needs of the companies. Mostly, though, he wanted to get back inside, out of the constant, damp wind that swept across Camp Ellis. He called out company assignments as his eye fell randomly on names.

Company I needed two infantrymen. "Romanov, Tannenbaum, report to I Company, to your right," Mason croaked. Two men shuffled out of the line and marched to the gunnery sergeant who signaled to them.

Company K needed three infantrymen. "Hungh, Nu, Llewellan, K Company. Straight ahead." The three men shouldered their seabags and headed to the staff sergeant who signaled them.

Company L also required three infantrymen. "McNeal, Dean, Chan, L Company. To your left." Dean, McNeal, and Chan grinned at each other. They shouldered their seabags and marched to a utility-clad staff sergeant who stood looking at them somewhat disinterestedly.

Company L also needed a clerk. "Doyle."

The three looked at each other, aghast that they weren't getting away from Corporal Doyle.

"My name's Bass," the staff sergeant said when the four reached him. "Who are you?" His face was red and his breathing slightly labored—he'd been on liberty with Gunny Mason the night before.

Dean, McNeal, and Chan introduced themselves.

"Any of you have experience?" Bass asked before Doyle could give his name. Doyle's jaw snapped shut and he flushed.

"I do," Chan said.

Bass looked at him expectantly.

"Riot control on Euskadi," Chan said. "Peasant rebellion campaign on Ivanosk. Peacekeeping in the intersectarian wars on Cross and Thorn."

Bass shook his head at the mention of Ivanosk. "That's the fourth peasant rebellion we've had to put down there in the past half century," he said softly, almost as though he was thinking out loud. "I wonder when the Whites will realize their policies are causing the rebellions." Then, in a stronger voice, to Chan, "Well, PFC, with that much campaigning under your belt, how come you don't rate a starburst yet?"

Chan grinned crookedly. "Everybody up my chain of command lived a charmed life. We had no serious casualties, and nobody was reassigned. So no slots opened up for me to be promoted into."

Bass nodded his understanding. "How long were you with 14th FIST?"

Chan raised an eyebrow, thinking that Bass must keep very up to date if he knew which of the hundred FISTs had been on those three campaigns during the past couple of years. "Twenty-two months." Two months short of a full two-year tour.

"So they rotated you rather than keep you around where they'd have to promote you."

"That's about the size of it."

"And you two, this your first assignment?" he asked Dean and McNeal.

"Yessir," they said in unison.

"PFCs, I'm not an officer, I'm a staff sergeant. I work for a living. Don't 'sir' me."

They grinned. It was an old story by then, but the three PFCs thought they were going to like this Marine.

"Well, PFC Chan, fall those other two in and follow me."

Chan barely restrained a smile as he turned to Dean and McNeal and said, "Detail, attention!" The other two PFCs returned the smile and did as ordered.

Doyle was beyond simply flushing with embarrassment. "Staff Sergeant Bass," he snapped, "I'm senior man here. I should be the one to fall the detail in and march them where you want us to go."

Bass gave Doyle a "Who are you?" look, then said, "You're an oh-nine, isn't that right?"

Doyle drew his lips into a thin line. This staff sergeant had said that as though admin was an unworthy field. "That's right," he said tightly.

"What's your name?"

"Corporal Doyle."

"Well, Doyle, these Marines are going to the company

area to be assigned to platoons. You're going to battalion headquarters for orientation. Gunny Mason—you remember Gunny Mason, he was the one who gave the assignments—you know, the hungover one. Follow him. Chan, move 'em out." Doyle was dismissed. And Bass hadn't addressed him by rank.

Doyle glared at Bass, then picked up his seabag and stomped back to report to Gunny Mason. Gunny Mason ignored him too.

Bass didn't seem to mind that the three PFCs "marching" to the L Company area weren't in step—something the three of them, sweating and breathing heavily, appreciated by the time they reached the barracks a kilometer and a half across the rock-strewn, wind-swept base.

L Company was billeted in an H-shaped, two-story, wood-frame building. The wind that constantly blew on that part of Thorsfinni's World tore at the outside of the building so that it would need a fresh coat of paint in the near future. The central part of the building, the crossbar in the H, where Bass led the company's new men, held the offices and the officers and staff NCO quarters of L Company and of 34th FIST's artillery battery. Bass held the door open for them, then brushed past when they stopped inside.

Inside, the barracks' floors shined from frequent polishing, brass decorations glinted, and glassed-in 2-D's of the FIST chain of command glimmered. The bulkheads and overhead—"walls and ceiling," in civilian—were newly painted and spotless.

"This way," Bass said, leading them toward a door alongside which stood an eight-foot-tall staff that was festooned for half its height with campaign and battle streamers. "Morning, Claypoole," he said to a passing PFC who looked wide-eyed at the new men. Through the door was the company office. Two of its four desks were unoccupied. Two doors led from the other side of the office. One of them was open, and a captain, probably the company commander, could be seen working at a desk.

"Drop your seabags there," Bass said, pointing to an open space next to the entrance. When they did, he led them to one of the occupied desks.

"Morning, Top," he said to the first sergeant.

The first sergeant, like Bass, wore garrison utilities. He looked up from his computer. "Morning, Staff Sergeant Bass. You over it yet? I heard Gunny Mason is still hurting." He had also pulled too much liberty with Bass and Mason the night before.

"I'm good enough for garrison duty, Top."

"So what can I do you for?"

"Well, Top, I was just over at battalion headquarters, checking in on Gunny Mason. You heard right, he's still feeling poorly. On the way back I found these." He jerked a thumb.

The first sergeant looked at the new men for the first time. "Oh? Found 'em, huh. What do you think we should do with them?"

"Well, I found 'em, I get to keep 'em."

The first sergeant leaned back in his swivel chair and looked up at Bass. "You do?"

Bass nodded confidently.

"I've got holes to fill all over this company. What makes you think you should get all the goodies?"

"Third platoon's six men short. Nobody else's more than three men short. I keep these three, that almost brings me up level with everybody else."

"That a fact."

"That's a fact. I've got more two-man fire teams than any of the other platoons. One of my squad leaders is a corporal. Half of my fire team leaders are lance corporals. One of my gun team leaders is also acting gun squad leader. I haven't gotten any replacements since I've been with the company. Anyway, if you really need to assign someone to one of the other platoons, we're also getting a new oh-nine." The PFC at the other desk looked up at that and started paying attention. "He seems like a hard-charger," Bass continued. "You could give him to one of the other platoons."

The first sergeant raised his eyebrows. "Now, that's a thought."

"Oh no you don't," said the PFC at the other desk. "We finally get a second clerk and you want to give him to one of the platoons? Come on, Top, I need some help here. Let me tuck that young man under my wing. I'll have him shipshape in no time, and you'll have the best-run company office you've ever seen. We'll be doing such a good job in here we'll rate as a force multiplier and you won't need to get the other platoons up to full strength."

"That a fact," the first sergeant said.

"You know it, Top."

"Not so fast, Palmer," Bass said. "The new man's a corporal. Got you ranked. He'll take you under his wing and teach you all kinds of bad habits you haven't had the chance to pick up on your own."

Palmer collapsed against his chair back. "A corporal? You mean I'm still going to be the most junior man in this office?"

" 'Fraid so."

Muttering to himself, Palmer went back to what he was doing.

The first sergeant rose to his feet. "I'm First Sergeant Myer," he said to his new men. "Call me Top, unless you've done something wrong and you're on my carpet for it—then you better pray to me as God. Who're you?"

The three introduced themselves.

"Welcome aboard, Marines," Top Myer said. "I want you to know that Company L, 34th FIST is the best company in the Marine Corps. There are few FISTs that have been involved in as many campaigns and other operations as the 34th has. And damn few companies that have been on as many independent missions as L Company, 34th FIST. You may have gotten a hint of that when you came past our streamers outside the hatch." He pointed at the door. "If you bothered to look at it, you saw a lot of Confederation Unit Citation streamers, Marine Unit Citations, and Meritorious Unit Citations. Between what we've been awarded as members of the FIST or larger units, and what we've won on our own, I don't think any company in the entire Corps has been cited as many times. While you're with us you can expect to see a lot of action. What I expect is for you to do your absolute best as members of this company. If you do, we'll get along just fine.

"Now, let's go meet the Skipper. Then we'll decide about what platoons to assign you to."

The captain they'd seen through the open inner door was indeed the company commander. Unlike the two senior NCOs, the captain wore his Bravo uniform, khaki shirt and green trousers. Several rows of ribbons were ranked above his left shirt pocket. The three PFCs came to a rigid attention one pace in front of his desk, eyes fixed on a piece of wall above his head. Top Myer stood at the corner of the company commander's desk; he didn't come to attention. Bass leaned against the door frame, not quite slouching.

"New men, Skipper," Myer said when the captain looked up. "PFCs Chan, Dean, and McNeal." To the new men he said, "This is Captain Conorado." Then back to the captain: "Two of 'em are fresh off Arsenault."

"And the other's got the Third Ivanosk Campaign

Medal and the Marine Expeditionary Medal with comet for second award," Captain Conorado said. "It's nice to get a junior man with experience for a change."

Chan held back a smile; he knew Dean and McNeal had to be wondering how the captain knew so much. Not only hadn't Bass or Myer said anything about his level of experience, the captain hadn't seemed to be paying any attention to them when they were at the first sergeant's desk. This was an old trick Chan had seen before.

"PFC Dean," Conorado went on, "you fired High Expert and were squad leader in Boot Camp. PFC McNeal, you were assistant squad leader. Speaks well of both of you. You apply what you learned on Arsenault and you should do well here. I expect you to do as well here as you did with the 14th, PFC Chan." He stood. The first impression he gave was that he was a tall, gangly man. It was only on second look that they realized he was average height and build.

"The Top already welcomed you aboard," Conorado said. "I'd like to second that. With some effort on your part, you'll fit in here very shortly. Now, as for assignments . . ." He glanced at a sheet of paper on his desk. "We've got holes to fill all over this company, but third platoon is more shorthanded than the others. I think I'll let Staff Sergeant Bass have all three of you. That'll almost bring his platoon up to the level of the others."

Dean blinked. Maybe it was some kind of game they were playing, showing the new men how much they knew.

"I'm short an officer," Conorado continued, "that's why your new platoon commander is a staff sergeant. Pay close attention to him. He knows more than any ensign I've ever known, and more than most lieutenants and captains as well. Matter of fact, Charlie Bass is something of a legend in the Corps."

It was Chan's turn to blink. He had heard of Charlie

Bass—but the Charlie Bass he'd heard of was a gunnery sergeant.

"He's got one problem, though. A lot of junior officers think he's insubordinate. And he's got no fear of the consequences when he takes action to back up his convictions." He sat back down. "That's it for now. Staff Sergeant Bass, they're yours. Get them processed in." He returned to the work on his desk.

Back in the outer office, Palmer took them through the company check-in process. It wasn't much more than sticking their wristbands in the reader to check them against the records netted to the company personnel files while they were walking from Battalion to the barracks. Palmer asked them a couple of confirming questions: date of birth, blood type, mother's birth name. Finally they looked into the retinal scanner for positive physical ID, and that was it. The processing-in for all three took less than five minutes.

"I'll take you to meet Sergeant Souavi later—he's the company supply sergeant," Bass said when Palmer was through with them. "First, let's go to the platoon squad bay. Grab your seabags. I'll introduce you to everybody and assign you to squads."

On the way, Bass told them that the left wing of the building, one of the verticals on the H, was the L Company area, and that the right wing housed the artillery battery. The company's living quarters proper were divided into small rooms, each housing the three men of a fire team—squad leaders had private rooms. First and second platoons were on the first deck—the ground floor. Third and the assault platoon were on the upper. A recreation room with two vidscreens, library cards, and various table games was in the rear of the second deck, and a weight room was under it.

CHAPTER
NINE

The wide-eyed PFC took a few more steps along the corridor, then spun back as soon as Bass and the strangers went through the office door. He dashed to the streamer staff and stood next to it, listening to the Marines in the office. When Top Myer led them into Captain Conorado's office, he darted into the office and spoke with Palmer in a hushed-rushed voice.

"New guys?" he asked. "Really? And they're being assigned to third platoon? Two of them are really boot?"

"So boot they still smell like Lincoln shoe polish, Claypoole," Palmer assured him.

"Sumbitch," Claypoole said when Palmer said it was so. "Thanks, Palmer. You just made me the happiest man in the company." He gave a quick glance at the men in the commander's office, then raced out and headed for the third platoon squad bay.

He hit the second level on the double and turned left. Halfway down the corridor he skidded to a stop, grabbed a door frame, and spun himself into the three-man room he shared with Lance Corporal Lupo "Rabbit" Ratliff, his fire team leader.

"No more 'New Guy,' Rabbit," he almost shouted. "I'm not 'New Guy' anymore. We've got two boots joining the platoon. They can be 'New Guy.' New Guy

One and New Guy Two even. I'm not 'New Guy' anymore. Got it?"

Ratliff didn't look up from the graphic novel that was scrolling across his vid. "New Guy," he said dryly, "you've always been New Guy, you'll always be New Guy. Go away, I'm busy."

Claypoole glared at him, then snarled something and twisted out of the room to dash farther down the corridor into NCO territory, where he grabbed another frame and spun into the doorway of Sergeant Wang Hyakowa, his squad leader.

"Sergeant Hyakowa, I'm not 'New Guy' anymore. Got it? Staff Sergeant Bass is bringing two new guys up. One of them can be 'New Guy.' *Both* of them can be 'New Guy.' I don't care, just so it's not me."

Hyakowa was playing a platoon-level tactical simulation game, part of a Marine Corps Institute correspondence course, in preparation for the tests for promotion to staff sergeant. He didn't bother looking at Claypoole when he said, "New Guy, you were born New Guy, you're going to die New Guy. Says so on your birth certificate. Now, stop bothering me while I'm studying." Still without looking up, he reached out and pushed his door shut in Claypoole's face.

Claypoole jerked back far enough to avoid being hit by the closing door and stood slack-jawed for a moment. Then, grimly determined, he began making a circuit of the platoon area, visiting every room, telling everybody he wasn't New Guy anymore. Some looked at him, some didn't. Some grunted, some were silent. None agreed to stop calling him New Guy.

"Attention on deck!" Bass's voice boomed out. "Third platoon, assemble in the rec room. Now."

All along the corridor heads popped out of rooms to see what was up. No officers were visible, so no one bothered to check clothing for proper military appearance before they headed for the company rec room. In little more than a minute all twenty-two men of the platoon were gathered. The first ones there grabbed chairs that were not occupied by the members of other platoons who were already in the room, reading or watching flicks on the big-screen vids. The later arrivals lounged against the walls. All looked expectantly at Bass, or curiously at the three men who stood somewhat self-consciously near him.

Bass gave them a moment to get a good look, then said, "We've got some replacements. This is PFC Chan. He was with the 14th FIST on Euskadi, Ivanosk, and Cross and Thorn. I'm sure he'll fit in with us right away. PFCs Dean and McNeal recently completed the best military training humanity has ever devised. It'll take them a little longer, but we'll all see to it that they quickly become productive members of the best platoon in the best company of the best FIST in the Corps."

"Then how come he's introducing them to third platoon instead of second?" one of the vid-watchers whispered to his neighbor.

"Two guesses," Bass boomed. "And neither of them is second platoon."

The man who whispered turned red. "Uh, excuse me, Staff Sergeant Bass," he said, and stood up. "We, uh, we shouldn't be in here while you're meeting with your platoon." He nudged the man he'd whispered to and the two of them quickly left the room.

Amusement flickered across Bass's face, then he asked the other Marines in the room who weren't in his platoon, "Any other comments?"

"No, Staff Sergeant Bass," one said and got up and left. Everyone else who wasn't in third platoon followed his example.

Bass waited until he was alone with his platoon before he laughed. "Looks like they all agree that third platoon is the best. Now, down to business.

"Everybody's equally shorthanded, each squad is short two men, so we'll do it by the numbers and each squad gets one replacement." He paused to look at them, particularly the squad and team leaders. "If anyone has any objections to how I'm making the assignments, speak up." There were many reasons Charlie Bass's men respected him, not least of which was his willingness to hear their ideas and accept the good ones. "Now, I don't like to put a new man or a man I don't know in the gun squad. Neru, you still want to be a gunner?"

A swarthy lance corporal said, "I sure do."

"Think you can train him, Hound?"

"I can make a gunner out of anybody big enough to carry one," Corporal "Hound" Kelly said.

"That okay with you, Wang? Do you mind having two replacements?"

"Not as long as one of them has experience," Sergeant Hyakowa answered.

"Okay, you've got Chan. I'll also give you Dean. Eagle's Cry, that leaves McNeal for you. Any questions? Any problems?"

Nobody questioned or objected.

"All right, squad leaders, let me know how you reorganize your squads so I can update the platoon roster. Dismissed." Bass left the rec room.

"First squad, on me," Hyakowa said, and the members of his squad gathered around him.

"Second squad, over here," Eagle's Cry said.

"Guns up," Kelly called.

"Let second team have the new guy, Sergeant Hyakowa," Claypoole said eagerly when first squad assembled. "Right, Rabbit? Second team gets the new guy. We'll train him right."

Hyakowa looked at him innocently. "All right, you got New Guy." He looked at Ratliff. "Think you can handle Chan?" he asked without expression.

Ratliff grinned back. "As many campaigns as he's been on? Yeah, I can use some help breaking in New Guy."

"I'm not New Guy anymore," Claypoole snapped.

"Chief," Hyakowa ignored Claypoole's outburst, "you're my most experienced fire team leader, you get the greenest one. PFC Dean, meet Corporal Leach. We call him 'Chief.' Don't ask why, nobody knows. All right, team leaders, get them settled in." Hyakowa looked around and saw the other two squad leaders were also finished making their assignments. He gave a signal and Eagle's Cry and Kelly went with him to report to Bass.

It took only a few minutes for Corporal Leach and Lance Corporal Justice Goudanis, the other member of first fire team, to get Dean settled into their room. With everything he owned in one seabag, Dean didn't have much unpacking to do. It didn't take Ratliff any longer to settle Chan in, even though Claypoole wasn't there helping—he was busy running back and forth between the rooms where the two replacements were, greeting them, calling them each New Guy, and making sure everybody in the platoon heard the two new men being identified as New Guy.

Other members of the platoon stepped into their rooms to meet the new men and introduce themselves during the unpacking, but neither Leach nor Ratliff let them stick around where they'd be in the way. Second squad's first fire team leader, Corporal Tim Kerr, who got McNeal, said it as well as any of the others: "Get out of here. When the new guy's unpacked, I'll bring him out for you to confuse with all of your names."

Nobody argued the point, not with the third man in the fire team, Lance Corporal Dave "Hammer" Schultz, standing there looking at them. Schultz was acknowledged as the platoon's crazy, and nobody wanted to cross him.

When he was almost finished unpacking, during a moment when nobody from one of the other squads was interrupting, Dean asked Leach, "Chief, how come everybody's hanging around in the barracks? I thought everybody'd be doing something."

"You mean like hand-to-hand combat training, or classroom work?"

"Yeah, something like that."

"You just got here, right?"

Dean nodded. "It's been less than an hour since we got off the Dragons at Battalion."

"How long did it take you to get here?"

Dean thought that was an odd question. Everybody who knew where Thorsfinni's World was knew how far it was from Arsenault. "Six weeks."

"Did you go home on leave after Boot Camp?"

"No. I came right here from Arsenault. A transport took us someplace where we split up. McNeal and me and a couple others transhipped directly onto an assault carrier coming here. We didn't even make planetfall; I don't even know what planet we orbited then."

"You're from Earth, right? That's what your accent sounds like."

Dean hadn't known there was such a thing as an "Earth accent." He'd always thought it was everybody else who had accents. "That's right, New Rochester."

"Let's see, a standard month from Earth to Arsenault, five standard months there, then a standard month and a half in transit here." He cocked his head. "You haven't seen a calendar in more than half a standard year, have you?"

"That's right." Until that moment Dean hadn't realized he hadn't seen a calendar in all that time.

Leach grinned broadly at him. "Well, Dean, nobody's doing any work because this is Saturday. We're all on liberty."

That didn't explain why they were all hanging around the barracks, though. Leach and Goudanis quickly filled him in. Payday was every other week, and last week had been payday. On payday weekends almost everybody left the base Friday evening for shore liberty in Bronnoysund, which the Marines called "Bronny" for short, the town right outside the main gate, and didn't come back until Sunday. Some went farther, to the larger cities of Troms or Bergen—or even went all the way to the other end of Niflheim to the big city, the capital, New Oslo. That day, between paydays, the Marines were preserving their money to spend tonight.

Claypoole came around to call Dean New Guy again and arrived in time to hear the end of the explanation.

"You have any money, New Guy?" Claypoole asked. "You must have money if you just got off ship. I'll take you into Bronny tonight, show you the sights. Hey," his eyes glowed, "I'll even take you to a real restaurant so you won't have to eat the swill they serve in the mess hall."

"You think he's got all that back pay in his pocket and he's going to pay for your dinner, right?" Leach asked.

"Go away, New Guy," Goudanis said. "*I'm* taking him on liberty tonight."

Dean didn't have a chance to tell them that in his entire time in the Corps he'd received only a few credits in pay.

The notes of the chow call bugle had barely died away over the parade ground before the men of third platoon were back in the barracks, making sure their garrison utilities were clean and squared away. Hardly anybody was going to stay on base to eat at the mess hall, not on a Saturday night, not if they had any money in their pockets.

"You haven't been paid yet, right?" Goudanis asked Dean.

"No, Lance Corporal. We didn't need any money on Arsenault and I didn't bring any from home."

"Call me Juice, Dean. Okay. Staff Sergeant Bass'll get you squared away at the finance office on Monday. Here." He handed Dean a wad of bills he took from a compartment in his locker. "Take this. It should cover you for tonight. You can pay me back when you get paid." The bills were green, blue, and white with a picture of a fierce-looking, bearded man on the front and an imposing public building of some sort on the back. The denominations were clearly printed in Arabic numbers in each corner. The wad added up to 100 kroner, whatever that was.

"Well, thanks," Dean said, flattered but at the same time embarrassed at the lance corporal's openhandedness.

"Don't mention it, Dean. We take care of each other in this platoon. See?" He tapped the touchpad locking device on his personal gear locker. It didn't activate when it came in contact with Goudanis's fingertips. "No locks on our personal stuff. We don't have any thieves in this company. That's enough cash to get you through a *good* liberty night in Bronny. Since it's Saturday, there's no curfew for Marines until midnight tomorrow. M'boy," Goudanis clapped Dean on the shoulder, "we're gonna see just how good you are with a schooner of beer this evening!"

"Juice!" Claypoole shouted from the doorway. "What's taking you so long!" Claypoole glanced at Dean, still in his Class A parade uniform. "New Guy, get a move on. You're holding up the whole Third Herd!"

Dean was beginning to tire of Claypoole. He reminded him of that bully long ago who'd tormented him on the playground about his middle name. But he sensed that Claypoole's foolishness was being tolerated by the other Marines in the platoon, and he understood instinctively that overreacting would be a mistake.

"Pipe down, New Guy," Goudanis muttered. "PFC Dean is 'PFC Dean,' until we come up with a new name for him, and as for you, reindeer face, you always were New Guy, you're New Guy now, and you'll always be New Guy."

Claypoole ignored Goudanis and said, "New Guy, you got money? You'll need money in town tonight." He dug deep into a cargo pocket and produced a wad of bills. "Here." He looked about defiantly. "See, it isn't like Chief said, I don't expect you to spring for me tonight. I know you haven't gotten paid yet."

"Uh, thanks, New Guy," Dean said, surprised a second time by the generosity of the men but determined not to give in to Claypoole's badgering. "Lance Corporal . . ." Claypoole snickered and Dean paused briefly. "Uh, Juice gave me some already."

Claypoole shrugged and put the money back into his pocket. "You run out, New Guy, give a holler. I'll be around. Unless you call me New Guy again. Then we got trouble. Okay, Juice, main gate? Fifteen minutes?" Goudanis nodded. "Hey, Juice," Claypoole added as an afterthought as he went out the door, "let's fix New Guy up with Big Barb tonight." Claypoole laughed raucously and ran down the hall, shouting to other Marines to meet him at the main gate in fifteen minutes.

"Uh, Juice," Dean was having trouble calling a lance

corporal by a nickname, "isn't it against regulations or something for Marines to go on liberty in utilities?"

"In a civilized place, yes. But you're on Thorsfinni's World, just outside Bronnoysund. This place is the tail end of the planet that's been called the lower colon of Human Space. There isn't much in the way of what anybody would consider civilized amenities. We're better off wearing clothes that can stand hard wear when we're on liberty. Besides, these people are as hard as the rocks in their fjords. So no frills with these folks, and the colonel doesn't play garrison dukshit games with his Marines. And do you think the 'Finnis up here care what a man wears when he's on the town? Did you know that in winter, when it's fifty below, they think it's *fun* to break the ice on the Bothnia and go *swimming* in the goddamned river?

"Now, it *is* against regs to wear civilian clothing around here, unless you go to New Oslo," Goudanis continued. "But for that you've got to take leave, unless you get lucky and pull courier duty to the embassy there. But let me tell you something about leave: so long as you're with the 34th, when you aren't deployed on a mission, you'll be training in the boonies, so you won't have much time to vacation. Save up your leave to use when you go to a real world, or cash it in when you're discharged. I been in six years now and got over a hundred days on the books. Man, that's more'n three months' pay! And if you ship over, well, you can go home or someplace." The way Goudanis emphasized "someplace," it was evident to Dean that he did not think much of wherever home was for him. "And remember this," he added, "travel time doesn't count as leave."

Dean zipped up his utility jacket. "Who's Big Barb?"

"You don't wanna know," Corporal Leach said as he

looked through the door to see if they were ready yet. Juice, you been tellin' him about Big Barb?"

"Nah, Chief, bigmouth Claypoole just had to bring the subject up."

Leach grinned. "Don't let him get on your nerves," he said to Dean. "Claypoole can be a pain in the ass, but when the going gets rough, he'll back you up. All right, people!" Chief shouted. "Transportation to the frigid delights of Bronny awaits us!"

The liberty bus bounced and swayed as it roared down the steep gravel road to Bronnoysund, snuggled in a bend of the Bothnia River about five kilometers from the mouth of the fjord emptying into the Nordenskold Sea. The town wasn't far from the main gate, within easy walking distance, but the Marines going on liberty rode the bus anyway. The bus wasn't going on its rounds to carry them, it was on its way to pick up the men who'd stayed in town overnight and were too hungover or otherwise disoriented to make it back to base on their own.

The twenty Marines seat-belted into straight-backed and thinly cushioned seats in the passenger compartment laughed and shouted back and forth, eagerly anticipating their night on the town. "You see, Dean," Chief shouted into his ear from the seat next to him, "we don't use liberty passes in the 34th. Most places you gotta get a pass from your first sergeant to go on liberty, if you're a sergeant or below: You sign it out from the duty NCO before you go out and sign it back in when you return. The duty NCO, who's usually a PFC or lance corporal who screwed up and got stuck with the duty, checks you out and checks you back in, and if you screw up, he'll log you in and the Skipper'll pull your pass for punishment."

Dean nodded.

"See," Goudanis shouted from the seat behind him,

"this is a hardship post, and they give us a break from the normal dukshit rules that apply throughout the rest of the Fleet, where the pogue Marines go."

Claypoole, sitting up behind the driver's console, began to sing, and several other men took up the tune in time to stamping feet and clapping hands:

> You ever been to the Grenadines
> Where the place is full of shade-tree queens?
> Oh, the grout is bad but the scabs is worse,
> So beat your meat for safety first.

"Pipe down back there!" the driver shouted over the intercom. "You're making so much noise I can't concentrate on the goddamn road!"

The noise level increased and the men began shouting in unison for the driver to turn the bus on its side.

CHAPTER
TEN

The bus ground to a halt and the driver pushed the button that whooshed the door open, but he was barely fast enough to keep the first men from slamming into it. "First fire team: lock and load!" Leach hollered as he rushed headlong out, followed by the rest of the platoon.

Bemused, Dean scrambled off the bus and stood in the settling dust a safe distance from the Marines who were still exiting. The bus was parked by itself in one corner of a huge graveled lot. The lot sat beside a dirt road lined with wooden buildings, none of which was over two stories high. At the end of the road, about half a kilometer beyond where the Marines stood, Dean could see the light from the setting sun glinting off the Bothnia River. The communications masts of several large commercial seagoing vessels poked up above the buildings situated down there on Bronnoysund's waterfront, the main commercial district of the town.

Much of the town was in the shadow of the rugged peaks that formed the walls of the fjord, and a chill wind swept small clouds of dust and pieces of wastepaper across the parking lot. Dean drew his field jacket closer.

Claypoole, his face flushed and eyes twinkling with amusement, slapped Dean on the shoulder. "Cold, New Guy? Hell, this is summer in these parts. Wait'll winter comes!"

Nobody took off right away; they gathered in an informal formation in front of corporals Eagle's Cry, Leach, and Kerr. Eagle's Cry, as senior man present, addressed the junior men. "Listen up," he said. "We've got three new people with us tonight. They don't know their way around Bronny, they don't know the people, they don't know anything about the local customs. Do not, I say again, do not let them wander off by themselves or otherwise leave them alone tonight. Be a damn shame to lose a man before he even gets to meet everyone in his squad. Also, don't let *them*—and don't *you*—get into any trouble you can't get out of on your own. We," he gestured in a way that included the other corporals, "don't want to have to dig you out of any pit you get yourselves into. And if you get into more trouble than we can get you out of, don't worry about what the Skipper or Staff Sergeant Bass will do to your sorry asses, worry about what *we're* going to do to you when you get out of the brig. Now, get out of my parking lot and have a good time."

Everybody scattered.

"C'mon, New Guy, we're goin' to see the elephant." Claypoole trotted off down the road.

Dean looked around for McNeal and Chan. The three of them fell in with Ratliff, Goudanis, and a couple of other Marines whom Dean had probably met but whose names he couldn't remember. They trailed along behind Claypoole. "New Guy can do whatever he wants to," Ratliff said. "But first we're going to Helga's for a steak."

Steak? Dean had had a real steak once, from a cow, a tough, well-cooked piece of meat about two inches square that he'd consumed in two bites. He hadn't liked it very much.

"C'mon, Dean," Goudanis said, putting his arm around

the new man's shoulder. "First we eat and drink, then we drink, and then we drink some more."

None of the citizens they passed on the street paid the Marines much attention. Many of them were big people, even the women, with fair complexions and light-colored hair, though there was a large minority of other physical types and complexions. Their cheeks were ruddy with the glow of good health and they wore simple, sturdy outer garments that looked to be made from natural fibers of some sort. Noisy vehicles running on oversized wheels lurched and sputtered along the rutted roadway.

"What's that smell?" Dean asked. Ratliff shrugged. "You'll get used to it. It's a combination of the wood and coal they burn to heat their homes, the cheap tobacco they grow in greenhouses to smoke, and the, uh, internal combustion engine. Yeah," he said when he saw the surprised expression on Dean's face, "their vehicles operate on gasoline-powered engines. This world has vast oil reserves and the stuff's easy to get at, so they got used to it. Now you go to New Oslo, which you will before you leave the 34th, they have modern energy systems there, but this place is several hundred klicks from New Oslo and four hundred years behind the rest of Human Space. This is the *frontier*. Enjoy it while you can, 'cause when we go on a deployment, you'll consider this real good living."

"And don't forget the fish," Juice said. "That smell's from the canning company that operates down at the waterfront. Fish, lumber, and reindeer meat are the major industries for the people who live in Bronny."

The signs they passed on the shopfronts and street corners were in a strange-looking language Dean had never seen before. The letters were the same as the Roman alphabet he was used to, but some had lines through them, and there were extra dots and circles in unexpected places. The conversations he overheard as they passed people along the street were in a guttural language that seemed to rise and fall in tone as the people spoke. "Hey, do they know English in this place?" he asked.

"Oh, yeah," Juice replied, "but they also speak the language they brought with them from Old Earth: Norwegian. These are very traditional people."

"Well, do they resent our being here or something?"

"Why do you ask that?" Ratliff asked.

"I dunno. Nobody's even nodded at us since we got off the bus. They just seem to be ignoring us."

Ratliff laughed shortly. "Sure they like us, Dean. What looks like them ignoring us is just their way of being polite. They think it's rude if you look at a stranger on the street. Nah, they like us sure enough. We spend our pay in their town, and when we get drunk we don't mind fighting with them. The 'Finnis love to drink and they really love to fight when they've been drinking. We have that in common."

"Hell, Dean, what do you think they have to do for entertainment around here but fight and drink?" Juice added.

"And fuck," McNeal said.

Ratliff laughed. "That too, but they don't talk about it—and they don't do it in public."

Helga's was a warm and clean family restaurant with a well-stocked bar along the back wall. A dozen tables, each set for four, filled a spacious dining area. Only one was occupied, by a middle-aged couple apparently in their late sixties, finishing a quiet meal. The man was wearing a large bandage on his forehead. He looked up and smiled when the Marines came in. Dean noticed he was missing several front teeth. "Hah, Rabbit," he shouted. "Ve haf gud fight last Saturday, yah?" He pointed to the dressing on his head.

"Yo, Mr. Malmstrom. Hi, Mrs. Malmstrom," Rabbit called to the pair. To Dean he whispered, "*She* put the bump on the old guy's noggin, not me. It was Claypoole who started the fight when he tried to pick up Mrs. Malmstrom. He mistook her for a whore. She was gonna bean him with a beer schooner, but Claypoole ducked and she bounced it off her old man instead." Goudanis led them to a corner near the bar, where they put two tables together and seated themselves. Instantly a huge blond woman bustled up to the Marines.

"Helga!" Juice shouted. "Food! Steak!"

"Ach, my boys!" she squealed. "You eat good tonight, but no fighting!" She wagged an index finger as big as a sausage at the Marines. "Oooh, who are dees gud-looking young men wit' you tonight?" she asked, hands on her enormous hips, looming over Dean, Chan, and McNeal like a mountain.

"New men," Ratliff answered. "This salty one here," he clapped a hand on Chan's shoulder, "is Chan. This is his second duty station. The dark one is McNeal, and the redhead is Dean."

"Ach, you are too skinny, my darlings," Helga crooned. "Helga vill fatten you up!"

"Beer and steaks, then," Ratliff ordered.

"Yes, beer," Juice cried, and then sang, "Beer, beer, beer cried the privates, merry men are we, there's none so fair as can compare with the fighting infantreeeee!"

When the steaks arrived, they completely covered the huge platters on which Helga served them. They were two inches thick, so tender and juicy they almost melted in Dean's mouth. He had never tasted such wonderful meat before.

"Where do they raise the cows this meat comes from?" Dean wanted to know.

"They're from reindeer," Ratliff mumbled around a mouthful, "the 'Finnis breed them special for eating." He swallowed and then chased the meat with a huge gulp of the potent pilsner that was another specialty of Helga's. "All the reindeer on this planet—there's more of them than people—are descended from three cows the first colonists brought with them, along with a sperm bank drawn from the herds that used to roam all over Norway back on Old Earth."

"You ever seen a reindeer?" Goudanis asked.

"Only pictures. They've been extinct on Earth for a long time."

"You'll see the real thing when we get out in the boonies. Let me tell you about reindeer. They're walking latrines with a clothing rack on their heads, and you get downwind of a herd, you'll wonder how such things can taste so good."

Gradually the other tables filled up with diners, some of whom nodded affably at the Marines as they took their places. Soon the air was hazy with pungent smoke from the large black cigars both the men and the women smoked, even while they were eating. The noise level increased and Dean found he had to raise his voice to be heard at their table. He didn't mind. They had finished two large schooners of Helga's beer each and he was experiencing his first alcohol buzz since before he'd enlisted in the Corps. He was also feeling warm, full, and very satisfied for the first time in more than six months.

Leach offered his companions cigars. Goudanis lighted his without hesitation, sucked in a lungful of acrid smoke, held it a moment, and then expelled noisily. "Ahhh," he sighed, savoring the flavor of the tobacco.

Dean had never smoked before. He couldn't afford

tobacco back on Earth so he'd never picked up the habit. Goudanis flicked a small blue flame from a lighter, and when the tobacco started to burn, Dean sucked the smoke deep into his lungs, as he had seen the others do. It burned intensely and he began to cough uncontrollably.

Goudanis laughed and pounded him on the back. "We didn't know how to smoke either, before we came out here. Try it again. You'll get used to it."

Dean doubted he ever would—or that he'd ever stop coughing. He looked around at the other diners, but nobody seemed to have noticed his discomfort. A sudden wave of dizzy nausea passed over him and he thought he was going to vomit, but the feeling passed as quickly as it had come. Cautiously, he sucked again on the cigar, expelling the smoke through his nose. Well, it wasn't half bad that time, he thought. In the next fifteen minutes he managed to smoke half his cigar down. Leach and Goudanis, on the other hand, had smoked theirs only about a third of the way. They winked at each other as Dean puffed happily away on his cigar.

"Now, m'boy," Rabbit said, leaning conspiratorially across the table, "it's time to introduce you to Big Barb."

"No," Juice exclaimed in mock horror, "*not* Big Barb, no, no!"

"Yep," Ratliff said as he motioned for one of Helga's waitresses, a buxom young blonde, to bring their check. The entire meal cost twenty-five kroner. "Leave a fiver for Miss Haraldsson," he told the other two and got to his feet. Dean stood up too quickly and almost lost his balance.

"Whoa, there, PFC Dean," Goudanis cautioned as he steadied Dean with one hand. "Watch yourself tonight. The beer these people drink is mighty potent." Dean gave an embarrassed laugh.

Outside, complete darkness had descended upon the

town and the temperature had dropped to a cool ten degrees Celsius. The brisk night air burned in Dean's lungs as he slowly breathed it in. Overhead in the clear night sky thousands of stars twinkled down at them. Being unfamiliar with the local constellations, Dean couldn't tell where he'd just come from, but he knew that not so very long ago, he'd been out there where the light from those stars had been generated hundreds of years ago. Now he was on Thorsfinni's World. When the light had started out from the star that had most recently shined on him, this place hadn't even been discovered yet. The thought made him catch his breath.

Dean never forgot that brief moment. He felt good, physically, but more important, he really felt good about himself. He was comfortable, with men he respected, and they were treating him as one of their own. And now they were off to see Big Barb, whoever that was.

Big Barb's was a combination hotel, bar, dance hall, bordello, and ship's chandlery and outfitter's that occupied a two-story warehouse along the waterfront. It was a favorite hangout for the Marines from Camp Ellis, as well as for the crews from ships in the harbor.

The "elephant" was Big Barb herself, one of the largest, most foulmouthed women Joe Dean could imagine. She did not allow cursing or fighting in her establishment, unless it was she who was doing them. And there was plenty of both all the time at Big Barb's. The fighting among her patrons was usually over the women, and the cursing took place over the prices she charged for use of the rooms on the second floor. Big Barb broke up most of the fights herself, and with great relish.

Big Barb did not waste money on decor. The dance floor was just a huge space cleared of tables. Patrons were served at the bar, beer only, in large earthenware mugs that cost nothing to produce but ten kroner if you broke one. Gambling was allowed and, next to the girls, was the place's chief attraction. Dance music was provided by the patrons themselves, those who could play some kind of musical instrument. Usually when one of the Marines danced with one of Big Barb's girls, they were serenaded by jeers and lewd comments from the other patrons. But nobody jeered when a sailor or two from one of the fishing boats danced a lively reel or hornpipe to a tune played on an accordion or a fiddle or harmonica.

Dean's first impression of the place was of the strong stench of stale beer. Only a few tables were occupied at that early hour. "Wait'll after midnight," Leach said. "Then this place'll be hopping."

A dozen men from third platoon had shoved two tables together near the bar and were well into many mugs of the powerful brew served there. Six of Barb's girls had attached themselves to as many Marines and were busy matching them drink for drink as one of the men sang a drinking song in a surprisingly good tenor.

> I'm Cap-tain Jinks of the Space Marines,
> I feed my men on flip and creans,
> And sport young la-dies in their teens,
> Though a cap-tain in the arm-y.

At the mention of Marines and army, the men around the table shouted catcalls and banged their mugs loudly.

The singer, Dean was astonished to discover, was none other than Staff Sergeant Bass.

"Get over here!" Bass shouted as he saw the three new men. "We've got some serious drinking to do before this night's over." He drained his mug with a flourish and wiped foam off his upper lip with the back of his hand.

Dean wondered if Bass had walked into town; he hadn't been aboard the bus. "Ahhh, you thirsty dogfathers," Bass shouted. "Beer, more beer for m'lads here." One of the women, a brunette and not that bad-looking, detached herself from her Marine—it was the missing Claypoole—and hastened to the bar.

"Beer, beer, beer cried the privates!" Claypoole shouted, and several others took up the song:

> Beer, beer, beer cried the privates,
> Mer-ry men are we!
> There's none so fair
> As can com-pare
> With the fight-ing infan-treee!

The song went on and on, through all the ranks up to colonel, with all of them shouting for beer, and when they got to the chorus, every man stood up and shouted for beer at the top of his lungs. The bare rafters rang with the sound of their voices.

Face flushed from the shouting, and his heart pounding with the effort, Dean found a seat next to McNeal. "I see you've managed to fit right in with this crew," he commented.

"I fit right in," McNeal replied, nodding gravely. "I fit right in," he repeated. Dean realized then that McNeal and the others had been drinking steadily since they'd arrived at Helga's. McNeal was well on his way to a monumental drunk.

"Joe, Joe," Fred began. "You are my best friend in the world, you know that?" He put his arm drunkenly around Dean's shoulders and leaned into him. "You know sumptin' else? I *fit right in* here. Yessir, I fit in."

The girl returned with a dozen big mugs on a tray, and Dean snatched one for himself. Nobody said anything about paying, so he just started drinking. The beer was cold and powerful, rich, full-bodied. Dean glanced at McNeal and was surprised and embarrassed to see a tear forming in McNeal's right eye. "Joe, you know what?" Dean shook his head. "All my life people been kickin' my ass around, starting with my old man, and you know what? That's over now, *o*-ver. That's over 'cause I fit in now and I ain't takin' no more shit from no-body no more."

Three cigars and several schooners of beer later, Dean's head began to swim sickeningly. Quietly, he excused himself from the table and staggered outside. The cold air seemed to refresh him momentarily, and then suddenly the heavy food, the cigars, the beer, the excitement, overcame him and he vomited in the street until he gagged on a completely empty stomach. Passing Marines hooted and shouted encouragement, but for long moments Dean was just too sick to care. Finished, he wiped his mouth and eyes, straightened his uniform, and, feeling like a new man, strode purposefully back inside.

Sometime around midnight Staff Sergeant Bass called for attention. Big Barb's was crowded by then and the noise in the place was deafening, but at their tables in the corner, the Marines could have been in church, so rapt were they when their platoon commander spoke.

"Gentlemen," Bass began, "it is time I was leaving." The men protested loudly, but Bass held up a hand for silence. "No, I must now seek my beauty sleep."

"You'll have to reenlist to get *that* much sleep!" Leach shouted.

"Silence, you miserable short-penis dogfather wretch," Bass said, feigning anger. "No, I must depart. But first, our anthem."

Everyone stood. Bass sang in his clear, natural tenor, not a trace of beer in his voice:

> We meet 'neath the sounding rafters,
> The walls around are bare.
> As they shout to our peals of laughter,
> It seems that the dead are there.

The rest of the men joined him in the chorus:

> Oh, stand to your glasses steady,
> We drink to our comrades' eyes.
> A cup to the dead already,
> And hurrah for the next who dies.

Dean couldn't sing the song with the others because he didn't know the lyrics. He just stood silently taking in the ritual. He knew a lot of beer had been consumed that night, but he also realized something very special was going on, a tribute to friends who'd been lost in combat. He understood this and sympathized with the veterans, but since he had not experienced that loss himself, his heart was not completely in it—not yet. As the song went on, the crowd in Big Barb's began to grow quiet, and soon the only sound was the voices of the Marines singing. Before the song was done, several of them were crying openly.

The other patrons, and even Big Barb herself, remained silent for several long moments after the Marines had finished.

CHAPTER
ELEVEN

In the fifty-two years Fleet Admiral P'Marc Willis had been in the Confederation Naval Forces, he had never seen anything as terrible as the sight before him in the dusty schoolyard.

"It is far worse in the outlying settlements, Admiral," Jardinier Dozois, the portly Confederation Consul, whispered beside him, a handkerchief clamped firmly to his nose and mouth to keep out the smell of putrefying flesh.

Almost overcome, Admiral Willis cleared his throat before speaking. He gestured helplessly toward the heaps of tiny bodies littering the yard. "How could something like this happen?"

"Too many mouths and not enough food—and the rebels," Kismayu Merka answered, virtually spitting out the last word. A small brown man with a black goatee, he had been president of the Republic of Elneal for only two months, thrust into the job after his predecessor's assassination. Unlike the arrogant tribesman who had preceded him, Merka immediately requested assistance from the Confederation upon assuming the duties of his largely ceremonial office. And Admiral Willis had come. That request for help had been the only time Merka had had the courage to make a political decision on his own.

The horribly mutilated children had been dead long enough for decay to swell their tiny bodies obscenely.

When the Admiral's party arrived only a few moments before, aides had to chase off carrion-eaters—fliers and crawlers—that were feeding greedily on the corpses. Innards and severed body parts lay everywhere, interspersed among piles of tiny corpses, two hundred or more of them. No ordinary person could possibly envisage what had happened here, the Admiral thought.

The fierce sun beat down oppressively on the small party. The Marine major commanding the Admiral's security detachment whispered into the mouthpiece of his headset, checking the dispositions of his men about the perimeter of the school. An oppressive silence hung over the group. Small dust devils swirling about the schoolyard only momentarily obscured the clouds of insects busily feeding on the bodies. A bright piece of cloth fluttering in the breeze caught the Admiral's eye. It covered what had once been a little girl, her now hairless skull covered with the remnants of parchmentlike flesh drawn tightly over the delicate bones of her face. The eye sockets were empty cavities; the scavengers had fed. Her arms had been hacked off. Ashes to ashes, the Admiral thought. In another day or so only bones would be left.

"The relief workers ran out of food and medical supplies more than a month ago," President Merka said. "We could not help them. What you see here is multiplied many times over throughout our poor land. The parents of these poor babies brought them here because they were dying themselves and hoped at least their children might survive with the help of the foreigners who ran this place."

"Not many crops were put in during last year's planting season," Dozois added. "And much of what the farmers could get in was destroyed or confiscated by the rebels. Their 'scorched earth' policy," he said bitterly, "seems to be working better than even they could have hoped."

"What happened to the adults who ran this place?" Admiral Willis asked.

The other men were silent for a moment. "Dead," Dozois answered shortly.

"How?"

The Consul paused before answering in a quavering voice. "By the rebels. Dragged out of their beds in the middle of the night, tortured, mutilated, nailed to crosses, and burned alive over there, on the other side of the swings. Then the scum ran amok among the children. No one found out about this massacre until yesterday. . . ."

The Admiral stared at Dozois.

"They were all young volunteers from other worlds in this quadrant," Dozois volunteered. "Good kids. Our people, Admiral," he added softly, meaning they were citizens of Confederation member worlds, not natives of Elneal, which was only in protectorate status. Elneal had always been a wild and dangerous place. Things like this happened there from time to time, but until recently, only on a much smaller scale.

"The rebels are Siad, the most important of the warrior tribes," President Merka said. "These," he gestured help-lessly at the bodies, "were the children of farmers and city people, less than human in the eyes of the Siad. They killed the foreigners because they were foreigners, but they killed these children as a civilized man would exter-minate pests." Obviously President Merka himself was not of the warrior tribes.

Admiral Willis was about to reply when a cadaverous man about the Admiral's own age cleared his throat. Large perspiration rings stained his expensive shirt beneath the armpits, and when his snow-white handkerchief wasn't blocking his sense of smell, it fluttered across his brow like the dead child's dress. He cleared his throat several more times until he was certain Admiral Willis had noticed. "Our mining operations have completely ceased," he said in a soft, wet, petulant tone of voice. "Nobody can move in the hinterlands. The savages have murdered hundreds of our employees." The Admiral only glanced at him out of the corner of his eye. "Something must be done, Admiral. Must be. Law and order must—"

"That's why I'm here, Mr. Owens," the Admiral said, cutting him off abruptly.

"Ah, perhaps the Admiral would like to review the photographic evidence of the atrocities committed upon our employees at—"

"No!" the Admiral replied sharply. He knew what the rebels had done and was disgusted by it, but just then he hated the thin man from Consolidated Enterprises for introducing the tawdry problems of his business partners into that charnel house of dead innocents. Locklear Owens and his friends cared no more for the lives of their slaughtered employees than for those of the murdered children and their benefactors, and although Admiral Willis would never admit it or even show it, he hated the likes of these pampered, overfed businessmen from the bottom of his heart. In reality it was they who were responsible for the suffering of the people of Elneal.

"Gentlemen, I've seen enough," Admiral Willis said. He turned and began striding toward the Dragon that had brought them out. He could not help but notice the President speaking softly and intimately to Owens trailing at the end of the line. Another sharp flash of anger shot through the old navy man. The mining consortiums had paid well to get at the huge molycarbondum deposits under the surface of this world. That money had enabled the tribes to buy the weapons and technology they needed to start the uprising. The companies were warned that would happen, but they had persisted. Admiral Willis even had a file on his desk that proved some of their executives had earned the rights fees back by selling large quantities of modern weapons to the tribes—paying the tribes half what it was worth for the use of their land and then charging them through the nose for the weapons they wanted. And there was no shortage of rogue mercenaries to teach the rebels how to use all that hardware— and they were all on the mining company payrolls.

Even now Owens was whispering some plot into the President's ear, some scheme to make some off-world entrepreneur even fatter. And the President would listen because he was the company's man. Hell, the Admiral reflected, what else could the old boy do in his position?

Admiral Willis stood beside his Dragon's ramp, looking back at the schoolyard as the other members of his party filed aboard the vessel. The security platoon moved with practiced swiftness, withdrawing from its defensive perimeter, the men mounting their vehicles, weapons at the ready. What must it be like to die like those children did, he wondered, nobody left to mourn them, much less remember who they were and give them a decent burial? He thought of his own great-granddaughter. She was seven, about the same age as that nameless little girl in the flapping skirt. Well, by God, I won't forget what happened here, the Admiral promised himself.

Before the Confederation transferred Admiral Willis to command of the Seventh Star Fleet over a year earlier, he'd been warned about Elneal. Public opinion had been building up for years, pressuring the Confederation Council to take action. Some members wanted intervention for humanitarian reasons alone—which, based on what Admiral Willis had just seen, was fully justified— others to protect the molycarbondum mines that provided an ore essential to the alloy used in building interstellar spacecraft, the economic lifeline of the Confederation worlds. But all agreed that intervention was a foregone conclusion. It was just a matter of time. And now was the time.

Settled originally by the descendants of nomadic tribesmen from the horn of Africa on Old Earth, from the beginning the inhabitants of Elneal had been a fiercely independent, warlike people who despised civilization and hated outside interference in their ancient ways. Subsequent migrations composed of dissident ethnic elements from other Terran cultures, unassimilable, fractious, and quarrelsome in their own way, only intensified the warlike xenophobia of the first settlers. Until the coming of the mining companies, the nomadic tribes had been content living in their desert fastnesses, venting their hatred on rival clans and, occasionally, the vastly outnumbered citizens in the few settlements on Elneal. The tribes hated the settlements because they saw them as breeding grounds for new ideas and government, the very concept of which drove them to murder.

By law, Admiral P'Marc Willis was the supreme Confederation authority in this quadrant of Human Space, with the power granted to him personally by the Confederation Council of Worlds to act on its behalf on his own initiative. He had already decided what had to be done, but now he must make it legal by going through the motions of soliciting opinions from his staff and the civilian representatives.

He walked up the ramp into his vehicle and the hatch closed with a hiss behind him. As he strapped himself into his seat he wondered, Now who in the hell am I going to send down here to straighten out this goddamned mess?

* * *

The briefing room on board CNSS *Robert P. Ogie*, Admiral Willis's flagship, was designed to accommodate a hundred persons. It was full when an aide announced, "Ladies and gentlemen, Fleet Admiral Willis." Everyone stood as the Admiral strode into the room. Nodding to Consul Dozois and his staff, Admiral Willis took his seat, a modified captain's chair taken from the bridge of the Admiral's first combat command, a Condon-class battle cruiser.

"Ladies and gentlemen," the Admiral announced, "as of 0001 hours this morning, the planet Elneal has been under martial law." An approving murmur ran through the room. Willis's N-3, his operations officer, sat straighter in his chair. He and his staff had worked all night to prepare the operations order for the relief of Elneal that now flashed onto the viewscreen before each participant. "Mr. President," Willis turned to President Merka, "you are now under my orders." An expression of relief passed over Merka's face; noting a faint scowl of annoyance on Owens's craggy countenance, Willis smiled to himself.

"Miss Ebben." The Admiral nodded at a young woman sitting next to Consul Dozois. As the chief representative of the Confederated Interplanetary Relief Association, Leenda Ebben was responsible for all humanitarian assistance operations in 7th Fleet's area of operations.

"Sir, we have stockpiled several thousand tons of relief supplies in the capital city, New Obbia, but over the past months much of it has been looted. Local police forces are unable to furnish adequate security in any of Elneal's settlements, much less the capital." Willis's N-2, his intelligence chief, nodded agreement. "We have adequate medical supplies and food for several hundred thousand people on Boradu. We can have it on Elneal in twelve to fourteen days, standard, depending on the availability of transportation. The details are in the logistics annex to N-3's ops plan." Her staff had been working all night too.

"We can get it there in that time, Admiral," the N-4, Fleet logistical officer, added.

"Admiral Nashorn," Willis turned to his N-2, "give us a brief rundown on the situation down there."

"It's bad, sir," Rear Admiral Jerrold Nashorn said gravely. A planetary map of Elneal appeared on the vidscreens. "Elneal has a total population of perhaps sixteen million. The last census was conducted twenty-four years ago and it was never completed. More than half of the census teams sent into the deserts to count the nomads just disappeared.

"About a million people live in New Obbia, the only city of any size on Elneal. The rest of them are spread out in the deserts that stretch more than three thousand miles from the ocean to the Honolato Mountains. These mountains rise to heights in excess of eight thousand meters and can be crossed only in a few places. Outside the city are numerous settlements—small villages and towns—but most of the people in the outback are nomads. They survive by grazing flocks of sheep and goats, just as their ancestors did on Old Earth more than three and a half centuries ago. The rest of the planet is virtually uninhabited. There are the Muong Song pirates on some offshore islands, as well as a small colony recently established by people from Boradu on an island continent a few degrees south of the equator, but the Democratic Republic of Elneal is the only body politic. The molycarbondum deposits are found only under the deserts of Elneal.

"The original colonists came from Africa, in the Somalia-Ethiopia-Kenya region. Their ancestors were rugged nomadic peoples who never submitted well to civilization. The initial wave of immigration was sponsored by the governments of various oil-rich emirates in an effort to dispose of these unassimilable people peacefully. It proved remarkably successful, and once the word got out, other Terran governments sponsored similar programs to rid themselves of their problem children. Subsequent waves of immigrants came from such diverse regions as Afghanistan, Southeast Asia, the British Isles, and, in the wake of the Second American Civil War, North America.

"The basic social unit on Elneal is the clan, a unit of a tribe. Over the last three hundred years they have developed along two lines, nomadic warrior clans and the families that dwell in the settlements and make their living by farming. The largest and most powerful tribe is the Siad, who are descended directly from the original North African immigrants. The Bos Kashi is the second-largest group. They came originally from Afghanistan and are responsible for importing the ancestors of the herds of wild horses that roam the grasslands and plateaus. They and the Siad constantly fight each other over grazing lands and water rights. The Muong Song from the Thai-Laos-Burma border region of Southeast Asia were among the third wave of immigrants. They emigrated when the opium trade upon which they depended for their livelihood died out. They eventually settled in the Sharja Islands, about two hundred kilometers off the coast, and took up piracy for a living. Finally there came the English-speaking elements, the Gaels from what was formerly Ireland on Old Earth, and the Sons of Freedom, an extremely militant North American group that arose in the wake of the Second American Civil War. These last two groups settled the temperate regions just across the Honolato Mountains, and for generations they have raided—and been raided—through the passes.

"There has been a lot of interbreeding among these

groups—women are valued property and are prime booty of raiding parties—and numerous schisms have arisen over the generations, which have resulted in changing the demographics of the various clans and tribes. For instance, the city dwellers and farmers were originally members of one nomadic group or another who split off on their own over quarrels now long forgotten.

"But one thing all the warrior tribes have in common is love of combat. Every male in the warrior clans—and many of their women as well—goes armed everywhere, all the time. You are not considered a man until you are proficient with a weapon in this society. Until about twenty years ago, when the mining operations began in the Siad and Bos Kashi lands, the weapons the clansmen carried were pretty primitive devices, mostly projectile launchers of various types. Now, thanks to the money the mining consortiums have invested in Elneal," here the N-2 glanced sharply at Owens, "some of them are almost as well armed as our own Marines. And since the Siad profited most from the mining operations, they are now the ascendant tribe on the planet.

"Also about twenty years ago," the picture of a fierce-looking bearded man appeared on the viewscreens, "this man, Shabeli the Elder, a very intelligent and charismatic leader, began to get some of the clans to cooperate with his own in raids on New Obbia and the coastal settlements. He was able to craft workable nonaggression pacts with the Gaels, Bos Kashi, and Sons of Freedom that have eliminated the episodic but disastrous interclan wars, while continuing the tradition of individual feuds and vendettas that all these people seem to relish so much. Before Shabeli's coming, raids on the settlements had been sporadic. Whenever one of the clans or tribes felt like tormenting somebody and doing a little looting, their men would take off for a month and raid a town.

Before Shabeli, no one had ever successfully kept the tribes from fighting among themselves. But Shabeli was a genius. When he died six years ago his son, Shabeli the Magnificent, as he styles himself, stepped into his sandals."

The older man's picture disappeared, to be replaced by a striking face: It was of a man in his early fifties. His skin was very dark and pulled tightly across high cheekbones. The lips were sensuous and full; his nose long and aquiline. His black eyes burned under shaggy brows. A thick, dark mustache blended smoothly into a short, sharp beard. It was a face of great intelligence and determination.

"How did we get those images?" Admiral Willis asked.

"They were taken by an off-world journalist. Somehow, she got the Shabelis' confidence and was allowed to make several visits to the rebel stronghold somewhere in the Honolato foothills. She disappeared completely about five years ago. Some think she perished in the desert. Others say Shabeli killed her. But there's a persistent rumor that she's now the mistress of Shabeli the Magnificent." The N-2 shrugged.

"That man is a devil!" President Merka blurted out. "Sorry, Admiral," he said sheepishly. "I could not control myself." Merka sank back into his chair, silent and brooding.

"This is a man to be reckoned with," the N-2 affirmed. "We estimate he has between six and seven thousand heavily armed men under his command. Over the past six months his raids have just about closed down any trace of government on Elneal; the mining operations have totally ceased. About a million people in New Obbia and the villages have died of starvation. Nobody really knows what it is he wants. He inspires his men with an appeal to their ingrained lust for combat and loot, but the big difference now is that he's convinced them the time has come for a crusade against the non-nomads and everyone else not of the warrior tribes. He preaches a vague messianic mysticism that promises complete restoration of the nomadic independent life their distant ancestors led back on Old Earth. He believes, as evidently do most of his followers, that the original plan has gone astray and now is the time to restore that vision of the past. I think what we have here is an ambitious and politically astute man who's seen a chance to grab supreme power and is taking it.

"What he's got is a small army that can do whatever it wants to whomever it wants on Elneal because there's nobody here who can stop him. And, ladies and gentlemen, make no mistake, this man and his people are not pushovers. If we send forces in to restore government on Elneal, there'll be fighting." The N-2 settled back in his chair.

"Thanks, Admiral," Willis said. "General Curry?"

Immediately the Forces annex of the operations order appeared on the screens. General Larray Curry, Commander, 4th Fleet Marine Force, cleared his throat. "Sir, as you can see, we propose a provisional brigade-size deployment force. It would be composed of the 121st, 62nd, and 34th FISTs. Each will establish a base of operations in one of the three coastal cities. After reestablishing order in the urban areas, they will move units into the outlying countryside and relief operations can begin. If we can feed and protect the people until the next crop gets harvested, about six months from now, then we can devote our full efforts to destroying Shabeli's forces. We estimate nine months, from start to finish."

"How soon can we have forces on the ground in Elneal?" Willis asked.

"Sir, the closest unit is the 34th FIST on Thorsfinni's

World, about two standard weeks away. The 121st and 62nd can be here in a month standard. Until the 34th gets here, we propose forming a provisional FIST from the Marines in the ships' complements in the fleet to secure a base for the 34th FIST in the capital city. The outlying settlements, I'm afraid, will have to make do on their own until our people can get here in force."

"The 34th FIST? Fine combat record." Willis then turned to the rest of his staff. "I want you to study this plan thoroughly for the next hour, people. Be back here and in your seats then."

Admiral Willis let his staff debate the operations order for another hour after they reconvened. Technical details concerning logistics, ordnance, quartermaster, transportation, communications, and medical support matters were adjusted. During that time Owens and the other civilians sat quietly, if impatiently, on the sidelines.

"All right," Admiral Willis announced at last, "that's it. The plan is hereby approved and ready to be executed. Captain," he turned to his chief communications officer, "dispatch hyperspace drones immediately to the President of the Confederation Council and Commander, Combined Forces Headquarters, the commanders of the deploying units, and all other commanders in the Fleet. Encode the standard deployment message to include the final version of the operation order. Fleet staff and Consul Dozois will prepare updates every seventy-two hours.

"Oh, one more thing. Mr. Owens?"

The Consolidated Enterprises executive looked up expectantly from a hushed conversation he was having with President Merka.

"Mr. Locklear Owens, you are under arrest."

Owens gaped at the Admiral as two Marines stepped

up to his side and grabbed his arms. "You can't be serious!" he managed to blurt out.

"Oh, yes, I am," Willis answered. "Never more serious, sir. Naval investigators have dug up enough dirt on your operations on Elneal to earn you a death sentence, Mr. Owens."

"What charges?" Owens demanded.

"Violation of the Intra-Confederation Arms Control Act of 2368, selling military weapons to civilians without a license."

"You'll hear about this, you certainly will hear about this! My company will not stand by and let you—"

Admiral Willis stopped the executive with an upraised hand. The conference room had fallen completely silent. "Sir, under the constitution of our Confederation, you have the right to a fair and speedy trial. As the supreme judicial power in this quadrant of Human Space, I guarantee you will get one. It will be over and sentence passed before your company even knows you've been charged. The Fleet Judge Advocate will assist you in finding counsel, and you will be given adequate time to prepare your defense." For the first time Admiral Willis displayed emotion. His face turned red with anger as he almost shouted at Owens: "I have asked the Judge Advocate to seek the death penalty for you, mister. Now get this piece of shit out of here," he said to the Marines, and turned his back on the prisoner.

Owens had gone white and his mouth worked silently as he tried to form words of protest. Nothing came out of his throat but a high-pitched wheezing noise. Stiffly, holding the quivering executive as if he might rub off on them, the Marines escorted him toward the door.

"Oh, one more thing, Mr. Owens." Admiral Willis whirled around in his captain's chair. "A complete copy of my investigative report will be in the drone to the Confederation Council. Before your superiors even know you're on trial, they'll be in court themselves. Take comfort in the coming weeks that misery loves company, Mr. Owens, and you are in very bad company."

Admiral Willis sighed and forced his breathing to return to normal. "Now, Bernie," he said, turning back to his communications officer, "get a drone off to the 34th FIST on Thorsfinni's World. I need those men out here yesterday."

CHAPTER
TWELVE

During the next month and a half the days and weeks passed in a whirlwind of activity. Dean, McNeal, and Chan were fully processed-in—including back pay—and the loans they'd received their first night were promptly repaid.

There was much to do: equipment issue; learning the names of everyone in the platoon and their chain of command; and learning how the infantry squad, platoon, and company really functioned in the Fleet. They learned that during the times they spent in the field—a minimum of two days a week, once for more than a week. In garrison, they cleaned the barracks—even when it didn't need cleaning—stood daily inspections, managed to stay awake during seemingly endless classroom lectures, and between running, calisthenics, and weight training, the newer men blossomed into the best physical shape any of them had ever experienced, surpassing even the conditioning they'd achieved in Boot Camp.

And then on Friday nights and Saturdays when they weren't in the field, it was the Weekend Ritual. Promptly after chow call on Friday night those men not on duty details and with kroner in their pockets headed for Bronny. Between 17 and 1715 hours every Friday when the 34th was not training in the field or on a deployment, the spotless barracks degraded into a trash dump, staying that way until Reveille Monday morning. Inevitably, their weekends began at either Helga's or Big Barb's, but gradually the new men were introduced to the other attractions of Bronny, which included fishing in the fjord, learning to operate the primitive vehicles the 'Finnis used for transportation, and impromptu midnight "picnics" along the Bothnia with as many local girls as were daring enough to go out with the Marines—and all of them, it seemed, were game. Inevitably, these outings ended with all parties swimming nude in the frigid waters and then warming up in intimate togetherness on the shore afterward.

Over the course of a week or so, members of the platoon gradually stopped calling Claypoole "New Guy," and soon after he stopped trying to pin that sobriquet on Dean and McNeal. Chan, the veteran who'd been through the ritual before, was quietly amused by it all. Not long after, more replacements arrived, and soon the third platoon and all of Company L were up to full strength.

They also learned more about Staff Sergeant Charlie Bass: who he was, and who he had been. It wasn't that he talked about himself or what he'd done, he never did; he let others do the talking, and they relished the opportunity, incessantly telling stories about him. The most recent concerned the incident on Fiesta de Santiago, which the barracks gossips embellished with unfeigned glee, especially when they got to the part where he beat up Mr. Daryl George—who in these renditions had become an icon for the despicable and unscrupulous civilian entrepreneur making a fat living selling shoddy goods to the Corps. But Bass had been a legend in the Corps for years now. Anyone who wanted to appear a veteran had a Charlie Bass story to tell, most with eye-witness reputability.

The first solid evidence the new men had that he was someone truly special among Marines was the first time the company fell out in dress reds for a FIST commander's inspection.

"Move it, move it move it move-movemove!" the squad leaders shouted in the rising staccato voice that always seems to be issued along with a sergeant's chevrons. "On the parade deck right now! Move it, move it move it move-movemove!" They strode up and down the squad-bay corridor like bos'ns on an ancient slave galley, exhorting the men at the same time to complete their preparations for inspection and form up on the company parade ground.

Inside the rooms the team leaders were everywhere, hovering over their men, breathing down their necks, in their faces, and sometimes calmly making final adjustments to a uniform—at times even their own.

"Okay, Juice, Dean," Leach said when he was satisfied at his men's appearance. "You're as ready as you're going to be. Let's hit that deck."

Dean tried to swallow, but his mouth was too dry. This was his first FIST commander's inspection since Boot Camp Graduation, and he was for some reason very tense. He'd been well-prepared for the graduation inspection; the recruits knew far in advance that it was coming, and the drill instructors worked with them for several days ahead of time getting everyone ready. For this inspection, though, they'd had only two days' notice. Nobody walked them through their preparations step by step—everyone from the company commander to the squad leaders expected each man to know what was expected of him. If it hadn't been for Claypoole, Dean wasn't sure he would have been ready.

"Snip off that Irish pennant, Dean," Claypoole said

with a trace of condescension, gesturing at a stray thread hanging from a buttonhole. "You don't want to meet the Brigadier looking like some kind of sloppy civilian." He shook his head sadly. " 'New Guy'? Everybody was right about not calling you New Guy, you're too boot to be salty enough to even be 'new.' " Claypoole spent so much time helping Dean prepare for the inspection, Dean wondered when he had time to get ready himself. Claypoole raised an eyebrow when Dean voiced his concern.

"Dean-o," he said calmly, "once you've been around as long as I have, you'll always be ready for a FIST commander's inspection. You get as much salt on you as I've got on me, you'll always be ready for anything." Goudanis guffawed at his boast and Claypoole glared at him.

"I got more time in the chow line than you got in the Corps, Clayhead," Goudanis muttered.

"What's the joke?" Dean asked, but Goudanis only shook his head. Claypoole nodded grimly at the lance corporal and went back to helping Dean get ready.

Dean was so concerned with getting his uniform ready he didn't notice the amused way Leach kept an eye on him and Claypoole, ready to step in at any time to make sure his most junior man was ready. But instead of intervening, Leach let Claypoole do the job he'd assigned himself—if nothing else, it was good practice for Claypoole, a good way for him to learn something about leadership. Ratliff approved also—he was glad to have Claypoole out from underfoot.

Finally, the day, the hour, the minute of the inspection arrived and the men of third platoon scrambled out of their rooms, down the stairs, and out to the parade deck for the ordeal. Dean barely noticed Bass as he passed him at the head of the stairs. It wasn't until they were outside, standing at attention in platoon formation, Bass front and center, that he had a chance to get a good look at his platoon sergeant in his dress uniform.

Staff Sergeant Bass was resplendent. The scarlet of his tunic seemed to burst into flame above the blue of his trousers with the bloodred NCO stripes running down their outer seams. His ebony NCO sword scabbard gleamed. But what caught the eyes of the men who'd never seen Bass in dress uniform before were the medals displayed across his left chest. The first, farthest to the wearer's right and occupying the "field of honor," as the precedence of personal decorations was called, had a navy-blue ribbon with a scarlet stripe down its middle, suspending a cross with a fouled anchor in its center— the Marine Medal of Valor, second only to the Confederation Medal of Heroism in the hierarchy of decorations. A gold comet pinned to the ribbon told the men he'd won the medal twice. Next came a medal with the ribbon colors reversed from the first, the Gold Nova. Then a Silver Nebula, once more two awards; then a Bronze Star with three gold starbursts, indicating he'd been awarded the medal four times in action against an enemy. After this, his Good Conduct Medal—it was short one silver comet cluster that denoted subsequent awards since his recent court-martial invalidated the award for that entire enlistment. His Marine Expeditionary Medal was so covered with comets the ribbon could hardly be seen through them.

Those six medals, slightly overlapping, formed the top row. Under them were clustered so many campaign medals they couldn't easily be counted or individually recognized. On his right chest were the rectangular ribbons for the Confederation, Marine, and Meritorious Unit Citations, again with multiple awards of each. The only mar on the uniform was a slightly darker swath of red under the gold chevrons that showed where a second rocker had once been. But no one in the platoon cared that Charlie Bass had once carried a higher rank, they only knew that they'd follow him into combat anywhere, under any circumstances. And so would any other professional who met him on the street, because what counted about Charlie Bass was not his "conduct," but how he conducted himself under fire.

"Listen up, people," Bass said in a soft voice that nonetheless carried clearly to every one of his men. "I've watched you prepare for this inspection more closely than you realize. I'm here to tell you we are going to ace it." It may have been only their imagination, but his men detected a trace of pride in his face as he looked them over. Bass drew his sword and held it at rest. "Sergeant Hyakowa, front and center."

The senior squad leader stepped briskly from his position and marched to face Bass, also drawing his ceremonial sword. The two NCOs exchanged salutes with their swords. The blades flashed brightly in the strong sunlight, slashing up and down in brilliant silver arcs.

"Sergeant, the platoon is yours."

"Aye aye, Staff Sergeant, the platoon is mine."

The two exchanged salutes again, then Bass sheathed his sword, about-faced, and marched to take his place among the platoon commanders where the company officers were assembled.

Hyakowa about-faced to look over the platoon. "First squad, one pace to the right." The men of his squad sharply shifted position to fill in the blank he had left when he stepped into the platoon sergeant's position. "Like the man said," he said when the platoon was again in crisp formation, "we're going to ace it." He paused for a moment, then cried out, "Third platoon! Pa-rade REST."

With a sharp thunk, the men of third platoon shifted their

left feet to a shoulder's length apart and leaned their grounded blasters out and to their right in the classic position. Hyakowa about-faced again and assumed the position of parade rest himself.

Hyakowa must have gotten a signal from somewhere, because he suddenly whirled around and commanded: "Platoon! A-ten-HUT! Open ranks for inspection, HARCH!" The first rank took one smart step forward; the second stood fast; the third took one step backward. "Platoon! In-spec-shun, HARMS!" In two sharp, perfectly coordinated movements, the platoon hoisted their blasters to the port position, bisecting the body at a forty-five-degree angle.

Abruptly, the FIST commander and his retinue were with the company officers. They went through the motions of introductions and stating briskly what was about to happen, and then the Brigadier walked the ranks, inspecting the men. He stopped briefly in front of each man and said a crisp, "Good morning, Marine," as the man operated the charging lever of his weapon, exposing the battery well, glancing down quickly into the empty well and then back up. The Brigadier then stepped to the next man. Once or twice per squad his hand shot out to take a blaster that was held at port arms. The Marine's arms snapped instantly to his side, fingers extended and joined, thumb placed carefully along the seams of his trousers, eyes fixed steadfastly to the front. He gave the weapon a cursory glance, simply going through the form of inspection, and then casually handed it back. The man snatched it out of the Brigadier's hands with a sharp smack as his own hands clapped loudly onto the weapon.

He stopped in front of Dean, who operated the charging bolt instantly, ready for the Brigadier to "inspect" his weapon. The Brigadier noted the Expert Marksmanship medal on Dean's tunic. "Name?" he inquired.

"Dean, Joseph F., private, serial number 21993014C, SIR!"

"You ever fire this weapon, Private Dean?"

"Yes, SIR! Zeroed in on the range last week, SIR!"

"Your chest won't be bare for long," he said to Dean. "Thirty-fourth FIST never stays on Thorsfinni's World for long." When he finished the inspection, which was more of a review than a true inspection, he took a place in front of the company to address the men. The company's officers stood behind him.

"The 34th Fleet Initial Strike Team is a proud unit." The Brigadier's voice carried clearly without need of amplification. "We have fought in more campaigns and expeditions than any other unit in the Confederation Armed Forces. It has now been more than half a year standard since we returned from our last mount-out. We don't know when next we'll receive orders to go somewhere, nor do we have any idea where we will be sent or what we will be required to do once we get there. Still, we have to be ready for any contingency. To that end, you will be going into the field tomorrow on a training operation of an at-this-time-undetermined duration. Your officers will be briefed at zero-seven hours as to the nature of this training exercise. They will then have one hour to formulate their preliminary plans and get the company ready to move out. Do well, whatever the mission is." He cracked a smile. "Right now, I don't even know what the exercise will be. My F-3 hasn't sent me the operations order yet, so I don't know what he's got planned for you. That is all." The Brigadier turned to the company officers and returned the company to them. He was gone as suddenly as he arrived.

Captain Conorado stepped forward and looked over

his company. "You heard the man, people. Be ready." He turned to Top Myer. "Company First Sergeant, the company is yours."

"Aye aye, sir, the company is mine."

The two exchanged sword salutes and Conorado led the officers into the barracks.

"Platoon sergeants," Myer bellowed. "Dismiss your men." He about-faced and followed the officers.

"Platoon!" the platoon sergeants cried out. "Dis-missed!"

Released from formation, the hundred-plus men of the platoons broke ranks and raced back into the barracks to strip out of their dress uniforms and prepare for the next morning's exercise. Sergeant Souavi, the company supply sergeant, got busy issuing weapons simulators to the platoon sergeants—just because they weren't using real ammunition didn't mean they wouldn't be able to tell where they were hitting, or that they were hit.

But 34th FIST didn't go into the field the next morning. The overnight arrival of Admiral P'Marc Willis's orders canceled the training exercise. Instead, the men of Company L fell out on the company parade ground to get new orders.

CHAPTER THIRTEEN

Many of the tribal leaders sitting around the brightly lighted cavern had traveled far for the council. It was the largest such gathering even the oldest among them could remember. Not even Shabeli the Elder had been able to muster as successfully.

Actually, the younger Shabeli did not need the other tribes called to the council; the Siad alone had sufficient manpower for his immediate intention. Publicly, of course, Shabeli maintained the fiction that he desperately needed their assistance in his great crusade to wrest control of Elneal from Consolidated Enterprises. His real motive in calling them together, however, was to bind them to him as allies. Then, if the Confederation sent in its forces, they would be obligated to fight on his side. He had gotten this idea from a vid he'd seen as a boy, in which a group of assassins, after murdering their leader, pledge allegiance to one another by staining themselves with his blood. If the Confederation intervened and there was serious fighting, Shabeli would sacrifice his allies to weaken the Confederation forces until he could defeat them. If the Confederation forces proved too strong, and defeated his "allies" so severely he knew his Siad could not beat them, he could conclude a favorable peace with the Confederation that would buy him time to lay other plans for seizing full power on Elneal.

Either way, Shabeli knew he would emerge as the single most powerful leader on the planet, with all others paying obeisance to him.

Sitting on Shabeli's right, the sword-arm side and hence the position of honor among the Siad, was his uncle, Wad Ramadan. Since Shabeli the Elder's death six years before, Ramadan had served faithfully as his nephew's adviser and counselor. But Shabeli the Magnificent only tolerated his uncle because of the old man's powerful connections among the other Siad leaders. He seldom followed the old man's advice and secretly wished him dead—honorably, of course—and safely out of the way. Now in his seventies, Ramadan was far older than most Siad, who, without the medical care available on the more advanced worlds, seldom lived much beyond their fifties. Shabeli hoped nature would soon take its course and remove the meddlesome old warrior.

On Shabeli's left sat his consort, Moira the journalist, one of the few outworlders ever to voluntarily remain on Elneal in the society of clans. Her white skin, golden hair, and blue eyes betokened northern European ancestry. Although it would be death to stare or even look directly for more than a few moments at the beautiful consort of Shabeli the Magnificent, the other men in the assembly managed to avoid that fate with sly glances. And she was someone to admire: Only a bit shorter than Shabeli himself, and taller than most of the other Siad or the Bos Kashi men, Moira was a full-figured woman. Some of the Siad resented her presence among them. She was an outsider, and to make matters worse, Shabeli had never formally taken marriage vows with this woman. Some thought she had an undue influence over him. Looking at her, the delegates could understand why. But she was Shabeli's most valuable adviser not because of her voluptuousness, but because she understood something none of these other men could ever know—the psychology of the Confederation. The only quality Shabeli admired as much as courage in a man was intellect in a woman; she did not even have to be beautiful to earn his respect—but Moira definitely was both.

Next to Moira sat the Bos Kashi delegation. Short, dark-skinned, wiry men, bow-legged from lives spent constantly in the saddle, they bristled with weapons, as did all the other clansmen present in the great underground hall. The one thing not even Shabeli could persuade these men to accept was to go anywhere unarmed. It would be more natural for them to walk about with their bottoms exposed than ever to be caught without weapons. The delegations from the Gaels and the Sons of Freedom, the transmontane tribes, were seated beyond Wad Ramadan. These men were light-skinned with fine hair and beards. The Gaels were known among the Siad as the "Potato Eaters," and the Sons as the "Beer Bellies." These nicknames belied the respect the Siad professed to have for them as fighting men, and many among them and the Bos Kashi sitting in peaceful conference in this very hall carried the scars from wounds inflicted by one or the other in past skirmishes.

Beyond the Bos Kashi were the representatives of the Shan, secretive, dark-skinned little men whose sharp facial angles contrasted with their slanted eyes. The daggers that bristled from their waist sashes bore hilts encrusted with precious gems. Even so, these were working knives.

Opposite the Shan were the Euskadi, the truly unknown quantity in the gathering. Where Shabeli was certain of how the Bos Kashi, the Gaels, and the Sons of Freedom would react to his proposal, and was fairly sure of the Shan, he had no idea what the Euskadi would say. The Euskadi representatives sat close, their heads together, whispering to each other in a tongue that was so unrelated to any language spoken by others on Elneal no one could ever learn to understand it.

The headmen of the other Siad clans completed the circle. Wad Mohammad, chieftain of the powerful Badawi clan, sat opposite Shabeli.

Wad Mohammad was the greatest threat to Shabeli's plans. The fearsome chieftain had never prostrated himself before Shabeli the Elder, and had sworn never to give the great man's son more honor than he had the father. It was most important to Shabeli that Wad Mohammad be kept under his eye, where he could work no mischief.

Among themselves the tribes spoke the various ancient languages of their clans—the Gaels and Sons an archaic form of English—but in conference they used modern English, the lingua franca of the Confederation. While none had—or would ever—accept a formal school system among them, with individual tutoring and a rude form of home schooling their young learned how to cope with life on Elneal. Leaders were expected to know not only the dialects of the other clans, but modern English as well. While the warrior tribesmen of Elneal hated government and the new ideas gradually filtering down to them from the other worlds in the Confederation, they realized the value of technology—and understood that to master technology, knowledge of English was mandatory.

Realizing this and wanting a secure base of operations for his clan, Shabeli the Elder had secretly contracted with the mining magnates to construct his underground complex and train a few men to run it. The subterranean complex had a modern communications center and more luxurious accommodations than most corporate dwellings in New Obbia and the coastal towns. Shabeli the Elder believed in austerity, but did not believe in being miserable. The son followed willingly in the father's footsteps. But the old man had been wise, and knew his son could benefit from knowledge of other cultures, so his military training was supplemented by the best tutors in the arts money could buy. His followers considered Shabeli's fondness for the literary arts and music his only weakness, but none ever dared say that in his hearing once he had succeeded to his father's place among the Siad.

Shabeli signaled for silence. "Brothers . . . ," he began in a deep, resonant voice that filled the large meeting hall. He paused to wait for total silence. "Brothers, we have met here today to resolve the vision of our ancestors . . ."

Shabeli talked for the better part of an hour. During that time all eyes were upon him. He played his voice like a great musical instrument, and used it to express every emotion, intense adoration for the memory of his ancestors, pride in the mores and fighting spirit of the tribes—here he extended his arms wide to embrace all the men in the hall—and hatred of anyone who would dare interfere in the independence of the nomadic clans. His words were perfectly phrased, and complemented by gestures intended to accentuate them powerfully: vigorous pounding of fist into a palm to underscore a point; hands extended palms upward, appealing to the delegates for their support; fists slapping the table—*boom, boom, boom*—in time to his thundering sentences; arms thrust mightily toward the sky, beseeching the heavens for confirmation. At times he would shout in a voice so powerful it echoed in the huge room. At other times he whispered in a voice so low and sibilant the men had to lean forward to hear him. Not a man dared to breathe deeply as Shabeli thundered on and on, building to a stupendous climax. In the oral tradition of the Siad, this speech was one of the most stunning ever delivered.

"Brothers! Cousins! Listen to me! The vermin in the city and the towns," here Shabeli gestured toward the distant ocean, "the dregs of our race, have cast their lot with this Con-fed-er-a-tion." He spit the five syllables out upon the table as if they were poison. "And what is this Confederation?" His voice rose on the last syllable and his lips twisted in a sneer. Shabeli paused. He glanced left and right, his arms flexed, palms open, fingers wiggling, as if saying, "C'mon, c'mon, tell me, tell me!"

One of the Gaels involuntarily farted, and in the silence it sounded like a gunshot, but so intensely were the delegates following Shabeli's speech, only one person noticed. Moira cracked a very tiny smile, just a twitch on the right side of her mouth.

"It . . . is . . . an . . . outhouse . . . stuffed . . . with . . . constipated . . . old . . . men, long dead . . . penises . . . dangling . . . in . . . the . . . shit!"

"Aaaarrrrgh!" One of the Gaels howled out his admiration for the original phrase, and the other men began pounding the table with the hilts of their daggers.

"They flit about like pretty little insects," Shabeli continued, "telling other men—telling us—what is good for us, what is best for us, what is right for us! And when they are done," here Shabeli raised his arms and looked about at the assemblage, "when they are done, brothers, when they are done, they will take away your arms, and you and your children will live as farmers, and people from the city will tell you when and where to shit!"

The room broke into pandemonium. Most of the delegates shouted their defiance at the cities and the Confederation and begged Shabeli to continue. Not the Shan, though. Those men held expressions so rigid it seemed their faces were veiled. The Euskadi wore expressions of disgust and murmured in their unintelligible language. Only Wad Mohammad among the other delegates maintained a dignified mien. In time the hall grew quiet again.

"Well, brothers, that won't happen," Shabeli said in a

quiet, determined, controlled tone of voice. "Our ancestors came here to live free, in the old ways, and we will, we will, we will!" Again pandemonium reigned—with the previous exceptions.

When a semblance of calm returned to the gathering, the Great Khang, headman of the Shan, rose to his feet. "Shabeli the Magnificent," he began, looking at everyone present except the man he was addressing, "you are a fool. I think you do not understand the power your plans will bring against us. The Confederation is monstrously strong. The only way we can treat with them is to go to the sea, or into the mountains and fight them in small bands there, where they cannot mass their forces against us. If you make any attempt to wage open war, you will guarantee that we will be vassals of the Confederation."

While talking he turned his gaze to Shabeli. "If you bring the Confederation against us, all the work and plans of the Shan will be for naught. We are close, very close, to concluding an arrangement with Consolidated Enterprises to export our drugs. If you will join with us in this enterprise, we will all become wealthy beyond your dreams. If you persist in your plans, you will bring poverty and ruination on us all."

The Great Khang signaled the rest of his delegation and led them from the cavern. None of them looked back at the disdainful eyes that followed them.

Shabeli raised a restraining hand before anyone could make a motion toward the departing Shan. What the Shan did was no more than he had anticipated. "Any other dissenters?" he asked.

Raymondo Itzaina, the head of the Euskadi delegation, stood. "The only safety for free men," he said, looking at no one because to look at a man other than a relative or a friend was to challenge him to a fight, "is in isolation. I trust the Shan no more than I trust the Confederation, no more than I trust the Gaels, no more than I trust Shabeli, no more than I trust anyone else who is not of my blood." Now he looked directly at Shabeli, and there was fierce challenge in his eyes. "If you mix with the Confederation, you will die. Just as treating with the corporation that controls the New Obbia government will ultimately kill you." He turned his head to look at the other delegates, the same challenge in his eyes. "All of you." He didn't have to signal the other members of his delegation; they were on their feet and moving with him before he completed his first step from the table.

Shabeli hadn't expected this from the Euskadi, but neither did it surprise him. He looked expectantly at the rest of the delegations.

The Gaels all stood and offered Shabeli their side arms in the universal gesture of fealty among the Clans. "None should speak of our being defeated by mere off-worlders," their leader growled.

Instantly, the other delegations rose and performed the same gesture. These men were no fools. They knew that their only safety lay in numbers. They knew Shabeli wanted something for himself out of the alliance, but they also knew that Shabeli was a leader and a fighter. Later, during the war councils, cooler heads would prevail and Shabeli knew he would have to use a different form of persuasion to get their cooperation, but right now, in this hall, after that rousing speech, the delegates of these tribes, the only ones who mattered, were committed.

"Did you hear the fart that bastard let during your speech?" Moira asked Shabeli. They lay snuggled under skins Shabeli had taken from the animals he killed on his hunting expeditions in the mountains over the years, watching an ancient flat-vid of a funny woman, her handsome husband, and their elderly neighbors. Shabeli laughed in genuine amusement at the exaggerated comic predicaments the woman got herself into. "What do you expect from a man who lives on potatoes and beer?" He laughed.

"What," Moira asked as she massaged one of Shabeli's nipples gently with a forefinger, "are you going to do?"

"Air out the meeting hall?" he replied. "I will kill many people," he continued, his voice serious now. "We will work out the details in council, but I'll start with an all-out campaign against the cities and the farmers who support them."

"That is what the Confederation has been waiting for," Moira said.

"So you've told me many times, my love. And as always, you are right. The Confederation will send in its Marines. They'll have to: The people we don't massacre outright will be starving, and I will control the mines. Molycarbondum is the key, my dearest Moira. I'll draw the Marines into our deserts and mountains, pick them off one by one, pin them down, embarrass their leaders. It will cost me the lives of many men, but in time I'll conclude a truce with the Confederation. Then you shall be Madam President, and when I am in complete control—"

Moira moved her hand lower and exclaimed in mock surprise, "Why, what in the world is this thing?"

Shabeli laughed. "It is the staff of life, my dear, something for you to write home about," he said, referring to her former career as a journalist. "And," he added, "the shaft of the Confederation Marine Corps." They both laughed at the pun. On the vid the funny woman was stuffing handfuls of candies into her mouth.

CHAPTER
FOURTEEN

When Reveille sounded, most of the men of Company L were already up, putting the final touches on the gear they expected to take into the field in the next hour or two. Their preparedness was wasted.

Staff Sergeant Charlie Bass stepped into his platoon's squad bay and announced in a voice loud enough for everyone to hear even through closed doors, "The training exercise has been canceled. Stand by for further orders. Until we receive new orders, we will conduct normal garrison duties. That is all." Then he turned and left before anybody could ask what was going on.

So the men of the platoon asked each other what was happening.

"We're mounting out, that's what's happening," Claypoole told Dean and McNeal with an air of superiority.

"Where are we going?" Dean asked him.

"What are we going to do?" McNeal added.

"We're going where the Marine Corps sends us and we're going to do what the Marine Corps tells us to," Claypoole replied haughtily. "Someone, somewhere, is going to pay a price for doing something they weren't supposed to do." He paused to glare at the two only slightly less experienced men, then continued, "When the Marines get called out, people die. You had best remember everything you've been taught, or you might be the ones."

Hammer Schultz walked over to the three and clamped a possessive hand on McNeal's shoulder. "New Guy," he said, the first time in weeks anyone had called Claypoole by that name, "I've seen to it that Freddy here knows everything he needs to. You worry about yourself." Holding McNeal's shoulder firmly, he turned and marched back to the fire team's room.

Claypoole swallowed. Even though Schultz never seemed to get out of line in garrison, the other men in the platoon used tales of his combat prowess to frighten those who hadn't yet had to fight. Schultz was not someone Claypoole wanted to be on the wrong side of.

Goudanis snickered.

Corporals Leach and Kerr had also been watching. They looked at each other.

"We're going to have to talk to Rabbit about that young man," Kerr said.

Leach nodded agreement. "He needs to get a couple operations under his belt before talking that talk."

Despite everyone's curiosity about what was going on, the next couple of hours progressed routinely enough. Between Reveille, at 06 hours, and 07 hours, when the company lined up to march to the mess hall for morning chow, they cleaned the barracks again, even though none of them thought it necessary. At 08 hours they were again in formation behind the barracks for roll call. They had to wait a little longer than usual for Gunny Thatcher to come out of the barracks and take his position front and center. Bass came out with him and took the platoon sergeant's position in front of his platoon. His passive face gave his men no clue about what was happening. The men of the company fairly buzzed, certain that they were about to be given orders to mount out on a campaign.

Except for the men of third platoon. They exchanged quick glances, wondering why Bass was in this position instead of coming out with the company's officers.

At Thatcher's command to sound off, the platoon sergeants each called out, "All present and accounted for." Gunny Thatcher about-faced just in time to salute Captain Conorado, who came out of the barracks a few paces behind him. There was a stranger among the company's officers as they took their positions behind the company commander. The stranger was an ensign who didn't look quite old enough to be an officer. The company's officers were all dressed in garrison utilities; the stranger was wearing the officers' dress uniform, scarlet, stock-neck tunic over gold trousers. One row of ribbons was arrayed above his shooting badges.

"Company L, all present and accounted for, sir!" Gunny Thatcher boomed when the Skipper raised his hand to return his salute.

"Have the company stand at ease, Gunny," Conorado said at the conclusion of the formality.

Thatcher about-faced, scanned the company, and called out, "Company! At ease!" The men relaxed their positions from rigid attention to something slightly more relaxed than parade rest.

The captain stepped forward, two paces to the right and one to the front of Gunny Thatcher. He stood easy, with his hands clasped behind his back. "I have one piece of new company business this morning, then Gunny Thatcher will turn you over to your platoon sergeants for the day's training."

A quick, almost inaudible buzz swept through the company, since it didn't sound as if the Skipper was going to tell them why the field exercise was canceled.

Conorado paused to look over the company; the way his eyes moved, it seemed that he looked directly at everyone. "As you have probably already noticed, we have a new officer in the company." He glanced over his shoulder, and the stranger stepped forward to take a position one pace to the right and front of Gunny Thatcher, next to the company commander. "This is Ensign Baccacio," Conorado said when the young officer took his place. "Ensign Baccacio reported in a few minutes ago. Over the next few days, as he gets settled in here, he will take command of third platoon." The men of third platoon exchanged quick glances and looked at Bass. Bass didn't move a muscle at the surprise announcement. "I have to apologize to Staff Sergeant Bass and the men of third platoon for letting them know in the company formation, but as I said, Ensign Baccacio reported in literally a few minutes ago and there was no opportunity to tell them in advance.

"This is Ensign Baccacio's first duty assignment as an officer, though he has notable experience as an enlisted man behind him. He was meritoriously promoted to lance corporal after only a year and a half of duty—that was on a bandit-chasing campaign on New Serengeti, where he earned a Bronze Star with starburst for valor under fire. A year ago, on a peacekeeping mission on Saint Brendan's, he was awarded a second Bronze Star, without starburst this time." A muscle visibly knotted in Baccacio's jaw when Captain Conorado mentioned the lack of a second starburst, which meant it was awarded for bravery other than in combat. "And he was selected for officer training. He also holds a Meritorious Unit Citation, as well as the Marine Expeditionary Medal with comet device for a second campaign." Everyone in the company noticed that the new officer didn't have a Good Conduct Medal. That must mean he had been selected for officer training well before he'd been in the Corps long enough to earn one, which was very unusual.

"I know that you will all make Ensign Baccacio feel welcome, and will help him quickly integrate into the company. Especially third platoon," Conorado added pointedly.

"That is all." He took a step back and turned to face Gunny Thatcher to hand the company back to him, but was interrupted by Top Myer, who ran out of the barracks to thrust a sheet of paper into his hand. The captain scanned the paper once quickly, then read it through more slowly. Finished reading, he faced the company again.

"Belay that last," he said. "You've probably been wondering why our planned field exercise was canceled." He paused briefly while a few men laughed nervously, but gave no other indication he was aware of an interruption. "Well, here's the reason," he said when quiet was restored.

"Thirty-fourth FIST has received orders for an operation. When you are dismissed from this formation, you will return to your squad bays and saddle up. The entire FIST will be heading off-planet on a humanitarian mission. Company L will be the vanguard. We will board a fast frigate for transport later today. The remainder of the FIST will follow along in the next few days. You will pack expeditionary." He paused briefly. "These orders don't say what our destination is, only the general type of mission. We'll get the rest of the information in transit. Right now, all I can tell you is be prepared for anything." Conorado faced Thatcher. "Company Gunnery Sergeant, the company is yours," he said, and returned Thatcher's salute. He hurried back into the barracks with the company officers in tow. An anxious-looking Top Myer held the door for them.

"Company, ah-ten-HUT!" Thatcher called out. He looked at each of the platoon sergeants. "You heard the man, saddle them up. Dismissed."

The gunny watched impassively as the Marines broke ranks and raced to the barracks to ready their gear and pack their personal belongings for storage, then signaled Bass to join him for a moment. He pulled his personal communicator from a pocket and punched in a code. He was just lifting it to his ear when Bass reached him.

"Hell of a time for a new officer to come aboard," Thatcher said to Bass, then turned his attention to the person who answered his call.

Bass took advantage of Thatcher's distraction to tell Hyakowa to oversee matters until he was finished with the captain, and so he didn't hear any of the gunny's conversation.

Thatcher had a far-off look in his eyes when he signed off and secured his comm unit. "This ensign walked into the company office right when we were getting ready to come out for roll call. You were there, you saw the way he walked right past me and the Top to report to the Skipper," he said. "Just talked to a buddy of mine in F-1." His eyes drew in their focus and he looked directly at Bass. "Baccacio reported in to FIST at eleven hours yesterday morning. At 14 hours they gave him directions to the company and offered him a driver to bring him here. It seems that instead of coming here, he went into Bronnoysund and stayed there overnight. Strange way to report in to your first command. Damn strange." He gave his head a shake. "Something tells me this is a young man we should keep an eye on."

Bass looked somberly reflective while Thatcher spoke, then grinned and said lightly, "I knew he was impressed with his own importance when I saw the uniform he chose for morning roll call." He clapped the other NCO on the shoulder and said, "Don't worry. I've straightened out young officers before, and I know you and the Top will give me any help I need with this one. Now, I shouldn't keep the Skipper waiting."

They marched into the barracks and went their separate ways—Thatcher to see how Sergeant Souavi was coming along with readying the supply room for shipping out and to find out how much help he needed.

In the office, First Sergeant Myer was busy packing his gear and overseeing Doyle and Palmer in readying the company's records and the headquarters equipment for transshipment. Through the open inner door Bass saw Captain Conorado seated at his desk, seemingly involved in mild conversation with Ensign Baccacio, who was standing at parade rest a pace in front of the desk. Without looking directly at Bass, Conorado signaled him to come in.

"Good morning, Skipper," Bass said as he entered the inner sanctum.

"Morning, Charlie. I'd like you to meet Ensign Baccacio. Ensign, this is Staff Sergeant Charlie Bass, the man you'll be receiving command from." Bass wondered if the slight ambiguity of the captain's phrasing was deliberate. It was. "Staff Sergeant Bass has been running the best platoon in the company. Third's the most squared away, and the most proficient in field tactics. That's despite the fact that it's been more understrength than any of the other platoons for most of the time he's been running it, and half of his NCOs are either acting in a grade above their ranks or are lance corporals acting as corporals. What I'm saying is, you're following a tough act. But it's not going to be as tough as it might, because Charlie will be there to teach you.

"Now, as of this morning you are nominally in command of third platoon. The key word there is 'nominally.' Staff Sergeant Bass will remain in de facto command until you get up to speed, and that won't be before we're halfway to where we're going, wherever that might be."

"Sir, if I may?" Baccacio said.

Conorado raised his eyebrows at the young officer's formal manner. Infantry officers were normally much more casual except on ceremonial occasions. He gestured a you-may.

"If Staff Sergeant Bass is such a good platoon commander, why isn't he an officer?"

Taken aback by the arrogance of the question, Conorado took a slow, deep breath before answering. "There are many reasons a man might not have a commission," he finally said. "There are more qualified enlisted Marines than there are officer slots. Some NCOs feel they are of more value as senior enlisted men than they would be as officers. Some *like* being enlisted rather than commissioned. There can be any number of reasons." He raised one shoulder in a slight shrug. "That's not a question that's always fruitful to ask."

"I understand, sir."

Bass studied Baccacio's face during the captain's explanation. He didn't think the ensign really did understand. Yes, he was going to have quite a job on his hands. He thought, not for the first time, that it was a shame the Corps didn't require men to be platoon sergeants before being selected for officer training.

"That's all for now, Baccacio," Conorado said abruptly. The significance of his not using the ensign's rank in addressing him in front of his platoon sergeant wasn't lost on Bass, or Baccacio either. "I trust you didn't completely unpack last night. Go to wherever your gear is and change into garrison utilities, gather everything up, and return here ready to ship out. You have one hour standard. Do it."

"Aye aye, sir." Baccacio snapped to attention, executed an about-face, and marched from the company commander's office. He didn't bother looking at any of the enlisted men as he marched through the company office.

Bass watched him wordlessly.

"Sorry about that, Charlie," Conorado said when Baccacio was out of sight. "The man's got the rank, I've got to give him the command."

"No problem, Skipper. How long's he been in?"

"Four years."

"Half a year Boot, a year officer training. That means he only has two and a half years' experience as an enlisted man."

"Minus transit time," Conorado agreed. "That's the way it adds up."

Bass shrugged.

"He'll get over it, Charlie. We're all going to be so busy during the next few days, he'll be racing just to stay in place. By the time he gets a chance to catch his breath, you'll have had ample opportunity to demonstrate to him how valuable you are. Just don't go hitting anyone."

Bass smiled wryly. "Aye aye, sir. Just don't anybody give me any reason."

Nearly all the men of Company L had mounted out before, most of them more than once. Several had done it on even shorter notice. All of them knew what it meant to "pack expeditionary"—they were taking only what they would normally carry into the field for combat training: their weapons and other combat gear and equipment, a pack with spare chameleons, boots, underclothing, and personal hygiene gear, tentage, and field mess gear. All dress uniforms, garrison uniforms, and personal, non-issue belongings went into lockable chests for storage in a Camp Ellis warehouse. If they were going to be gone long enough—and conditions were right—the chests would be delivered to them later on. Otherwise, the chests would securely await their return. Everyone, even those who hadn't mounted out before, was ready in less than an hour.

There was only one bit of grumbling. That was when Bass told them, "Secure your chameleons. This is a humanitarian aid mission, not combat. We wear garrison utilities."

After that the hurry-up became hurry-up-and-wait.

The hurry-up-and-wait was interrupted at 1030 hours when two trucks came by to pick up their storage chests. Two men from each platoon were dispatched with the trucks to observe the secure storing of the chests. That was the official explanation; in fact, they went along as a work party to do the storing.

At 1215 hours, the company fell in behind the barracks to march to the mess hall for noon chow. Nobody lingered over the meal, and the last straggler was back at the barracks ten minutes before 13 hours.

Shortly after 15 hours, two platoons of Dragons pulled up behind the barracks. In minutes Company L was aboard the ten vehicles and on its way to the navy spaceport. The fast frigate HM3 *Gordon* was in orbit waiting for them. With only a pause for directions, the Dragons drove aboard four Essays. As soon as the vehicles were secured, the Essays were cleared for takeoff and launched to orbit. In orbit, two of the Essays mated with the *Gordon*'s two cargo bays, and the Dragons drove into the ship's hold. After off-loading, the Essays dropped back out of orbit to the surface. The second pair of Essays mated to the frigate and, rather than off-loading their Dragons, secured to the ports for hyperspace transit. The

Gordon didn't have entry shuttles of its own capable of landing the Marines, and these would be needed at the end of the voyage.

On board, the Marines were quickly assigned berthing. The 107 enlisted men of Company L below the rank of staff sergeant were assigned to a crew bay that was normally home to twenty-five sailors. The six officers shared a compartment designed to house three of the ship's officers. The company's six senior NCOs had it the best; they got a chiefs' quarters that normally berthed four. It would have been worse had not the fifty-one men of the transportation company, who were part of the advance party, chosen to berth in the cargo hold with their Dragons.

The navy had spent most of the day installing extra bunks in the crew compartment. The Marines quickly secured their gear and weapons to stanchions and pilasters, then climbed into the bunks, mostly because there wasn't room for them anywhere else. There was only one tense moment.

Commander Kahunii, the ship's captain, objected to the Marines having their weapons at hand while aboard his ship. This was only to be expected, as navy officers usually object to having anyone aboard a ship armed except for designated security personnel. But the *Gordon*'s small weapons locker was already filled with the few weapons the ship carried for emergency use. Captain Conorado strenuously objected to Kahunii's suggestion that the Marines' weapons be stored in the officer or staff NCO quarters—there simply wasn't room, he insisted. Kahunii grudgingly relented when Conorado assured him that none of the weapons had batteries installed and couldn't be fired. But Kahunii had the final word—if there were any weapons incidents, the weapons would be secured in the officer and staff NCO quarters, even if that meant the officers and staff NCOs had to cram themselves into the already overcrowded troop hold in order to make room for them.

While all this was going on, the *Gordon* left orbit and came up to full space-3 speed, headed for the nearest hyperspace jump point, which it reached in three hours. Since a jump into hyperspace was best done on an empty stomach, the embarked Marines didn't get evening chow until some hours later than they were used to in garrison. Then it was Taps.

Still nobody in Company L knew where they were going. Commander Kahunii did, of course, but he didn't bother telling Captain Conorado.

CHAPTER
FIFTEEN

Nine men and one woman sat around the conference table deep in the bowels of Shabeli's mountain retreat. One wall of the room was covered with a viewscreen display map of Elneal. The details were perfect, the result of map surveys made by the mining companies—Shabeli had better maps than the Confederation, which had to rely exclusively on satellite surveillance since the companies' maps were proprietary and not available to the military. The details provided for the transmontane and oceanic regions, however, were much less accurate than for the Siad and Bos Kashi lands, because the companies had no interests in those regions. That was fine, since Shabeli did not expect any action to take place there.

The Bos Kashi, Gaels, and Sons of Freedom had each sent their chief war leaders and their deputies to this council. Shabeli himself, Wad Mohammad, and Wad Ramadan represented the Siad. The tenth member of the council was Moira, and she was the topic under consideration at the moment.

"Either she leaves or we do," Erne Foyle of the Gaels said. The other representatives nodded.

"It is not that we distrust her, Shabeli," Obeh Rud of the Bos Kashi added. "But she is a foreigner and we will not discuss our war plans in the presence of a foreigner."

Shabeli bristled, as he knew he was supposed to over

such a demand. He was not afraid of any of the men and they were not afraid of him. He had discussed this probability with Moira before the council. Her departure, after some perfunctory blustering, would make the chiefs think they'd won a concession from him, but in reality Shabeli was setting them up. Were the truth known, he himself often wondered if Moira were a spy. Therefore, he never told her all the details of his plans.

Shabeli turned to his uncle, pretending with a gesture to seek the old man's guidance. Not a party to the charade, the old man nodded. Going along with the ploy, Moira swirled out of the conference room without a glance or a word to anyone.

Shabeli sighed. "Brothers, the first phase of our campaign is proceeding well." The map display zoomed in on the capital city of New Obbia and its suburbs. "Two nights ago my cousins carried out the raid against the foreigners' relief operation in the suburbs. Admiral Willis was there yesterday. By now he will have decided to intervene."

"President Merka's government is virtually helpless," Ramadan said, "and our raids against the other settlements have been totally successful." He nodded to the others. "The mines are in our hands," he added.

"Fine," Mallow Ennis, Foyle's deputy, interjected. "But when do we get into the picture?"

"Yes, Wad Shabeli," Prairie Dawson of the Sons said. "Our compliments. The Siad and the Bos have upheld their part of the plan. But we want to get in on the action." He glanced at his deputy, a tall, dark-haired man named Blaine Flathead, who nodded.

"When the Marines get here, brothers," Shabeli answered. "The Confederation forces in New Obbia will send for reinforcements. I expect them to begin arriving in force within the next two weeks. Meanwhile, Admiral

Willis will form a provisional force from the Marine complement in his fleet to secure at least New Obbia as a base of operations for the first of the subsequent contingents. I expect the advance party to begin landing within hours. When the reinforcing contingents arrive, their first mission will be to secure the city and then extend relief operations into the outlying territories. Once that is done, we will destroy them piecemeal."

There were no comments. Everyone around the table had already figured out this scenario for himself. They also knew that if they were not successful tying up the Marines in the towns and farmlands, the full force of Marine arms would, in time, visit total destruction upon their own people.

Wad Mohammad was the only one who spoke of their concerns. "The Confederation Marines have aircraft more fearsome than the rocs of legend," he said. "Their soldiers are armed with fire-guns. They ride in fire-breathing dragons. How can we stand against such might?"

"Pfaugh!" Shabeli spat on the polished floor at his side. "Yes," he said angrily, "the Confederation has aircraft more fearsome than rocs. Yes, their rifles shoot fire instead of bullets. Yes, they ride in fire-breathing dragons, swifter than the jinn. But as fighters, their men are as women." He spat again, and glared at the men facing him. "Had you not insisted that she leave, Moira could tell you that. She was born into them and lived with the Confederation people until she came to Elneal and met real men—true fighters and warriors. When she saw that their men are as women to our men, that their men are not even as strong as our women, she disowned her own parents and people so she could live with true men, men of courage. Us!" He bellowed the last word. "Does any man here question that?"

The war chiefs hung their heads and glanced at each other, but none met Shabeli's eyes.

"No, Wad Shabeli," they murmured. "No, Magnificent One," they said. Faced with the anger of Shabeli the Magnificent, they could do nothing else.

Shabeli glared at them again, let the silence continue until they shifted uncomfortably and finally became still again. In the end, Wad Mohammad was the only one who raised his eyes to Shabeli.

"All right, then, let us continue." Shabeli gave a signal to someone unseen and a table of organization and equipment for a Marine FIST flashed on the vidscreens. "This is what we're up against," Shabeli continued. Next to the FIST Table of Organization and Equipment appeared the diagram of a breakout of allied forces. In contrast to the Marines, Shabeli's forces had no air support, no artillery, and very little in the way of logistical support. "Our advantage lies in mobility, knowledge of the countryside, and the valor of our men," Shabeli said.

"Many will die," Jabal Rustak, Obeh Rud's deputy, muttered.

"Is there anyone here who is not ready for death?" Shabeli asked. There was no response. After a pause Shabeli continued. "We are a light, highly mobile force. My plan is that each of you will provide two thousand men. Each of you will target specific towns where you will conduct urban terrorist operations. The Bos Kashi will relieve my men now in position around New Obbia because they are closer to the capital. You brothers of the Sons of Freedom and the Gaels may decide between you which will join the Bos Kashi to attack the surrounding settlements and which will attack the farther towns.

"Brother," Obeh Rud said, "since your men are already in place, why don't you attack the Marines in New Obbia and let us be the reserve force?"

"Because we are better armed and can deal on a nearly equal basis with the Marines after they have settled in the countryside. None of us can stop them from doing that, brothers. But you can keep them off balance and delay their timetable. Once you control portions of the cities, you will hold the populations hostage so the Marines won't be able to use their airpower and heavy weapons against you. They will have to fight house-to-house, street-to-street, man-to-man, and therefore their weapons advantages will be greatly nullified. You can inflict severe damage on them. The Bos Kashi are brave and resourceful fighters, all know that. You will kill many of the Confederation Marines. You will know how to make them think they have killed many more of you than they do in truth." He shifted his gaze from Obeh Rud to include all of the other tribal war leaders in what he said next.

"Remember, when I give you the signal, you will melt into the surrounding countryside and disperse to your own lands. That is when I will tell the government we are suing for peace. They will believe we have been defeated." He snorted at the preposterousness of the idea. "They will have no more desire to fight us after the losses the Bos have inflicted on them. Then they will go into the countryside peacefully and confident. There we will kill them all."

The others cheered.

Since it was the Siad who had received the bulk of the payments the mining companies had made on Elneal, it was they who possessed the more modern weapons and communications systems. Everyone at the conference knew this, but what they did not know was how many men Shabeli had been able to outfit. He let on it was only a few dozen, but in reality he had more than five hundred well-equipped men under arms. What nobody outside his immediate circle knew was that he also had aircraft, two

A-5B Raptors—old, second-generation, and as yet poorly armed for a ground-attack mission, but a devastating surprise for any foe. They were piloted under contract by renegade airmen trained originally by the Confederation Naval Forces. Shabeli passed them off as foreign technical advisers required to keep his headquarters power plant running. The machines were kept well-hidden in a remote valley two days' march from the headquarters. The pilots were already on their way there, to prepare the aircraft for combat. He also had a company of Siad warriors armed with the same blasters the Confederation Marines carried.

"We shall leave at once," Obeh Rud announced.

"We must move with caution," Shabeli said. "Until you actually get inside the city, you are not safe from attack by Willis's ships."

"Yes," Mallow Ennis said. "It will take us several days to get our men across the mountains, and then perhaps a week to reach our targets. We'll move in small groups." He glanced at Prairie Dawson. A long white scar down the center of Dawson's forehead was a reminder of a blow Ennis had once given him at a wedding party. Dawson smiled. Under Ennis's shirt was the long, broad scar of the wound Dawson had given him at the same party. "We'll move at night, groups of no more than twenty men," Dawson said.

"We'll agree later on which towns to attack and which passes through the mountains our parties will use," Foyle proposed. The Sons of Freedom nodded.

"Good," Shabeli announced. "I expect the first major Marine contingent, probably the 34th FIST now on Thorsfinni's World, will be here in about two weeks. Be inside New Obbia and near the towns by then."

Several hours of discussion followed, during which details were agreed upon. "Brothers," Shabeli concluded, "you have all sworn to obey my leadership. Tactical decisions will be left up to you and your local leaders, but I must be informed of everything that is going on in each sector. Strategic decisions are to be made by me—in consultation with you—but they are mine and mine alone to make. Once made, they will be obeyed. That is understood?"

Each man presented his side arm toward Shabeli, re-affirming acceptance of his leadership. They filed out of the conference room to make their separate ways home to prepare their men for the campaign.

Shabeli the Magnificent stood alone in the empty conference room and smiled. He knew full well how quickly they would have turned on him if they'd known he already had an emissary on his way to negotiate a cease-fire with Admiral Willis.

Moira opened the door to her apartment expecting to greet Shabeli. Instead, ancient Wad Ramadan stood there, his pure white hair and beard reflecting the dim light shining through the doorway.

"Miss Moira, may I come in?" the old man asked politely. Wad had always played the gentleman toward Moira, and she liked him for that even while suspecting he didn't trust her any more than she did him. She motioned him inside.

Ramadan declined her offer of refreshment. He stood silently in the middle of the sitting room for a few moments as if marshaling his thoughts. "Miss Moira, if you have any influence over my nephew, I beg you, use it to dissuade him from this insane plan."

Moira, completely taken by surprise, said nothing.

"I must confess, my dear," Ramadan continued, taking a chair, "my kinsmen do not support me in this. I am completely alone among the Siad in opposition to my nephew's ambitions. They can't see as clearly as I that what he is about to do will bring total ruin down upon all of us." The old man looked into Moira's eyes.

"The Confederation has been bluffed before. Shabeli can do it again," Moira responded.

"No." Wad Ramadan shook his head firmly. "So long as we killed only our own maybe that would've been true, but when we seized the mines and killed the foreigners, we went too far. And when we kill the Marines, that will be the end of our independence because the Confederation will never tolerate such defiance. We must seek peace with the Confederation now, if we wish to survive with any degree of independence."

"Wad Ramadan," Moira replied, "they tell me no one was a fiercer warrior and hater of foreigners than you when you fought beside your brother, Shabeli the Elder. Now you, of all the Siad, want to make peace with the Confederation? You know that will mean making some concessions to President Merka's government in New Obbia."

"And I know that Shabeli would fly into a towering rage if he knew of my opposition. I, like every other man of the Siad, am committed utterly to following his lead. But what has happened to me, you ask? I'll tell you, my dear, what has happened to me will someday happen to you; I've grown old." They were both silent for a moment. "The Confederation sends its ships to the farthest reaches of Human Space. We will never, never be permitted to stand in their way if we oppose them."

"Not so, Wad Ramadan. Not too many years ago the Confederation forces withdrew from—"

Wad waved his hand impatiently. "No, no. Here it is a matter of economics and also a matter of humanitarianism. When a man can feel that he is doing good for the people while making money for himself, he will stop at nothing, and the Confederation has all the resources it needs to reduce us to nothing. We are a strategic threat to them because we've stopped the mining. They cannot permit that. Also, in their eyes, we are evil. I strongly advised Shabeli against killing those children at the orphanage. You should have known that was a mistake, Miss Moira! Your people will never deal with men who murder children."

Moira didn't tell Wad Ramadan that in fact she had advised Shabeli against attacking the orphanage, not because she cared about the victims, but because, like Ramadan, she knew it would make the Confederation more determined than ever to eliminate the Siad. "I will speak to him about this," she agreed.

Wad Ramadan smiled weakly. He did not believe her. It would still be up to him to talk to his nephew, and he already knew that would do no good. "Thank you, my dear," he said, resigned. "Now I will accept your offer of a sweet drink."

"You must kill the old fool," Moira told Shabeli. "He is against you and—"

Shabeli struck her on the side of the jaw with the full force of his open palm. The blow threw her back upon the bed, shocked. Instantly, she leaped to her feet, fumbling with the dagger she kept under her robe. Shabeli grabbed her wrist in a grip so crushing she screamed aloud in pain and the dagger clattered harmlessly to the floor. He spun her around and pushed her facedown on the bed, her arm twisted painfully behind her back.

"My love, you understand much I will never comprehend, but know three things about the Siad: Never accuse a man of cowardice, never insinuate he's had sex with his own mother, and never suggest a Siad murder someone in his own bloodline. If ever you say something like that again, I will kill you."

Shabeli allowed Moira to get up. The right side of her face was already turning bright red from the blow. In the years she had known Shabeli, this was the first time he had hit her. The Siad in general derived no honor from abusing women, unless for political gain. She cursed herself for the remark. She should have known better. But despite her distrust of Uncle Wad, she too was desperately afraid Shabeli's plan would end in disaster and bring ruin upon all of them.

Shabeli flopped down on the bed and flicked on the flatvid viewer. He motioned for Moira to join him. He put his arm around her. "Nature will take care of Uncle Ramadan," he whispered. "He is powerless anyway. But he is respected, and as long as he lives, I must defer to him in public."

Moira was about to mention her own misgivings but decided it was definitely not the right moment to disagree with Shabeli the Magnificent. Instead she asked, "Would you really kill me?"

Shabeli pretended to think hard about this for a moment, then replied, "Only by fucking you to death."

With Moira sleeping soundly beside him in the darkness, Shabeli the Magnificent thought about his plan. While the others were wasting themselves in the settlements, when he was ready, he would ambush the Marines in the countryside. He would wait until the other clans had dissipated their strength in urban warfare, and then, when the Confederation, disgusted over its losses and impatient at the delay in its relief operations, believed it had finally gotten the upper hand on Elneal, he would strike a devastating and totally unexpected blow. Afterward, he would offer peace, and the concessions would be granted to him.

Ah, he thought, it is all a gamble! He had purposely ordered the attack on the orphanage because he knew it would bring matters to a head. He also knew that with Confederation intervention, the stakes were now infinitely high and his position utterly precarious. But that was what made life so enjoyable. He lay back and within moments was sound asleep.

CHAPTER
SIXTEEN

On the second day out, Captain Conorado held an all-hands briefing for the 173 men of 34th FIST's advance party, Company L, and half the transportation company. He held the briefing in the crew's mess, the largest open space on the *Gordon*.

The space was never meant to hold so many people at one time. The men crammed into the room, and those fortunate enough to get seats at the tables were hip-to-haunch so tight they were almost in each other's laps. Some sat on the tables and tried not to obstruct the view of too many of the others. The rest squeezed tightly into the aisles. The senior NCOs bunched together at the hatch. When all were assembled, Captain Conorado entered from the galley, followed by the other officers and Staff Sergeant Bass. The men of third platoon noticed that Ensign Baccacio didn't look happy. The company commander took his place in a small open space next to a large vidscreen that was set into the wall, the other officers grouped together around the hatch to the galley.

"Company, atten—"

"Don't anybody get up," Conorado said, interrupting Top Myer's call to attention. "There isn't enough room for you to move in here."

The Skipper slowly looked about the crew's mess before beginning his remarks. If it seemed to his men as though he looked each of them in the eye, it was because he very nearly did. There was no waiting for their attention; each man had fixed his eyes, ears, and thoughts on the company commander as soon as he entered the room. Neither did Conorado have to gather his thoughts; he knew what he was going to say. It was much the same as his own commander had said a dozen years earlier when the company in which he'd been a platoon sergeant was in transit to Haguri, where he was given a direct commission on the battlefield. Conorado paused before speaking now because he wasn't sure that what he had to say was any more accurate than what his company commander had said then. Haguri was supposed to be an easy, low-key mission with no fighting. It turned out to be one of the bloodiest campaigns he'd ever been involved in.

Well, he was a Marine; when in doubt, act decisively.

"We are on a humanitarian relief mission to Elneal," he began without preamble. "Elneal is both a backward world and a backwater. It has little trade with the other worlds of Human Space other than in molycarbondum, and there has been almost no immigration into it for several generations. Its molycarbondum deposits are the only thing Elneal has of value. That's mined by Consolidated Enterprises under contract to the planetary government—and giving legitimacy and providing laborers to the mining operation seems to be the only thing the central government does. The government appears to have control only in New Obbia, the capital city. The rest of Elneal is populated by nomads and isolated pockets of back-to-earthers—at least 'back-to-earthers' is how they're officially characterized—none of whom answer to any power above their own clan or settlement.

"For several years the nomadic tribes have been warring against each other and with the independent settlements. This has not been sporadic warring, but constant, and recently it has become very serious—some observers have called it genocidal. The best-case estimate is the fighting has reduced the planet's population by twenty-five percent. Some estimates go above fifty percent. Because of the fighting, agriculture has failed and famine is now endemic. Hundreds of thousands of people have died of starvation on Elneal in the past two years.

"The Confederation hasn't stood by idly while the fighting has been going on. There have been repeated and continuing attempts to get food and medical supplies into the countryside to feed the starving people. In many instances, food convoys have been attacked and the food taken by the raiders or destroyed in place. In such cases, the crews of the attacked convoys have been killed almost without exception. In places where food and medical supplies have been flown in and central distribution points established, those points have been attacked, the food and medical supplies taken or destroyed, and the staffs killed. Social order on Elneal, such as it is, is on the verge of collapse, as is the entire population."

The Skipper paused for a moment, to let his words sink in, before continuing. "A few weeks ago, the leaders of the major warring factions agreed to lay down their arms if the Confederation would guarantee their safety so that food and medical supplies could be distributed. That's our job. Company L, 34th FIST, is the lead unit of a Provisional Marine Brigade being assembled and sent to Elneal to guarantee security of food distribution to end the famine, and secondarily to oversee the disarmament of the warring factions so that the central government can resume control over the world.

"Now I'm going to hand the briefing over to First Sergeant Myer. I'm sure he'll give you the detailed information you need in a forthright manner that I could not match. First Sergeant." Without waiting for acknowledgment, Captain Conorado left. The other officers followed him.

"Aye aye, sir." Top Myer bounded to the top of the closest table and crossed the room rear to front by jumping from table to table over the seated men.

With the officers safely gone, Top Myer nodded at Gunny Thatcher, who closed the hatch and dogged it. The first sergeant took his time looking at the troops. He knew what he had to say was accurate, since he'd gotten it direct from the lips of other senior NCOs who had recently been on Elneal—and he himself had served a short tour many years earlier with the security detachment at the Confederation consulate in New Obbia. The information he was about to present wouldn't appear on any official document or in any command-sanctioned briefing. He took his time getting started because he wanted to impress on the men the seriousness of what he was about to say.

"Listen up and listen up good," he began, his voice gruff. "Gunny Thatcher secured that hatch because the brass wouldn't like what I'm about to tell you, and I don't want them walking in while I'm saying it. We're going up against a bunch of bloodthirsty savages." Eyes popped open throughout the mess. Not even the men who'd been on several operations had ever heard a first sergeant begin a briefing with a statement like that.

"The Skipper told you the central government only seems to control New Obbia, the capital city. Well, New Obbia's all the central government has ever controlled. The only reason any kind of official government exists on Elneal at all is because the Confederation needed one to conduct official dealings with Consolidated Enterprises on their mining operation. Otherwise C.E. could have gone in, strip-mined the place down to the moho, and the only accurate record of how much molycarbondum they took out would be in a set of books the tax man never sees.

"There's a story that Elneal was named after the obscure late-twentieth-century American philosopher L. Neil Smith. Smith had the cockamamie idea that if everybody went around armed to the gills, there wouldn't be any violence, there wouldn't be any need for government, and everybody would live in a state of utopian bliss.

"I don't know whether that story's true or not, but it happens that the first settlers were nomadic and seminomadic tribesmen from the deserts of northeast Africa and the mountains of southwest Asia who objected to their national governments' wanting to disarm and urbanize them. Most likely, the planet was named after a North African clan leader called El Nelffi. He was the one who came up with the idea of emigrating.

"Anyway, Elneal got settled by some pretty xenophobic and otherwise unsociable people. Less than a generation later, the British realized there was a world out there where people went around armed and fighting each other, so they rounded up as much of the Irish Republican Army as they could find and exiled them to Elneal. The Spanish thought that was such a great idea, they did the same thing with the Basques. Somewhere in there, the old United States put a lot of pressure on the U.N. to mount a major operation against the opium-producing tribes of Southeast Asia. When those tribesmen realized that this time they were going to lose the war, they sued for peace and offered to move to Elneal. They figured the Kurds, Afghanis, and Tuaregs already there would like a bit of smoke, and they could always refine opium into heroin if the Irish and Basques preferred needles to pipes. Along about that time, the few remaining American pistol-packers, those who believed as L. Neil Smith did, decided it was time to 'get out of Dodge,' as they would have put it, and they moved to Elneal. Hardly anybody else has moved there. There's been no intermarriage between the different groups, though there's been a lot of inter-breeding. The nomads steal women from each other on raids."

Top Myer stopped talking and slowly looked the troops over again. "Are you getting a picture here?" he asked. "This world was populated almost exclusively by people who want to carry firearms and don't want to answer to any government.

"I have spent my entire adult life under arms. So has Gunny Thatcher. Every man among you, from Staff Sergeant Bass on down to the newest Marine—who's that, Clarke?—every last one of you lives under arms, and will as long as you are a member of the Confederation Marine Corps. That's a condition of being a Marine. Marines go in harm's way, and we must be armed in order to survive and do our jobs. We expect to have to use our weapons. Most of us have. Those of you who haven't yet, will soon. That's part of being a Marine.

"If you're not prepared to use a weapon, you shouldn't carry one. We expect to have to use ours, and we're pre-pared to. But there's a universe of difference between carrying a weapon because you expect to have to use it, and liking to be good with it because that's a skill you've mastered, and carrying one because you *like* the power it gives you. If you like to carry a weapon because of the power it gives you, you're a danger to everybody around you. In that case, sooner or later you're liable to use it on someone needlessly.

"However it goes, if you carry a weapon, whether for the reasons we do or for some other reason, sooner or later you're going to use it. And that's what happened on Elneal. With no government to keep them in check, the tribesmen and various other groups quickly found themselves at war with each other."

Top Myer paused a moment, then went on: "If you're thinking that not every individual descendant of the original colonists wants to carry weapons and fight, you're right. Not all of them do. Those who don't, generally don't live to become adults—they get killed during their juvenile training. Some manage to run away to New Obbia. Most of them, though, prefer death rather than the shame of running away. The people of New Obbia are universally considered to be lower than human—to go there is to suffer the greatest shame.

"If they were using swords, or bows and arrows, or other ancient weapons, it wouldn't be too bad. But they started out with projectile-throwing firearms, which are much more devastating. I don't have any hard confirmation on this, but there are rumors that some of them have blasters today. Without the controls imposed by a social order larger than the clan or tribe, when people are well enough armed, they go around slaughtering everyone who isn't a member of the same clan or tribe. You can put that down as a law of nature. It's happened time and again throughout all of human history. It's happening today on Elneal.

"On most worlds in Human Space, citizens can walk about with reasonable expectation of not being molested. They do it unarmed. There's no need for them to carry deadly weapons. On Elneal, they've created a world where no one can walk around expecting that nobody will try to kill him. It's a world where anyone unarmed is in extreme jeopardy. Hell, anyone who isn't in a large band of heavily armed men is in constant danger." He shook his head. "Supposedly that's stopped now. The clans and tribes and other groups want to end the famine and are willing to stop fighting—or so they say. I'll believe it when I see every last one of them disarmed."

He stopped talking, and stood for a long moment looking someplace only he could see. When he resumed, his voice was much softer than it had been.

"We are not going in on a combat operation. We are going in to provide symbolic security for the distribution of food and medical supplies. We are also going to oversee the disarming of the warring factions—or at least see to it that they go about unarmed. We are not expected to do any fighting. That is the official word from the top. They believe it so much they made us leave our chameleons behind." He suddenly became gruff and serious again. "But we damn well better be prepared to fight. Because anyone who isn't prepared to fight is most probably going to get killed.

"That is all. Platoon sergeants, the platoons are yours." Top Myer made his way through the crowded room to the back, where Gunny Thatcher was undogging and opening the hatch. The two top NCOs left together.

Sergeant Hyakowa, Company L's three regular platoon sergeants, and the transportation company platoon sergeants, looked at one another. They had to meet with their men and continue the briefing by platoons, but Top Myer was a tough act to follow.

Because the men of the transportation company were conducting maintenance on their vehicles, and half the Dragons were in the two Essays mated to the *Gordon*, a breathable atmosphere was maintained in the Essays. Hyakowa only wished the transportation chief hadn't been so condescending about graciously allowing third platoon to cram itself into one of the Essays for its meeting.

Sergeant Hyakowa told the men of third platoon about

some of the humanitarian aid and peacekeeping missions he'd been on, and about things that went wrong with them. Then he had everyone else in the platoon with experience on such missions talk about them. He thought it was curious that no one had a story to tell about a humanitarian relief mission on which nothing went wrong.

As Captain Conorado predicted, Ensign Baccacio was very busy indeed. His two primary official duties were assisting in planning operations, and meeting and getting to know the men in his new platoon.

Now that they knew where they were going and what their duties would be once they got there, the company's officers, assisted by Top Myer, Gunny Thatcher, and Staff Sergeant Bass, who was still de facto platoon commander until Captain Conorado decided that Ensign Baccacio was up to speed, worked on their operational plan.

Company L, reinforced by the transportation platoons, was to land at New Obbia, meet with the Confederation Consul for assistance in establishing a base of operations, and prepare for the arrival of 34th FIST's command element, which was expected to arrive in two or three days. Part of that preparation would consist of updating the month-old information they now had on the situation on Elneal. Using this probably already-obsolete information, they were choosing which localities should receive the first deliveries of food and medical supplies.

They considered the topography of various sites, usability of existing roads between the capital and the sites, terrain conditions where roads were lacking, and other factors affecting accessibility. They took into consideration population size and density, and were concerned with the level of famine—what percentage of the population at a site might be saved by timely arrival of relief supplies. Other concerns included the location, number, and condition of existing food and medical supplies—distressingly few and small outside the city. They made guesstimates about the likelihood of hostile action from groups that weren't yet ready to lay down their arms and end the starvation. They factored in the number, type, and condition of local-government and Confederation delivery vehicles.

When all this information was before them, they weighted everything and assigned priorities to more than a hundred distribution sites, first those within two days' land travel of New Obbia, then within easy air transport distance of the city. Then they spread out farther.

Finally, they examined their own manpower and transportation resources to determine how they might bring the greatest benefit to the largest number of people in the several days between when they began distribution of food and arrival of the rest of 34th FIST, or elements of the other FISTs in the provisional brigade.

In the end they had a plan for a crude kind of triage. Many people would still die, which was frustrating, but more would be saved.

They knew they would have to redo everything once they landed on Elneal and got updated information, which was also frustrating, but at least they had a matrix for the plan—and that would cut days off the time between the landing and the dispatch of the first relief convoy.

For his other official duty, Ensign Baccacio dutifully went about with Staff Sergeant Bass to meet everybody in the platoon. He asked each man the usual questions:

"How long have you been in?" Dean, McNeal, and a few others had been in less than a year. Sergeant Hyakowa had twelve years' service.

"How much action have you seen?" None for Claypoole, Dean, McNeal, and a few others, ten operations and campaigns for Leach. Everybody else was somewhere in between.

"Do you plan to make a career of the Corps?" Those on their second or subsequent enlistments all said they were making a career of it; the rest were about equally divided between thinking about it and no.

"How old are you?" Their ages ranged from twenty-two to thirty-five.

"Where are you from?" Most of them were from small cities, towns, and rural areas of Earth, though there were an appreciable number from other worlds. Few were from major cities.

"What do your parents think of your being in the Corps?" Their parents were uniformly proud—how else would you answer that question?

"How many brothers and sisters do you have?" None to eight.

"Are any of them Marines?" A few.

"How much education do you have?" Mostly college, very little graduate work.

"What was your study major?" They studied computer science, history, engineering, liberal arts, philosophy, fine arts, premed, business—the usual gamut.

"What are your interests or hobbies?" Baccacio was distressed at how many of them said drinking and chasing girls.

"Do you have a steady girl?" He shouldn't have been surprised that none of them had a steady relationship with a woman—not with marriage banned for Marines under the rank of staff sergeant—but he was.

"What do you like to do on liberty?" Nor should he have been dismayed that what they most wanted to do was drink, chase women, and generally carouse.

"When was your last leave?" On average, none of them had taken leave in more than two years.

"Where did you go on it?" Most of them went home for leave.

Before he was through meeting them all, Ensign Baccacio became convinced that none of his men were living up to his potential and he had a major job ahead of him, straightening out this platoon.

Ensign Baccacio also assigned himself an unofficial duty. He got on good terms with Corporal Doyle so he could have greater access to the personnel records than a junior officer under his circumstances normally did. He was most interested in Charlie Bass's record. He wanted to know why, if Bass was as great a leader of men as Conorado said, he was only a staff sergeant. Of course, it was all there in the records.

Several days into the voyage, at the end of a long planning session for contingencies in event of hostilities, Bass noticed Baccacio staring at him intensely. Sensing that the younger man was looking for an opportunity to assert his authority, Bass didn't follow the officers out of the ship's secondary ward room, which had been assigned to the Marines as their operations center. Instead he sat down again and waited, calmly looking at the ensign.

At first it seemed Baccacio was going to follow the other officers out of the ward room, but he stopped when he reached the door. Looking both ways along the passageway outside, he stepped back, pulled the hatch shut, and dogged it. Then he turned back to Bass, who casually gestured for him to take a seat.

Baccacio hesitated. He didn't want it to appear that he needed the NCO's permission to sit down, but if he remained standing, he would seem to be declining the offer, which might mean he was losing control of the situation before he had a chance to say anything. So he sat down across the table from Bass.

"The men seem to like you, Staff Sergeant Bass," Baccacio said after the two men studied each other for a moment.

"Yessir, it does seem that way," Bass replied noncommittally.

Baccacio nodded. It wasn't quite the response he expected, but it gave him another opening. "You treat them well."

Bass nodded.

"You even go on liberty with them. Do you think that's wise?"

Bass raised an eyebrow. "It's not precise to say I go on liberty with the men," he said. "It's more that I sometimes go on liberty to the same places they do."

"Is there a difference?"

Bass shrugged. There was, but if Baccacio didn't want to see it, he wasn't going to argue the point.

"Noncommissioned officers, like commissioned officers, should distance themselves from the men, don't you think?"

Bass dipped his head in a slight nod, wondering where this conversation was going. Surely Baccacio wasn't going to take him to task for a situation that wouldn't arise anytime in the foreseeable future.

"Officers and NCOs have to send men into harm's way," the ensign said. "Sometimes, we have to send them into situations where we know they're going to get killed—"

Bass sharply interrupted him. "A good leader never sends a man into a situation where he knows the man will get killed."

"It happens all the time," Baccacio snapped back, to cover his shock at the way Bass had spoken to him.

"Mr. Baccacio," Bass said in a slow, calm voice that was nonetheless threatening, "I don't know how many missions, operations, and campaigns I've been on. I'd have to go and count all of my campaign medals and the comets on my Marine Expeditionary Medal to tell you. Far more than twenty, I do know that. On all but the first few of them, I was an NCO, responsible for the conduct and the lives of the men under me. Not once did I ever knowingly send a Marine to his death. I've seen many Marines die along the way, including more than I'd ever want to think about who were in my charge. But none of them ever died because I told them to go out and get themselves killed. The same holds, to the best of my knowledge, for every platoon and company commander I ever served under, and to every NCO up and down my chain of command. Marine leaders send their men, or lead their men, *to* kill, not to *be* killed. We know that some of our Marines might die in an action, but we never deliberately send them to their deaths."

Baccacio leaned back in his chair and drummed the fingers of his left hand on the table. "So you're insubordinate as well," he said when the silence between the two stretched long enough to become uncomfortable.

"As well?"

"I know about you, Bass. This is your third time as a staff sergeant. You've been busted three times. Once from corporal to lance corporal, once from gunnery sergeant to sergeant, and most recently from gunnery sergeant to staff sergeant." He leaned forward and tapped a fingertip on the tabletop to emphasize his words: "And you have the nerve to say what noncommissioned officers do and don't do? This most recent time," he sat up and threw his arms out, "you were court-martialed for assaulting a civilian! How can you justify assaulting a civilian? What kind of example are you setting for the men when you do that?"

"If you checked it out closely enough, Mr. Baccacio,

you know I assaulted that 'civilian' because he pushed a piece of defective equipment that got a lot of good Marines killed. When I hit that man, I was standing up for a lot of needlessly dead Marines. That's a fine example to give." He leaned forward and reached under the table. His fingers fell exactly where he wanted them to: on the opening of the special pocket on the thigh of his trousers, where he kept his ancient K-Bar.

Baccacio did his best not to swallow and blanch when his platoon sergeant withdrew the knife—he couldn't believe the man was threatening him. Was he?

"Do you know what this is, Mr. Baccacio?" Bass asked. He didn't wait for an answer. "It's a K-Bar. This isn't a reproduction, or a museum replica, it's the real thing. This knife is nearly four centuries old."

The young officer stared at the knife. Its blade was seven inches long. Once, the blade had been an inch and a half wide, but sharpening had worn it down to less than an inch. The metal was blackened. Unlike the knife he carried as a Marine officer, it didn't start tapering until near the end, where it became double-edged. Bass turned the knife so Baccacio could see the legend USMC stamped into one side of the blade, and KA-BAR OLEAN, N.Y. into the other. The knife's hilt was made of broad, leather disks packed tightly together. Some of the washers had dried and split over the centuries and been replaced. The remaining original disks were a deep, shiny black, polished smooth from generations of handling, and looked as hard as gemstone or volcanic glass.

"There's no way of telling how many of those old American Marines carried this knife before one of them took it home with him when he was discharged," Bass said, "instead of returning it to his company supply sergeant. Those old Marines called themselves a 'band of brothers.' This knife, handed down through generations of Marines, is a symbol of that brotherhood. Carrying it reminds me that I am part of that. We Confederation Marines are the spiritual if not the lineal descendants of those United States Marines. We are no less a 'band of brothers.' Brothers don't send each other out to be killed.

"Now, listen up and listen up good, Ensign. The men don't like me because sometimes we wind up in the same place on liberty and I buy a round of drinks. They like me because I take care of them. I don't waste their lives. I stand up for my men and I back them up when they get into trouble. And they know that if they get into trouble of their own making, they have to answer to me for it. They respect me for that, Ensign. They know that's fair.

"Every man in this company respects every NCO in it, and until you arrived, they respected every officer. You have yet to show anyone that you deserve respect. Nobody knows if you respect them, if you'll back them up, if you're fair. Nobody knows that you won't waste their lives. Here's a lesson you better learn in a hurry. Officers and NCOs who aren't respected don't last long. Yes, I know what they say, respect the uniform. Well, there's a man inside that uniform. The men will obey the orders that come from the uniform even if they don't respect the man inside it. They're Marines, and that's one of the rules they live under. But if they don't respect the man inside the uniform, they won't obey the orders as well as they will when they come from a man who is respected. Some unrespected officers and NCOs wind up getting killed because nobody's looking out for them. For others, their units develop low morale, which means they get bad marks on their quarterly reports and eventually they get kicked out of the Corps.

"You said I'm insubordinate, Mr. Baccacio. If that's so, then what I'm about to say must be insubordinate as all hell. I've long maintained that nobody should be selected for commissioning before he's reached the rank of staff sergeant. You've got the training, Ensign. But you don't have the experience to back it up." Bass stood abruptly, stuck the ancient K-Bar back in its scabbard, and left the ward room. He left the hatch swinging idly behind him.

Ensign Baccacio sat stunned, staring at the space Bass had sat in. Instead of taking full command of the platoon as he'd planned, he had just been read the riot act by an NCO he'd been determined to put in his place.

CHAPTER
SEVENTEEN

"Fast frigate" is a class of warship. From its designation, one might reasonably expect a fast frigate to be fast, probably faster than any other starships. And it is—but only in Space-3, normal three-dimensional space. In hyperspace all ships are locked into the exact same amount of travel-time for a given distance; the same 6.273804 ad infinitum irregular number of light-years-per-day speed, known as the Beam Constant, allowed by the Beam Drive, applies equally to a fast frigate and a slow-boat-to-China, assuming that such a scow would be spaceworthy at all. So even though travel by fast frigate rather than by troop transport can cut transit time between planetary systems by several days, the HM3 *Gordon* spent the same twelve days in hyperspace as did whatever transport ship the rest of 34th FIST followed on.

A vagary of interstellar travel that most people aren't aware of is the effect of the irregularity of the light-year-per-day distance on navigation. When a navigator plots his course, he doesn't know with any real precision where his ship will pop back into Space-3. For that matter, two starships jumping in tandem from the exact same spot and using the exact same destination coordinates, won't come out of hyperspace in the same place. This phenomenon has caused some people to say that the Beam Constant is a variable as well as an irregular number.

Astrophysicists say that's not so, that the uncertainty is caused by the interstellar dance of the spheres, and by the resulting shift in the normal curvature of space-time.

Whatever, interstellar navigators have to plan a margin of error when they plot their courses. The plotted arrival point is always at greater distance from the outbound jump points than the radius of the sphere of error, as it's called. It really wouldn't do to have an inbound ship suddenly return to Space-3 in the same spot from which an outbound ship is attempting to make a jump. When two or more ships are traveling together, they also have to consider each other's plotted arrival points to avoid coming out in each other's spheres of error. Just in case. Since the margin of error increases with distance traveled, ships in convoy go in short jumps and reassemble in formation each time they return to Space-3. Otherwise, on a long trip, they would be scattered over a horrendously large sphere on arrival at their destination. Which won't do at all for warships going into a hostile situation.

The CNSS FF HM3 *Gordon* was traveling alone, so it was able to go from Thorsfinni's World to Elneal in one jump. But at slightly more than seventy-five light-years' distance, it was going to take the ship longer to reach orbit once it returned to Space-3 than the three hours it took from orbit to jump point at Thorsfinni's World. And if it had the misfortune of coming out near the far rim of its sphere of error, even at a fast frigate's high rate of three-dimensional speed the trip from there to orbit would take the best part of a standard day.

Captain Conorado broke the seal on a packet of orders he was given moments before he left the barracks back at Camp Ellis. The staff major who handed him the packet gave him very specific orders: "Do not open this packet until you are planetside wherever you are going, or on approach if the ship comes out of hyperspace with at least a twelve-hour flight time to orbit."

They certainly had more than twelve hours' flight time, so he opened the packet. A smile slowly spread across his face as he shuffled through the pages. Finally. He wondered why Commander Van Winkle, the battalion commander, wanted him to wait with these orders. They were dated the first of the month, and it was already mid-month.

"Lieutenant Humphrey," he said to his executive officer. "Get the Top. I want all officers and platoon sergeants assembled in the ward room in ten minutes. Include transportation in that." Orders in hand, he headed for the bridge to get permission from Commander Kahunii to use the crew's mess for an unscheduled, all-hands assembly.

The Marine officers and senior NCOs were in the ward room waiting for him when Captain Conorado arrived with Commander Kahunii's permission to use the crew's mess for the next hour. Without a word, he handed out pages of orders to each of his platoon commanders and the senior officer from the transportation detachment. He noted, but didn't comment on, the way Ensign Baccacio grabbed for the orders he handed him, quickly scanned them, and shoved them toward Staff Sergeant Bass, the only NCO in the room who didn't look over an officer's shoulder to see what the orders were.

"All hands in the crew's mess in ten minutes," he said when everyone had seen the orders and was passing them back. "Top, do you have, or can you get, what we need?"

"Anything I don't have, I can get," First Sergeant Myer replied, grinning broadly.

In ten minutes all 173 Marines were crammed into the crew's mess.

"Marines, I'm sorry we can't do this under more cere-monial conditions," Conorado said once everyone was settled. "But I'm sure you'll forgive me for that over-sight." He looked at the jammed room and at the tiny open space in front of him and shook his head. "We're about to have a demonstration that Marines really can do anything, anyplace, at any time. As I call out your name, front and center."

He called out six names from first platoon. The first couple of men looked surprised, then everybody caught on to what was happening and they all became excited, especially the men whose names were being called. Five men were called from second platoon. Then it was third platoon's turn.

"Sergeant Eagle's Cry, Sergeant Kelly, Corporal Ratliff, Corporal Saleski," four more names, and the last was "Lance Corporal Chan," followed by three names from the assault platoon and five from the transportation detachment.

The twenty men whose names were called scrambled, crawled, and climbed from wherever they were to stand at attention in a tight formation in front of the captain. Other Marines howled at them and took good-natured swings as they bumped into and stepped on people in their rush to get to the front of the room. In hardly more time than it took Conorado to call out the names, they were at attention in front of him.

Captain Conorado held up the sheaf of orders and began reading from the top page. " 'Know ye all men, that placing special trust and confidence . . .' " He read from the Marine promotion warrant, a text that hadn't changed its wording in centuries. All twenty men standing in front of him had been holding positions higher than their ranks. Each one was being promoted to the rank the table of organization specified for his position.

Conorado turned his head to the commander of the transportation detachment. "Lieutenant Drabek, do your honors, sir."

"Aye aye. With pleasure, sir." The transportation commander accepted the promotion warrants for his men from Conorado, and he and his top NCO, the company's gunnery sergeant, handed each of their five newly promoted men his promotion warrant and pinned the new rank insignia on his collar.

When they finished, Conorado said, "First Sergeant Myer."

"Aye aye, sir." Myer and the captain stepped to the first man in line.

"Sergeant Eagle's Cry, congratulations," Conorado said, shaking his hand and giving him the warrant.

"Thank you, sir," Eagle's Cry said, barely containing his grin.

Myer pulled a pair of sergeant's chevrons out of a pocket and handed one to Conorado. Together, they removed the corporal's stripes from Eagle's Cry's collars and pinned on the new insignia.

When Conorado stepped on to Kelly, who was the next man in line, Myer leaned close to whisper to Eagle's Cry, "I'll see you later, when there aren't any officers around."

Eagle's Cry grimaced and said, "Not if I see you first, Top."

Myer chuckled and moved to Kelly.

When a Marine was promoted, for a day or two every Marine of equal or greater rank got to hit him on the shoulder, once for each stripe of his new rank. So, every newly promoted enlisted Marine had sore arms for a while. No one was allowed to hit hard enough to cause injury. But if that should happen, the Marines had another custom that dealt with anyone who hit too hard.

* * *

Once the newly promoted Marines had been congratulated by their commanders, received their warrants, and were wearing their new stripes, Captain Conorado had one more piece of business for everybody before planetfall.

"I'm sure First Sergeant Myer told you the rumor that at least some of the warring factions on Elneal have energy weapons. I want to emphasize the fact that it is only a rumor, there is no verification. All the fighting, to our knowledge, has been done with projectile weapons and chemical reaction explosives. Our shields give us significant protection from blasters and other energy weapons, but as far as a flying piece of metal is concerned, a shield is just another piece of air. A shield does absolutely nothing to stop, deflect, or slow down a bullet or chunk of shrapnel. So we'll be wearing body armor in the event that someone down there hasn't gotten the word and wants to tangle with us. Unfortunately, our orders came so suddenly and we had so little time to prepare before embarking that battalion was only able to pack enough body armor in our landing load for a reinforced platoon.

"Th—make that *first* platoon, and a section from the assault platoon, will be issued the armor and go planetside on the first wave." He'd wanted to send third platoon, but with something wrong between Bass and Baccacio, he decided not to send them into a touchy situation until the problem was cleared up. "Top Myer and I will be with the first wave. Lieutenant Humphrey and Gunny Thatcher will bring down the rest of the company once we've secured the landing zone. I'm sorry there isn't enough armor for anyone in transportation to have any but, at least at first, you'll be inside your vehicles most of the time and that'll give you some protection from any projectiles that might come our way.

"In case anybody's wondering, the Top and I don't get armor either. Ensign Kracar, Staff Sergeant DaCosta, you will issue the armor to your platoon and the assault section in reverse order of rank. If there's not enough to go around, and I'm not sure there is, you go as bare as I do.

"Are there any questions?"

"Sir, when do the rest of the men get armor?" Gunny Thatcher asked. He knew the answer, but he knew the men didn't and were probably wondering.

"Good question, Gunny. Sorry, I should have said this without prompting. The rest of our load, including enough body armor for everybody, will arrive with the advance command unit, which should be in about three days, depending on where they come out of hyperspace."

He looked around the room. "Anything else?" There were no other questions. "All right then, when you're dismissed, squad leaders, see to it that your men are ready for planetfall. Officers and staff NCOs to the ward room." He gave the Marines of his reinforced company a last look, then turned and left through the galley.

"Com-PANY!" Myer shouted, then bit his tongue. No matter how much he wanted to call the company to attention, there wasn't enough room in the crew's mess.

After what felt like an interminable wait, a voice boomed over the ship's intercom system, "Commander, Landing Force, prepare the landing force for landing."

Everyone, even those slated to land later, checked their gear to make sure everything was ready. The platoon sergeant of first platoon and the section chief of the assault section joining first platoon in the first wave issued their squad leaders the batteries for their squads' weapons. Out of deference to Commander Kahunii's concerns, the squad leaders wouldn't issue the batteries to their men until they were aboard the Dragons, where the men would load their weapons before launch—the ride to planetside would be too rough for them to be able to load before the Dragons stopped in New Obbia. The men of the first wave lined up and, on order, made their way quickly to the cargo hold the Essays were attached to.

Moments later a whoosh was heard throughout the ship as the Essays were launched. An hour later a ship's mate led the rest of the company to the hold, where they boarded the Dragons already aboard the Essays, which had returned for the second wave. Twenty minutes later second and third platoons surged out of the Dragons into the main square of New Obbia, the capital city of Elneal, and fell into the parade-ground formation their NCOs called for.

New Obbia wasn't much as cities went. It was even less as a planetary capital. The great majority of its million inhabitants were about equally divided between broken-spirited refugees from the wilderness and similarly dispirited immigrants who wished nothing more for themselves than passage off that forsaken world. The city reflected its inhabitants. Few buildings rose more than two stories, and nearly all looked in need of repair—certainly in need of painting and cleaning. The rubble that littered the streets wasn't the leavings of people who had so much they could afford to waste it; it was the detritus of a decaying infrastructure. There was little in the way of goods in the windows of the shops, the clothing of most of the people in evidence was the gray of too many washings, and the people wearing those garments seemed just as gray.

Only the managers of Consolidated Enterprises and the higher reaches of government bureaucrats looked less worn than their city. But they never walked its streets; they sped past in limousines with darkened windows on their way from well-appointed modern office buildings to luxurious living quarters. When visiting the mines, they flew; when they relaxed, they flew to one of the well-guarded resort spas established for their exclusive use in the uninhabited regions of the planet.

The two-acre city square on which the Marines formed up was paved with cracked and pitted flagstones laid on an unevenly packed foundation. A thin line of scraggly trees bordered the square, but wide gaps exposed the brooding entrances to the official buildings that surrounded it. The few benches arrayed in a smaller rectangle within the square of trees were unoccupied.

Still, Dean looked around in awe of the undistinguished burg. In the first twenty-three years of his life, he'd never gone farther from New Rochester than New Columbia District. This was the third foreign planet he'd set foot on in less than a year.

McNeal looked around and spat on the ground. New Obbia looked entirely too much like what he'd wanted to escape when he enlisted in the Marines.

"Living here must be worse than going through Boot Camp," Claypoole said softly. "And I thought Arsenault was the asshole of Human Space."

Chan shook his head. "Reminds me of Cross and Thorn. Whoever's in charge here doesn't care about the physical well-being of the people."

"That's enough chatter in the ranks," Sergeant Hyakowa said. They all stopped talking.

At that moment, Captain Conorado and First Sergeant Myer, accompanied by three well-dressed civilians and a Confederation Navy Admiral, came out of the four-story building the formation faced.

"Comp-ANY, a-ten-HUT!" Gunny Thatcher bellowed.

The click of heels coming together and thuds of blaster butts snapping to the ground echoed hollowly through the square. Thatcher timed his about-face to coincide with the arrival of Conorado and the others. His hand snapped up in a salute. "Company L and attachments, all present or accounted for, sir."

The company commander smartly returned his salute. "Thank you, Company Gunnery Sergeant. You may take your place."

Thatcher took a sharp step backward, then turned equally sharply to his right and marched to his parade position parallel to the front row of the formation.

Conorado took a step forward to stand in the same spot Thatcher had and stood at attention. "Company L and attachments," he said in a voice loud enough to clearly be heard throughout the square, "first platoon and the assault section that came with it in the first wave have already been briefed on the current situation and are in security positions around this part of the city. Here to address you are Fleet Admiral P'Marc Willis, the highest-ranking representative of the Confederation on Elneal; Confederation Consul Jardinier Dozois; and Planetary President, the Honorable Mr. Kismayu Merka." He turned to his right. "Admiral."

The navy officer stepped forward. "Thank you, Captain," he said. He faced the company and began, "I can't tell you how glad I am to see a reinforced company of Marines here. I'm sure the Marines of the provisional FIST I assembled from the ship's complements of my fleet are as glad to have you here as I am. Now they can begin to return to their regular duties." He paused briefly and pretended he didn't notice the soft wave of snickering that swept through Company L at his mention of the ship's Marines. "As I'm sure you are well aware, the situation on Elneal has gone beyond mere desperation.

People are dying of starvation all over the world. There have been repeated massacres by hungry people trying to seize food from other hungry people. Now, after months of difficult negotiation, the fighters have agreed to put down their arms and put their conflicts behind them so that people can be fed."

Three things then happened in such rapid succession they seemed to happen almost simultaneously. First came the sound of explosions, muffled by distance. Almost instantly, a navy petty officer raced out of the government building. A shrill whistle preceded a puff of gray smoke that erupted in a corner of the square before the petty officer reached the Admiral, and chunks of rock and metal flew about and clattered to the flagstones.

As experienced as many of the Marines were, it was a second or two before any of them understood that this strange noise was a mortar explosion.

"Into the Dragons," Conorado shouted as soon as he realized what was happening. "Those are chemical explosives!"

CHAPTER
EIGHTEEN

Conorado unceremoniously grabbed both Admiral Willis and President Merka by their upper arms. He shoved one at First Sergeant Myer and the other at Gunny Thatcher. "Get them inside," he snapped. He looked around for Consul Dozois and saw that the diplomat was already sprinting for the safety of the government building. Only then did Conorado race back into the government building himself, to the command center he'd hastily set up in a room of Admiral Willis's suite, near the entrance of the building. Still in the square, Lieutenant Humphrey oversaw the loading of the Dragons before following. From his vehicle, Staff Sergeant Drabek, of the transportation platoon, ordered the ten armored vehicles into positions affording them some protection from the incoming mortar rounds while covering all the approaches to the square. Three mortar rounds exploded in the square. The Marines in the Dragons waited tensely for more, which didn't come, and for their company commander to issue further orders.

Inside the command center three flat-screens hung on the walls. Only one, the largest, was lit. It showed a picture of the city center projected from the string-of-pearls satellites. Eight points were marked in green in a tight circle around the blue point that indicated the command center. Two of the green points, one to the southeast and one to the west, had red splotches near them.

"Bring in the view," Conorado ordered. The scale of the map on the screen immediately changed so that the circle of green reached almost to the edges. He looked at the view and shook his head. Buildings were in the way. From its angle of view, the satellite couldn't pick up enough detail of what was happening on the streets.

The Marine captain didn't even glance at the navy admiral before beginning his intelligence, assessment, planning, and action sequence. Admiral Willis, for his part, may have been the senior man present, but he knew when to defer to the expertise of others and stood quietly out of the way, regathering his dignity after being hustled out of the square.

"What are you getting from your UAVs, Cowboy?"

"Cowboy" Bill Flett, the company's unmanned aerial vehicle chief, sat with his head encased in a virtual reality helmet and his hands and feet on the controls of his remote-controlled reconnaissance drone. On the other side of the room Corporal "Speed" MacLeash, the company's other UAV man, was operating another recon drone.

"OP Delta is under attack by unidentified people inside two facing buildings," Flett answered. Observation Point D, OP Delta, was represented on the map by the green spot to the southeast. The eight OPs, located at a distance of three blocks from the square, were each manned by three Marines from first platoon. The assault section that came down with them in the first wave was on building tops immediately around the square.

"Any idea how many attackers, or how they're armed?"

"They're using projectile weapons, Skipper, I can see

that much. There might be a reinforced squad, it's hard to tell. I'm looking for the mortar."

"Find it." Conorado turned his attention to the other UAV man. "What do you have, MacLeash?"

"OP Golf is under assault. I see about two squads maneuvering through the street toward them." He paused, wondering if he should continue, then added, "You're not going to believe this, sir, but they're wearing skirts."

"What? Golf is being attacked by women?"

"Nossir, not unless the women here have hairy faces. It's men with beards, but they're wearing skirts and blouses."

"Skirts. Right." Conorado concluded they were probably Bos Kashi. The Siad wore robes MacLeash would have described as "dresses." A corner of his mouth twitched as he realized the briefings he and Myer gave the Marines on board the *Gordon* hadn't included enough ethnic information on the inhabitants of Elneal. MacLeash had one small unit under observation. Conorado wondered if one of the other warrior tribes was also in the city. Was one of those groups attacking Delta, or were they ready to attack elsewhere in the city? And who was on the mortar?

"Do you see anybody on rooftops?"

Both reconnaissance men answered in the negative.

"Do you see anybody else?"

"Not in the patterns we've been flying," Flett answered. Inside his helmet, he was able to switch points of view between the UAV he controlled and the one MacLeash was flying, which he did frequently enough to be on top of what his assistant was observing.

"Radio," Conorado said.

"OP Delta reports no casualties," replied the company's senior communications man, Corporal Escarpo. "They think they took out two of the men with projectile weapons, and fire has slackened. OP Golf reports they've got their attackers pinned down and unable to return fire. No other OPs report any hostile activity."

Conorado nodded to himself. These attacks on the two observation points could be isolated actions undertaken by a few Bos Kashi who wanted to demonstrate their lack of fear of the Marines before laying down their arms. It didn't have to mean any real resistance was going on, but making a wrong assumption could be disastrous. He needed more information.

"Get me third platoon's command unit," he told Escarpo, and put his helmet on. "And send them a map."

The communications man touched several buttons on his radio.

Almost immediately Conorado heard Lance Corporal "Moose" Dupont, third platoon's communications man, in his earphones acknowledging the call.

"Three Four," Conorado said—he almost said "Three Actual," but remembered in time that Bass was no longer the platoon commander, "this is Six Actual. Do you see the map yet?"

There was a brief hesitation before Bass answered, "I've got it."

Conorado imagined Ensign Baccacio handing over the commander's locator, and knew he'd have to explain to him why he was giving his orders to the platoon sergeant instead of to the officer in charge. But that could wait. He also knew he should be giving these orders to Ensign Baccacio, but he wanted an experienced man in command of the situation. Too much, including the lives of his men, depended on the man in charge. He leaned over Escarpo's shoulder and tapped a few keys on the pad. "Your position is marked in blue. OP Golf is green. The red-speckled area west of Golf is approximately two squads of Bos Kashi with projectile weapons. They are pinned down. Take your platoon and round them up.

Recon Two will fly for you. I want at least one live prisoner. Any questions?"

"They have projectile weapons, and we don't have body armor," Bass replied.

"You're in armored vehicles."

"On our way, sir."

Conorado flicked off his radio and glanced at MacLeash to make sure he got the message to fly reconnaissance for third platoon. "Recon, project," he said. The two smaller wall screens blinked on, slowing the view from the two UAVs. Recon One, being flown by Flett, was well above the city, flying a quartering pattern in the direction the mortar rounds had come from. Recon Two gave a clear picture of the street where OP Golf was fighting. The two squads of Bos Kashi had good cover from their front, but most of the fighters were fully exposed to their rear.

"Do you see what I do, Charlie?" Conorado asked into his radio.

"That's an affirmative, Skipper," Bass replied. "We can walk right up on them. Just make sure Golf knows we're on our way."

"Sir," Escarpo interrupted before Conorado could acknowledge Bass's request. "Delta reports heavier fire from the buildings and requests suppressive fire."

Conorado looked at Willis for the first time since entering the command post. "Sir, how hard do we have to try to avoid damaging the buildings?"

There was a cease-fire in effect, and someone had violated it. Because of the cease-fire, the Marines came in unequipped for all-out combat; they were peacekeepers who were attacked. More, Admiral Willis had seen the carnage the Bos Kashi and others had inflicted on innocent civilians. As far as he was concerned, they were vermin to be disposed of as quickly as possible. He didn't have to think about it before saying, "The Negev Protocol is authorized, Captain." He then looked toward an apparently blank stretch of wall and added in a strong, clear voice, "For the record, I am P'Marc Willis, Fleet Admiral of the Confederation Navy. I hereby authorize the Marines on Elneal to put into effect the Negev Protocol." The microphone concealed in the wall dutifully recorded the Admiral's statement.

Twenty years earlier, the Marines had a peacekeeping mission on Alhambra. A squad came under heavy fire from a large number of men in a village in the Negev district. The squad leader, seeing that his men were severely outnumbered and in extreme danger, called in an air strike, which leveled the village. Two hundred civilians were killed, along with every man in the unit that had fired on the Marines. The Marine brigadier in command of the mission immediately backed up the squad leader's decision and announced that any further attacks on Marines would be met with overwhelming and devastating force. No one fired on a Marine for the remaining four standard months of the mission—and no villagers harbored armed men who wanted to resist the peacekeepers. Such a strong response became known as the "Negev Protocol." There was no clear policy on when the protocol should be used. It was left up to the commander on the scene to determine if his forces were in danger of unprovoked attack and if massive retaliation was appropriate.

Admiral Willis thought it was appropriate in these circumstances. Captain Conorado unhesitatingly agreed—those were his men out there with their lives in danger.

Conorado activated the all-hands circuit in his helmet radio. "All hands, now hear this," he said. "This is Captain Conorado, commander of Company L, 34th FIST." He used his name and position to make it absolutely clear

to everyone who was speaking. "Until further notice, the
Negev Protocol is in effect. If anyone shoots at you, or
threatens you, you are authorized to use all necessary
lethal and destructive force to stop whatever threat you
are faced with. That is all." Then he turned on the circuit
to the assault platoon headquarters unit and ordered, "Get
a section to where it can support Delta. Knock down as
many buildings as you have to to convince whoever's
shooting at those Marines that it's a bad idea."

From the instant Bass realized Conorado was leaving
him in command of the platoon, he carefully avoided
looking at Baccacio. He could imagine what was going
through the young officer's mind. When he got a moment,
he'd think of a way of explaining to the ensign that this
was a good training opportunity, but in the meantime he
had a strike to plan and execute. Bass spent a few seconds examining the map on the locator. Both his position
and OP Golf's were precisely marked—where the Bos
Kashi were located was more generally indicated. As he
moved forward to the crew chief's station he took stock
of who was in the Dragon. He had his own first squad
and one assault gun team, along with half a squad from
second platoon.

The crew chief was examining his own map of the
area, which showed not only the same positions that were
marked on Bass's map, but all the vehicles of his platoon.

"How does this look to you?" Bass asked, tracing a
route that would bring the two armored vehicles to less
than a block behind the pinned-down Bos Kashi.

"If we do it this way," the crew chief traced two lines
on his map display, "we get them caught in a three-way
cross fire, and neither of my vehicles blocks the other."

Bass thought about the suggestion for a second or two
and saw it would take only half a minute longer for them

to arrive at the two-way positions. He clapped the crew chief on the shoulder. "Let's do it." If they didn't run into anyone else along the way, it would be fairly easy.

The crew chief gave his driver a hand signal and spoke into his radio. The two Dragons carrying third platoon and part of second roared out of the square at high speed.

Bass glanced at the crew chief's map to get the designations of the two vehicles and flicked on his radio. "Foxtrot Five is going to November Twenty-seven," he said, reading off the map coordinates of his vehicle's destination, "and Foxtrot Six is going to Oscar Twenty-eight." He pressed the button on the locator that sent the map image to the Heads Up Display in the squad leaders' helmets. "When we get where we are going, third platoon will dismount and take positions on line facing the Bos Kashi. The members of second platoon who are with us will dismount and take defensive positions facing the rear, and will be the reserve. When we are in position, I will hail the Bos Kashi and demand surrender. We are here to capture them, not kill them. Nobody fire until I give the word, or unless fired upon. Questions?" There weren't any. Bass didn't turn off the HUD transmission; his squad leaders could cancel it individually when they had seen enough to know where they were going and what they'd do once they got there.

Baccacio had come up next to Bass as he was transmitting, and the platoon sergeant now looked at him.

"Just like an immediate reaction drill," Bass said. "Except lives are on the line."

Baccacio's jaw was locked too tightly to speak. He nodded curtly.

It took less than two minutes for the two Dragons to get into position to dismount their passengers, but that was long enough for Conorado to come back on the radio with his all-hands message.

"Negev," Baccacio said, a skull-like grin splitting his face. "You don't hail them, Bass. We get in position and fry them."

Bass gave Baccacio a steady look. "The Skipper wants a prisoner. We hail first."

"Negev, Bass," Baccacio repeated. "He didn't say anything about prisoners this time. He said Negev. We fry them."

Bass kept his eyes fixed on the ensign's as he flicked on the company command circuit. "Question for Six Actual, this is Three Four. Do you still want a prisoner?"

Conorado's voice came back immediately. "Capture all of them if you can, but don't hesitate to kill as many of them as you have to. I want at least one prisoner. I say again, I want at least one prisoner."

"I hail them," Bass said after signing off.

Baccacio glared at him.

The Marines within hearing studiously avoided looking at them.

The chemical reaction explosions from the gunfire the Bos Kashi were directing toward the Marine observation post that had them pinned down, combined with the crackling of shattered masonry from the Marines' blasters, kept them from noticing the noise of the approaching Dragons, so the vehicles were able to get as close as Bass wanted. When Foxtrot Six radioed that it was in position, Bass gave the order to dismount. "Squad leaders, you know what to do," he added.

The squad leaders did know, and in fifteen seconds the men of third platoon were under cover and deployed, facing the Bos Kashi who were still pinned down by OP Golf's fire.

As soon as Bass assured himself that his men were in position, he filled his lungs and bellowed, "Bos Kashi, you are surrounded by Confederation Marines. Surrender and you will live."

"We are Bos Kashi," shouted back a defiant voice. "We do not surrender. We kill!" More gunfire erupted from the Bos Kashi, but Bass's voice had echoed off the walls, so they couldn't tell where he was and their bullets went wild. Bass was about to order one fire team in each position to return fire when more gunfire broke out behind his other unit, and he heard Eagle's Cry over the radio:

"We're being hit from the rear by a force of unknown size. I am redeploying to face it."

CHAPTER
NINETEEN

"Kerr, can you move?" Eagle's Cry asked his first fire team leader as soon as he finished his report.

"I think so," Kerr answered, but he didn't sound certain. He'd faced projectile weapons before, but this was the first time he'd faced lead bullets without wearing body armor. "They don't seem to be hitting near us." They weren't. The Bos Kashi attacking from the rear were concentrating their fire on the rear guard from second platoon.

"Stay low," Eagle's Cry told him. "Get to that building to your left, then go around it and see if you can flank them. We've got Recon Two. I'll let you know as soon as I hear anything from them."

"On our way." Kerr signaled to his men, Schultz and McNeal, and started crawling on his belly toward the house to his side.

McNeal looked across the rubble-littered pavement toward the building they were headed for, saw it was only twenty meters distant, then flattened himself on the ground and began following Schultz's inchworming body. No sooner had he started than a bullet cracked over his head. He'd thought he was already flat on the ground, but the nearness of the projectile made him somehow hug it even closer. He crawled and crawled, scraping his face so close to the pavement he thought he might never have to shave again. He pressed his chest, belly, and thighs so tightly to the ground he was certain he was fraying the material of his uniform right off his body.

When he felt that he'd gone far enough to be well behind the building, he raised his head to look for Kerr and Schultz. Kerr was on his feet, hunched over, looking around the building's far corner. Schultz was a few meters behind the fire team leader, on one knee, looking back and grinning at McNeal.

Schultz pumped one fist up and down in the "Hurry up" signal. "You taking a nap back there, McNeal?" he called. "Get a move on."

McNeal groaned—he had covered only half the distance.

The crack and sizzle of Marine blasters was louder than the bang and zing of Bos Kashi bullets, building blocks cracking thunderously from being hit by Marine fire almost completely drowning out the whine of projectile ricochets. The sounds told McNeal that the Marines had the upper hand in this firefight. They had to, didn't they? Didn't they? Still, he felt more naked than he ever had in his life. Without thinking about what he was doing, he surged to his feet and reached the cover of the building in three rapid strides.

Still grinning, Schultz shook his head. "Good going, bright eyes. You just told them where we are."

Hyperventilating as he was, McNeal barely heard Schultz's words, but still managed to understand them. "But . . ." he gasped, "how did you . . . ?"

"Don't worry about it," Schultz said. "You get caught in the open like that another time or two, you'll learn how to crawl fast." He turned his head toward Kerr and added in a lower voice, "If you live that long."

Kerr pulled back from the corner of the building and faced his men. He studied McNeal a brief moment, then decided the young man's expression indicated anxiety and not panic. He was sure McNeal could work his way through the anxiety, and that it wouldn't affect his ability to function. He gestured for McNeal and Schultz to come closer. Quickly, he shifted pebbles, chunks of masonry, and bits of wood to make a three-dimensional map.

"This is OP Golf." He plunked down a broken brick. "These are the buildings lining the street, running away from it." He laid out two parallel strips of scrap wood with one end at the brick. "This is first squad." A scattering of pebbles went behind the far end of one of the wood scraps. "This is second squad." Another scattering of pebbles behind the far end of the other scrap. "This is our building." He touched the building they huddled against with one hand while the other placed a small chunk of masonry to the left rear of the second-squad pebbles. "Here's the fire team from second platoon." Three pebbles went into place farther from the strips of wood indicating the street; another scrap placed at an acute angle across their front showed the far side of the street the second platoon fire team was blocking; a chunk of masonry to the right front of the one indicating the building they were behind showed the next building over. "I couldn't see anything around the building, but Recon Two reports there's a squad of Bos Kashi here." He scattered a few pebbles just beyond the second masonry chunk. "Recon Two doesn't see anyone else, so we go here." He used his finger to line a route behind their building and the next one to their right front. "Is that clear?"

Schultz leaned back from where he squatted to look beyond the building. He saw the next building, and how to get from here to there. "Got it," he said.

McNeal also looked, and nodded.

"They have us outnumbered two or three to one," Kerr continued without expression. "They have projectile weapons. We do not have body armor. No prisoners; we fry them. They are dead. Do you understand?" He looked directly at McNeal as he spoke.

McNeal wanted to answer yes, but his throat was too dry. He tried to swallow so he could speak, but his mouth was even drier than his throat. He simply nodded. His hands gripped his blaster so tightly his knuckles turned white.

"Let's go." Kerr stood bent at the hips and sprinted toward the far end of the next building. Schultz gave McNeal a push to get him going and brought up the rear.

The Bos Kashi gunfire was much louder and clearer here. Kerr had Schultz and McNeal stay in place while he slithered farther to precisely locate their target. He was back in a minute.

"They're right over there," Kerr said, pointing. "There's eight of them. We can get behind that wall," he indicated a low, masonry wall with breaks in it, "and have a clear view of their flank. Hammer, you see the break in the middle of the wall?" Schultz nodded. "That's where I want you. McNeal, you see the break five meters to the right of that break?" McNeal looked at the wall and nodded also. "That's your position. I've got the next break. When we get in position, the closest one of them will be less than twenty-five meters away. They're bunched up in a short line. Hammer, you start with the near one and work your way to the middle. McNeal, you start in the middle and hit anything that moves. I'll start at the far end of their line. When we open up on them, it'll be like a bomb hitting in their middle. They should all go down in a hurry. Nobody shoots until I do. Any questions?"

"What are we waiting for?" Schultz asked.

McNeal merely shook his head.

"Me first, Hammer, and McNeal. Let's go." Kerr lowered himself to the ground and scrambled on elbows and knees. He reached the break in the middle of the wall in seconds and paused to make sure Schultz knew this was his position. Then he went five meters farther and placed McNeal, then moved on to his own position. He looked through the break in the wall and saw the Bos Kashi were still where they had been, then back to make sure his men were ready. Schultz was watching him for a signal to open fire. McNeal was sighting along his blaster toward the Bos Kashi. Kerr motioned to Schultz to take aim, then sighted in on his own first target.

McNeal had seen violence and death growing up on the streets of New Rochester. He'd seen death going through Boot Camp on Arsenault. But he'd never witnessed a killing, and had largely avoided the violence around him while he was growing up. The deaths on Arsenault were a suicide and an accident. This was the first time he'd ever set out to deliberately kill anyone, and the prospect made him tremble in horror. A weakness pervaded his body. His breath became rapid and shallow. His vision tunneled down until he could see nothing beyond the sights of his blaster and the hairy, fierce face of the man he stared at through them. It appeared to McNeal that the face was that of a man who had no fear, who had no respect for anyone but himself and his companions. A man who didn't know what mercy was and gave no thought to those weaker than himself.

Abruptly, McNeal's horror of killing was replaced by fear—fear of the man he was about to kill. What if he missed? What if his first shot didn't kill that man? Surely, the Bos Kashi would turn on him and kill him, and his companions would slaughter Kerr and Schultz. He had to do this right, he had to, had to had to. And when this first man was dead, he had to kill the next man and the next man and the man after that. If he didn't, he would be dead himself, and Kerr and Schultz would be dead and it would be all his fault.

McNeal was so tightly engrossed in these thoughts that he almost missed Kerr's command through his helmet comm unit, "Fire!" It seemed to him that a long time passed between the order to open up and the time he could order his own fingers to press the firing lever and send a bolt of deadly plasma toward his target, but actually, he fired before the bolts from Kerr and Schultz reached their targets.

Instantly, he shifted his aim to the next man and blasted him, and then the next one and the next one and the one after that, and he kept firing and looking for more targets until suddenly his blaster was yanked out of his hands. He twisted his body, rolled away from his firing position, and reached for his knife as he leaped to his feet. He expected to see a bearded face, a skirted man attacking, and was instantly ready to defend himself.

"They're all fried, McNeal, you can stop now, there's no one left to shoot at."

It took a moment for McNeal's eyes to focus on the source of the voice, but its familiarity made him hesitate long enough to see it was Kerr. Then he collapsed against the wall and slid down it, to sag into a sitting position, wide-eyed and panting, feeling too weak to move. Did they do it? Did they actually do it? He was still alive—he thought he was, he was pretty sure he was. Did he do well enough that the Bos Kashi weren't able to kill any of the Marines? Kerr was standing there and didn't seem to be bleeding, so he was all right. But what about Schultz? Had his slowness in responding to the command to fire given the Bos Kashi enough time to kill Schultz? McNeal jerked and twisted to his right, terrified that he would see Schultz's broken, bleeding body.

"We're so good." Schultz stood casually, looking over the carnage. "They were fried before they knew we were here." He blew on the fingernails of his left hand and buffed them on his shirt. His eyes narrowed to slits and he said harshly, "Nobody messes with Marines. Nobody." He spun and started walking back toward the rest of the squad.

Kerr held a hand out to help McNeal to his feet. "You did good, Marine."

McNeal accepted the hand. Standing, he took several slow, deep breaths to calm himself in the quiet sunlight. Suddenly, he cocked his head, listening. He didn't hear any gunfire, no blasters going off.

"It's over," Kerr told him. "A whole platoon of Bos Kashi is either dead or captured."

While McNeal was getting his baptism of fire in the flanking maneuver against the Bos Kashi attacking the rest of second squad, Dean and Claypoole got theirs against the Bos pinned down by OP Golf. They too were outnumbered by the Bos Kashi, but not by nearly three to one, and there were many more Marines surrounding them. They hadn't felt the weight of the fight as heavily as McNeal had, and they stopped firing on their own when their part of the small battle was over. Still, they'd all fought in their first action, acquitted themselves well, and survived.

Then the shooting was over and Doc Hough, the medical corpsman assigned to the platoon, was doing his best to save the one wounded Bos Kashi who survived the one-sided fight.

Chan stood and looked over the carnage. "Claypoole, Dean," he said, seeing their pale faces. "It was a good fight and you did good." He looked back at the slaughtered Bos Kashi and softly added, "Anytime you survive a firefight and the bad guys don't, it's a good fight and you did good."

Staff Sergeant Bass, supervising collection of the bodies and weapons a few feet away, was close enough to overhear. He knew better. He'd been in fights where he survived and the bad guys didn't that he couldn't call good fights and say he'd done good. His feeling was that a leader does good only when he brings all of his own men back, alive and uninjured. Casually, he took in Chan and the others. Dean and Claypoole were looking intently at Chan, absorbing his words. What the lance corporal had to say seemed to hearten them. Bass nodded to himself and said nothing as he turned back to the killing zone and returned his attention to policing the bodies and weapons. Chan wasn't quite right in what he'd said, but Bass knew that anything that helped a man make it through the aftermath of killing was right and good.

Elsewhere, at the same time third platoon went to the aid of OP Golf, a section from the assault platoon leveled two buildings in support of OP Delta. So far as anyone could tell, all the Bos Kashi in them were killed. Flett and MacLeash located the mortar team that had opened the fighting, and a navy Raptor attached to Admiral Willis's provisional FIST struck from the sky, killing it and its crew.

On the outskirts of the city a platoon from the provisional FIST that consisted of technicians and clerks was attacked by a company-size group of Bos Kashi. The "cooks and bakers" platoon handled them easily and suffered only three casualties of their own—one dead—in breaking the attack. The fleeing Bos Kashi were caught in the open by a flight of Raptors and wiped out. Less than a half hour after its main body landed on Elneal, elements of Company L had maneuvered, faced, and killed more than thirty enemy soldiers while suffering no casualties of their own. They also took one prisoner, whose wounds might even let him live long to tell the Marines why the Bos Kashi had made the suicidal attack.

Meanwhile, Bos Kashi attacks in other settlements and villages wrought greater damage, since the Confederation Marines weren't there. But when Company L and the provisional FIST beat off the attack on New Obbia, these attackers melted into the countryside. Soon after, word came to President Merka from Shabeli the Magnificent, who said the attacks had been made by renegades— renegades who were being dealt with by tribal authorities. It was time for peace, Shabeli said. Time to heal wounds and distribute food to all who needed it.

A few days later the rest of the 34th FIST made planetfall. Company L headed into the wilderness as soon as Captain Conorado was able to make his report to Commander Van Winkle.

CHAPTER
TWENTY

The village of Tulak Yar lay in the Bekhar River valley 140 kilometers east of New Obbia. The river was now as high as it got, except during floodtime. When Tulak Yar had been founded 300 years before, the settlers built their homes on the bluffs high above the river so they wouldn't be swept away in the spring floods. The silt from the floodwaters was what made the Bekhar River valley one of the richest farming lands on Elneal.

At first nobody noticed the distant low droning that slowly grew louder and closer. Eventually a disconsolate group of starving villagers gathered along the narrow roadway that wound its way up the steep slope from the floodplain. They glanced up briefly with disinterest as a flight of Raptors drifted high overhead. A frail old man, a gnarled walking stick grasped tightly in one bony fist, pushed his way to the front of the small crowd that gathered by the roadside. Shielding his eyes from the glaring sunlight with one hand, he peered intensely at the approaching vehicles. A huge pillar of dust floated in the silent, stifling air at their passing, stirring dimly remembered legends and folk tales brought to this world by his ancestors, a pious people who had always lived in desert places, where they felt very close to their gods. Something else stirred in the old man too, memories of long ago, when he was young and did great deeds.

"Achmed, your eyes are keen," the old man said to a skinny adolescent standing by his side, "tell me what you see down there."

"Many vehicles, Father," the young man answered. Everyone in the village referred to the old man as Father. As the eldest, best-educated, and most experienced man among the five hundred or so souls who populated Tulak Yar, he was looked upon as both a spiritual and temporal guide.

"I know that, you young fool," the old man snapped. "But what kind of vehicles, lad, what kind?"

Achmed was silent for a moment as he strained to make out details. "Some are trucks, the kind the city people use to carry goods. There are others of a kind I have never seen." He paused, peering closer at the approaching vehicles, trying to decipher the fluttering he could see above the lead vehicle. "One is flying their flag, Father," he said shortly. "Their" flag was the green and gold banner of the Democratic Republic of Elneal, but the people of Tulak Yar owed their loyalty to whatever force was in command of their area at the moment, which just then was the Siad. The flag told the old man that in a few moments that would change again, if only for a while. Until recently, the Siad had left them in relative peace, tolerating the people of Tulak Yar because they provided goods and services needed by the clansmen— mostly crops, meat, and women.

"Stand easy, boy," the old man said, "I think it is help." At the mention of help, a murmur ran through the small crowd, and now everyone peered intensely at the approaching vehicles.

When the convoy reached the fork where a roadway split off from the highway along the bottom and climbed to Tulak Yar, several of the vehicles turned and began climbing while the others waited below.

* * *

The lead Dragon's front skirts lifted high over the roadbed where it flattened out at the top of the bluff, the armored vehicle blowing a storm of dirt and pebbles about. The driver saw there was no one in his path and hit the accelerator to speed to the far side of the village. A moment later four ground-effect trucks trundled over the final hump and roared into the village square, where they re-formed from in line to on line. A second Dragon brought up the rear. Instead of proceeding into the village, it spun around to face the way it had come, and dropped its ramp. A squad of Marines ran down the ramp and sprinted to the sides, alternating left and right, to take defensive positions overlooking the bluff and to the sides of the village, where they linked up with the twenty Marines who had done the same at the plateau side.

Another group of Marines and civilians dismounted the vehicle less rapidly and strode to the square. One, the obvious commander, watched the people as they slowly, painfully assembled. His face showed no expression when he saw how pitifully thin and bent they were, how the children stood about dull-eyed and unresponsive, swollen bellies protruding through their ragged clothing, making them look like tiny old men. After a moment he spoke, clear and loudly enough to be heard by everyone who was watching.

"Who is the headman here?"

"English!" the old man croaked, the long-unspoken tongue rusty in his mouth. "I am," he said, then had to clear his throat and say it again when the unfamiliar words stumbled on his tongue. He approached the Marines, and as he walked, a transformation began: His stride lengthened, his back stiffened, and the years seemed to melt away. Coming to attention before the small knot of Marines, he rendered a smart hand salute and announced in impeccable English, "Corporal Mas Fardeed, 5th Mechanized Infantry Battalion, McKenzie's Brigade, Second Division, Fifth Composite Corps, reporting, Captain!"

The Marines stared at the old man for a few moments and then Conorado returned his salute. "I'm Captain Conorado, commanding officer Company L, 34th FIST, Confederation Marines. We have brought food and medical supplies for this village. You are the headman?"

Mas Fardeed bowed. "I am indeed the headman of this poor village, Captain."

"Were you at the relief of Manning on Saint Brendan's in the First Silvasian War?" Bass, who was in the command group, asked, his voice touched with respect.

"Yes, Sergeant!"

"Jesu!" Top Myer whispered. To have been present at the relief of Manning was an honor for men of the twenty-fifth century comparable to having been at Agincourt or Seward's Ride around Fresno to warriors of earlier eras. The Marines stared at the old man in disbelief. They had all studied the details of that almost legendary campaign, and although it had been an army show, Brigadier Ran McKenzie was one of their heroes. He had fought his brigade through a thousand kilometers of enemy territory to relieve the garrison at Manning and break the siege. According to many historians, it had been the turning point in the First Silvasian War.

"Headman Mas Fardeed," Conorado said formally, "may I present Mr. France Savik of the Confederation Blue Crescent Relief Agency. He is here with food and medical aid for you."

One of the civilians stepped forward and bowed to the old man. "With your leave, headman," Savik said in a language that sounded to the Marines like someone gargling with gravel, but which was very close to the local dialect, "I will have my assistants construct a kitchen in the center of this square and begin feeding your people in less than half an hour."

Mas Fardeed returned the bow and answered, "You have my leave."

"If you have sick among you," Savik continued, "my medical personnel can have a clinic started even sooner."

While the kitchen was still being set up and the clinic was seeing its first patients, Conorado and Myer paid their final respects to Mas Fardeed and left. "We have other villages to bring aid to," Conorado explained to the headman. "But I am leaving a platoon of my men behind to protect you."

McNeal and Schultz were in a defensive position, lounging behind some rocks outside the northeast corner of Tulak Yar.

"Nothing's here," Schultz grumbled, his hands caressing his blaster. "Nobody out there." He scanned the barren landscape with practiced eyes. "We're wasting our time. We should be out chasing bandits instead of baby-sitting a bunch of farmers."

McNeal lay on his back with a forearm shading his closed eyes. He didn't need to keep watch; he knew Schultz was doing enough watching for both of them. "We don't 'baby-sit,' the bandits'll come in and steal the food and kill the relief workers. We ain't wasting our time."

Schultz snorted and turned his head to spit. "Company," he said.

McNeal spun into a prone position and put his blaster into his shoulder. His eyes darted from spot to spot around the barrens. It looked the same as it had the last time he looked. "Where?" he asked as he flipped down his infras.

Schultz snorted again. "Behind us. Kids."

McNeal looked back over his shoulder and flipped up

his infras. Three small children, so dirty, hollow-eyed, and emaciated he couldn't tell whether they were boys or girls except for one who wasn't wearing pants, stood a few meters away looking dully at the two Marines.

"Look at these kids!" he exclaimed. "Sweet Jesu, look at them. They look like they haven't eaten anything in a month."

Schultz made a noise. "They'd be dead if they hadn't eaten in that long."

McNeal sat up and groped in his pack.

"What are you doing?" Schultz asked.

"Feeding them," McNeal said. "We don't feed them, they die, and all our work here don't mean squat." He took out a packet of emergency ration bars, tore it open, and offered them to the children. None of them moved. McNeal opened the wrapper on one of the bars and mimed eating it. The boy without pants took a tentative step forward. McNeal gestured again. The eyes of the three children were now riveted on the bar, but they stood as though their feet were rooted to the ground. McNeal sighed and tossed the bar lightly so that it landed at the boy's feet.

"He takes a bite of that, he's gonna think you're trying to poison him," Schultz said dryly.

The bars were high-energy ration supplements that the Marines carried in the field in case they ran out of their regular rations. An adult could live off one bar a day, not well and perhaps not willingly, but it contained all the vitamins, fat, carbohydrates, and calories an active adult needed to sustain him during a twenty-four-hour period. They did not taste very good, but they could save your life in a pinch.

Flylike buzzers swarmed about the film of dried mucus that caked the boy's upper lip, but he was too apathetic to brush them away. Slowly, he bent over and picked up the emergency bar. He briefly looked at it, then raised his eyes again to McNeal. McNeal again mimed eating. The boy looked back to the bar, then slowly, uncertainly, he unwrapped it and took a small bite, then another, bigger one. The transformation was almost instantaneous, and afterward McNeal swore he could see the life come back into the boy's eyes, which suddenly went wide with the excitement of returning physical energy. He turned his head to the other children and chattered something that, despite his high, reedy voice, still sounded to the Marines like gargling with gravel. The other two piped something back, and were answered. The boy looked at McNeal again and lifted one hand as though saying, "My friends are hungry too." McNeal started to shake his head; he wanted them to come to him and take the bars from his hand, but then realized they probably were as frightened as Schultz had said and tossed the other two bars. But he didn't throw them as far and the children had to come closer than the other boy to pick them up. They skittered back to a safe distance before eating. Their faces lit up brightly as they ate.

"Come here," McNeal said.

"Give them time," Schultz said, and turned his back on the children to resume watching the barrens. He reached into his own pack for emergency bars and got a packet ready for when the children joined them.

McNeal sighed and turned to also watch. "Sad, what was done to them."

"You're good with kids," Schultz said. Despite his show of gruffness, he too was moved by the plight of the children. The two returned to watching the barrens. McNeal turned slowly at a light touch on his shoulder and looked up into the wide eyes of the pantless boy. The other two stood silently behind him.

The boy said something that McNeal guessed meant

thanks. "You're welcome," he said back. "Always glad to feed a hungry kid." Looking at the other two, he added, "Did you enjoy yours as well?"

One of them, he guessed a girl because her hair was longer, said something back.

"Glad to hear it."

Schultz turned to the children. "Still hungry?" He opened the packet of bars he'd set aside and held them out. The children grabbed them quickly and skittered out of reach to eat in safety.

They were back in a few moments, this time all three smiling and touching and talking. McNeal sat up and gently wiped the face of the pantless boy with a bandanna. "You're a handsome little fart, with some of that crud off your face," he said.

Just then they heard a thin shriek, and saw a woman running toward them, waving at the children to get away.

Schultz held up a hand to her. "It's okay, ma'am," he said calmly. "They aren't bothering us."

The children chattered at the woman and ran toward her. McNeal and Schultz couldn't understand them, but from their gestures and excited motions, it seemed they were telling her how the Marines had fed them and that they were good men, not to be feared. At first the woman didn't listen to them, instead clutching the children and trying to draw them away. But the children resisted and talked even more excitedly, and then she stopped and listened, questioned them, and finally looked at the Marines and spoke to them.

McNeal reached into his pack for another emergency bar and mimed eating it. "They're good kids. I fed them."

The woman's jaw worked at the miming of eating and she took a stumbling step forward.

"That's right, for you."

The pantless boy ran to McNeal, snatched the bar from

his hand, and ran back to thrust it into the woman's hand. She looked at it uncertainly, and the boy took it back, tore the wrapper off, and held it to her mouth. She took a small bite, her face lighting up as the energy coursed through her system, then sank to the ground, sobbing as she ate the rest of it.

McNeal started to get up, but Schultz put a restraining hand on him. "Leave her alone," he said. "She'll get over it on her own."

Reluctantly, McNeal stayed where he was. After a while the woman levered herself painfully to her feet and approached the Marines. Laying her thin hand on McNeal's shoulder, she spoke to him earnestly. Although he didn't understand the words, he realized she was saying thanks. The way the children gleefully clung to her, McNeal knew she was their mother. He and Schultz gave her several more of the energy bars and the bandanna.

"Whoo!" McNeal whooped after the woman led her son away. "That made me feel good."

With Captain Conorado gone, Ensign Baccacio and Staff Sergeant Bass established their command post inside an abandoned warehouse while the rest of the platoon prepared fighting positions that doubled as their living quarters. The next day they had to make new defensive positions several hundred meters away from the village in the surrounding hills, because the flocks of children who constantly swarmed about the Marines were too much of a distraction. But as the days passed, the men took great pleasure playing with the children when off duty, and everyone took pride in watching them change from pitiful, starving waifs into bouncing boys and girls.

But nobody was more pleased at the changes among the villagers of Tulak Yar than old Mas Fardeed, and he saw to it that his hut became an off-duty gathering place for the men of Company L, most of whom quickly developed a genuine fondness for the old soldier.

"I came back here after the war," he told a small gathering one evening. They were sitting around a warm fire in the kitchen. One of Mas Fardeed's daughters bustled about, making sure each Marine's earthen mug was kept filled with the old man's barley beer. "I was young and stupid. I thought I could do something about life here," he said bitterly. "We are worse than slaves, the way the Siad treat us. They keep us like we keep our sheep. I thought I could change that." He spit into the fire. The six Marines sitting about the hearth were respectfully silent.

"Give me one of those," he muttered, gesturing at McNeal's blaster, "and I could change a lot of things around here." The Marines nodded. "But the bureaucrats in New Obbia, they said, 'No reason to arm the peasants! We can protect them!' Ha! Those bastards, all they've ever done is cower in the cities and lick the privates of the mining executives! The guns went to the clans. Governments hate and fear citizens with guns, lads, that's a bitter lesson I've learned during my eighty-two winters. When men give up to their government the right to defend themselves, they give up their right to live as men. The Siad at least realize that."

The old man sighed and was silent for a moment. "Oh, I know," he continued, "the people of this village aren't warriors, and I am not the man I once was. Were we to stand up to the Siad, they would just cut us down. But we would die fighting and we would take some of them with us. How a man dies is as important as how he lives. Before you came here, we were going to die like our sheep."

Nobody wanted to comment on that sentiment. "What did you do, then?" Dean asked.

The old man shrugged. "I survived. We survived. We accommodated. The Siad are not fools; our crops and livestock are of great value to them. So they tolerated us and left us to live what little lives we have in this miserable place." He shook his head. "Until recently. Now, one day the crops will fail entirely and our sheep will all die, and then they will swarm down on this village and destroy it out of spite. Or that's what I thought, until you came here."

"We do what we can," Claypoole said lamely. Every man in L Company knew that the old man was right, and every man hoped and prayed they would not be pulled out of the village until the Siad and their allies had been dealt with. There was not a doubt in any man's mind that once the Marines were let loose on the clans, they would deal with them permanently, and every man looked forward to that day.

"You are proof that there is a God and that He loves us," Mas Fardeed told them, his voice strong and steady. "You are proof, too, that there is good in mankind. I pray that your leaders are as brave as you."

CHAPTER
TWENTY-ONE

Third platoon quickly settled into a set-your-time-piece-by-it routine in Tulak Yar. All the Marines on the perimeter stood careful watch during the last hours before dawn—the time when most people are in deepest sleep, the time hardest to stay awake, a favorite time for a sneak attack. Once the sun rose, those in most need of sleep slept, some of the others maintained a watch on the surrounding countryside, while others prepared for the arrival of the daily resupply hopper. At 10 hours, when the hopper dropped off its precious cargo, part of it was stored for distribution to the citizens of Tulak Yar and the immediately surrounding area, and the rest loaded into the Dragon that was left with the platoon. At 11 hours, it was delivered to one of the other villages within an hour's drive of the base with a squad along for security. At midday a fire team with a gun team went out into the foothills on a security patrol; it was gone anywhere from two to four hours. An awning was set up on the side of the Dragon when it returned from its run before 16 hours every day, and every day at 16 hours, Ensign Baccacio held an all-hands meeting in the shade of that awning. After the meeting, some members of the platoon returned to perimeter duty and the rest relaxed until nightfall, interrupted only by evening chow, when they went back on perimeter security for the night.

Staff Sergeant Bass wasn't terribly comfortable with the supply run leaving at 11 hours every day, but at least it never went in the same direction two days in a row. He had a serious problem, however, with the 16 hours all-hands meeting.

At the daily meeting, Ensign Baccacio gave his men a brief report on the progress of the relief effort on Elneal, in 34th FIST's area, on Company L's area, and on third platoon's sector. Concerning third platoon, the leader of the daily foot patrol into the hills gave his report on what his patrol had—or more usually, had not—seen. Doc Hough, the medical corpsman, reported on medical progress in Tulak Yar—there was enough illness, mostly malnutrition, that it was several days before he was able to go out with the Dragon to provide any kind of medical assistance to other villages. That was pretty much the extent of the goings-on, and Bass felt that most of the men could have done without it.

The second time the platoon commander called his 16 hours meeting, Bass said, "Mr. Baccacio, this is the same time we did this yesterday. We're in danger of fixing a schedule. Everybody's going to know that at sixteen hours we don't have anybody on the perimeter. Anybody who wants to attack us will do it when we're in this all-hands meeting."

"Staff Sergeant Bass," Baccacio replied, "having a schedule and sticking to it shows everybody that we are in command of the situation here. As for anybody's attacking, we are Marines. I don't believe anybody on this planet is dumb enough to attack a platoon of Confederation Marines. Not after what we did to the Bos Kashi in New Obbia."

"That was the Bos Kashi. The Siad are supposed to be much more powerful. This is territory claimed by the Siad."

"I don't care. If they're dumb enough to attack us, they deserve everything we'll do to them. We're having the meeting now."

The third day, Sergeants Hyakowa, Eagle's Cry, and Kelly found Bass when the ensign was nowhere around.

"What's that man trying to do, get us all killed?" Hyakowa asked.

"It's like a patrol never comes back on the same route it went out on," Eagle's Cry said. "You have a routine, you get killed."

"I talked to him," Bass answered. "So far he's not listening. But pretty soon I think he'll see there's no need for a daily meeting. Or maybe I'll get the point across to him."

"I think we should let him call his meeting and not show up," Kelly said.

"Belay that kind of talk, Hound," Bass snapped. "That's disobedience. It doesn't matter if you're right, no one has yet been hurt by these meetings. You don't show up, you get court-martialed. If nothing has happened because of the routine, it'll be tough to convince a court-martial board that you were right in deliberately disobeying a direct order."

The squad leaders grumbled, but none of them was willing to face a court-martial.

"Don't worry, it won't last," Bass reassured them. "The Skipper and the Top will be back tomorrow or the day after. If Mr. Baccacio is still holding us to a routine then, I'll kick it up to them." But Bass was worried; if he'd been an opposing commander, he would have taken advantage of the Marines' routine as quickly as possible.

Captain Conorado and First Sergeant Myer had come out during the first day of Ensign Baccacio's routine, when nobody yet knew it would become a routine. Then first platoon ran into distribution conflicts between the

Basque and Montanan settlers in Verde Hollow, which occupied the attention of the company's top men for several days. Then some of the suddenly sated Burmese settlers in Mogaung Gap overdid their eating and got sick, and Conorado and Myer had to go there with representatives of the Blue Crescent to convince the people that the food wasn't poisoned. What with one thing and another, it was a week before the Skipper and the Top made it back to Tulak Yar, by which time Charlie Bass was developing a mutinous state of mind. The stress of maintaining a routine in a potentially hostile area was wearing on everybody else in the platoon as well—except for Ensign Baccacio, who absolutely *knew* he was doing exactly the right thing, no matter what his ill-disciplined men thought.

It happened that Conorado and Myer arrived just in time for the daily all-hands, and Bass didn't have to say anything at all. The two senior men were accompanied by a fire team for security and by Corporal Doyle, the company's senior clerk.

Conorado stood under the awning attached to the Dragon and saw too many Marines in front of him. He turned and stood close to Baccacio so he could speak softly enough not to be heard by anyone but the young officer. "Who's on security? It looks like the whole platoon is here."

"The whole platoon is here, sir," Baccacio said in a slightly louder voice. Those close enough to hear tried as unobtrusively as possible to hear more. "Security's no problem. Nobody's interested in bothering these people now that we're here. Anyway, there's a couple goatherds and some kids acting as crow-chasers out there. They'll let us know if anybody's coming."

Conorado stared at the ensign for a few seconds, then looked past him to Bass. Bass was blandly looking at the men of his platoon, for all the world as though he had no idea of what was being said between the two officers.

"Some goatherds and crow-chasers," Conorado said. "That's what you're relying on for security."

"Yes, sir."

"Do you really believe that children will be able to give adequate warning?"

Baccacio blinked. Of course he did, and he said so.

"Put some Marines out there."

"But—"

"Do it."

Flushing, Baccacio turned to Bass. "Platoon Sergeant, put out three two-man security teams."

Bass looked at him for the first time since Conorado had begun talking to him. "Aye aye, sir," he said in a voice as bland as his expression. He looked back at the platoon. "Squad leaders, each squad put two men in security positions in your squad sector."

"Aye aye," Hyakowa replied for all three. In seconds, three two-man teams were sprinting for the village's outskirts. Everyone in the platoon felt a great sense of relief—except for Ensign Baccacio, who felt humiliated.

Finally, they got into the usual substance of the daily all-hands. Conorado reported to the men on what had been going on in the rest of the company's sector. He told of the problems between the Basques and Montanans of Verde Hollow in a way that almost made blood feuds sound funny, and got some laughs. His description of the solemn antics of the Shan headman at Mogaung Gap had them roaring. Then he got serious.

"There have been no incidents of violence involving Marines or anyone we're protecting since the Bos Kashi were wiped out in New Obbia. But—and this is an important but—neither has anyone come forward to turn in his arms. Satellite surveillance shows the Siad moving. While they seem to be congregating, they aren't doing it in any way that we can absolutely identify as threatening. So we don't quite know what to make of their movement. The Sons of Liberty have retired to their strongholds, though not all of the strongholds seem to be occupied. We think they've consolidated into fewer, stronger locations. Nobody knows what, if anything, that means. The Gaels have managed to vanish, and that's bothersome. But again, nobody knows what significance to attach to it.

"Since we moved into the countryside, a number of relief workers have decided to risk taking convoys to other villages, villages that don't have Marine protection. Most of them have made it with no incident. The few incidents have mostly been caused by clansmen robbing them of a portion of their food and medical supplies. Only once that we know of have raiders attacked a convoy and killed everyone and taken or destroyed everything.

"On the whole, everything is vastly improving throughout Elneal. In little more than a week, relief has reached more than ten percent of the population. The work is speeding up and the current estimate is that fully half the population will be saved within a month of when we began to move into the countryside, and the whole planet in a month and a half, or not much more." He was interrupted by cheers.

"We've done a marvelous job, but don't get too happy about it. It's going to take another month or longer to get to everybody. Remember, there's a planetwide famine. Tens of thousands more, maybe hundreds of thousands, are going to starve to death before relief can reach them." He stopped talking for a moment to let that sink in.

"And remember, we don't know what the Siad, the Sons, or the Gaels might be up to. Even after the people are fed, we need to disarm enough clansmen that people can live in peace.

"Now," he said briskly, "on to other matters. As you know, our Corps is not a static organization. The Confederation Marines Corps is a vital, living corps. One way that vitality is continued is through innovation and the adoption of new tools and technologies to help us do our job better, and help us survive when we go in harm's way. A new piece of equipment has been tested and is now being distributed throughout the Corps. The first sergeant has brought one along and will tell you about it before handing it over. Incidentally, some of you may have noticed Corporal Doyle is with us, and you might be wondering why." There were a few muted laughs at the mention of Corporal Doyle, who normally stayed as close to headquarters as possible. "The first sergeant will tell you about that too. Top." Conorado stepped aside and Myer stepped forward.

"What we have here," Top Myer began as he took a black box approximately twelve inches high, eight inches wide, and two deep from Corporal Doyle, "is the Universal Positionator Up-Downlink, Mark Two, commonly called the UPUD." He carefully avoided looking at Bass. "The UPUD Mark One, the original version of this piece of equipment, was intended to replace the radio, geo position locator, and vector computer for calling in air strikes and artillery missions that every unit from platoon on up, and sometimes squads as well, had to carry. That was three pieces of equipment the Mark One was supposed to replace. The UPUD Mark Two," he placed an emphasis on *Mark Two*, "still replaces those three. It does more than that, though. The Mark Two also replaces the motion detector. Which makes the Mark Two one piece of equipment to carry instead of four. Somebody in every platoon is going to be mighty happy. Now, I'm sure some of you are aware," this time he did glance at Bass, "of problems that were encountered when the UPUD Mark

One first saw action. That's why this unit is a Mark Two. The problems with the first model have been corrected."

He turned and faced Bass directly to say his next. "When the Mark One was originally fielded, every unit that received one turned in its existing radios, geo position locators, and vector computers. That was a mistake. You are going to keep your existing equipment until such time as the UPUD Mark Two is properly integrated into your operational mind-set. Is that clear?"

Bass gritted his teeth but gave a sharp nod. Only then did Myer look back at the rest of the platoon.

"Now, the reason Corporal Doyle is with us today is he has been thoroughly trained in the care and feeding of the UPUD Mark Two. When the Skipper and I leave, he will stay with you to train everyone in its use." Someone whooped. Myer ignored it, but Doyle glared out at the platoon, trying to spot who had laughed.

"If anybody has any questions, I'll be happy to answer them. If not, the Skipper and I have to deliver UPUDs to the other platoons."

"It's not like last time, Charlie," Myer said. "You're keeping your existing equipment. No risking men's lives this time on something we don't know for sure works."

Conorado stood silent a few feet away. He'd known Bass was going to resist the UPUD and didn't want to have to give him a direct order. He was relying on Myer's persuasiveness.

"What you're telling me is, instead of carrying four different pieces of equipment, now we have to carry five, one of which might not work."

Myer shook his head. "Charlie, it's not as if you're out there chasing bandits on foot and weight matters. You use the UPUD here to communicate with Company and to guide in the resupply hopper. You put it on the Dragon when it makes its run to the outlying villages, and try out its capabilities there. You still have your old equipment here, your Dragon still has its old equipment. The UPUD doesn't work, you've got backup you know does work. Think of it as a field test under controlled conditions."

"This isn't controlled conditions, this is a live operation."

"You've got your regular equipment to use as backup, and to confirm any data from the UPUD. That makes it controlled conditions."

"Who made it?"

"It doesn't matter who made it. It's made to Confederation Marine Corps spec, that's what matters."

"It matters to me."

Myer hesitated, giving Bass a hard look. "Terminal Dynamics. And they fixed the problem, Charlie. I checked that out myself, went out to where I didn't have line-of-sight communications and used the damn radio. It bounced off the satellite."

"I still don't trust it."

"You shouldn't. Never trust anything the first time you see it. Never believe manufacturer's claims. When they don't lie outright about their equipment's capabilities, they exaggerate them. All I'm saying is try it—with your existing equipment as backup."

Bass's internal struggle was evident on his face. Myer stood without saying anything to give the platoon sergeant a chance to work his way through it. Finally, Bass said, "All right, I'll test it." He took the UPUD Mark II from Myer's hand. "But the first time this piece of shit doesn't work, it's gone."

"Fair enough, Charlie."

Bass looked into Myer's eyes, hard. "I'm going to take it out on a foot patrol myself. I'm going to put it through its paces like it's never been tested before." He turned to

Conorado. "Skipper, you said the Siad are on the move. Where?"

"All over their territory. But other than a few stragglers and small groups, none of them within seventy-five klicks of here."

"How long would it take for them to mass here?"

"They're on horseback. It would take two days for enough of them to gather and get here in strength to do any damage—but only if they were willing to kill their horses doing it."

"Then tomorrow I'm taking a patrol out on the relief run and have it drop us off twenty klicks away. We'll test this," he hefted the UPUD, "on the walk back."

CHAPTER
TWENTY-TWO

"You see where we are?" a glaring Staff Sergeant Bass snarled at Corporal Doyle. "That damn thing better work," he couldn't bring himself to call the UPUD Mark II by name, "and you better know how to use it, or just maybe none of us will live to see Tulak Yar again."

Doyle swallowed. He could see perfectly well where they were—in the anteroom of some medieval hell. Populate it with a few dozen tormented souls, and it was a landscape that could have been painted by Hieronymus Bosch, had Bosch been a Copt instead of Flemish and known what a desert looked like. It was barren, colored light brown and light tan, and all the browns and tans in between, with occasional splotches of pink and rust-red and blue—and those were just the rocks erupting from the sand. Nowhere did Corporal Doyle see the greens and reds and yellows of life. The fantastically twisted and contorted land, with its spires of rock, tumbles of stone, and drifts of sand, made him shudder. High fliers drifted on the currents. Doyle wondered if they were carrion-eaters. They must be, he thought. There can't possibly be anything here to hunt. But where did the carrion come from? Must be from animals that accidentally wandered into this area and died from it—or people who went into it on foot when there were better places to go or vehicles to ride in. He really didn't need Bass's glares and barely veiled threats to let him know they were in a deadly place where the Mark II and his expertise in using it could make the difference between life and death.

Bass's question was rhetorical and he didn't wait for an answer. Instead he simply added, "Don't turn that damn thing on until I tell you to." Then he snapped, "Move out," at his patrol, and led them in a direction perpendicular to that of the Dragon, which had dropped them off in the middle of . . . "nowhere" seemed too inadequate a word to describe where they were, so Bass shook his head and didn't try to assign a label to the place. The air cushion drone of the armored vehicle that was now out of sight beyond one of the nearby table-lands rapidly diminished into silence. Encumbered by little more than a large supply of water and a holstered side arm, Bass set a brisk pace for his twisting route through the badlands. The other men had to struggle to keep up—they were carrying larger weapons, more ammu-nition, and other gear as well as their water. An hour later, when he was sure none of his men knew where they were—he certainly wasn't sure where he was—he stopped in the shade of a monolithic boulder that thrust out of the ground.

Bass had been in a bad mood from the minute he woke up that morning. He didn't want to field-test the UPUD Mark II in the first place, but he had to regardless. So if there was a flaw or hidden problem in the UPUD Mark II, he was determined to find it.

"If by some miracle this thing works, I want men from each team in the platoon to be familiar with it," he'd growled at his squad leaders after morning chow. "Hyakowa, Eagle's Cry, I want one man from each of your fire teams. Kelly, I want a gunner and an assistant gunner from you." The squad leaders exchanged glances; they'd never seen Bass in so vile a mood. "Soft covers, no helmets," Bass said, giving instructions on what the men should bring. "Weapons, a spare battery, one day's rations, one day's water, basic medkits. Now do it." He spun about and stomped off to get his own gear.

"Aye aye, Staff Sergeant," Hyakowa murmured toward Bass's back. He tipped his head at the other two and they followed him away.

"You pissed off enough at anybody to send him with Bass?" Eagle's Cry asked before they went their separate ways to their squad areas.

Hyakowa shook his head.

"I'm never that mad at anybody in my squad," Kelly said.

"So what are we going to do?" Eagle's Cry asked.

"Ask for volunteers," Hyakowa told them.

"Do we tell them what kind of mood the boss is in?"

Hyakowa sighed. "Use your own discretion."

"Gotcha."

So it was that Corporal Dornhofer, Eagle's Cry's second fire team leader, Lance Corporals Schultz and Neru, a gun squad gunner, and PFCs Claypoole, Dean, and Clarke, a new guy in the gun squad, volunteered for something that they began having second thoughts about as soon as they gathered around Staff Sergeant Bass.

Long before the Dragon dropped them off out in the middle of . . . of—"Does anyplace like this exist in the real universe?" Claypoole asked when he saw where they were—every one of them had revised his previously sterling opinion of Staff Sergeant Charlie Bass and resolved never again to volunteer for anything.

"I'm offering odds on none of us ever seeing civilization again," Schultz muttered during the fast-paced trek into the badlands. Maybe nobody could mess with Marines and get away with it, but this land was bigger and meaner than anybody Schultz had ever run into.

"You can't offer odds long enough to get any takers," Dornhofer said sotto voce to Schultz when Bass finally halted in the shade of the boulder.

A long, high, riftlike cliff stood opposite the boulder a couple of hundred meters away. A jumble of mounds and hillocks cut off their vision less than a hundred meters to the rear. The farthest they could see other than up was less than five hundred meters ahead, where a high hill or low mountain began its climb to the sky. There was no way they were in line of sight of another UPUD Mark II.

"Turn that damn thing on now," Bass snapped at Doyle when the panting corporal caught up with him and slumped against the boulder.

Doyle gasped once or twice, then pulled the UPUD Mark II from its carrying pouch, flipped on its power switch, and opened the lid.

"Ask it where we are." Bass pulled a standard geo position locator out of a pocket and queried it. Doyle looked accusingly at the GPL. Bass wasn't being fair about blaming him for anything that might happen if the UPUD Mark II didn't work right. With that GPL, they wouldn't get lost.

Bass grunted when Doyle read off coordinates that agreed with the ones his GPL gave. He wished he had a good map to compare the readings to, but there weren't any reliable maps for that part of Elneal. He looked at the sketchy one he had and decided it might as well have a large X, labeled in a shaky hand, "Here Lie Treasure," and a large blank area with the legend "Tygers Be Here." Disgusted, he jammed the map into a pocket.

"Crank up the radio and raise the Six," he ordered. As far as he was concerned, this was the most important test. If the radio didn't work, he was going to borrow somebody's blaster and slag the damn thing.

Doyle pressed a sensor, spoke into the mouthpiece, waited, spoke again, and handed the unit to Bass.

"Lima Three Six," Bass said into it, "this is Five Actual. We are at," he read the coordinates off his own GPL, "and proceeding as planned. Over."

"Lima Three Five Actual, this is Lima Three Six Actual," Baccacio's voice came back. "Use correct radio procedure."

Bass looked at the Mark II as if he wanted to strangle it; he couldn't believe that Baccacio was chiding him about radio procedure.

"Roger yours, Six Actual. Out." If Baccacio didn't like his radio procedure, let him chew on that one—the senior position, in this case the platoon, Baccacio—was supposed to be the one to sign off first in radio communications.

He handed the Mark II back to Doyle. "Set a homing vector for us. And turn off the radio." He punched the appropriate commands into his GPL and decided that part of the Mark II was working properly, for now anyway, when Doyle read off the same azimuth the GPL gave him. "Give it a tangential vector of 045 degrees. We'll follow that for a while and see how that damn thing behaves. Deviation of five degrees." He set his GPL the same way. This was a test to see how the homing vector changed as they moved away from the line of their original direction, and to see if the Mark II would alert them if they were shifting too far from their intended direction.

They went three kilometers in the tangential direction. The UPUD beeped within seconds of when Bass's GPL did to warn of course deviation. The homing vector on the Mark II changed the same as on the GPL. So far, the UPUD was performing properly.

"Next test," Bass snarled when he called another stop. This was a place where the land dipped and rose and twisted back and around on itself. It was pitted and pimpled so severely that half an army could be hidden in it so well that not even infras could pick up signs of anybody nearby.

So far the locator was working properly and so was the radio—Bass had Doyle make the half-hourly situation reports. "No change, proceeding with mission," Bass said, and didn't bother to speak into it himself, not even when Doyle tried to hand it to him. They couldn't test the vector computer for calling in air strikes, but they were going to test the motion detector.

"You stand here looking in that direction," Bass ordered Doyle, and went back to where the rest of the patrol waited for him.

Doyle stood where he was told and wished he had the courage to look in a direction other than the one Bass had indicated. He was shaken by a sudden fear that Bass was going to lead the others away and leave him there to find his own way out of the desolation. Not even the thought that he had the UPUD Mark II and that it was working properly could quell his trembling. But Bass didn't have any ideas about abandoning Doyle or anyone else out there. What he really wanted was for the UPUD to flunk a test so he could slag it.

"Sit down and find a rock to lean against," Bass suddenly said from right behind Doyle.

Doyle jumped at the unexpected words. He dropped into a sitting position and, with a whoosh, let out the breath he hadn't realized he was holding. He took a couple of deep, slow breaths, then scooted around until his back was against the shady side of a boulder that stood higher than he was tall.

Bass sat next to him. "I didn't want you to look back because I didn't want you to have any idea where I was sending people," he explained. "I want any motion readings you get on that damn thing to be real readings, not affected by anything you know. Understand?"

Doyle nodded. "I understand. No problem." Still, he couldn't keep the relief at not being abandoned out of his voice.

"The rest of the patrol is out there somewhere, moving around. Maybe. Turn on the motion detector and see what it picks up. Use its lowest setting." Bass wanted to test its sensitivity along its entire range.

Doyle managed to tap in the commands without fumbling. He studied the shifting colors on the viewscreen for a moment, then his eyes opened wide and he looked up. A puzzled expression took over his face, and he looked back at the screen, then back up again.

"It can't be."

"What?"

"It's showing two men moving over there." He pointed at a flat area fifty meters away.

Bass nodded. "There's a gully over there. Claypoole and Dean are following it."

"But I've got the setting so low it shouldn't pick up anybody at that distance, not unless he's moving in the open."

Bass raised his eyebrows, impressed. "Very good. See anything else?"

Doyle shook his head.

"Notch it up."

Doyle did and studied the screen again. Abruptly, he dropped the UPUD and scrambled to the side of the boulder to look around it. Neru and Clarke were approaching the boulder from behind.

"No!" Doyle exclaimed. "It can't be." He looked back at Bass. "It's not possible for a motion detector to pick up movement through stone at that setting."

Bass considered what Doyle said. He thought the company clerk might be right. If he had the UPUD set right, that is. He looked suspiciously at the UPUD. "Check your setting."

Doyle came back and examined his settings. "Second lowest."

"Odd."

Doyle nodded agreement.

"Everybody in," Bass called out.

"My God," Doyle murmured as the screen went crazy with all the motion that suddenly appeared on it.

"The motion detector's more sensitive than we expected," Bass said when his men were assembled. "On its lowest setting it picked up you two in that gully," he said to Claypoole and Dean. "On the next setting up, it caught you two coming up behind us," to Neru and Clarke. They gaped at him.

"I want to see what happens if you really wind it up."

Everybody moved to where they could see the screen. Doyle obligingly shifted to make it more easily visible. His hand paused over the controls. The motion detector was so sensitive on its two lowest settings he was a bit apprehensive at what it might do at its highest. He entered the commands. The viewscreen suddenly filled with fluttering ghosts and tiny, swimming dots.

"What the . . . ?"

"Sweet Jesus Mohammad."

"What's it doing?"

Doyle studied the manic images and looked in the directions it indicated. "It's showing us breathing," he said in an awed voice. "Look at that." He put a fingertip on one of the ghosts. "See how much more it's moving? That's me talking. Dorny, say something."

"This can't be," Dornhofer said. "I've never heard of

a motion detector doing that before." A different ghost shimmered rapidly when he spoke.

"Schultz, you say something."

"What are all those little dots in between?" A third ghost responded to Schultz speaking.

Doyle peered at the moving dots on the screen. "I don't know, but they seem pretty close." He made an adjustment to focus the image tightly on one of the moving dots, then, holding the UPUD in one hand, moved forward and began crawling, shifting his eyes between the viewscreen and the ground in front of him. After a few meters he stopped and lowered his face toward the ground.

"It's picking up bugs," he said, so faintly that Bass had to ask him to repeat himself. "It's picking up bugs. Look at this."

Bass knelt next to him and looked closely until he saw a tiny mitelike bug crawling along the rock surface. He looked at the viewscreen, back at the bug, then at the screen again. "It's picking up bugs," he said, as awed as Doyle. His face contorted through several exaggerated expressions, then he angrily shouted, "It's picking up goddamn bugs! A motion detector isn't supposed to pick up goddamn bugs! It's worthless!" He grabbed for the UPUD, but Doyle jerked it out of his reach. Top Myer had made it clear to him that he was responsible for the UPUD, and he was afraid Bass would damage it and he'd get blamed.

"Put it on the ground and step back, Doyle," Bass snarled as he scrambled to his feet. "Somebody give me a blaster. I'm going to slag that damn thing."

"*No!*" Doyle squeaked, and clutched the UPUD to his chest. Nobody offered Bass a blaster.

"The Mark One got a lot of good Marines killed." Bass

turned slowly, glaring at each of his men in turn. "I'm going to kill this one before it can hurt anybody."

The instant Bass's attention turned away from him, Doyle ducked behind a boulder and found a crack in the stony ground to hide in. He couldn't let the platoon sergeant slag the UPUD, no. The Top would have his hide if he did. Doyle had a fleeting image of a human skull with the top of its cranium cut off sitting on the first sergeant's desk. Being used as an ashtray for those awful cigars the first sergeant smoked. *His* skull. No, no way he could let Bass slag the UPUD.

In the background he heard Bass haranguing the other men. Nobody had given him a blaster yet, but Doyle knew it was just a matter of time. He had to avoid Bass until the platoon sergeant cooled off. Then maybe Bass would get over his desire to turn his skull into an ashtray for the Top. He'd turn down the setting on the motion detector to where he could use it to help him evade Bass. He looked at it to make the adjustment and stopped when he saw the screen.

"Look at this," he shouted as he clambered out of his hiding place. "I don't believe this."

"What?" Bass snapped. He clenched and unclenched his fists from wanting a blaster.

Doyle looked into the far distance, into the sky. He saw nothing but a few high, wispy clouds in the blue. Those clouds weren't what the UPUD was picking up. "Here." He showed the screen to Bass and indicated two flecks the motion detector showed at a range of eighteen kilometers and moving in a tight pattern at more than a hundred kilometers per hour. He punched in a new command and the motion detector closed in on the image.

Bass pulled out his GPL and compared its homing vector to what the UPUD screen showed.

"Those are Raptors," Doyle said softly. "They're over

Tulak Yar." He shook his head. "I've never seen a motion detector that could pick up aircraft at eighteen kilometers."

Bass studied the image for a few seconds, then said softly, "That's not a demonstration flight, they're flying a ground-assault pattern. Tulak Yar is under attack." He checked the time. It was a few minutes past sixteen hours.

Claypoole and Dean jumped to their feet and began trotting in the direction of the village. After a few paces they stopped and looked back.

"Shouldn't we go back right now?" Claypoole asked when he saw the others still huddled around the UPUD.

"We're eighteen kilometers away," Bass said without taking his eyes from the viewscreen. "Whatever's going on will be long over by the time we can get there. Besides," now he looked at Claypoole and Dean, "what do you think the eight of us can do against a force large enough to take on a platoon?"

"They're breaking off," Doyle suddenly said.

Bass looked back at the screen. The Raptors were no longer swinging and swooping in a ground-assault pattern. Instead they were gaining altitude and flying away from Tulak Yar. But instead of heading south toward New Obbia, they were flying north, toward Bass and his patrol.

"Turn on the radio and raise Platoon," Bass said softly. "I need to find out what's going on."

Doyle adjusted the focus of the motion detector so they could follow the northward flight of the Raptors, then turned on the radio. The viewscreen flashed bright and a jolt of electricity shot through the UPUD and into his hands. Doyle fell backward and tumbled over. The UPUD dropped to the ground. A wisp of smoke rose from a hairline crack in the viewscreen. The unit couldn't handle the power needed to use the motion detector and the radio simultaneously.

A roar came out of the sky. Bass looked up and saw the Raptors streaking far overhead. He pulled out his binoculars and studied the aircraft while Dornhofer bent over Doyle to check the extent of his injuries.

When the Raptors disappeared over the northern horizon, Bass lowered his glasses. "Those are Model B's," he said softly. "I haven't seen a Model B in ten years. They're retired." He looked at Dornhofer. "How is he?"

"He'll be all right," Dornhofer said. "I think he was just knocked out."

CHAPTER
TWENTY-THREE

It's a military truism that no intelligence system, no matter how good or how thorough, ever provides enough information to the people who need it the most—the fighting men. Marine, navy, and Confederation intelligence on Elneal failed to provide a couple of vital bits of information to Ensign Baccacio. Of course, if the intelligence establishment had had those two bits of information, all of the Marines on Elneal would have been operating in a different manner to begin with.

One missing bit of intelligence was Shabeli's Raptors. They were a well-kept secret, though many people had been involved in that deal and there had been plenty of time to ferret out the information. But no one ever considered that such weapon systems might have been imported for use by people as primitive as the Siad.

The other very important detail they didn't know was that Shabeli had adopted the tactic of the ancient Mongol horsemen, whereby his warriors each had several mounts and changed them frequently as they rode into combat. That enabled them to travel much faster and farther than the fleet intelligence officers, most of whom had never even seen a horse much less ridden one, imagined was possible. Intelligence was just not worried about the Siad horsemen as a military threat. After all, with Raptors, hoppers, Dragons, and the whole inventory of modern weapons available to the Marines on Elneal, who would have considered horsemen much of a threat?

The way Ensign Baccacio saw it, Captain Conorado was "micromanaging" when he'd ordered him to put out security during the daily all-hands. Today, with the company commander off "micromanaging" one of the other platoons that didn't need his meddling, and with Staff Sergeant Bass, who Baccacio was convinced was incompetent, away on his totally unnecessary field test of the UPUD, Baccacio found himself free to run his platoon in what he thought was the right way, without interference. Third platoon adhered to the routine that he knew could only build the morale and self-confidence of the people of Tulak Yar and the surrounding area.

At 16 hours, the few security watches on the village's perimeter were called in for the daily all-hands meeting. Even if the Siad had any hostile action in mind, Baccacio knew that as of yesterday they were two days' ride away. Even if the Siad came, the goatherds and crow-chasers would be able to give more than adequate warning.

That's what Ensign Baccacio believed to the core of his being.

Six-year-old Mhumar was one of the crow-chasers in the fields below Tulak Yar. He knew that he had the extra duty of watching for Siad raiders and giving warning to the Marines if any appeared. He was very proud of that responsibility. The Marines who came to save his village were the greatest and bestest men he'd ever seen. Life had changed quickly for young Mhumar and his friends since then. Now he couldn't wait for each morning, to get out and watch the Marines at their routines. Life in Tulak Yar was a lot of fun again for a six-year-old crow-chaser.

And they were nice to him, not like the Siad, who hit

him when he came too close or when he tried to admire one of their horses or look at their sharp knives.

Mhumar would do anything he could to help his friend "Maknee Al" and the other Marines. When he grew up, he wanted to be just like them. Maybe, if he did a really good job of warning them if the Siad came, when he grew up they would let him be one of them. After all, old Mas Fardeed had gone off when young and fought bravely in many battles, and the Marines all respected him, so why not him?

The thought of becoming a Marine swelled Mhumar's tiny chest with pride, and he promised himself he would be good enough that they would let him join them. He remembered something that Maknee Al had told him.

"A Marine is always ready for anything," Maknee Al had said. "Every time he goes someplace, he is always looking around to see where the enemy might be, where they might come from, where he can find cover, how he can fight to win. A Marine always plans for whatever might happen."

It was a difficult thing to understand. There was very much that a Marine had to do all the time and everyplace. It was harder to understand because Maknee Al spoke a language that even now, a whole week after the Marines came to Tulak Yar, Mhumar hardly understood at all. What Maknee Al told him was translated for him into Afghan by old Mas Fardeed. Mas Fardeed nodded his head sagely and added in Afghan that the dark-skinned Marine was a man of surpassing military wisdom. Someday soon, Mhumar would have to make the old man tell him what "surpassing" meant.

But one thing Mhumar did understand very well: "A Marine always plans for whatever might happen." So Mhumar had made his plans for what he would do if the Siad came.

When the Siad came to Tulak Yar, mostly they came from the mountains to the northwest. But sometimes they came through the fields here where he was chasing crows from the crops. Once in a while they even came from the other side of the Bekhar River, but only when the water level was very low, and it wasn't low now. When they came from the west, they rode tall and proud on their horses and trampled their way through the crops. If they came that way, he would be able to see them a long way off.

Mhumar looked a long way off to the west. He didn't see any Siad riding their horses through the crops. Then he looked to the east, where the road ran up to the top of the bluff. He was a lot closer to the road up the bluffs than he was to a long way to the west. Yes, he would have time to run to the road and run up it if he saw the Siad a long way to the west. Before he reached the top of the road, he would start yelling for the Marines, to tell them the Siad were coming. But what if he was chasing a crow and the Siad were not all of that long way off before he saw them? He looked at the bluff, and behind the row of trees that shaded its base he saw the crease in its face that he and the other children used to climb to the bluff's top when the adults couldn't see them. None of the mothers in the village wanted the children to use that crease in the bluff. They said it was dangerous. But Mhumar and the other children could climb the bluff faster on that crease than they could running up the road. Besides, climbing up the crease was more fun than using the road.

Satisfied that he had planned for everything, and that he would be able to give warning if the Siad came this way, Mhumar looked around to see if any crows were sneaking in while he was making his plans to help the Marines. There was one! He ran at it, waving his arms and yelling. The crow twisted its head around on its scaly neck to glare at him, then ran and flapped its wings until it got off the ground. As it flew away, Mhumar looked around for more. He didn't see any others in the crops, though he did see many flying in the sky. He watched them for a few minutes, wondering why so many crows were flying and so few of them were landing in the crops to eat the food that the people of Tulak Yar were growing for themselves. Then he decided that the ways of crows were mysterious and he shouldn't question them. If he did, the crows might all decide to eat the crops at the same time and he would have to run around a lot to chase them off and he would get very tired.

He decided to go over to the bluff, where he had left his water bag in the deep shade of the trees to keep cool. Halfway there he froze. He thought he saw something in the shadows behind the trees. Something that shouldn't be there. His heart started fluttering in his chest and his entire body began to tremble. What he thought he saw wasn't possible.

Unwilling to approach, but needing to know, he resumed moving toward the bluffs, but angled toward the road to the top. Then what he thought he saw moved and he knew.

A mounted Siad warrior eased his horse into a walk from between the trees and the base of the bluffs, on a course to intercept Mhumar. All the strength suddenly went out of Mhumar's legs and a frigid wave of nausea swept over him. Involuntarily, the boy's bowels emptied. Now the boy could see a column of Siad advancing behind the lead warrior, all nearly hidden in the deep shadow behind the row of shade trees. Far in the back of his mind, where he was barely aware of it, Mhumar realized that there was more to understand about the things a Marine did than he knew. It had never occurred to him that the Siad might come in a way other than the ways they always had.

The lead warrior didn't seem to be looking at him. Mhumar had only one chance, run as fast as he could and hope he got far enough before he was spotted. And so he ran, faster than he had ever run before.

But the Siad warrior did see him. His sun-darkened face split into a grin, revealing a mouth full of broken teeth. Casually, effortlessly, as a man born to ride, he heeled his steed into a trot and then a gallop. As fast as Mhumar ran, the horse was far faster. Its hooves kicked up clods of rich dirt and thundered over the ground, echoing eerily behind the trees. Mhumar's voice shrilled thinly as he tried to call out a warning, but he was too small, and his voice couldn't carry to the top of the bluffs. The Siad pulled his horse out from behind the line of trees and galloped through the crops, trampling them in his wake. The horse's nostrils flared wildly as his rider spurred him on. Standing in the stirrups, the warrior rose and leaned forward against his mount's neck, extending an arm. The bayonet on his rifle glinted harshly in the sunlight just before it slammed into Mhumar's back and drove on all the way through his chest in one swift motion.

The Siad reined his horse to a stop in a swirling cloud of mud and shredded crops. He stifled the war cry he wanted to shout out, and instead victoriously thrust his rifle arm skyward, Mhumar's still-wriggling body impaled on its bayonet. He looked back toward the trees, where the line of warriors followed, and grinned. The boy's warm blood gushed wetly down the warrior's arm and dripped onto his saddle. Not much of a prize, the man thought, but first blood was first blood. Then he thrust his arm forward and down, flinging the tiny corpse onto the ground. Raising the back of his hand to his mouth, he tasted the blood there in the age-old Siad ritual of the kill.

The Siad were not detected again until, screaming war cries, they swarmed over the lip of the road where it leveled out at the top of the bluffs. But that wasn't until after Shabeli's Raptors struck.

Ensign Baccacio looked at his platoon and smiled to himself. It didn't matter that this was a rump unit, with only twenty-two of his twenty-nine enlisted men. With Bass out of the way and Captain Conorado gone, for the first time he had the opportunity to show these men how the Marine Corps really functioned, how real Marines operated on a humanitarian mission. A daily commander's briefing to the men was important for morale and unit cohesiveness.

"If there are any of you who don't remember what Captain Conorado reported yesterday," he began, "I'll recap it. The Sons of Freedom have retired to their strongholds and don't pose a threat to anyone. The Gaels have simply retired, they evidently understand that they're totally outclassed and have decided to stop their depredations on the people of Elneal. The Siad, who are the ones we'd have to concern ourselves with if they were going to cause any trouble, have gone into the steppes where they can play Mongol horde without being a threat to anyone. Simply by landing an operational FIST on Elneal, the Confederation has stabilized the entire world."

Hyakowa nudged Eagle's Cry and whispered, "Is that the way you remember what the Skipper said?"

Eagle's Cry shook his head. "I think our boy is reading the wrong things into what could be a tactical withdrawal to regroup."

"Me too." Hyakowa noticed Baccacio looking in his direction and nudged Eagle's Cry again. Both sergeants stood erect and looked at their platoon commander as though they were gratefully absorbing his words of wisdom.

Mentally, Baccacio tallied a point for himself. It looked as if those two were beginning to stop conspiring against him. As soon as they did, he was certain, the rest of the platoon would follow right along. He didn't miss a beat in his presentation about food and medical aid being distributed unhindered all around the planet as he glared at another minor disturbance to the side. It was McNeal, one of the troublemakers, and Goudanis, looking at the sky over their shoulders. Baccacio was gratified when Corporal Leach directed their attention back to him without his having to say anything. During his presentation about the importance of the UPUD Mark II and what it was going to mean to future Marine operations, more of his men began nudging each other, mumbling among themselves, and looking to the northwest. He was losing them, and that couldn't continue.

"Platoon! Atten-SHUN!" he shouted. A few of the men glanced at him, but none of them snapped to attention. Baccacio saw red. Someone was going to suffer for this breach of discipline.

Just then Hyakowa turned and asked, "Mr. Baccacio, are we expecting any fast fliers?"

The question was so unexpected that Baccacio didn't say what he'd been about to. Instead he looked into the sky in the same direction as his men. He quickly picked up two objects moving in their direction. Now that he saw the aircraft, he heard the dim roar of approaching engines. They grew rapidly as he watched, and resolved into a flight of Raptors heading straight toward them at low altitude.

If he played this right, he wouldn't look like a fool to his men. "As you were, people," Baccacio said. "FIST

HQ has decided to make a demonstration overflight, to show the good people of Tulak Yar how powerful we are." Miffed at the unexpected interruption, he promised himself to say something to somebody, raise some hell, really, about the need for higher headquarters to let local commanders know ahead of time when something like this was planned.

"I don't think they're ours, sir," Hyakowa said. "They don't have Marine markings on them."

The two Raptors flashed low overhead, the sonic shock of their engines at such close range shaking buildings in the village and sending dirt devils spinning. The Marines all ducked to cover their faces.

Eagle's Cry shouted, "They don't have navy markings either."

"Now this is absurd," Baccacio called out. "If they aren't Marines and they aren't navy, they don't exist. So they have to be ours. Everybody, eyes front."

Hyakowa was one of the few who faced him. "Sir, they exist and they aren't ours. What are we going to do?"

To the southeast the Raptors were beginning a turn that would bring them all the way back around to the northwest for another overflight.

Hyakowa counted to two. When the young officer didn't give any orders, he did. "Everybody, to your positions."

The Marines sprinted to their fighting positions outside Tulak Yar as though their lives depended on it. In seconds Baccacio stood with jaw gaping, alone in front of the Dragon—its crew had already mounted and was starting it up for action.

The two Raptors completed their turn and came in again from the northwest. This time four lines of plasma burned through the village. Baccacio had seen firepower demonstrations before, but nothing like this, not this close up, and certainly never as a target. He felt the intensity of the heat on his face as structures burst into flame, and smelled the sharp, tangy odor of mortar and rock liquefying under the plasma bolts.

For an instant the villagers were stunned, frozen in place, the attack was so sudden and overpowering. One old man stood gaping at a plasma bolt as it sizzled along the street and vaporized him in a bright flash. The horrified ensign thought he heard a loud *poof!* as the man disappeared. Then everything dissolved into chaos. Men cried out in terror, grabbed their women and children, and ran for whatever protection they could find. Other men ran about, searching for wives and children who weren't near them. Women screamed, for their children, their husbands, their lives. Children screamed and cried for their mothers, for the protection of their fathers. Many of them flashed into ash as the spitting streams of Raptor fire lanced through them. Houses exploded in the line of the Raptors, those made of wattle and reeds erupting into flames so hot they were vaporized. A conflagration sprang up in the path of the Raptors, and more people were caught in the flames and incinerated. The Raptors passed the village and turned again, more tightly than before. This time they swooped over the village from due north. The sonic boom of their passage knocked over structures weakened in the first pass and by the strafing. The air displaced by their passage sent burning debris flying about, spreading the fire already consuming a swath through Tulak Yar.

But the Raptors didn't fire this time; their gun batteries held only enough power for one strafing run. Shabeli had thought that would be enough to terrorize the people and panic the Marines, to pave the way for his horsemen. The Raptors made another, tighter turn and ripped over the village again from the southeast, the turbulence of their passage spreading the fire even farther.

Then four hundred horsemen came screaming over the top of the bluff.

As the Raptors made their strafing run, Baccacio dove over the Dragon's ramp as it closed. Inside, he tried to shout commands to its crew, but Corporal Manakshi, the crew chief, was already calmly giving Lance Corporal Bwantu directions to move the vehicle out into the open where it would have maneuvering room. The Dragon lurched into motion and Baccacio had to grab hold of whatever he could to keep from being thrown about its interior. The Dragon had passed the outermost buildings of Tulak Yar when the Raptors made their run from the north. Rodriguez, the gunner, was ready for them when they made their final pass from the southeast, and he fired the assault gun; but the Dragon's fire-control computer wasn't designed to track targets moving that fast and that close.

Kerr and McNeal reached their fighting position and dove into it while the Raptors were making their approach from due north. The concussion wave from the Raptors' low passage knocked them down and left them stunned and disoriented for a moment. Dirt and sand blasted in through the openings in the shelter, scouring their exposed skin. Pebbles pelted them like hail, and fist-size rocks clattered off the low walls of the position. But the dirt they'd so carefully slagged into firm walls when they built the position held firm.

Kerr flopped on his belly as soon as he recovered and looked back through the entrance toward Tulak Yar.

McNeal knelt over him and looked past his head. Flames were spreading through the village, the screams of the dying horrible to hear, even at a distance. The saliva seemed to freeze in McNeal's mouth.

"Here they come again," Kerr shouted, and flattened himself even lower than he already was.

McNeal ducked down to where he could see the Raptors through the entrance.

Then the Raptors swooped low over Tulak Yar from the southeast. The sonic concussion flattened the flames and put out parts of the fire. It also threw about burning debris, and fire ignited in parts of the village that hadn't yet been touched by the conflagration.

"Why aren't they shooting?" McNeal asked.

"They don't need to, that's why," Kerr answered, awed by the way the wind from the Raptors spread destruction.

The sound of the Raptors' engines changed from a full-throttled roar to a low, receding drone that moved toward the north. More screams, some of them louder than any they'd heard before, came from Tulak Yar. McNeal twisted around and looked out a firing slit. He saw the Raptors climbing to the north.

"They're going away," he said. Anger fought with confusion on his face. "Who are they? Why did they do that? Those people weren't hurting anybody." He pushed at Kerr to move him through the entrance. "Let's go, we've got to help those people."

"Watch the other way," Kerr snapped back. "An air strike usually means a ground attack is coming. Or didn't they teach you that?"

"Who—"

"Here they come."

McNeal looked over Kerr's shoulder. A mass of screaming men with painted faces, wearing furs and feathers, suddenly swarmed through Tulak Yar on horseback.

"Spears?" McNeal croaked. "They're using spears?"

Kerr put his blaster to his shoulder and sighted in on one of the horsemen. "Those aren't spears, they're rifles with bayonets," he said as he pressed the firing lever. The Siad warrior he fired at suddenly flashed, then tumbled off his horse, a blackened shell.

"They're using what?" McNeal was shocked.

"Put on your body armor," Kerr ordered.

McNeal did as he was told, struggling fiercely and awkwardly into the unfamiliar equipment. "Okay," he said, finished, "I've got it on. Trade places and you can put on yours."

"I'm busy," Kerr snapped as he shot another horseman. "You watch our rear. They're probably coming from more than one direction."

"But we would have seen them," McNeal objected.

"Do it, Marine!" Kerr snapped. Even if McNeal was right, which he might be, the fighting position was designed to defend from an assault from out there, not one from the village—there wasn't room for both of them to fire to the rear of the position. McNeal watching the rear did nothing, but it kept him out of Kerr's way as the corporal fired and fired again. The Siad weren't coming from the front of the Marine positions; instead they fought in a primitive manner—a full charge from one direction until they were inside their enemy's position, followed by an every-man-for-himself melee.

Other Marines around the village began firing into the mass of Siad and more of the horsemen fell, blackened cinders. So did many of their mounts—horses' screams added to the cacophony from the village. But the Marine fire was sporadic; too many villagers were caught in the melee, and the Marines didn't want to risk hitting them.

McNeal split his attention between watching the front, as Kerr told him to, and looking at the village over his fire team leader's head. The fire continued to spread. A gasp escaped him when he saw, at the place where he'd befriended young Mhumar soon after the Marines arrived, a mother running with a small child clutched to her breast. The building she was running past was ablaze. A Siad horseman raced his horse up behind her, his bayoneted rifle extended to impale her. A rock rolled under the horse's flying hooves and caused it to stumble, the Siad's thrust missing the woman, but the flank of the off-balance horse slammed into her as it passed and knocked her out of sight through a collapsed wall into the burning building. The Siad looked back in time to see her disappear into the building and screamed in triumph, but it was a short-lived victory; before he could straighten around in his saddle, blasts from at least three Marines slammed into him and turned him and his horse into a pyre.

McNeal thought he could hear the woman's scream, and her child's thinner wail. Seconds later she came staggering out, her clothes blazing, carrying a second, smaller fire in her arms. She danced in the flames for a long moment until they sucked the last of the life out of her and she collapsed on the ground to join her child in death.

"No more," McNeal growled, and clawed his way past Kerr into the open. He stepped aside so he wouldn't block the other's field of fire, dropped into a kneeling position, and began shooting past the villagers still fleeing the flames and the Siad, into the attackers. With his first bolt he had the satisfaction of seeing a rider lifted off his horse and thrown away. Then he turned to another target.

The spreading flames, lack of victims, and increasing casualties inflicted by the Marines, who were able to fire more freely as the villagers either escaped or were killed, forced the Siad out of Tulak Yar. Some of them raced after the easy targets of fleeing villagers. Many of them didn't live long enough to complete their charges. The others, singly, in pairs, and in small groups, charged the eight Marine positions, shooting their rifles as they came.

Now that the Siad were in the open and no longer surrounded by villagers, the Dragon was able to open fire with its big gun. Its first blast incinerated a half-dozen Siad who were charging one position. Manakshi ordered Bwantu into motion, and the heavy vehicle slammed into a trio of horsemen, pulping them.

McNeal wasn't the only Marine who'd left the protection of his fighting position to be able to fire on the attackers. More of them were in the open than were protected inside their fighting positions—but unlike McNeal, they were behind their positions and had some cover during the Siad charge. Nearly half of the original four hundred horsemen were either dead or still chasing the fleeing villagers. The Marines had a Dragon and blasters against the horsemen's rifles and bayonets, and many of the Marines had struggled into their body armor. But the Siad horsemen had the speed of their mounts and still outnumbered the Marines by at least ten to one. Even so, the Marines were steadily evening the odds as more and more of the Siad were crisped.

Manakshi kept a cool head in the Dragon and had Bwantu run over horseman after horseman, while Rodriguez flamed others with the vehicle's big gun. But there were too many horsemen. The Dragon had to stop shooting when the Siad reached the Marine positions or it would hit its own men.

Corporal Ratliff stayed cool, behind his position, calmly crisping the Siad charging at him. He never saw the horseman who galloped up behind him and speared him with his bayonet. As the horse leaped over the position, Chan crisped the victorious rider, who fell screaming and writhing in flaming agony. But, swathed in flames, the Siad staggered to his feet and charged, a long dagger clasped unsteadily in one hand. A second bolt disintegrated the man's dagger arm, but he still came on, howling and burning, collapsing only a few feet from the Marine, the flesh sloughed off cheekbones, nose, ears, lips, his eyelids burned away, his teeth clenched in a dying rictus. The image of the man's hair burning in a bright blue flame stayed with Chan for a long time after the fight was over.

A few yards away Lance Corporal Lanning sighted on a rider at the very moment the heavy slug fired from a Siad leaning under his running horse's belly crashed through his brain.

Lance Corporal Goudanis, behind a different position, heard several horsemen galloping at him from the rear and spun about to meet the threat. He took out three of the five while their bullets ricocheted off his armor, before a bullet found his unprotected shoulder, mangling flesh and shattering bone, spinning him around.

McNeal heard thudding hooves from the side in time to twist around and avoid a bayonet thrust. The horse that followed trampled over him. The third man in that group reined in and fired his rifle into the position's entrance. Kerr shot back and killed the Siad, but not before two bullets thudded into Kerr's torso and took him out of action. Two other horsemen milled about the front of the position for a moment, then galloped toward Tulak Yar. Manakshi spotted the two Siad, who appeared to be carrying a wounded warrior out of the fight, and ordered Rodriguez to fire at them, but the gun couldn't swivel fast enough to bring to bear on them.

Suddenly, an ululating cry sounded over the battlefield and the surviving Siad broke off the fight to race to the north, into the nearby hills. The Marines and their Dragon poured fire after them and took down many before they reached the shelter of a fold of land.

"Let's get them," Rodriguez shouted, still aiming his gun at the point where the Siad disappeared.

Bwantu hit the accelerator to chase after the Siad and was yanked out of the driver's seat by Baccacio, who screamed, "Belay that! We aren't going after them. They ran too easily, they were winning. That's probably a ruse to lead us into an ambush."

Manakshi didn't agree, but he looked into the ensign's near-panicked eyes and decided not to argue. He used his opticals to scan the battlefield. "They weren't winning," he said softly. "It looks like we killed half of them. They're running away."

"I'm not sure Kerr will pull through," the corpsman told Hyakowa and Eagle's Cry as he closed a stasis unit on Ratliff. Kerr was already sealed in one. "He has massive internal trauma. I think one bullet sent something into his heart. I know it tore all hell out of one of his lungs. Ratliff'll live, but it'll be a long time before he goes into the field again. That bayonet severed his spinal column and did other damage to internal organs. He could be bleeding to death internally." The stasis units would hold the wounded until they reached a surgical team.

The two most severely wounded Marines attended to, Hough turned to Goudanis. He had to heavily sedate him because of the pain, but was able to stop the bleeding and secure the shattered bones of his shoulder so they wouldn't cause any more damage.

"Raise Bass," Baccacio ordered Dupont, his communications man. "Find out where he is and how soon he can get back here." Then he ran to where Hough was treating the lesser casualties.

"How much longer is this going to take?" he demanded.

Hough looked around at the waiting wounded men. "Half an hour, I don't know. Doesn't look like anybody else is bad off. The civilians, though, that's a different matter. I need a whole damn field hospital to deal with them."

Baccacio merely grunted. He abruptly turned and went back to Dupont.

"I can't raise him, sir," Dupont reported. "No reply of any kind."

Shocked, Baccacio looked north. "There's more of them out there," he murmured. "They caught Bass's patrol and killed them," he said with finality. "Squad leaders up!" he shouted, turning in a circle, scanning the horizon, looking for the Siad to return any moment.

"I also called for medical evacuation," Dupont said. "They said it'll take at least a half an hour to get a hopper here, maybe longer. We should put any serious casualties in stasis units."

Hyakowa and Kelly trotted over before Baccacio could reply to Dupont. Hyakowa had a field bandage on his arm. Eagle's Cry was slower coming because he was limping from a leg wound.

"They caught Bass," Baccacio said as soon as the three reached him. Hyakowa thought he heard a hint of satisfaction in the ensign's voice. "There's only us left, and we're hurt. Get everybody into the Dragon now, we're heading back."

The order stunned the squad leaders.

"We can't go," Hyakowa protested. "McNeal's missing. We can't leave without him. Besides, we're supposed to be protecting these people. If we go, the Siad will come back and slaughter them."

"McNeal's dead," Baccacio snapped. "I saw him go down. The Siad swarmed all over him."

"How do you know Staff Sergeant Bass is dead?" Eagle's Cry asked. He did not believe the platoon sergeant was dead. The Skipper, he could be dead, and so could the Brigadier, but not Bass.

"They're dead! They're all dead!" Baccacio shouted. "The Siad already slaughtered them! If we hadn't been here, this wouldn't have happened." The squad leaders couldn't tell whether he meant Bass and the men with him, or the villagers. But they clearly heard the panic in the ensign's voice.

"But—"

"No buts, Sergeant. Get the men aboard the Dragon now."

Hyakowa couldn't believe this was happening. Marines never left their men behind and they never withdrew while they could still fight, and the sergeant was still full of fight.

"Goddamn you, Mr. Baccacio!" he shouted. The veins stood out in Hyakowa's neck and spittle flew from his lips. Now, like a man getting rid of a bad meal that had been too long in his stomach, the sergeant blew up. "You fucking worthless piece of shit! You goddamned coward!" As he shouted, one part of Hyakowa's mind could see himself standing there, the words roaring out of his mouth like unleashed demons. At the same time, a small voice inside his head seemed to be telling him calmly and very clearly that he had gone too far, now he was finished, a court-martial and the brig were the next stop for him. But the curses kept coming, and despite the fact that Sergeant Hyakowa knew the small voice was right, that he would soon face charges of mutiny and would wind up in one of the Confederation's penal colonies, he had never felt more satisfied about anything in his life than he did at this disastrous moment.

Baccacio's face went white and his eyes bulged. Slowly, almost calmly, he drew his weapon and leveled it at Hyakowa. The sergeant stopped at that moment, but only because he was out of breath. Perspiration poured off his face.

Kelly and Eagle's Cry, who had been standing open-mouthed, rooted to the earth as Hyakowa screamed at the ensign, came to life now and stood between the two men. Kelly grabbed Hyakowa by the arms and shoulders and roughly pushed him toward the Dragon, while Eagle's Cry stood in front of Baccacio—he didn't think the ensign would try to shoot Hyakowa through him. Hyakowa went without resistance, totally drained now.

Baccacio stood there, breathing heavily, staring after Hyakowa. The other Marines who had witnessed the scene shifted their feet uneasily. Doc Hough said something. "What?" Baccacio demanded as he spun around.

"I said I'm staying behind with the wounded civilians," Hough repeated. He fixed Baccacio's eyes with his own until the ensign was forced to drop his gaze.

"You've got wounded Marines to care for. You do that in the Dragon on the way. I mean it," he added, and gestured menacingly with his weapon. Doc Hough knew enough to realize that Ensign Baccacio was dangerously close to going over the edge. Reluctantly, he started for the Dragon, and the others followed him.

In two minutes the Marines were aboard the Dragon, heading for FIST headquarters, north of New Obbia, 240 kilometers away.

CHAPTER
TWENTY-FOUR

Schultz considered the broken UPUD Mark II, then wordlessly offered his blaster to Bass.

Bass shook his head, looking at the line of smoke that still dribbled from the UPUD. "We're taking it back. I want whoever was responsible to know that damn thing malfunctioned. Then I want them to find out why and fix it." He looked at the group. "The Mark One cost the lives of a lot of Marines I was with when its flaw was revealed, and I reacted strongly—some say too strongly. We just found a flaw in the Mark Two. It didn't hurt anybody. Well . . ." He glanced at Doyle, who was just regaining consciousness. "It didn't seriously hurt anyone. That damn thing is coming into the Fleet Marine Force whether I like it or not. So we need to make sure it doesn't have any flaws that will get more Marines killed. Or we have to know every flaw it does have so that our ignorance doesn't get Marines killed."

Doyle was still a bit groggy, but it didn't sound to him as if he was being blamed for the malfunction. He sat up without assistance and wiped the perspiration away from his eyes.

Bass looked at Doyle and solicitously asked, "Are you okay?"

"I've been better," Doyle said, "but I'll get over it." The other Marines looked at him with surprise. This was the first time they'd heard him talk like an infantryman.

"Good. Glad to hear it. Now, aren't you glad I made you carry a regular radio? Get it out and raise Tulak Yar so we can find out what happened."

Doyle blanched. "I don't have it," he said weakly.

Bass looked at him as though waiting for him to continue. The others edged back; this wasn't a good sign.

"You didn't bring the radio, is that what you said?" Bass blinked, then wiped at a line of sweat that dribbled past his eye. "After I specifically told you to bring a radio in case that damn thing didn't work?"

Doyle hung his head and mumbled something into his chest.

"I can't hear you, Doyle," Bass said with forced patience. "What did you say?"

Doyle raised his head and looked at Bass defiantly. It wasn't his fault he didn't have the radio. "Ensign Baccacio told me not to bring it. He saw me when I was putting it in my pack and took it away from me."

Bass looked away from Doyle. His face darkened and his fists clenched so tightly his knuckles turned white. "I'm going to have that man busted back down to private," he said through gritted teeth. "I'm going to have him court-martialed and kicked out of my Marine Corps." He turned back to Doyle. "And you, Corporal, are going to be my star witness."

Doyle swallowed.

"All right." Bass shook himself and calmed down with visible effort. "Here's the situation. Eight of us are out here in the middle of, of . . ." He paused, then began again. "We're eighteen kilometers from the nearest friendly forces. Those forces, the rest of our platoon, have just been attacked by enemy air, and probably by ground forces as well, but we have no way of knowing for sure. Because we don't have any communications. Eighteen kilometers doesn't sound like much. Even in terrain like this, we could cover that distance in three hours or so. But we have to assume that there are hostile forces between us and Tulak Yar, so we'll go slow and figure on reaching Tulak Yar tomorrow morning."

He looked at his somber men for a few seconds, then asked, "Did anybody bring a motion detector?" They shook their heads. Bass hadn't thought anybody did—the motion detector was squad leader's equipment, and if they had one, it would have been his responsibility to bring it, but he hadn't suspected they'd have any need for one.

"We have no communications, no motion detector, no infras—I don't imagine anybody brought their infras." He paused for confirmation. Nobody had infras. "Marines, we have just become a low-tech deep reconnaissance patrol. At least I have my GPL. We won't get lost."

"And we have water. Everybody did bring water, didn't you?"

"One day's worth," Dornhofer said.

Bass nodded. One day's worth. That was more than he thought they would need. Now they might need more.

"Water discipline is in effect now. One mouthful every hour. Move out. Schultz, take point."

As the afternoon wore on, the heat rose and the sweat evaporated from their bodies as fast as it popped up.

Two hours later they heard the clop-clop of horses' hooves. Bass snapped his fingers to get everybody's attention, then waved his arm in the signal to get down and take cover.

They were in a dry watercourse too broad to be a mere erosion gully. The dirt was a crumbly, light grayish-tan studded by the occasional boulder that was washed downstream during floods. The only vegetation in it was an occasional sprig of something that didn't grow high, or a low-lying wash of green. Here and there, where the most recent torrent had undercut the bank, large clots of dirt had fallen from the bank two and a half meters above. Some of the clots had space behind them. Those spaces and behind boulders were where the Marines went to ground.

Bass listened carefully to the echoes for a few moments and realized the echoes were all he heard, there were no clops or voices that sounded clear, as they would if the horses or men were very close. He glanced up and down the arroyo to make sure his men were all hiding, then eased deeper into the half-concealed split in the bank he was hiding in and found hand- and footholds to climb near its back end. He kept glancing to his rear as he climbed toward the other side of the arroyo, but saw no movement in that direction.

A small, spreading bush grew at the top; its roots kept the split from expanding. Bass used the bush as concealment while he eased his head up high enough to see over the lip of the arroyo. Little more than a hundred meters away he saw a line of hills. Between the hills and the arroyo in which the Marines hid was a score of horsemen with a small herd of replacement mounts. The riders were armed with projectile weapons. They were headed north, away from Tulak Yar, and frequently turned to search the sky to the south. They bantered among themselves and cried out victory whoops. A couple of times while he watched, one of them prodded a large sack flung over the back of one of the few horses used as pack animals. The horsemen shook their rifles at the sky and swung them in wide, horizontal arcs.

Bass couldn't understand any of the guttural words the horsemen yelled out, but he could guess their meaning. The horsemen were telling each other they'd won their fight, this land was theirs uncontested.

These men had to be from the force that had attacked

Tulak Yar, Bass thought. He wondered how men who had reverted to such a primitive state could have Raptors. Surely they were allied with the aircraft the UPUD Mark II had shown attacking Tulak Yar, if they—or their commander—didn't actually own the attack aircraft.

They were a score of horsemen armed with rifles, nearly a hundred meters away. Bass had seven Marines with him. At that range, with the element of surprise, he and his men could easily take these Siad warriors. He considered the situation for a long moment; race a hundred meters back up the dry watercourse and get into an ambush position. Then blast away when the horsemen came abreast. It could be done; he and his men could wipe them out before they were able to respond and hurt anyone in the Marine patrol. But these men couldn't be the only Siad survivors of the fight. They were too happy, acting too victorious. Where were the rest of them? He slowly looked around a complete 360 degrees and saw no one else. That was the problem.

Bass stayed where he was, watching the horsemen pass by and recede into the distance. A fight would make noise and other Siad would hear it and come. Maybe, probably, too many for the Marines to deal with. It was best to let these go. When the horsemen were out of sight around a low hill, Bass slid to the bottom of the split and stepped out into the open.

"They're gone," he called out softly, but loud enough for all his men to hear. Briskly, he went from Claypoole, at the rear of the patrol, to Schultz, leading off to tell them what he'd seen.

Schultz looked at him accusingly. "We could have taken them."

"You looked?"

"I looked. We could have taken them. Easy."

Bass nodded. "You're right, we could have taken those

few. But where are the rest of them? How fast would the others have gotten here? How soon would there be so many of them here we wouldn't have had a chance? What if they called those Raptors back to strike us?"

A corner of Schultz's mouth twitched, the only acknowledgment he would make that Bass was right. He turned away and led the patrol south.

During the next two hours they had to stop three more times to hide from Siad war parties. Their pace continued to slow. At dusk they settled in for what turned out to be a very cold night. Bass set a twenty-five-percent watch.

It took time in the morning for them to work the stiffness out of joints that had spent too many hours in too cold air lying on too cold ground. As softly as they could, they hawked and spat the night phlegm from their chests, those who didn't have the last watch. They wordlessly excused themselves for whatever momentary privacy they could find in cracks or behind scraggly bushes to void themselves; they worked saliva about their mouths and wiped at fuzzy teeth with dirty fingers. It was the kind of morning they'd all been through before.

Bass checked his GPL while Schultz and Claypoole scouted for sign of overnight enemy activity in their vicinity—or current enemy presence. When the two came back to report all clear, Bass gathered the men around him.

"We're still six kilometers from Tulak Yar," he began. "My guess is the Siad who attacked aren't there anymore. Probably they've all left this area. But we don't know that for sure, there might still be a few of them around, maybe observers to report to Shabeli about the Confederation response to the attack, maybe a reaction force to take on targets of opportunity. And we don't know what kind of communications they've got. If they have watchers with radios, and those watchers see us, we could have a Raptor flight on our asses." He paused to look at his men. They understood what having Raptors on them meant. "We'll move the way we did yesterday. We're not out of it yet. Order of march will be the same; Schultz on point, Clarke, me, Doyle, Dornhofer, Dean, Neru, and Claypoole bringing up the rear. Slow and easy. Water discipline is still in force. Chow down now, but eat lightly; these rations have to last longer than we expected. Maybe a lot longer. Questions?"

Nobody asked any. Bass signaled Dornhofer and Schultz to sit with him while they ate. He gave Schultz the GPL to study so he'd have an idea of how to proceed when they started moving.

After fifteen minutes he stood and said, "Saddle up, we're moving out."

Two minutes later they were on the move. They left no trash to mark their passing. They went slower than they had the day before, and frequently stopped to look and listen for any sign of other people. They heard nothing but the cries of wind and wild animals.

Bass paused on a low ridge facing forward on their line of march and spat out the small pebble he'd had under his tongue to induce the flow of saliva in his mouth. The others stopped and dropped into security positions, facing outward, weapons at the ready. They panted in the intense heat. Down on one knee, Bass checked his GPL heading again, then looked back to the south. He tried to ignore the carrion-eaters he saw wafting in the sky beyond the ridge, tried to tell himself they were crows being kept aloft by village children guarding the fields.

"Recognize this place?" he asked the others. Bass busied himself for a moment selecting another pebble and popped it into his mouth. The others followed his example.

"Big Barb's and a schooner of beer must be just over

that ridge," Claypoole joked, pointing to the south with a grimy forefinger.

Bass smiled briefly. He knew that if Marines could joke, they still had fight left in them. "Just over that far ridge there," he said, "is Tulak Yar and the river."

"Omigod!" Dean whispered as he staggered forward.

Bass held out a restraining arm. "Not so fast, Marine. We aren't home yet. Until we know different, we will assume the village is occupied by the Siad, and we're going to approach it just like any other unknown position."

The Marines said nothing, just stared at him. Then Claypoole nodded. Bass was right; rushing toward the village without knowing what was waiting could mean death. "Dean, you come with me. The rest of you cover up here and watch us. We'll signal if everything is okay."

The sun was well beyond the meridian when the pair at last crawled to the crest of the ridge beyond which lay the river valley and the village of Tulak Yar. On the way, Dean could think only of Mas Fardeed and his snug little hut and the happy hours the platoon had spent there during their stay in the village.

Cautiously, Bass crawled behind a clump of desert grass and, using the vegetation as cover, peered over the ridge. The village was just a burned-out ruin on the lip of the bluff about five hundred meters from the ridge. The few buildings still standing were deeply scorched. Nothing moved down there but dust devils and minor debris blown about by vagrant breezes. And the carrion-eaters that hopped ungainly from spot to spot, tearing at lumps on the ground. He wondered where the Dragon was, whether its not being there meant some of the others got away, or if he now had to worry about the Siad having an armored vehicle. Then he put the Dragon and the rest of the platoon out of his mind.

Bass knew nothing was alive down there but the buzzards. Still, he lay for a long time watching. Once, a long time ago, the company in which he'd been a lance corporal walked into an obviously dead village—just like Tulak Yar now—only to discover the village had been surrounded by an enemy battalion using it as bait. He wasn't going to walk his few Marines into a trap. Neither was he going to assume that there weren't a few Siad left in Tulak Yar scavenging whatever booty wasn't destroyed by the fire.

He lay there for the best part of an hour, watching dust devils, debris, and carrion-eaters, then got to his feet and motioned Dean to come up beside him. Dean could not help an involuntary gasp of horror at the sight.

"The Raptors," Bass said. "You've never seen that before, have you?" he asked. "A raptor is a bird of prey. That's what they do. They kill." And the Raptors that struck here, he said to himself, were old Model B's.

Dean sank to his knees beside him.

"Signal the others to come up," Bass said tiredly as he slumped down beside Dean.

The sun was just setting when the others joined the pair on the ridge. The small group lay disconsolately on the ridge looking down at the destroyed village. They knew there was no use searching for survivors. Still, the wells should be full, and that meant a temporary end to water discipline for them. Yet Bass hesitated to move forward. He was waiting for night to fall. That would hide them from any Siad who might be roaming in the vicinity, and it would reduce their exposure to the horrors he knew lay amid the ruins, the seared and blasted remains of people his men had come to think of as friends.

Silently, they picked their way through the rubble of Tulak Yar. There was no moon, so the Marines moved almost as much by memories of how the village had been laid out as by sight. Heaps of slag lay all around and everything was covered by a thin layer of ash that filled their nostrils and irritated their lungs as it drifted up from under their feet. An eerie silence pervaded the scene, and that was the hardest thing for the Marines to endure. Only the day before, the village had been full of smiling, happy people, and the contrast was numbing.

And now that the sun was down it had turned cold again.

It took them an hour to find a well that wasn't half filled with ash or didn't hold a decaying body. The water was cool and sweet and plentiful.

"Don't get too used to it, people," Bass said. "We've got a long walk ahead of us and we don't know when we might get more water."

After refreshing themselves, the Marines located the still-standing portion of a wall and made camp behind it for the night. They huddled together for warmth. Two watched the darkness while the others tried to sleep. An hour slipped by and then two. The guard changed.

"Fuck it, nobody can sleep," Claypoole muttered.

"Well, try, goddamnit!" Bass whispered. "If you can't sleep, just lay still and rest." He rolled over onto Dean, who let out a grunt. "Sorry," Bass muttered.

"That's okay," Dean replied, "I wasn't asleep either." They were all silent for a few minutes. "Remember the last time we were at Mas Fardeed's house?" Dean whispered to no one in particular. They were all silent again for a long moment.

"Yeah," Claypoole answered.

"I could never get enough of that goat's milk cheese," Bass said.

"I wonder if any of 'em got out?" someone wondered aloud. There was silence again for a while.

"Well," Dean said, "old Mas Fardeed said that our

presence in his village was proof that there is a God and he really loves us, or something like that, remember?"

"Yeah," Dornhofer said. "I wonder what kind of a God would let something like this happen to good people like them," he added from the darkness.

"Just my thought," Dean responded. "I mean, we weren't religious in my family or anything, and I never thought much about God or any of that stuff until I came here. But old Mas Fardeed, he was a very religious person and he believed in some kind of God."

"God's a Marine," Schultz said sarcastically. "He just kicks ass and takes names."

"I mean, it just figures there's got to be somebody in charge," Dean insisted.

"Maybe," one of the others said, "but maybe not."

"No, no, I think maybe there really is a God, but he's just there, behind the scenes, kind of, watching us try to figure things out," Claypoole offered.

"God is an idiot, then, to have made so many stupid assholes," Schultz snorted.

"I believe in God," Bass said from where he lay, sandwiched between Dean and Claypoole. "He's a joker," he continued. "He—or It—is like a kid who likes to put small animals into glass jars and watch 'em try to get out. But I'll tell you one goddamned thing: tomorrow morning, two hours before dawn, we are gonna get up and start walking about 240 kilometers in that direction," he pointed due west, "back to HQ. And when you dukshits are all safe back on Thorsfinni, drinking beer at Big Barb's and trying to snatch a passing titty, you'll know one thing for sure: a Marine is the finest thing God ever made, he knows it, and he's satisfied with it. Now shut up and let me sleep, 'cause I got a big day tomorrow."

CHAPTER
TWENTY-FIVE

At first Fred McNeal was aware of a roaring noise that barely penetrated the red haze of his pain. After a few moments, just as he regained full consciousness, the noise resolved itself into the beating of his pulse.

McNeal was tightly bound to a cross that had been erected so that his feet barely touched the ground. The weight of his body hung heavily from leather straps bound tightly around his chest and under his rib cage. His arms were stretched above his head and out to the sides. The major source of the pain that throbbed throughout every fiber of his body came from the excruciating pressure hanging in this position put on the broken humerus of his right arm. Gradually he became aware of the other injuries he had sustained when the Siad horsemen trampled him. The blood from a scalp wound that congealed over the front of his head stuck his eyelids together, and despite the agony of his other injuries, he fought down a surge of panic that he might have been blinded.

McNeal groaned.

"Aha!" Shabeli the Magnificent exclaimed. "The beautiful dreamer has awakened to join us!" Shabeli tossed a bucket of water into McNeal's face. The cool liquid washed enough of the gore away that McNeal could now open his eyes. It also reminded him that he was burning up with thirst.

"Water," he croaked. He flicked his tongue about the inside of his mouth, only to find that besides everything else, he was missing most of his front teeth.

"You won't need any water where you're going, Mr. Confederation Marine Corps man," Shabeli responded. McNeal's vision cleared. The man standing before him was big and very dark-skinned. He was so tall that his eyes were almost level with McNeal's. They were very bright eyes, and looking into them, McNeal felt the first twinge of real fear since the attack started—when? He had lost track of time. Suddenly it became very important for him to know how long he had been this way.

"H-how long . . . ?"

"Since this time yesterday," Shabeli answered. "We tried everything to bring you back to consciousness and were afraid at one point you'd die before experiencing the hospitality we've arranged for you." Shabeli's laugh was deep and resonant and full of menace.

But the fact that he'd been unconscious for a whole day raised hope in McNeal's mind that a rescue party must long since have been launched. He remembered clearly one of his drill instructors saying that only one Marine had ever remained a prisoner for more than seventy-two hours.

"Of course," Shabeli continued, "we needn't keep you alive for what we have in mind. You'd serve our purpose equally well dead. But," Shabeli pretended resignation with a sigh, "it will be so much more interesting now that you are conscious and can fully appreciate our little tradition." Shabeli laughed again, this time flicking the tip of a sharp dagger against McNeal's side. The point gouged a nasty wound just below his rib cage, but with all his other injuries, the Marine hardly noticed the new damage.

"Your friends have proved very uncooperative," Shabeli informed McNeal. At the mention of "friends," McNeal's spirits soared. Some of the others had survived the attack! "Oh, they will come 'round!" Shabeli crowed in a jovial tone of voice. Suddenly his voice hardened. "They will give up all hope when they see what will happen to them!" With each word Shabeli poked McNeal's chest with his knife, each blow drawing blood. "Oh, you will be reunited with them, Mr. Confederation Marine Corps man! Yes, indeed! They will be so surprised and impressed! But you, alas . . ." Shabeli shrugged.

For a long moment Shabeli was silent, gazing intently on McNeal's battered body. "There is nothing personal in any of what will soon transpire, I assure you," he said in a calm, sad voice, as if denying a bank loan to an indigent customer.

"Ah, go fuck yourself!" McNeal gritted through his broken teeth.

"Tsk tsk. You will never do that again, sadly. We Siad have elevated torture to an art form. With us it is almost a religious rite. We can induce the most exquisite pain in our victims. They scream and scream until they are hoarse, but they never lose consciousness."

"Eat shit!" McNeal shouted.

"First we will let our women use you. Ah, they have the most ingenious methods! They will put certain parts of your body into other parts in such a way it will astonish you. The act of . . . ah—'separation,' shall we say?—will be most painful, but afterward you will be fed a most original meal and you will savor the flavor of certain personal objects such as few men have ever done."

McNeal went cold with terror as he realized what this man was telling him. His only chance was to hold him off until rescue came. His mind raced. What could he say to stay this madman's plans?

"Then," Shabeli continued in a conversational tone of

voice, "the ladies will hand what is left of you over to certain gentlemen of my acquaintance who will finish the job begun under their feminine auspices. You will last for many hours, Mr. Confederation Marine Corps man. Finally, we will deposit your corpse where your comrades will find it. And when they do . . ." Shabeli raised his hands in a gesture of helplessness.

Shabeli lapsed into another long moment of silence. McNeal's heart raced. He had never been so frightened in his life, but he was determined not to show it before this man, or any of them. At the same time a tiny voice inside his mind told him he'd crack, badly, once they got started. He willed himself to die. No damned good, he thought. Why couldn't I have been killed outright in the attack? Does it all come down to this?

"You are almost like me," Shabeli said, putting his brown arm up against McNeal's naked chest. "We are black men, Mr. Confederation Marine Corps man!"

"Fuck we are!" McNeal croaked. "I'm black like a man! You're black like a piece of shit, you dirty motherfucker!"

Shabeli gasped and stepped backward as if McNeal had slapped him. "You—You—" Shabeli gasped in a paroxysm of rage. "You have a big mouth!" he shouted.

Suddenly McNeal was reminded of Corporal Singh and his admonishment so long ago back in New Rochester, "Recruit, you have a big mouth!" The utter incongruity of the memory, triggered by Shabeli's outrage in this desperate situation, was so bizarre that McNeal began to laugh. Despite his broken mouth and other terrible wounds, Fred McNeal roared in laughter.

Shabeli the Magnificent was astonished. Never had he seen a man act like this in the face of the Siad torture ritual. Most begged and screamed, some went mad, others raged and cursed. But none had ever laughed like this Marine. Whatever else their failures as human beings, the

Siad admired courage in a man, and to Shabeli, McNeal's laughing defiance was the highest form of physical courage he had ever witnessed. Such a man should die like a man. With one swift, spontaneous thrust, Shabeli the Magnificent buried his dagger to its hilt in Fred McNeal's chest.

Private First Class Frederick Douglass McNeal saw the flash of the blade, and in that instant he knew his life was ending. The last thing that flashed through his mind was that Staff Sergeant Neeley had said only one *live* Marine had ever remained a prisoner for more than seventy-two hours.

Shabeli turned to the circle of men who had been squatting silently, watching the tableaux. "Cut him down!" he ordered imperiously, stooping to clean his knife in the sand before stomping off to his tent.

CHAPTER
TWENTY-SIX

They didn't stay in Tulak Yar in the morning; there were too many bodies to bury. There was also the threat of the Siad coming back—or still being nearby. They knew other Marines might be coming back soon, to pursue the Siad or to aid any survivors, but still, they didn't, couldn't, stay. And with the sun came heat, and the two-day-old corpses began to stink.

The Siad observers in the hills were surprised to see the Marines leaving the village in the morning; they hadn't seen them enter it the night before.

The Siad had Raptors. The Siad had computers. The Siad had a sophisticated intelligence system in place within the planetary government. But their observation post overlooking Tulak Yar didn't have a radio. The commander of the observation post sent a rider on fast horses to the field headquarters of Shabeli the Magnificent.

Within two hours of receiving the report from Tulak Yar, Shabeli the Magnificent had a report from his intelligence sources on who these Marines were and where they had come from. Soon after, Wad Mohammad rode south at the head of a six-hundred-man-strong troop. Other Siad chiefs also rode with their warriors. Shabeli followed with sixty of his best warriors, all armed with blasters. He had more than two thousand men in pursuit not because he thought eight lost and isolated Marines were so strong that he would need that many to best them, but because the Martac Waste into which they had walked was a place where eight men could easily hide. He needed that many men to find them.

Once they were found, Shabeli the Magnificent, attended by his blaster men as an honor guard, would deal with them personally. But first he had a surprise for these Confederation Marine Corps men.

"I know the river is the obvious way to go," Bass said patiently. "Yes, if anyone comes looking for us, they'll probably follow the river valley—for a distance. Bear in mind, 'anybody' includes the Siad. We don't have any communications—that means we can't call anybody to come and pick us up. There's almost as good a chance of the Siad running into us as there is of a Marine patrol finding us along the river. That's one reason we're going cross-country." He looked at his men expectantly.

Dean was the one who had a question. "You said 'one reason.' Does that mean there's another reason?"

"Cross-country's half the distance. The maps we have of Elneal aren't much, but I studied them. According to them, right here the Bekhar River is near the top of a big bend to the north. About forty klicks downstream it takes a turn back to the south, and then the southeast, before it heads west again. We go twice as far if we follow the river all the way, or we go cross-country from where it bends south, and then we'd have to cross a mountain range.

"The way I see it, our best chance is to go cross-country from here. It's a lot shorter, and if our people might not find us there, we also have a smaller chance of running into the wrong people. Any other questions?" Nobody had any. "All right, then, look around for canteens and waterskins. Fill as many as you can carry. There are probably water holes out there, but we have no way of knowing where they are. It might be a while before we can get any kind of resupply. Do it."

Immediately, they scattered to find whatever containers they could to carry water and fill them from the one well they thought might not be contaminated. They'd still use purification tabs. If they were lucky, they'd have enough tabs to last the entire trek. If not, they'd all be sick by the time they reached New Obbia, unless they got rescued fast.

"PFC Dean, are my eyes deceiving me?" Bass asked when he saw Dean trotting toward him bearing a carton.

"Not unless I'm dreaming and you're in it," Dean replied.

"I'd have to be in his dream too," Claypoole said, coming up behind Dean. "And I refuse to be in his dreams. This is real."

Bass grinned and shook his head in wonder. One carton of field rations would feed a squad for three days, almost enough to supply four full days for the eight of them.

"We may run short of water," Bass said, "but this is enough chow to get us all the way home." He eyed the carton suspiciously. "Unless it's been contaminated somehow."

Dean shook his head. "Wrong. First thing I thought when I saw it was it was booby-trapped. So I looped a field cord around it, got behind a wall, and tugged. When it came loose, I checked it. The outer wrapping isn't broken anywhere, it can't be contaminated."

Bass nodded. "You're probably right." He studied him for a moment, then said, "Now you know why I never busted on you and McNeal for sneaking food to the villagers."

Dean gaped at him. He wasn't supposed to know they'd been giving cartons of rations to some of the villagers.

Bass laughed when he saw Dean's expression.

In another ten minutes everyone was back, loaded down with filled water containers. They all looked at the carton.

"We'll divide up the rations evenly," Bass told them, "along with the water." He broke the carton open, dumped its contents on the ground, mixed them up without looking at the pile, then began randomly grabbing packages and handing them out. There were fifteen different meals in the carton, two of each. Some were more desirable than others. Blind, random distribution was the only way to make sure no individual got stuck with all of the less desirable ones. After the rations and water were evenly distributed, Bass stood and checked that all his gear was secure on his body.

"Let's move it out," he said. "We'll chow down when we get away from this—" He looked around sadly. "—charnel house. Schultz, take point."

Minutes later the eight Marines were quietly headed east, into the Martac Waste. After an hour, Bass figured they were far enough away from the carnage of Tulak Yar to stop to eat.

They walked for three more hours, with Schultz looking back at Bass every few minutes to make sure he was still headed in the right direction. Bass frequently looked at the GPL he carried in his hand. He rarely had to do anything other than nod at Schultz—the man had an excellent sense of direction, which was one reason Bass wanted him to stay on the point. When the day's heat began to rise, and the sweat evaporated almost as fast as it beaded on their skin, Bass called a halt in the shade of a rocky outcrop.

"We'll stay here until sunset," he said. "It'll be best if we do our walking at night and in the morning." He didn't say that he wanted a good start on this morning to put as much distance as possible between them and Tulak

Yar, with its memories and its devastation. And the possible danger that lurked there.

While his Marines shrugged off their loads and collapsed gratefully in the shade, Bass scouted around their position. The Martac Waste wasn't as rugged as what they'd passed through north of Tulak Yar, but it was far from flat. Outcrops such as the one they stopped by dotted the landscape as far as he could see, flat-topped hills with sheer sides and masses of scree at their bases. Some of them were so narrow that if they had names, they'd be called towers or needles. Others were broad enough to be mesas. The hard ground between the outcrops and hills looked flat to a quick glance, but was filled with a tracery of small erosion gullies from the infrequent rains and simple cracks from the arid conditions. Most of the gullies were shallow enough that a man could step into and out of them without breaking stride. Most of the cracks could be stepped across without stretching. Most of them. There were a few major rivercourses, and some of the cracks Bass had seen were too wide to cross without bridging equipment, and looked to be bottomless. The little vegetation that existed here was low and scraggly where it lay in the full glare of the sun. Some grew where the hills or outcrops shaded it during the middle part of the day, and there it grew to the height of a man, though it was still scraggly. The only movement Bass could see was a few specks drifting high in the sky, hunting fliers or scavengers, he supposed. He saw nothing moving on the ground, not insects nearby nor dust devils farther out—the ground was too hard for dust devils to form.

So far as Bass could tell, the eight of them were quite alone. But he knew how deceptive apparent aloneness could be. While his men rested in the shade, he wanted someone watching their backs. He found a shaded spot on the west side of the outcrop from which most of the southern exposure could be watched. As the sun moved across the sky and its heat and brilliance filled this spot, he'd find another. One-hour watches, one man each. When all of them, including him, had had a turn, they would start out again.

Bass nodded to himself. It would do. They'd made good time during the four hours they walked. He estimated they'd covered more than sixteen kilometers. When they started again, they should do double that or more before he called another stop. Unless they came across an impassable rift, they should reach the outskirts of New Obbia in five or six days.

They moved out when the sun was low on the horizon and walked another twenty klicks by the light of the stars before Bass called another break. Then they slept until two hours before dawn and set out again.

Schultz, on the point after two and a half hours of walking, came to a stop. He didn't abruptly halt in his tracks, nor did he slow down over several paces until he was no longer moving forward. He just came to a stop and stood there with his chin on his chest, not moving, not seeming to do anything but stand there. The others stopped and faced outward when they saw Schultz stop. Some of them lowered themselves to kneeling or prone positions.

Bass watched as Schultz raised his head skyward and cocked it as though listening to something in the far distance. He walked forward. Schultz was on one knee when he reached him. The pointman turned his head toward Bass, but his eyes didn't look at him; they were scanning the horizon.

"You feel it too, huh?" Bass asked.

Schultz nodded. "Someone's out there."

"See anything? Hear anything specific?" When Bass

had listened, all he heard was the distant cawing of fliers. Their specks in the air was all his probing eyes could see.

Schultz slowly shook his head. "Just a feeling."

Bass knew the feeling, a crawling between the shoulder blades, a tensing of the neck muscles when there was nothing obvious to cause it. Bass had had it a few times. Each time, someone was there whom he couldn't see or hear. One time he felt it when some civilians were traveling the same road behind his unit. Another time it was a Marine unit converging through the jungle with his. The other times, maybe a half dozen throughout his career, it had been the enemy and the feeling saved him and other Marines from getting ambushed or caught unaware from behind.

"Any idea of where? Direction, distance, anything?"

Schultz nervously licked his lips and shook his head again. "There's someone out there somewhere, probably behind us, that's all I know."

"Could be someone looking for us."

"No shit."

A smile flickered across Bass's face. "I mean Marines, looking to rescue us."

Schultz looked directly at Bass. "You really think so? How'd they know to look out here instead of following the river?"

"Maybe they spotted us on satellite reconnaissance."

Schultz shrugged. "Maybe."

"Well, we'll keep going and be more alert. See that high place over there, looks like about a kilometer and a half?" Bass pointed. Schultz looked and nodded. "Let's go there. There's shade to rest in, and maybe it's a defensible position."

"I want rear point."

"You got it." Bass turned back to his other men. "Claypoole, up," he called softly.

Claypoole jumped up from where he'd been resting and watching the horizon and trotted to the head of the short column.

"You're taking point," Bass told him.

Claypoole looked startled. Pointman was the most important position for a patrol on the move. "This operation is my first real action. I don't have any more experience than Dean or Clarke. Dornhofer and Neru have more experience than me. You sure you want me on point?"

"Neru's got the gun. You've got plenty of training experience. You've got the point. Be alert, very alert. I can't say for sure, but I have a feeling someone is out here with us."

Claypoole looked at Bass oddly, but all he said was, "Aye aye, boss." He headed toward the outcropping Bass pointed out. His eyes probed everywhere in his path and to the sides. Whoever it was that Bass had a feeling about, Claypoole was determined to spot them if they were anywhere near his path.

At first glance the outcropping wasn't what Bass could have hoped for. It gave the shade for which he hoped for their daylight rest, but didn't have good positions from which to watch their rear. On the other hand, an erosion gully led past it. The gully was two meters deep and, as far as Bass could tell, meandered for several hundred meters in the direction of their march and past another rocky outcrop.

When everybody was in the deepest shade they could find, Bass looked at Schultz, who nodded and hooked a thumb back the way they'd come.

Bass nodded back and said out loud, "Listen up, everybody. There might be somebody following us. It could be another Marine patrol looking for us or it could be a nomad family just doing what nomad families do. Or it could be a Siad war party hunting us. We have no way of knowing until we see them." He paused for a second, but continued before anyone could ask questions. "If Siad are following us, they probably know exactly where we are. So what we're going to do," he pointed, "is go into that gully there and travel in it to the next outcrop. Don't anybody point, and don't look too obviously. But you see where I mean. We'll wait here for a half hour or so—I don't think anyone following us will do anything right away." Most of them noticed that even though Bass gave two options other than a Siad war party, everything he was planning was to counter the Siad. "If you're hungry, go ahead and chow down. If you're tired, take a nap. Any questions?"

"Why do you think it's safe to wait a half an hour?" Clarke asked.

"They're probably several kilometers away. Unless they want to make a long charge straight at us, it'll take them a couple of hours—or longer—to get into a position to do anything."

That explanation satisfied Clarke and everybody else. Even if it didn't fully satisfy Bass himself.

Thirty-five minutes later, one by one, they slithered on their bellies from the shade into the gully. Then, bent over, they trotted the several hundred meters to the next outcropping. From there they had a very good view of where they had just been. Bass put two men in covered positions watching their back trail and another man watching their rear; the watches changed every two hours. He let the others sleep. He kept watch himself. The day passed uneventfully. At a half hour before sunset, Bass and Schultz were the only ones who hadn't decided nobody was out there, so they were the only ones who weren't surprised to see a dozen figures creeping up on their earlier position from the rear.

CHAPTER
TWENTY-SEVEN

·

A hopper sped Captain Conorado back to New Obbia. He looked in on the men of third platoon where they were temporarily billeted in one of the government building's cafeterias, but didn't enter the room. He didn't have to count heads; the brief glance he took told him there weren't nearly enough Marines in that cafeteria.

"Where are the rest of your men?" he asked Ensign Baccacio.

Ensign Baccacio looked a bit green. He swallowed. "They're gone, sir. The Siad . . ."

Conorado waited expectantly, but when the young officer didn't continue he crooked a finger at him and led him to the room that was designated as his temporary office.

Conorado sat behind the desk in the room, but didn't offer a seat to Baccacio. "Tell me about it," he said.

Under Baccacio's air of discomfort was a touch of something else. "There's not much to tell," he said. "During the afternoon all-hands, a flight of Raptors hit Tulak Yar." Conorado blinked at Baccacio's mention of the all-hands but didn't interrupt. "The Raptors made several strafing passes over the village. They killed a lot of people and set off fires all over the place. Then several hundred Siad horsemen charged into the village and killed more people." He shook his head. "We took our

317

defensive positions as soon as we saw the Raptors coming. When the Siad attacked, we tried to fight them, but the way they were mingled among the people, it was hard to do much damage to them. When most of the villagers were dead and the rest fleeing, the Siad attacked our positions. We beat them off, then I ordered a withdrawal."

Conorado drummed his fingers on the desktop for a moment, then said, "Tell me about your casualties."

"Two men killed, three are in the infirmary—two of them had to be brought back in stasis units. There are other wounded, but they're walking wounded. They're with the rest of the platoon."

"Who was killed?"

"McNeal and Lanning."

"Who's hospitalized?"

"Kerr, Ratliff, and Goudanis."

The only sign of Conorado's mounting anger were his raised eyebrows. "Two dead and three serious casualties? I looked in that cafeteria. You're missing a lot more than five men." He held up his hand to stop Baccacio from saying anything and sat silently for a moment that stretched into several moments, watching his third platoon commander struggle to not fidget. Finally he said, "You let a bunch of savages straight out of the gunpowder era chase you off." He shook his head. "Now. Tell me about the circumstances of your withdrawal."

Baccacio's discomfort vanished and what had only been hinted at below it came to the fore: confident arrogance. "We had been severely bloodied by the Siad. I had ten men dead, including the Bass patrol, three severely wounded, and many of the others were also wounded. The Siad feinted a retreat to lure us into an ambush where they could finish us off." Conorado's eyes widened slightly at the way Baccacio's story was changing from what he had first said, but he didn't interrupt. "The villagers were all either dead or scattered," the young officer continued. "A medical evacuation hopper was at least half an hour away. Help was farther away. I ordered my men into the Dragon so we could get out of there before the Siad came back and finished what they started."

Baccacio brought himself to an erect and rigid attention. "Sir, I wish to bring charges of willful disobedience of orders in the face of the enemy against Sergeant Wang Hyakowa. When I gave the order to withdraw, he opposed me. He swore at me and threatened me. I had to draw my side arm and place him under arrest before he could rally any of the men to his side."

He had more to say, but Conorado interrupted him. "Let's go back to your dead. You say you had two men killed at Tulak Yar. The battalion medical officer only has one body, Lanning. Where's McNeal's body?"

Baccacio didn't even flinch. "Sir, we didn't have time to collect it."

"Then how do you know he's dead?"

"I saw him in the open. A group of Siad horsemen trampled over him. I never saw him again."

Conorado splayed his hands on the desktop for a moment and stared at them. When he looked up, he asked softly, "How do you know they didn't take him prisoner?"

Baccacio swallowed but couldn't find anything to say.

Conorado didn't let a silence stretch this time. He immediately asked, "Then you said you had ten men dead, including the Bass patrol. Tell me about that."

Baccacio grimaced. "Staff Sergeant Bass had a patrol out, testing the UPUD. I don't know how they found them, but the Siad got to them."

"How do you know that?"

"I tried to raise them on the radio and got no response."

The captain's neck muscles tightened and his jaw worked as he struggled to keep himself under control.

When he spoke again, there was no mistaking his anger.
"Mr. Baccacio, there are circumstances under which the
UPUD Mark Two will fry its insides. One reason for that
test was to see how likely it was to happen under actual
field conditions."

"Sir," Baccacio blurted, "nobody told us that!"

Conorado nodded—a slow, rigidly controlled nod.
"That's right. The test wouldn't have been valid if the
testers knew about the potential problem."

The company commander sat leaning back in his
chair for a long moment, drumming his fingers on the
desktop. "I've already read everybody else's reports, Mr.
Baccacio," he suddenly said. "They're all telling the
same story, and their story is at variance with yours. The
squad leaders, the surviving fire team leaders, and Corporal Manakshi all agree that the Siad had suffered about
fifty percent casualties and were in full flight. Manakshi
wanted to pursue, and you bodily removed his driver
from the Dragon's controls so he couldn't. The villagers
weren't all dead or scattered, at least not according to
Doc Hough. He said there were many civilians waiting
for his attention. He even volunteered to stay behind
to give aid to them, and you refused. According to
everyone, there was ample time between the end of the
fight and your withdrawal to retrieve McNeal's body—if
indeed it was there. Beyond one radio call, you made no
attempt to contact or locate the Bass patrol.

"Mr. Baccacio, the way I read all the other reports, you
fled in the face of a defeated enemy. You abandoned men
in the field. There is no worse dereliction of duty that can
be committed by a Marine officer. Rest assured, there
will be a court of inquiry. Unless new evidence appears, I
will urge that court of inquiry to recommend a general
court-martial for you." He stood abruptly. "Confine your-

self to quarters, Mr. Baccacio," he said as he stormed out of the office.

Ensign Baccacio stood rigid, his face blanched, his eyes wide and staring at nothing. He didn't seem to be breathing.

"Wild Bill," Conorado said, entering the command center, "bring in your UAVs and refuel. I've got a new mission for you."

Sergeant Flett shook his head. "No can do, sir. We're grounded."

"What do you mean grounded?"

"Someone's jamming us."

Conorado looked at him incredulously. "Who could be jamming you here? This planet isn't that technologically advanced."

"That may be so, Skipper, but somebody's using as sophisticated a jamming system as I've ever seen. I can't control my birds in flight, much less get any images from them." It was his turn to show incredulity. "It's so sophisticated a jamming system, we aren't even getting good resolution on our images from the string of pearls."

Bass watched the Siad warriors and wondered if they were the only ones, or if there were more nearby. He bitterly wished he had a motion detector, or satellite communications, even his helmet with its infra goggles to get a better look at the landscape. If the Siad he could see were alone in this area, he and his Marines could take them out. If there were others nearby, though, it could easily be a different story. Of course, that would depend on how many there were. Or if any ran off to alert a larger group. This situation was too much like the first day, when the UPUD Mark II committed suicide and the first band of Siad came past. The best thing for them to do might be nothing, let these go their way as they had the horsemen, and then surreptitiously continue on without alerting anyone that they were there.

While Bass was thinking that, the Siad completed their approach to the outcropping. Suddenly, with war cries that were clearly audible even at more than three hundred meters, the Siad leaped to their feet and ran around to the north side of the outcrop, firing their projectile rifles in a wild and ragged fusillade that ended even more abruptly than it started. He watched as the Siad darted about, yelling. Some of them threw their arms into the air; a few fired shots at the sky.

"You're slick, Staff Sergeant Bass," Claypoole said. "We really faked them out."

"What do we do now?" Dean asked. "They're in range and they're just standing around. We can get them easy from here."

"Where are their friends?" Bass replied.

Schultz nodded. He wasn't watching the Siad who attacked their earlier position, he was looking around for others.

Dornhofer saw the puzzled expression on Dean's face and said, "Maybe that's an isolated group. If it is, you're right, we can take them. But if they're out in force looking for us, shooting just tells them exactly where we are and all of them can come after us. Just like what would have happened two days ago if we'd shot the first horsemen we saw."

Dean didn't say anything to that.

"We wait and see what they do," Bass said. "Then we decide what we do." Seeing what the Siad did included watching for more of the nomads. He assigned men to a 360-degree watch; he kept watch on the ones he knew about.

"Do you think they'll find our tracks and follow us?" Dean asked.

Bass slowly shook his head. "I kept an eye on the ground while we were following the gully. It looked pretty hard. I didn't see any tracks left by the men ahead of me. Hammer, how about you?"

Schultz shook his head; he hadn't seen any footprints either.

"But this is their land," Bass cautioned. "They might see things we can't."

Just then one of the Siad gave out an excited cry. He pointed into the gully where it passed the outcropping, then dropped into it. The others raced to him.

"They can see things we can't," Bass murmured. "Neru, how many of them can you get with one burst?"

The gunner looked at the Siad. Nine or ten of them were standing bunched together next to the gully; the others were out of sight inside it. "Right now, maybe all of them."

"Do it."

"Aye aye. Clarke, spot for me." Neru quickly set up his gun on its bipods and took aim. Clarke lay down next to him, an extra battery in his hand, ready to reload the gun if Neru expended the battery in it. "Wish I had a spare barrel," Neru muttered.

Bass nodded wryly. No need to carry weight that they wouldn't need, he'd thought. Well, he'd thought wrong and there was nothing to do for it now.

"Ready?" Bass asked the gunner.

"Ready."

"Fire."

Neru pressed the firing lever and a stream of fiery bolts shot through the air in an elliptical cone. The bunched Siad collapsed. He released the lever.

They waited. After a few seconds a thin keening came

toward them; at least one of the Siad was wounded, not killed.

Bass grimaced. A nonlethal hit at that range was a horrible wound; it left a man disfigured and crippled—if he didn't die a lingering death from the injury, or go into convulsive shock and die from that.

A Siad jumped out of the gully and ran toward the wounded warrior. He didn't make it. Schultz calmly took aim and shot him. "Only one or two left," he said.

"Right," Bass said dryly. "And we've got to take out that one or two so they don't get back to others and set them all on us."

"What if . . . what if there are more close enough that they heard the gunfire?" Dean asked.

"Then they're already on their way." Bass looked at his men. "Everybody, stay sharp. Watch all around. Dornhofer, you're in charge. If anybody pops his head up, take him out. Hammer, you come with me. We're going to get them."

Schultz didn't wait for further orders. He darted to the gully and into it.

Dornhofer realized that with Schultz already on his way, Bass didn't have any time to spend on further preparations. "I've got everything under control, boss," he said.

Bass took off after Schultz. He had to race to close the gap, and even running as fast as he could without exposing himself, they were halfway there before he caught up.

It was a wasted effort. The Siad survivor—or survivors—was gone.

"Look, there's a track," Schultz said, pointing. "We can follow him."

Bass shook his head. "Probably not very far. Remember, neither you nor I saw the tracks we made. The Siad spotted them right off. This is their land. Their tracks will be harder to spot than ours. Let's get out of here. We have to leave this place now, before he comes back with his friends."

Schultz didn't speak or nod, he just turned back.

"We'll be harder to track at night," Bass said. He wasn't sure if he was telling Schultz or was trying to reassure himself.

When Bass and Schultz reached the rest of the patrol, the eight Marines set out as fast as they could without running. By nightfall they were two kilometers away from the scene of the fight. Bass looked back into the dying embers of the day. He couldn't see any moving figures silhouetted against the setting sun. Darkness made them slow their pace, but they kept it as fast as they could manage.

CHAPTER
TWENTY-EIGHT

"By the grace of God who is above all Gods, Wad Mohammad, we know where they go," the survivor of the attack at the rocks reported. He knelt on the rocks before his clan chief, who sat on an elaborately carved folding chair. His subchiefs and attendants stood in an arc behind him.

"There was an arm of you, and you are the only survivor?" Wad Mohammad asked. His voice was level, but disbelief and danger were in his eyes.

"By the grace of God who is above all Gods, Wad Mohammad, this is the truth." The survivor trembled slightly, but managed not to quake in his fear.

"There were how many of these off-world Marines?"

"Eight, Wad Mohammad."

The clan chief knew without being told how many Marines there were. Having the survivor admit to the small number gave truth to the man's story. Had he said there were so many off-world Marines that anyone could understand them defeating a Siad arm, then he would be lying. If he was lying, Wad Mohammad would kill him now. "Twelve of you and eight of them." Wad Mohammad's voice developed a distinctly cold edge. "You alone of us survived. How many of their heads did you take?"

The survivor threw himself prostrate and stretched out pleading hands to grip the hem of Wad Mohammad's gown. "None, Wad Mohammad. These off-world Marines are more skillful at invisible movement than any man could expect. We watched the off-worlders take shelter from the sun in rocks. Alakbar, may his soul rest in heaven, was the leader of our arm. He made plans for us to attack them from their rear before the sun set, when they would be feeling most confident, most invulnerable, and therefore be the most vulnerable. They would be eating and drinking and preparing to begin their night's trek. Alakbar, may his soul rest in heaven, alone kept watch while the remainder of us rested. At the appointed time we moved from our resting place to the rear of the off-worlders' resting place. As the Great God is my witness, Wad Mohammad, a desert viper could not have known of our approach, so skillfully and silently did we move. On the command of Alakbar, may his soul rest in heaven, we attacked with great fury.

"The off-world Marines were not there. They had moved without us seeing them go. A shallow gully passed nearby. I looked into it and found their tracks. The off-world Marines do not yet know how to walk without leaving their marks behind. Bhufi, may his soul rest in heaven, came into the gully with me. He was reporting to Alakbar, may his soul rest in heaven, about the tracks when the off-world Marines rained balls of fire on us from their flame guns. They had hidden in other rocks almost a long rifle shot away. Bhufi, may his soul rest in heaven, jumped out of the gully, for what reason I do not know. Another fireball came from the off-worlders and sent him to attend God who is above all Gods.

"I hid away from there. The off-world Marines came to look for me, but they were unable to find the tracks I did not leave, so they left. I followed long enough to be sure where they were going, then I came back here with the greatest speed."

Wad Mohammad, leader of the Badawi clan, stared west for a long moment. Abruptly, he stood. "You will show me where these off-worlders have gone," he said to the survivor. "When we attack, you will have the honor of being the first man they see."

"Thank you, Wad Mohammad," the survivor said, leaping to his feet and bowing. "You are most gracious and kind to one such as me."

"You!" Wad Mohammad snapped to one of his attendants. "Ride like the wind to the tent of Shabeli the Magnificent and report this to him. He has a gift he wishes to place in the path of the off-worlders."

The Marines heard the carrion-eaters before they saw them. Then sun glints reflecting from their scaly feathers became visible against the dark sky directly in the Marines' line of march as the birdlike creatures circled lazily on a dawn thermal. The vultures started drifting to the ground beyond a rise. At first Bass thought of skirting the scene—anything dead in the desert was of no interest to him and his men. But they needed to put as much distance as possible between them and the Siad to their rear before the heat made them stop. One hundred fifty meters beyond the crest of the rise they passed along the edge of a shallow dip in the ground where a substratum had collapsed, making a sheer-sided hollow about twenty meters wide and little more than one deep. The carrion-eaters had landed there and were squabbling over the feast that drew their attention; the Marines slowly came to a halt as soon as they saw what it was.

Schultz was the first to react to the sight—he spun toward it and flamed a half dozen of the vultures before the rest could scatter, screaming, into the air.

A human body stood grotesquely askew, impaled on a stake, the sharpened point of which jutted out just behind his right shoulder. Bass gave an abrupt hand signal and his men took up defensive positions around the rim of the shallow hollow. Schultz and Claypoole raced beyond the corpse to defend from that direction. Doyle stood dumbly where he was, gaping at the gruesome sight. Even as badly mangled by the torture the body had undergone, and torn by vultures' beaks as it was, Bass immediately recognized McNeal.

Bass stood still, transfixed by the horror confronting him. He had to will himself to step closer for a better look. He had to fight down his own gorge at the sight before him. He had never seen anything to match the mutilations the Siad had performed on what was once one of his men. Then a piece of paper caught his eye and he leaned closer.

From behind, someone vomited and another man cursed. Dean stumbled down the slope and stood beside his platoon sergeant.

"Get back up there, Dean," Bass muttered, his voice tight with suppressed emotion. "Nothing you can do down here."

"But—"

Bass whirled on Dean. "I said get back into position, Marine!"

Dean stood rooted to the spot. Then the full realization of what the Siad had done to his friend dawned upon him. "Fred . . . Fred . . ." Dean gasped, and then he began to cry helplessly. "Shut up and listen to me!" Bass commanded. He shook Dean several times. The crying stopped. "McNeal was dead before they did that to him. There's no blood, the wounds are all dry. They put him here as a message to us."

Seizing Dean by his equipment harness, Bass slammed the young man's blaster into his hands and shoved him back up the side of the hollow. He watched until Dean assumed a position, facing outward on the lip. Satisfied that Dean had himself under control, Bass turned back to the body and reached for the piece of paper that had caught his eye.

It was a note. The writing was gracefully curved and the letters were more horizontal than vertical, but it was recognizably English. It read:

Marines of the Confederation, trespassing on my land:

Your fame precedes you. I look forward with great anticipation to our meeting. Which will happen soon now that you are in my tent. Then you will become mine, and your fame will pass on to my possession.

Shabeli the Magnificent

". . . now that you are in my tent," Bass read again, and swore. McNeal's body wasn't put here as a message—it was here as the bait in a trap.

Cursing himself for falling for it, Bass yelled, "On your feet, we're moving out." It might be too much to hope for, but since the Siad hadn't attacked, maybe they hadn't arrived yet, at least no more than came to plant McNeal's body and leave the note. Maybe they could reach a more defensible position before the Siad were ready.

"Claypoole, Dean," Bass continued with his orders, "you're carrying this body. Marines don't leave their dead behind." Dean and Claypoole jumped up and ran to him. Before they reached him, he turned to McNeal's body and wrapped his arms around it as tightly as he could. Jerking from side to side, he loosened the impaling stake and yanked it out of the ground with the corpse still on it. As rapidly as he could, he laid out his ground cover and rolled the body into it.

"Claypoole, give me some of your line," he snapped. He took the offered spool of monofilament and used a length of it to tie the ground cover securely in place. Stone-faced, he ordered, "Use the pole to carry him."

Claypoole grimaced but reached for one end of the pole.

Dean flinched and looked as though he was about to cry.

"It's the best way to carry him," Bass snarled. "It'll be easier on you if he's not hanging between you like a sack of loose corn." His voice softened. "He's dead. It won't hurt him. If he knew, this is the way he'd want you to carry him."

Dean nodded and brushed the back of his hand at his eyes. "We'll take care of you, Fred," he croaked. Then he squatted and grabbed the end of the pole opposite Claypoole. "On three," he said in a clear but still weak voice. "One," his voice was stronger, "two," stronger yet, "three!" He sounded now as if no Siad had better show his face to PFC Joseph F. Dean, not today, not tomorrow, not ever.

Bass looked at Schultz, stuck his right hand up, twirled it in a quick circle, then thrust it forward to the west—move out. Schultz moved out. Bass sprinted to catch up; he wanted to take bearings and give Schultz a spot on the horizon to aim for. Just as he reached the pointman and was checking his GPL, a gunshot rang out and rock splintered in front of him. He heard the whine of the bullet as it ricocheted away.

"BACK!" Bass bellowed as he spun toward the hollow where they found McNeal's body.

Neru and Clarke hadn't gotten away from the hollow before the shot rang out and were still in it. Dean and Claypoole were already disappearing over its rim with their burden. Dornhofer was calmly assigning positions and fields of fire. Schultz raced Bass for safety. Even Doyle was scrambling to get under cover and ready his weapon.

"Did anybody see where that came from?" Bass called out as he dropped down with only the upper half of his head showing above the lip of the hollow.

Schultz was the only one who answered. "Somewhere to the right." Bass already knew that much.

He was looking that way. The terrain appeared flat to the north, but he was looking at it from ground level and couldn't see if there were indentations or gullies, though he knew there must be. There were no major outcroppings of rocks within rifle range where the shooter could be hiding, but boulders studded the landscape. He saw a couple dozen places where the shot could have come from.

"All right, everybody, look sharp. Whoever's out there will get around to showing himself. Dornhofer, make sure we've got all directions covered, they could be anywhere." And were probably everywhere. That shot had just been intended to make them stay in place, he was sure of that. He was equally sure there was more than just one sniper watching them. How many were there, and how long would they have to wait for something to happen?

Long enough to begin to sap their strength. There was no shade in the shallow hollow. The sun beat down on them hard, harder, hardest as it climbed the sky. They had walked all night, since just before the previous sunset. They were tired. Bass blinked sweat out of his eyes. If the Siad wanted to, they could keep them pinned here until they ran out of water and died from dehydration. Bastards. He didn't think the Siad would wait that long; they had too high an opinion of themselves as fighters. Maybe they'd be pinned down here all day with nothing more than an occasional shot aimed at them. If so, maybe they could slip away after nightfall. He looked up at the sky. The sun wasn't far above the morning horizon. No, he didn't think the Siad would wait long enough to give them a chance to slip away under cover of night.

"Watch your water, people," Bass said when he saw Clarke taking a long drink. "It's going to have to last longer than we thought."

Another shot rang out, from the southwest this time. They all ducked, but the bullet cracked harmlessly high overhead. Just something to let them know there was more than one man out there, Bass thought.

Several more minutes passed before another shot rang out, from the south. The Marines stayed low, watching tensely, waiting, hoping for someone to show himself and make a target for them to shoot back at. But the Siad didn't show themselves, and ten more minutes went by before another bullet flew toward them—from the southeast.

"Wait a minute," Claypoole shouted. "Northwest, southwest, south, southeast. There's only one man out there. He's circling around and firing from different places, trying to make us think we're surrounded."

No sooner had he spoken than a shot from the northeast ricocheted off the rock and sent stone splinters into Doyle's face.

"I thought of that," Bass replied to Claypoole. "But he couldn't have gone that far around us since the last shot."

"Right," Claypoole said. He covered his embarrassment by scuttling to Doyle's side to see how badly he was hit. The company clerk waved him away; the only injury he'd suffered from the rock splinters were a few scratches.

Bass rolled over and looked at his men. They all looked more tired than he was. He had to do something about this or they might be too tired to fight well when the time came. "Dornhofer, Schultz, Claypoole, Clarke, go to sleep.

Neru, watch the south. Dean, east, Doyle, north. West is mine. We'll change watches in an hour."

Dornhofer and Schultz glanced at him, then pillowed their heads on their folded arms and closed their eyes, but Clarke gaped at him. "Go to sleep?" he croaked. "How are we supposed to sleep? People are shooting at us!"

"That's right." Bass nodded. "Shooting, but not hitting. Don't worry, I'll wake you up if anything interesting happens."

Bass gave them a couple of minutes to get settled, then dropped below the level of the basin rim and scuttled around to the men on watch to make sure they had the entire 360 degrees covered.

"How you doing, Doyle?" Bass asked when he flopped down next to him.

"Staff Sergeant Bass, I'm the goddamn company clerk," Doyle said indignantly. "I'm not supposed to be doing this bad-ass stuff." With several days' worth of grime coating his uniform and his exposed skin, and thin streamers of drying blood on his face, Doyle didn't look like a "goddamn company clerk." He grinned nervously and his voice became serious. "But I'm probably as good here as a boot lance corporal."

Bass clapped him on the shoulder. "Well, promote yourself to boot lance corporal, Doyle, you're doing a good job."

Doyle beamed at Bass as the platoon sergeant moved on.

"How long are they going to make us wait?" Dean's voice was rough; he had trouble controlling it.

"Until they're ready, PFC, until they're ready," Bass said calmly.

"Instead of waiting, we should go get them."

Bass thought he heard a touch of accusation in Dean's harsh tone. "No we shouldn't." He had to restrain himself from snapping. "We don't know how many of them there are or where they are. They might just be waiting for us to do something dumb like that and they'll take us all out at once. What we should do is wait for them to do something we can do something about. Maybe they'll make a mistake that we can take advantage of."

"They've got a reputation as tough fighters. How likely do you think it is they'll make a mistake?"

This time Bass did snap. "Their reputation is mostly from attacking and brutalizing unarmed civilians." He took a deep breath to calm himself, then continued, "They're probably a bit better than the Bos Kashi. You saw how many mistakes they made in New Obbia. If the Siad make only half as many mistakes, they'll make one we can take advantage of."

Dean grunted and kept his eyes sweeping his quadrant.

"I know you're upset about McNeal, PFC. I am too. He wasn't a friend, like he was with you, but he was one of my men, and it always bothers me to lose a man. Remember him, never let him go. He was a good man, and you were lucky to call him friend. When the Siad come after us—and they are going to come after us— remember to fire low so you don't waste your shots over their heads. Pick your targets and make every bolt count. And kill them, PFC Dean. Kill some of them in revenge for your friend, if that's what you have to do. But mostly kill them for the Marines who are alive here. We all depend on you to keep us alive. Every Marine depends on every other Marine. Understand?"

"I understand." His voice was thick.

Bass patted his shoulder and moved on.

Despite his protests, Clarke was snoring softly when Bass reached the position he shared with Neru.

"Sleeping Beauty's going to be okay," Neru said. He grinned at Bass. "Did you think you could sleep the first time you came under fire?"

Bass laughed ruefully. "On my first combat operation, I got so tired I slept right through a firefight."

Neru gave him a disbelieving glance. "Sure you did," he said, and returned his attention to his quadrant.

Bass returned to his position facing west. When the hour was up he woke the sleepers so he and the other three could grab an hour's rest. That hour was almost up when Dornhofer woke him.

"I think they're getting ready to do something," the corporal said.

Bass looked up and saw the sun was more than halfway to the zenith. "What do you see?" He looked all around the horizon, but saw nothing moving.

Dornhofer shook his head. "I didn't see anything; it's what I heard. Someone's to our west."

Suddenly, a high-pitched ululating scream, the war cry of a Siad clansman, rent the day.

On the opposite side of the basin the cry woke Dean with a start. He listened and the cry came again, from a different direction. He had never heard anything so terrifying, yet at the same time so wildly exciting—that one lonely, soaring cry fully embodied the utter disdain of men who believed in their souls that a death in combat was the most glorious and magnificent death a man could achieve.

The war cries woke Claypoole, who shuddered at their sound. He understood now how Chinese bugles in the night and Scottish bagpipes coming over the hill in wars fought centuries ago could be so frightening to the men they were directed against.

Doyle's eyes snapped open at the first cry and he slithered to his fighting position, blaster extended over the lip of the basin, eyes searching for enemy movement. "Someone's going to pay for disturbing my sleep," he growled at Schultz, who lay a couple of meters away.

Schultz looked at him and wondered what had got into the pogue. Maybe there was a real Marine underneath the clerk.

Bass finally saw movement. At 150 meters to the northwest, a single Siad warrior stood in the open. He shook his rifle at the sky and called out something in that same ululating voice; it sounded like a challenge. The Siad stopped yelling, brought his rifle down to his shoulder, and aimed toward the Marines. Before he could fire, he pitched backward with a blazing hole through his chest.

Bass looked to his right rear, where he'd heard the crack-sizzle of a blaster, and saw Schultz tick off a mark on the air with his finger.

Then he didn't have any more time to look at his men. A hundred Siad warriors leaped to their feet from less than a hundred meters away and charged while screaming their ululating war cry.

CHAPTER
TWENTY-NINE

"Neru! Get your gun on them," Bass shouted as he glanced at his men to make sure they were all wearing their body armor. Satisfied that the Marines had as much protection as they could, he sighted on one Siad and pressed the firing lever on his blaster. "Dean, get over here next to me. Claypoole, watch our rear," he said, still giving orders. He was dropping a second attacker as Dean fell into position next to him and took aim at the onrushing Siad. "Dornhofer, Doyle, watch the flanks." He didn't bother telling Schultz what to do; Schultz was already flaming a Siad.

"Remember what I told you, Dean," he said quietly to the man next to him. "Keep your shots low, make them count."

"Roger that," Dean said, and got off two quick shots at a Siad in the center of the line who seemed to be directing the others. The head of that Siad suddenly erupted in flames. His body ran on for a couple of steps before it staggered and fell.

Neru got his gun set up and hosed a line of fire from left to right at the line of Siad. Many of them fell with arms blasted off, leaving charred stumps in their place. Others dropped with holes burned through their torsos. But the mass of Siad was close and moving too fast for the gunner to get more than a portion of them. Bass, Schultz, and Dean accounted for more, but the gun and three blasters weren't enough to convince the Siad to stop their suicidal charge. There were many fewer than had begun the charge, but they were only fifty meters away and closing.

"Everybody fire," Bass bellowed. Dornhofer and Doyle turned from where they were watching their flanks to fire at the ends of the Siad line. The line shortened. Claypoole raced across the basin and dropped into position next to Bass, opposite Dean. His first shot went wild; his second took the leg off a screaming warrior.

The Siad were now only thirty meters away, close enough for Bass to make out their expressions. Their eyes were wide and manic, their mouths twisted grotesquely as they continued to scream out their wild war cries. Their shots flew less wildly at this shorter distance—one bullet smashed into the rock next to Bass and riddled his side with stone shards. Thank goodness for body armor, Bass thought.

But there were only thirty Siad left.

Neru suddenly bounded out of the basin, raced a few paces to his left, then spun and, holding his gun clamped tightly to his hip, sprayed fire across the front of the Marine position at the Siad. Three of the Siad shot at him, but their bullets barely staggered him as they pinged off his armor. With one long burst Neru took out the entire middle and one side of the Siad line. But eight of the attackers were left, and he was directly in their path.

"Neru, drop!" Bass screamed. He snapped off a shot and plasma bored through the chest of a Siad.

Neru dove away from the few remaining attackers and scuttled toward the safety of the basin. A bullet whanged off the rock inches away and sent a rock shard into his arm. He didn't pause in his crawling.

Dean gut-shot a Siad who was trying to bayonet Neru's unprotected neck. Schultz calmly stood up and fired over the crawling gunner, taking out two more. Claypoole hit one below the knee, tearing his leg off. Doyle fired three rapid shots and screamed, "I got one!" Dornhofer hit one in the neck, burning it half away. Clarke realized that without the gun to assist with, he could use his own blaster; he picked it up and drilled the last attacker still on his feet.

Sudden silence, except for the wailing of the Siad whose leg Claypoole had burned off, fell over the battlefield.

"Back to your positions," Bass ordered after a few seconds.

"But—But we beat them," Dean said. "It's over."

"No it's not," Bass snapped. He grimly scanned the surrounding landscape. "That was just the first wave. There's more of them out there."

"How do you know that? We killed everybody."

"No we didn't. Not by a long shot."

As if to punctuate Bass's words, the legless Siad screamed shrilly, then grated something in the harsh tongue of the desert nomads. He groped about for his rifle, found it, and fumbled with it. If he was going to heaven in the next few minutes he was taking some of these infidels with him.

Schultz climbed out of the basin and walked over to the man. He drew his knife and leaned over to slit his throat. He was almost too late, the Siad had his rifle in his shoulder and was taking aim. His finger twitched spasmodically when Schultz killed him, and his rifle fired. The bullet whanged into the air and away.

Bass faced into the middle of the basin so he could see all of his men when he spoke to them. "Before that assault wave, we heard them screaming all around. They only came at us from one direction. There's more of them out there. They're going to come after us again. We don't know what direction they'll come from next, so we have to be ready for anything. That was just a test to see how we'd perform, what kind of fighters we are." He didn't say the other thing he thought: that the Siad commander must suspect they weren't carrying many extra batteries for their blasters, and was spending the lives of some of his men to make the Marines expend power.

Dean looked to the west, shaking his head at the hundred bodies that littered the landscape. "They kept coming at us," he said weakly. His dazed eyes hardly noticed the carrion-eaters that were already landing among the corpses, hopping from one to another to make sure they were dead and cooling before beginning their feast. "We were killing them and they kept coming. Why did they keep coming, how could they do that? They must have known they didn't have a chance."

Bass looked at Dean. "What would we have done if they had run when we started killing them?"

Dean didn't say anything, simply kept shaking his head.

Schultz spoke for him. "We would have shot them in the back."

Bass nodded. "That's right. If they had run, we would have killed them just the same. By continuing their charge, they had a chance, some of them, of reaching us. If enough of them made it, they might be able to overwhelm us in hand-to-hand combat. Once they reached a certain point, their only chance was to keep coming." He looked at his gunner. "If Neru hadn't done one of the dumbest things I've ever seen a man do in a firefight and got so many of them in an enfilade, some of them would have reached us."

Neru shrugged. "It wasn't that dumb; I knew I could get most of them with one burst."

"Yeah, but you didn't get the ones closest to you."

Schultz spat over the rim of the basin. "That was our job. Marines depend on each other. We got the ones closest to him." He gave Neru an approving look.

A sudden cry had everyone looking outward. "MARINE, YOU DIE TODAY," a harsh voice called.

"They speak English," Dean gasped in surprise.

"YOUR LOVED ONES WILL WAIL," another voice immediately yelled. The two voices were in different places.

Bass shook his head. "No they don't. They're just mouthing noises somebody taught them."

"THE VULTURES WILL GET FAT EATING YOUR BODIES," a third voice in yet another place called.

"It's an old trick," Bass continued. "Learn how to insult the other guy in his own language." He grinned. "I've done it myself a few times." He wondered if he'd have the chance to use any of the local insults he'd learned in Tulak Yar.

Schultz stood and shouted back, "COME AND GET US, WE'LL FEED YOU TO THE BUZZARDS!" He pointed his blaster upward. "LOOK UP! THEY'RE WAITING FOR YOU." So many carrion-eaters were gathering in flocks drifting on the thermals, they seemed to darken the sky.

Clarke gaped at Schultz with disbelief. Claypoole grinned, wishing he'd shouted back an insult himself.

Dean looked at him with admiration. "Way to go, Hammer," he said under his breath.

Bass simply shook his head. Schultz knew the odds against them. Bass knew that Schultz didn't care. What he didn't know was why the man was so willing to defy death, to take on any challenge.

The Siad answered Schultz's taunt with a heavy fusillade of gunfire. Schultz dropped behind cover and giggled. "Show them who's afraid of who," he said. "Show them who's got more." He grabbed his crotch and gave it a quick jerk.

"Belay the johnwayne, Schultz," Bass said.

"They're real good at fighting farmers and women,"

Schultz said back. "This time they're up against Marines."
He looked out; the Siad had stopped shooting.

"They took on third platoon at Tulak Yar," Bass said.
"Nobody's at Tulak Yar anymore." Schultz looked at him
and opened his mouth to make a retort, but Bass cut him
off. "Don't say it, Schultz. Don't say it. There were good
Marines at Tulak Yar. We don't know how it happened, all
we know is they were driven off by the Siad." He looked at
the ground-cover bundle that contained McNeal's corpse.
"And we know they killed at least one good Marine."

Schultz twisted his mouth in disgust, but didn't say
what he was going to about Ensign Baccacio's leadership.
Bass stared at him until the lance corporal turned around
with a disgusted grunt and began watching outward.

The Siad resumed their taunting calls. Schultz yelled
back at them, but stayed down.

Bass looked at his men. He had three Marines besides
himself who were combat-hardened by several campaigns. Three others had seen their only previous combat
action against the Bos Kashi in New Obbia. Today
had been Doyle's baptism of fire. Against them were
arrayed hundreds, maybe thousands, of Siad warriors. He
restrained himself from shaking his head. He wished
Hyakowa or Eagle's Cry was with him. And Goudanis,
Lanning, and Chan—experienced men all, men he knew
were good in a fight.

But he didn't have them. He had to make do with
Claypoole, Dean, Clarke—and Doyle. And make do he
would. They were Marines, the product of the best military training in the history of mankind. And every one
of them had been blooded and acquitted himself well
enough. Even Doyle. He glanced at the clerk again. He
hadn't gotten sick when he killed a man, he'd cried out in
triumph. The thing Bass had to concern himself with
wasn't how they'd do when the shooting began again,

but how they were dealing with this waiting. Once the shooting started, either you fought or you ran. None of these men had given any indication of wanting to run when the Siad made that suicidal charge. It was the waiting that could bring a brave man down.

"You're probably wondering why they aren't attacking again," Bass said in a voice calculated to keep his men calm. Dornhofer, Schultz, and Neru kept watching outward. The others turned to look at him. "Keep watching," Bass told them. "I'll talk loud enough you won't have to watch my lips to see what I'm saying." The four turned outward. "They could attack again now. If all of them came at us at once, they'd overwhelm us with no problem; we wouldn't stand a chance. But you saw what happened to the hundred of them who already assaulted. We killed them all. Well, the Siad saw that too. They know that even though they'd get all of us, we'd kill so many of them it would be a pyrrhic victory. So they're playing a game with us. We're trapped in the sun, there's no shade here, no relief from the heat. They want that to work on us for a while, to wear us down. They want us strung out, tense. That way we won't kill as many of them. They want us to get anxious, so that when they come again we'll be so nervous our aim won't be any good.

"None of that's going to happen. We know what we can do to them—we can hurt them, we can hurt them bad. We've got plenty of water, so we aren't going to get parched and dehydrated. And we're going to keep calm, because we know what they're doing and we won't let it work."

He was going to say more, but was interrupted by a shot from Schultz's blaster, followed by a quick scream from out there. He scrambled to Schultz's side.

"What?" he asked, looking over the side.

"I saw one of them crawling between rocks and took

him out." Schultz pointed. "See that boulder, about fifty
meters away there? It's the one with the horizontal crack
in it."

"I see it."

"Pile of rags ten meters to the left of it, that's the bandit.
He was crawling from a boulder farther out. I couldn't see
much of him, he must have been in a crease in the ground.
The crease wasn't as deep as he thought it was."

A Siad moving to a boulder fifty meters away, that
bothered Bass. It meant maybe the Siad were closing the
distance between themselves and the Marines, keeping
under cover all the way. If they managed that, then he
and his men were truly done for.

"Has anybody else seen any movement?" Bass asked.

"I thought I did," Dean said. "But it was so quick
I wasn't sure it was something real, or if it was a heat
shimmer."

Bass swore. "All right, people, I think they're trying to
slip up on us. Everybody, look sharp. Let me know if you
see anything. Don't, I say again, do not fire at any movement unless you've got a clear shot. Anybody else?"
Nobody else had seen movement.

One Siad definitely approaching from the north,
maybe one from the east. No movement seen anywhere
else. Maybe the Siad weren't closing. Maybe those two,
if there were two, were just getting closer to snipe at
them. But fifty meters was awfully close for sniping, too
close. Unless the close-in snipers were supposed to keep
the Marines' heads down while another assault started.
That might make sense.

A rifle shot cracked from the southwest, the bullet
it announced zinging by low enough to hit any head in
its path.

Claypoole snapped a shot back. His bolt shattered a

small boulder sixty meters away and exposed a Siad who was hiding behind it.

"Hold your fire," Bass shouted before anyone could shoot at the crawling man. "I think he's wounded."

"He should be dead," Schultz growled. He put his blaster to his shoulder and aimed at the Siad, but didn't touch the firing lever.

"Someone will have to tend him," Bass said. "One wounded man takes two out of the fight." Exposing as little of himself as possible, he slowly turned in a complete circle. The crawling Siad was the only movement he could see. If that Siad was one of his men, wounded and exposed, he'd have everyone lay down suppressing fire while someone ran out to get him. The Siad let him crawl alone.

Wad Mohammad sat on his carved folding chair in the shade of the pavilion his attendants erected beyond the rise east of the small depression where the Confederation Marines were trapped. He glowered at the fast-riders Shabeli had sent ahead with the Confederation Marine corpse and wondered again why they had put it in that depression where the Marines had cover. If the fools had placed the corpse in the open, the Marines would be fully exposed to his men's fire and might all be dead by now. Instead he had lost a hundred men while not wounding even one of the Marines. Then he glared at the fool who knelt between two of his warriors, the fool who had fired at the Marines before they were far enough away from the depression that they couldn't return to its cover. Wad Mohammad couldn't do anything about the fools Shabeli had sent ahead, but he could do something about the fool who had given the Marines warning. Wad Mohammad stood.

"Alambar," Wad Mohammad intoned.

The kneeling fool prostrated himself.

"This day your eagerness for battle needlessly caused

the death of one hundred Badawi Siad warriors," Wad
Mohammad continued. "The Badawi Siad are wise warriors. A wise warrior gives his enemy time to make a
mistake. You were not a wise warrior this day. You are
the one who made the mistake. You allowed the Confederation Marines the chance to take cover from the rifles
of the Badawi Siad." While he talked, Wad Mohammad
walked toward the prostrate man. He paused when he
reached him, gave Alambar a chance to speak, to give
word to his guilt, to his impetuousness.

Alambar made no attempt to speak with his voice; his
body spoke for him by quivering uncontrollably.

"You are unworthy to be a Badawi warrior, Alambar.
The only way you can redeem yourself is to serve the
brave warriors whose deaths you caused this day. I grant
you leave to do so in heaven." Wad Mohammad turned
and walked slowly back to his seat under the pavilion. He
ignored the keening that came from the condemned man,
keening that was abruptly cut off. When he turned to
again sit facing the attendants, subchiefs, and fast-riders
arrayed before his pavilion, the executioner was walking
away, wiping the blood from his ceremonial scimitar.
Two attendants were dragging the body away. Alambar's
head was already impaled on a spear standing erect as
symbol and warning. Blood dribbled slowly down the
spear shaft to join the puddle at its base.

"Now we know what kind of warriors these Confederation Marines are," he began, as though nothing had just
happened. "They shoot well—rapidly and accurately. We
cannot attack them on foot, running is too slow. Even if
we attack in large enough numbers to reach them and kill
them with our blades, they will kill too many of us before
we reach them and the Badawi will no longer be the
strongest clan among the Siad." He paused to listen to an
attendant who ran to the pavilion from where his warriors

were closing on the Marines, whispered an order, and sent the attendant back from whence he came.

"I have just received a report," he said to his audience. "Moving from rock to rock to close on the Confederation Marines will also cost us too many brave warriors. We must close on the Marines rapidly." If we are to defeat them and gain that glory for ourselves instead of waiting for Shabeli and his fire-weapons, he added to himself. "The only way we can close on them rapidly is on horseback. But a horse charge is on too broad a line, the Confederation Marines are on too narrow a front; it would cost us many men and horses to gain their small position."

"Great Wad Mohammad," a tall, darkly bearded man interrupted.

"Yes, Wad Kadj?" Wad Mohammad said patiently.

"As you say, Great Wad Mohammad," Wad Kadj said, "if we charge on line the Confederation Marines will kill many warriors and horses, and still we might not be able to reach them because we will be spread out too far. But if we get into a column, perhaps ten men and horses wide, and charge that way, the Confederation Marines might kill many warriors and horses in the front of the column, but there will be too many and we will reach them in sufficient numbers to kill them with our blades."

Wad Mohammad considered this tactic for a moment. It had been used to great effect by a great warrior king of the Francois some six centuries earlier. Yes, the Confederation Marines would kill many warriors and horses at the head of the column, but he thought Wad Kadj was right about the great mass of horsemen being too much for the defenders, just as the Francois king's tactic had proved too much for the Britishers and Rooskies.

"You are right, Wad Kadj," he said. "Your plan will work. I grant you the honor of being the lead in this charge. By the grace of God who is above all Gods, we will do this. We will defeat these Confederation Marines, and when Shabeli the Magnificent reaches us, we will present him with the heads of his enemies.

Nothing more happened for half an hour after Claypoole wounded the Siad attempting to creep up on them.

"What's that?" Dean suddenly shouted. "Does anybody feel it?"

Bass concentrated for a moment, and then he felt it too. There was a faint rumbling in the rock, as though something heavy was moving. The rumbling increased until he imagined he could hear the rapid thudding that made it. His eyes popped wide as he realized what it was.

"Everybody, face east," he shouted, and scrambled across the basin. "They're making a cavalry charge! Get ready!"

A growing thunder in the near distance resolved into the thudding of horses' hooves—far too many horses' hooves—and a mass of horsemen in a column ten horses wide suddenly swarmed over the rise 150 meters to the east.

Bass could hardly believe his eyes—a cavalry charge against modern weapons. The Siad were in a column! What kind of idiot would send horses charging into modern weapons in a column? The kind of idiot who didn't have any idea what modern weapons could do, that's what kind, he realized.

"On my command," Bass roared, "fire on line, slag the rock in front of the horses." He looked quickly to the sides to see that his men were ready. "FIRE!" he commanded, and the Marines opened up.

Their bolts struck the rock in front of the column, Neru's gun swishing its greater fire back and forth in the same place. The rock heated, softened, turned liquid in the path of the charging horses. Gouts of lava spattered

up and into the mass of them, the injured steeds screaming
in agony and fear. The lead rows of horses tried to rear
and spin away from the flying magma, but the mass of
horses barreling behind them wouldn't let them turn and
flee—the momentum of the charge pushed the leaders
forward, tumbled them into the molten rock. The next
rows of horses and riders slammed into the fallen, burning,
scrambling horses and men, and tripped over them,
spilling themselves into the growing lava flow.

The charge was stopped, and riders tried manically to
control their panicked horses. All they managed was to
create an ever-tightening mass that couldn't spread out,
couldn't retreat—couldn't fight in any way.

"Lift your fire," Bass bellowed. "Shoot into them!"
The Marines raised their fire and burned holes in the
milling mass of horses and men. Neru's gun burned a
swath from the front all the way to the farthest he could
see. Around the sides and rear of the Siad cavalry, individual horsemen began to break away from the mass.
Some fled to the north or to the south; most raced for
what safety they could find behind the ridge over which
they had so confidently charged. A few, a very few,
skirted the area of devastated rock and continued their
mad charge toward the Marines.

"Schultz, Dornhofer," Bass commanded, "shift your
fire, get the ones coming at us." He shifted his own aim
to one of the oncoming horsemen and blew the man's
shoulder off. Dornhofer and Schultz also made clean
kills with their first shots. The others kept firing into the
mass, slaughtering horses and men indiscriminately. The
mass thinned, partly from more Siad breaking away to
flee, more because of the Marines' murderous fire. Still, a
few of the Siad who succeeded in getting away managed
to round the molten rock and continue their charge.

Bass wanted to shift more of his men's fire to the Siad

who were still coming toward them, but the main force had to keep dying or they'd reorganize and resume their charge. But he could also see that too many were coming for him, Dornhofer, and Schultz to get all of them before any reached them.

Suddenly, one of the Siad was there and leaped over him, into the hollow. Bass twisted around and blasted the rider as the warrior tried to spin his horse around. Then more of them reached the Marine position.

"Everybody but guns, use knives!" Bass shouted, and drew his own fighting knife. The eleven-inch blade glinted fiercely in the sunlight.

The Siad screamed in defiance and the Marines' knives clashed loudly on the steel of thrusting bayonets as the Siad warriors stood in their stirrups, jabbing wildly at the Marines feinting and slashing and dancing between their horses' flailing hooves.

Doyle's anal sphincter nearly let go out of sheer terror. Use a knife to fight men on horseback? Men with rifles and fixed bayonets? Was Bass out of his mind? Then he only had time to act and his reflexes took over, rolling him out of the way of a horse bringing its front hooves down to trample him. The horse tried to stomp on him! It so infuriated Doyle, he leaped to his feet and struck the horse in the eye with his knife. The horse screamed and reared back. Its rider fell backward and landed hard on his back. Abruptly, Doyle remembered he was supposed to be fighting the men, not the horses. He bounded onto the Siad, landing on him as the warrior was struggling to refill his lungs, which had the air knocked out of them when he landed. The Siad's eyes widened and his mouth gaped with the effort to suck in a breath. Doyle jammed his blade upward into the open mouth and its point broke through his palette into the Siad's brain case, killing him instantly.

Claypoole surged to his feet and thrust up with his knife; its blade sank deep into the gut of a horse leaping over him and ripped its belly open. The horse screamed wildly and bucked in midair as its entrails tumbled out. It hit the ground on its side, its legs kicking frantically. The rider struggled to get his pinned leg out from under his mount, but Claypoole was on him before he could free himself. With one quick swipe, he nearly decapitated him.

Bass reached high over his head and pulled a frantic rider from his saddle, slammed him on the ground and gutted him in one swift movement, and then, rising swiftly, raked his bloody knife along the flank of another rider's horse, slashing the man's leg to the bone.

Dean hamstrung a horse and it came crashing to the ground, breaking its rider's neck.

Schultz stood to squarely face a charging Siad. The horseman leaned over the neck of his horse and extended his bayoneted rifle to skewer the Marine. Just as the bayonet was about to jab into his chest, Schultz spun aside. He grabbed the foreguard of the rifle with one hand and thrust his knife into the side of the Siad with the other. The horse sped on without its rider, who hadn't let go of his weapon. The Marine continued his spin, swinging the mortally wounded Siad at the end of his arm, and smashed him into the chest of another horse. The horse crumpled with a broken shoulder, throwing his rider hard onto the rocks at the far end of the basin, cracking his skull open.

Two Siad converged on Dornhofer. He rolled out of the way of the first and just missed being impaled on the Siad's reaching bayonet. Then, to avoid the bayonet thrust of the second Siad, he rolled under the skittering hooves of the first horse. Defenseless on the ground, he had to get to his feet. He grabbed the tail of the first horse to yank himself up, and when the horse reared and tried to spin around to bite its tormentor, it rammed into the second horse and the two were momentarily hung up together, with the second bucking to throw off the first. Dornhofer reached up with one hand and grabbed the belt of the first horse's rider, jerking him down onto his thrusting knife. He turned and twisted his arm to let the falling Siad slip off his blade, then dropped a knee onto him and stabbed him in the heart. The riderless horse tried to continue its turn, knocking the other Siad off his still-bucking horse. Dornhofer turned to him, but the man hadn't fallen hard and was on his feet before the Marine reached him. The Siad swung his rifle butt at Dornhofer, but the Marine was already inside the arc of his swing. Dornhofer swung his knife upward from his hip, slicing into the man's belly and thrusting his blade deep into his chest, mangling his heart.

In thirty seconds it was all over, dying horses in the Marines' position kicking and screaming while riderless mounts fled back toward the Siad lines, empty stirrups flapping wildly from blood-streaked saddles. Blood and lather from the animals' flanks splattered the panting Marines.

Schultz finished gutting the Siad he was kneeling on and looked around for another to kill. None were there. There were seven bloody bodies within two paces of him. Without someone else to knife, he picked up his blaster and began firing at the milling horsemen.

Throughout the close combat, Clarke had assisted Neru with the gun as it burned wide swaths through the mass of Siad horsemen still trying to unscramble themselves. Now the other Marines returned to firing at their enemy.

"Cease fire!" Bass bellowed as the last of the Siad disappeared over the rise.

CHAPTER
THIRTY

"Get those bodies out of here," Bass ordered before the last of the retreating Siad disappeared over the rise. "Make barricades. Don't bother with the horses, they're too heavy. Stack the bodies on the east side. And put a few around the rest of the perimeter."

The Marines immediately set to stacking the Siad corpses on the eastern rim of the shallow basin, where another cavalry charge would come from—if there was to be another cavalry charge. Bass didn't think there would be, this one had been too costly. He counted five horses and more than a dozen Siad who had fallen inside the basin—and an equal number of Siad an arm's length or not much farther outside of it.

Bass stood and surveyed the landscape over which the Siad had charged. More than two hundred badly burned Siad had gone to their warrior's heaven. Here and there to the east, wounded Siad inched their way toward safety. He didn't try to count the horses, though more than fifty had to have been killed in the second charge. Some of the horses, not yet dead, whinnied or weakly screamed out their pain as they vainly tried to struggle to their feet. For men to go into battle and fight and die was one thing. Nobody had put a gun to Charlie Bass's head and told him to enlist in the Marines and to fight battles. Any one of the Siad warriors who'd died today could have chosen another path. But the horses had no choice but to ride unknowing into the maelstrom of Marine fire.

He shook his head to rid it of such thoughts. He had more important things to do. The Siad had charged twice and lost badly each time. They would try again. How would they do it next? He looked away.

The carrion-eaters, made almost mad by the sheer size of the feast laid out for them, descended on the horde of dead and dying.

Wad Mohammad surveyed the battlefield from his vantage point in the shade of a rock outcrop several hundred meters to the south. He had lost too many warriors in these futile attacks. No more. No matter the pride of the Badawi warriors or their desire for vengeance. Too many wives would wail tonight, too many children must now seek succor from men who weren't their fathers. His only consolation was that Wad Kadj, whose idea this mad formation had been, was among the dead. He snapped his fingers and his attendants immediately attended him.

"Go to the subchiefs. Tell them one warrior out of twenty-five is to fire his rifle at the Confederation Marines. That man is to make one magazine last one hour. No warrior is to expose himself to the Confederation Marines. We will keep the off-worlders in place until Shabeli the Magnificent arrives. I will let him lose his men in the next assault. No more Badawi warriors will lose their lives until we can attack and win." He snapped his fingers again and the attendants sped off on their errand.

Again Wad Mohammad scanned the battlefield. The rocky land to the east, over which his brave horsemen had charged, was almost aglow with heat shimmer. Somehow, carrion-eaters hopped about on that hellish landscape without being cindered by its heat. He shuddered almost imperceptibly. Never had he seen such carnage and destruction. The Marines' blasters had melted the rock over which his horsemen had attempted to charge. The rock was too hot to charge over even now. The Confederation Marines truly used weapons of hell.

A sniper's bullet spanged off the rock and thudded into the body of a horse just in front of where Charlie Bass lay, spraying him with flecks of half-congealed blood and bits of horsehair. He should be getting used to it, he thought, but each bullet that zipped overhead, thudded into the barricades, or ricocheted off the rock frayed his nerves more. Mentally, he again took stock. They had plenty of water left from the refill at Tulak Yar the day before. But the men were drinking it too fast for it to last beyond the day.

"Remember your water discipline," he said again, and thought of how hard it was to not drink under the beating sun. But they would have to drink more; there was no shade and they were active, not sleeping.

Their rations were good for another couple of days. They had used half their batteries. At best, they could withstand two more assaults. He was sure there were more than enough Siad still around for two more assaults. After that it would be hand-to-hand. If the Siad reinforcements didn't arrive until after dark, then he and his men might be able to slip away. They still had the GPL. He patted the GPL holder on his belt. He froze.

The pouch was shredded. He twisted and looked toward his side where the pouch was. He yanked out the GPL. Its casing was cracked, its screen was dark, blank. The GPL was dead.

Well, Staff Sergeant Charlie Bass had been in tighter spots. At least that's what he told himself. Maybe not tighter, but just as desperate. They knew the general direction of New Obbia from where they were. They could make it there using dead reckoning if they got away—when they got away, he corrected himself.

He thought back to the incident on Fiesta de Santiago, when they had been pinned down by bandits and he'd joked with Lieutenant Procescu about fixing bayonets. Now that possibility was no longer a joke, except that the blasters didn't have bayonets, which was why they used their knives when the horsemen broke through. Next time they had lunch, he'd discuss that with the commandant, he thought wryly. He gazed for a moment at the ground-cloth bundle at the bottom of the basin which was McNeal's corpse. He would never let these men come to an end like that, he vowed. If it came to that, he would kill each one himself. He drew the ancient K-Bar from its special pocket and examined it in the late-morning light.

The K-Bar was lucky, and with it there riding on his thigh, Bass imagined he carried a living link with the spirits of the long-dead Marines of the ancient Corps; that when he fought, they fought again beside him. He smiled. The fantasy had always made him feel better when things got tough. He slid the K-Bar back into its pocket and patted it affectionately. "We'll get through this, Jarhead," he whispered.

Time for business. Charlie Bass looked into the sky. It was another clear, hot day in the Martac Waste. The Siad wouldn't come again from the direction of the rising sun, not the way the rock was slagged and still almost smoldering. They'd find another way to come. And then another way after that. Two more assaults and the Marines would be overrun. Loss of power in their batteries would see to that.

Briefly, Bass surveyed the men around him. Some of them were sleeping, sprawled in the awkward poses of men suddenly overcome by sheer physical exhaustion. Doyle lay with his mouth wide open, snoring. That young corporal acquitted himself well when the horsemen over-rode them, he thought. Surprisingly well. He might have made a good Marine one day. Claypoole, now a hardened combat veteran—would he still be a goof-off if he survived this action?—lay on his back, breathing quietly. A joker and a wise-ass in garrison, Claypoole had proved himself a good man when the chips were down. Clarke had gone to sleep, head folded over his knees, and now a long line of saliva dribbled down his chin onto his utilities. Dean reposed with his face against the rock. Now, there was a young lad with something in him. Bass regretted nobody might ever see how far he could go.

Shabeli the Magnificent alighted from his horse in one fluid motion and embraced Wad Mohammad. Several hundred of the surviving Badawi warriors were behind the rise, about three hundred meters from the Marines' position, quieting their horses. They stood ready for whatever commands they were given.

"Wad Mohammad, may God smile upon you always," Shabeli uttered in perfunctory greeting.

"And you, my lord," Wad Mohammad answered.

"Our enemies?" Shabeli asked.

Wad Mohammad gestured beyond the rise before them. "They have not exposed themselves or returned fire since our last assault."

"They cannot escape?"

"We have them surrounded on all sides. They do not dare expose themselves. I have many snipers firing into their position, and for one of them to stand is for that man to die. They cannot possibly escape."

Shabeli grunted. "You have attacked?"

"Twice. One time a hundred men on foot, to test the

Confederation Marines. That was from the west. The off-worlders used their hell-weapons to kill all of them. The second time was horsemen from the east. The assault was broken with heavy casualties."

"At what price to the off-worlders?"

Wad Mohammad's jaws locked. This was a question he didn't want to consider. "None. All of them survived."

"All eight of them," Shabeli said scornfully. This weak-kneed fool would have to be eliminated, he thought. One last, determined rush this morning would have overrun the Confederation Marines. Now the Badawi were crouching here—beyond the rise like old women—and hidden in other places around the off-world Marines. Well, the balance of power had just changed.

Shabeli gave a curt command to the captain of the small company he had led here. The sixty men dismounted. They all carried plasma weapons and knew how to use them. "Deploy your men behind the crest of this ridge. Let no one fire or expose himself until I personally give the order."

"What do you propose, my lord?" Wad Mohammad asked.

Shabeli smiled. "I propose a small demonstration. Those off-worlders down there must almost be out of firepower. When they see what I have brought, they will surrender. Or they will die. Either way, it is of no conse-quence. We have dealt the Confederation a powerful blow. I'll have their Marines alive, or I'll have their bodies dead."

A plasma bolt lanced out from the rise and seared its way into the rock just short of the man-barricade, where it exploded in a brilliant flash, spattering molten globules of magma into the corpses. The stench of burned flesh washed over the Marines.

"That got my attention," Claypoole said as he casually shook a small chunk of charred flesh off the stock of his blaster.

"The balance of power has just shifted," Bass commented quietly. This changed everything. He was not surprised at what followed.

"Confederation Marines!" a booming voice echoed over the waste. "Listen to me. I am Shabeli the Magnificent, leader of all the Siad. I am here with overpowering force. Surrender! Surrender and I will spare your lives." Shabeli stood on top of the rise, clearly visible to the Marines. In his right hand was a portable voice projector.

"Surrender, hell," Schultz muttered.

"Belay the chatter," Bass commanded. "That's Shabeli himself. He's got a very high opinion of himself." Old Mas Fardeed had schooled Bass well in the ways of the Siad, and Bass had filed the information away for possible future use. Bass had long thought that it was very good to know as much about your enemy as possible, even his curse words. Bass smiled. There might yet be a chance.

Quickly, Bass stripped off his body armor and utility shirt.

"What are you doing?" Doyle exclaimed.

"Going for a little walk," Bass answered. Chest bare, he looked at his men. "If this doesn't work, you're in charge, Dornhofer. You know what to do."

Dornhofer nodded wordlessly.

"Don't surrender if you don't want to wind up like McNeal. If they take you alive, these bastards'll use you as hostages and then torture you to death. Take as many of them with you as you can. Save a bolt for yourself. Do not wait until they get in among you.

"Do not, I say again, *do not* attempt to support me out

there, no matter what happens." He looked each man in the eyes until each indicated he would obey.

Without a further word, Staff Sergeant Charlie Bass stood erect on the lip of the basin and waved his arms at Shabeli the Magnificent.

"Come forward!" Shabeli commanded. Bass wended his way cautiously among the corpses, walked the still-steaming area his men had slagged, and headed toward Shabeli. It was a long walk.

Shabeli watched the lone figure approaching. A negotiator. He smiled. This would be easy.

When Bass at last reached a spot about thirty meters from the top of the rise, within good speaking distance, Shabeli ordered him to stop.

"I demand the immediate surrender of you and your men," Shabeli shouted.

"That's interesting," Bass replied. "I came to accept yours." He kept his face expressionless, despite the way his heart thudded in his chest.

Shabeli blinked in disbelief. Then he realized his men could see how calmly the off-worlder stood and knew he had to make the man quail or risk losing respect. "All who Shabeli the Magnificent does not kill surrender to him," he roared. "All whose surrender Shabeli the Magnificent does not accept, he kills!"

Bass remained motionless for a moment and then drew his issue knife and raised it above his head. "I do not surrender. You must try to kill me," he roared back.

At the sight of the drawn knife, clearly a challenge to individual combat, the Siad gasped in wonder. Shabeli regarded the lone man through narrowed eyelids. What an idiot! But a brave man still. The man was not as tall as he, but he was thick through the chest, and the muscles in his arms looked powerful. White teeth glinted through the fierce smile on his sun-darkened face.

"You are women, not men!" Bass shouted. Only Shabeli could understand the English words. They were meant only for Shabeli. Bass motioned for a prone blaster man to join him where he stood.

"That's right, you mewling coward! Cut me down! Otherwise, I'm coming up there to spill your stinking guts all over the ground!"

Shabeli hesitated to give the command to open fire. "Who are you?" he demanded.

"Staff Sergeant Charles H. Bass, Confederation Marine Corps, and I have come here to cut your stinking balls off, you gut-eating, puking, dogfather. You feed off the refuse other men eject through their assholes. I will cut out your tongue and send you back to your women, so they can teach you how to cook and real men will turn you over and use you like a whore!" Bass shook the knife and roared. His shouting was so powerful the men back at the basin could make out his words.

The other Siad, although they could not follow Bass, knew he was hurling insults at their leader. Shabeli's eyes widened. It was clear this defiant man expected him to come down there and fight. More to the point, his warriors were catching on that the Marine was offering a challenge for personal combat, something no Siad warrior could reject with honor.

Shabeli smiled to himself. It had come to this? An expert in hand-to-hand combat, he knew he could take the man easily. It would be best just to have him incinerated and get on with his plans, but— Bass interrupted Shabeli's thoughts and made his mind up for him.

"Shabeli!" Bass shouted in the language of the Siad. "Shabeli the Inconsequential! You! You fuck your mother up the ass!" Bass hurled the insult old Mas Fardeed had taught him to pronounce with perfect inflection. All the Siad heard the insult and each man leaped to his feet with a roar of outrage.

In one swift motion Shabeli stripped off his robe, unbuckled his side arms, and drew his own knife. It could have been the twin of the blade Bass brandished on the slope below. Shabeli strode down the ridge and came to a stop a few feet in front of Bass. All the Siad rushed to the top of the rise and stood there, outlined against the horizon, the remaining Marines crouched below completely forgotten.

But the Marines below hadn't forgotten the Siad; they were watching with rapt attention.

"What's going on up there?" Dean gasped.

"He's challenging the big boss to a man-to-man fight," Dornhofer answered.

"Why?" Claypoole asked.

Schultz stood watching the tableau, smiling softly to himself. "He's showing us how to do it," he said quietly.

"How to do what?" Doyle asked.

"How to die."

Shabeli and Bass squared off. Shabeli stood a head taller than Bass and, while he lacked the compact musculature of the Marine, he had the sinewy agility and strength of the practiced swordsman. Shabeli lashed his foot out with blinding speed at shoulder level. Bass took most of the force of the blow with his shoulder, but Shabeli's boot glanced painfully off the top of his head. Still perfectly balanced, Shabeli whirled around and slammed his body full into the Marine, who staggered backward with the force of the contact, raising his knife arm just in time to counter a thrust. The weapons clashed with a loud metallic ring, and as Shabeli withdrew into a defensive stance, his blade left a long gash down Bass's left arm, which instantly flowed with blood. The Siad on the ridge above let out a victorious roar.

Breathing heavily, unmindful of the painful wound Shabeli had just given him, Bass crouched, prepared for the next attack. Shabeli remained just out of range, carefully circling the Marine, looking for an opening. Bass tossed the knife into his left hand to distract his opponent and lunged. Watching the knife, Shabeli was caught momentarily off guard and Bass rammed his head into the bridge of Shabeli's nose, which cracked audibly. Blood flowed from the Siad leader's nostrils.

Stunned, Shabeli fell to one elbow, but rolled away as Bass leaped at him. Striking awkwardly across his body with his knife arm, Shabeli buried his blade into Bass's left buttock. Bass grunted and the Siad roared again. Bass jumped to his feet just as Shabeli slammed into him. Holding his knife in his left hand, now slick with his own flowing blood, the impact of Shabeli's full weight caused him to lose his grip and the knife fell between his feet. Shabeli kicked it away with one foot. Bass managed to grab Shabeli's knife arm with his right hand, deflecting it away from his carotid artery, but still the blade sliced a long furrow down the side of his face and glanced agonizingly off his right collarbone before he stopped it. The two struggled silently for a few moments. Both men were breathing heavily now, bloody perspiration dripping off their contorted faces. Shabeli took the lobe of Bass's right ear between his teeth and bit it off, at the same time twisting his body powerfully. Bass lost his balance and they fell heavily to the ground, Shabeli on top. The Siad on the ridge roared victoriously.

"Now you die!" Shabeli rasped through clenched teeth. He bore his full weight down upon Bass's upraised arms. A horseman from infancy, like every Siad warrior, Shabeli's legs were strong and they held Bass's own hips and legs in a viselike grip, allowing Shabeli to bring the full power of his upper-body strength to bear as he drove the knife homeward inch by inch.

Abruptly, Bass wrenched his head sideways and let go of Shabeli's arms. The plunging blade buried itself into the ground beside Bass's left ear. His right hand free now, Bass snatched the K-Bar from his thigh and thrust the point up into Shabeli's belly. The blade glanced off Shabeli's pelvis just above his genitals and slid into his bladder. Shabeli screamed in agony and his legs spasmed violently, releasing Bass from their hold. Bass flipped Shabeli onto his back and, gripping the handle of the K-Bar with both hands, sliced him open all the way to the sternum. The ancient blade snapped cleanly at the hilt just as its point sliced Shabeli's throbbing heart into two equal halves.

Shabeli the Magnificent uttered one long, high-pitched scream that echoed in the clear morning air and then lay still, his innards spilling in bloody, steaming coils upon the sand. Slowly, Bass rose to his feet. The hundreds of Siad standing along the ridge above him were completely silent. He stooped and retrieved his knife from the sand. In his right hand he still held the handle of the now-forever-useless K-Bar. The blade had broken and the USMC logo was buried in Shabeli's lifeless heart.

Bass, standing erect so as to not show how near he was to exhaustion, raised his good knife to the sun and shouted up at the dark figures clustered along the ridge, "Who's next?"

The Siad did not move. They remained completely silent, with their eyes fixed on Shabeli's gutted carcass even as Bass turned and, shoulders squared, marched back to his waiting Marines.

Bleeding, bruised, exhausted, Bass managed to stay

erect and not stumble until he stepped over the body barricade and back out of sight of the surrounding Siad. Still the Siad stood quietly on the ridge behind him.

"What now?" Dean asked as he and several others eased Bass down onto his back. Claypoole broke out an aid kit and began attending to his platoon sergeant's wounds.

"Now?" Bass asked. He let out a long sigh. "Now we go home."

The Siad watched, still enveloped in silence as the Marines gathered up their weapons and equipment and resumed their walk toward New Obbia. They walked erect with heads held high, almost marching, as though daring the Siad to attack again. Slung between Dean and Claypoole was the battered corpse of PFC Frederick Douglass McNeal. When they were finally out of sight behind a low ridge of hills, Wad Mohammad detached himself from the mass of warriors and walked to where Shabeli the Magnificent's ruined corpse lay. He stood regarding his leader's remains for a long moment and then kicked them—hard. He kicked the corpse again, and then again and again. Other Siad descended from the ridge and joined in. On the long ride back to their mountain fastness, the warriors carried Shabeli the Magnificent's head, genitals, and other body parts suspended on bayonets. Wad Mohammad was their leader now, and under him things would be different on Elneal.

CHAPTER
THIRTY-ONE

They didn't stop walking until shortly before nightfall. Bass wanted to put as much distance as possible between his men and the Siad. But something perhaps worse than running into more Siad happened. Two days later they ran out of water.

"Don't throw that away, Dean," Bass croaked when he saw Dean about to discard a water container he'd just drained during a break. He worked his jaw to force some saliva, then said to everybody, "Keep two water containers each. When you have to piss, don't water the rocks, they won't appreciate it properly. Use one of your empties. We'll stop soon and I'll teach you how to distill water from urine."

Clarke looked ill at the thought of drinking urine. Then he looked scared as he realized he had already dropped all of his water containers. Neru nudged him and handed him one of the three he was still carrying.

Dean grunted. "I don't think I want to drink out of a bottle Claypoole pissed into." He was surprised that he was able even to make a joke under these circumstances.

"That's all right," Bass responded seriously. "If the water Claypoole makes is all that'll keep him alive, I don't think he'd want you drinking it anyway."

Dean chewed on a strip of dried skin where his lip was splitting. "We're in deep trouble, aren't we?"

Bass nodded. "But we're not dead yet, Dean. Hey!" Bass raised his voice. "Any of you guys crap out on me now and I'll drag your body back to New Obbia and give it a court-martial. Now, on your feet! Only forty kilometers straight that way and we're out of here. Another day, day and a half, and I'm going to buy you all a cold beer."

"Look!" Doyle croaked. "Scavengers! Look!" They looked where he pointed. Sure enough, it was one of the scavenger fliers, drifting lazily on a thermal high above them. "It's coming for us. It's coming for McNeal," Doyle shouted.

"Aw, belay that crap," Claypoole muttered. "McNeal's hermetically sealed, and besides, we aren't—" Doyle charged his weapon and fired a bolt into the sky.

"Jesus Muhammad," Bass sighed as he watched the scavenger disintegrate in a bright flash, "that was probably your last bolt, Doyle. Secure that weapon and get on your feet; we've got to keep moving." That Bass had not jumped Doyle more severely for his rashness was an indicator of how exhausted even the inexhaustible Charlie Bass had become.

Wearily, the men got to their feet and staggered on.

Wad Mohammad knocked gently at Moira's door. She had fled to her chambers shortly after the war party returned, with what was left of her master and lover. Wad Mohammad knocked again. "Please open the door, my lady. I only wish to speak to you." He stood patiently in the hallway and knocked a third time.

Eventually the door was opened by one of Moira's serving girls. Wad Mohammad gently nudged the girl aside and entered the room. Moira lay on a couch, one arm flung across her face. "You bastard!" she hissed through clenched teeth. "You damned bastard!"

"My lady." Wad Mohammad bowed respectfully.

She sat up and faced him, her eyes red and cheeks wet. Even in her present condition, it was plain to see why Shabeli had honored the woman. In a culture where the women were short and dark, Moira's tall fairness was extremely exotic to the men of the Siad. "I am without protection, but I swear, Wad Mohammad, you touch me . . ." Suddenly her hand filled with the bulk of an ancient pistol, one of those chambered for center-fire metal cartridges loaded into a cylinder. Carefully, she cocked its hammer, readying the pistol for firing and leveling its huge bore straight at Wad Mohammad. He eyed the pistol with interest. It was an ancient and beautiful instrument, this pistol, and he vowed that one day he would own it.

Wad Mohammad held his palms out toward her. "You have nothing to fear from me, my lady. I have come here to pay you my compliments and to ask for your help." He gestured toward a chair, and she nodded. Wad Mohammad seated himself with a sigh and stretched his legs out before him.

"I am now the chieftain of all the Siad," he announced matter-of-factly. "Shabeli received the punishment he deserved." Wad Mohammad held up his hand to silence the protest she was about to voice. "He got many of our best men killed, my lady. His plot to defy the Confederation was insanely irresponsible from the beginning. Oh, yes, old Wad Ramadan was right all along. These Marines, these devils, are not to be defeated by us. They are extremely brave and better armed than we are, even with the weapons Shabeli stockpiled. You know these people better than we. If Wad Ramadan, his own uncle and father's closest confidant, couldn't influence Shabeli, you were in no position to do so either. Besides, who would dare defy Shabeli the Magnificent?" Wad Mohammad grinned and spread out his hands.

"Well, one man did, my lady," he continued. "One of those Confederation Marines. He killed your man. Oh, you should have seen that fight! Already our poets are composing songs about it. Those off-worlders have some fine men. It is no disgrace to be defeated by such as he, my lady. We know that one's name, and generations of Siad yet unborn will thrill to the songs of how he and Shabeli the Magnificent fought to the death.

"But that is over now. We must look to the future, make peace with the Confederation, and preserve what we can of our old ways."

She observed Wad Mohammad closely as he spoke. How much he reminded her of Shabeli the Magnificent. And yet there was something to Wad Mohammad that Shabeli never had—sincerity. He really meant what he was saying; he didn't radiate the impression he was planning things for his own glorification. Carefully, she lowered the revolver's hammer and placed the weapon in her lap. Wad Mohammad smiled. "What is it you wish of me, my lord?" she asked.

Wad Mohammad's smile widened, then disappeared, and he leaned forward briskly, all business now. He would get to know this magnificent woman better later. "Everything has changed on our world and we will have to change too. I want a video hookup to the Confederation officials at New Obbia, and I want you to translate a message for me. I have a present for the Marine commander, the lives of some very brave men."

Corporal MacLeash suddenly stiffened at his instrument console. Just before the screen went blank, the drone's opticals had focused on a small group of men far below. He hadn't been able to make out any of their faces in the brief look he had—a playback later could focus on them and come up with the ID—but in that instant the corporal clearly saw there were eight Marines staring up at the UAV. "Skipper!" he called to Captain Conorado. "It's just like that bastard told us. We found 'em!"

"Charlie, you old *kwangduk*, it's good to see you again!" Captain Conorado sat beside Staff Sergeant Bass as the battalion surgeon and his assistants tended to his wounds.

"I lost my K-Bar, Skipper," Bass groaned sorrowfully.

"I know, I know," Conorado soothed, and then he realized Bass was putting him on. "Charlie," the captain shook his head, "will you never cease to amaze me?" Both men laughed. Bass started to cough.

"Hey, Marine, easy there!" the surgeon said. "I know you're a tough one, Staff Sergeant, but how about lying still for a while, make our work easier for us, huh?"

Bass nodded and smiled. Then his smile vanished and he said to Conorado, "Baccacio—"

"Ensign Baccacio," Conorado interrupted, pronouncing "Ensign" sarcastically, "ran off and left some of his men behind. He's responsible for what happened to that fine young Marine, McNeal, Charlie, and had it been in my power to do so, I'd have shot Baccacio in front of the entire FIST." Conorado's voice grated and the blood rushed to his face as he spoke. Then, calmer, he went on, "But instead I just relieved him of command and sent his worthless ass back to Admiral Willis's flagship. If he doesn't resign, he'll be court-martialed for cowardice and dereliction of duty and a dozen other things I can think of, besides being a first-class ass. I think the young ensign will resign and save us a lot of work. By the way, that Sergeant Hyakowa, he's definite officer material." Conorado nodded. "Keep your eye on him, Charlie."

Conorado was silent for a moment. "Charlie, you and your men showed 'em, didn't you? We thought you were dead, but goddamn . . ." He paused. "I couldn't command this company without you . . ." He paused again, to get control of himself. "It was you, that nasty old K-Bar of yours," he went on, "and seven scraggly-assed Marines, who changed everything for the better on this miserable chunk of rock. You are a piece of work, Staff Sergeant Charles H. Bass," he concluded lamely.

"Skipper," Bass replied, "I think the Corps owes me one this time."

"It sure does, Charlie! I've already started writing up the citation for—"

Bass held up his hand. "No, sir, no medals, please. Not for me. I've got enough of those. Give them to my men. Every one of them rates at least a Bronze Star with comet. Neru should get a Silver Nebula. You should have seen him when he took on that first assault."

Conorado stared speculatively at Bass for a moment. Finally he said, "You'll disappoint your men if you don't accept a decoration. They all think that fight you had with Shabeli certainly rates one."

Bass shook his head. "Maybe some of them think so, but not all of them. Don't try to put me on."

"Everyone," Conorado repeated, "even Schultz."

"Schultz?" Bass said sharply. "The Hammer believes anything that doesn't kill you doesn't rate a medal. He says anytime you can walk away from an action, all you did was your job."

Conorado nodded. "That's right, that's the Schultz who thinks you rate a Silver Nebula. Probably means you deserve at least a Marine Heroism Medal."

Bass shook his head. He couldn't believe that Hammer Schultz thought he deserved a medal for bringing the patrol across the Martac Waste.

"If you want medals for your men, go ahead and write them up. I'll pass them on with my endorsement. I'm sure Admiral Willis will see to it that they get whatever you recommend them for."

"All right, I'll write them up. But none for me. I really don't need any more."

Now Conorado grinned. "You'll have to take that up with Admiral Willis. When your men told him what you did, he told me he expects a citation written and on his desk by tomorrow morning. I may be a bad-ass Marine company commander, but Charlie, damned if I'm tough enough to deny a full Fleet Admiral when he tells me he wants something."

Bass looked levelly at Conorado for a long moment, then sagged and swore under his breath. He straightened. "The citation you put on the Admiral's desk for me is going to be underneath the citations I write for my men. Understand?"

Conorado nodded. "Fine by me. Just have them in my hands before I leave for the flagship." He stood to leave.

"Not yet, Skipper," Bass said, stopping him. "There's still the matter of the thing I *do* want."

"What's that, Charlie?"

Bass motioned for the captain to sit down and lean close.

"He wants what?" the Brigadier exclaimed. "And he wants it how?" The Brigadier thought for a moment, then said, "Well, since it's for Staff Sergeant Bass, I'll give it a try."

"He wants what?" Admiral Willis asked his chief of staff. "And he wants it how?" The Admiral leaned back in his chair. "Well, get it for him and let's not keep the

374 David Sherman & Dan Cragg

man waiting." Then he added, "Have you finished processing those citations yet? I want the awards made before this operation is finished so I can pin the medals on them myself."

Admiral Willis assigned a commander to escort the six large metal containers to the FIST's infirmary where Bass was recovering. A sailor broke the seal on one and left them alone with Bass and Captain Conorado. The captain reached inside and lifted out an ice-cold, one-liter bottle of Reindeer Ale, which he handed to Bass. Bass motioned for the Skipper to take one for himself. Each container held twenty-four bottles of beer.

Bass snapped the top and drank. "Ahh!" he sighed. "There really is a God and He really does love us, Skipper."

"There's a hell of a lot of beer here, Charlie," Conorado said.

"Yessir. One more request. Would you get the men who were with me in the desert, and ask them to come in here for a while? Even Corporal Doyle—he turned out to be a better Marine than any of us expected. I promised them all a beer when we got out. Give us thirty minutes alone and then send in the rest of the platoon."

The party that night was one that lived on in platoon legend for decades.

The spirit of the Bos Kashi was broken in the battle of New Obbia. After some jockeying for position by rivals, Wad Mohammad became undisputed leader of the Siad and brought an end to Shabeli's disastrous raids on the farmers who fed the world. Moira, the off-world journalist, was first his translator, then his ambassador to the Elneal government in New Obbia. The Gaels and the Sons of Freedom decided that following the lead of men who wore dresses wasn't such a good idea and went back to raiding each other. The Muong Song, in their ocean fastness, nodded sagely about the foolishness of the lowland round-eyes and continued searching for lucrative ways to transport their drugs off-planet. The Euskadi, happy about being left alone, ignored the remainder of the planet.

The situation on Elneal returned to normal. After three months overseeing distribution of food and medicines, and with a new crop of grain and vegetables sowed and growing, the Marines left.

And the Siad did sing songs to honor the deeds of the Confederation Marine they called Siraj Bhats, and his bold men.

EPILOGUE

About midnight Dean stepped outside Big Barb's for air. He carried his beer and a lighted cigar with him. The cigar end glowed brightly in the darkness as he sucked the acrid tobacco smoke deep into his lungs. He held it there for a long time before exhaling. He sighed with pleasure. Since Elneal, small things, like a good smoke, had become very important to him.

The first night of liberty once the 34th FIST was back in garrison on Thorsfinni's World was anticlimactic. The men of the Bass patrol—including Corporal Doyle, whom they now accepted as one of their own—were still too close to the events on Elneal to relax, but once granted liberty, they headed for Bronny anyway, trying very hard to convince themselves they were going to have a monumentally good time that night. But their minds were still in the desert on that tragic world. They drank a lot of beer, sang the same old songs, joked with the waitresses, but nobody felt like going upstairs, and to the civilian patrons at Big Barb's that night, as they huddled together in a far corner of the hall, they seemed to be trying too hard to convince themselves they were having a good time.

Dean drew on the cigar again. The door opened, splashing Dean in light, noise from inside washing over him. Claypoole joined him and stood silently at his side for a while.

"Cold," Claypoole remarked at last.

"Yep." Dean nodded.

"I love the cold," Claypoole continued. "I never want to be hot again." He laughed nervously.

Dean smiled in the darkness. They were both silent for a time, looking up at the brilliant stars in the heavens.

Dean was thinking of Fred McNeal. The loss of his friend had subsided to a dull ache inside his chest that would always be there. He thought of his mother, who had died while he was trekking across the desert on Elneal. Someday he would go home and visit her grave. But when Captain Conorado had first broken the news to him on the way back from Elneal, he had displayed no emotion at all. At that time, the thought of leaving the company for the long voyage back to Earth never occurred to him. Dean sensed, and Captain Conorado knew from experience, that recovery from the ordeal on Elneal could only come among the comrades who had shared it. Besides, his mother would have been dead three months before he could ever have reached home.

The door opened behind them to let out a couple of Marines who were on their way elsewhere, and briefly the pair was illuminated in the light and engulfed in the boisterous clamor from inside. Staff Sergeant Bass's voice was clearly distinguishable in the hubbub, raised loudly in song. The door closed abruptly, plunging them once more into darkness and a silence that descended again as soon as the departing Marines were gone. Dean smiled. The platoon sergeant had told them earlier that evening, "I've lost a lot of friends since I've been in the Corps. You just never get used to that. But remember this: The ones who die are always with you," he tapped his chest, "and the ones who survive," he took in the entire table with outspread arms, "become closer to you than family."

A shooting star streaked silently across the sky. Dean finished his beer in one long gulp and belched loudly. He regarded the star-studded heavens. Way out there, beyond the unimaginable gulf of space, was Earth—home. No, Dean thought, not anymore. The 34th FIST was his home now.

PFC Joseph Finucane Dean took another deep drag on his cigar. "Fuck Earth," he said.

"Roger that," Claypoole said.

**Lethal, invisible, silent—
they go where no one else can.**

BACKSHOT

STARFIST: FORCE RECON

BOOK 1

David Sherman and Dan Cragg

**The first book in an exciting new special-ops
adventure from the battle-tested vets
who created the Starfist series.**

"Vivid characters, amazing but believable
technology, and explosive action combine in
a riveting adventure . . . Military fiction of any
age or type simply does not get better than this."
—MICHAEL LEE LANNING, author of *Inside Force Recon: Recon
Marines in Vietnam* and *Inside the Crosshairs: Snipers in Vietnam*

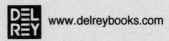 www.delreybooks.com